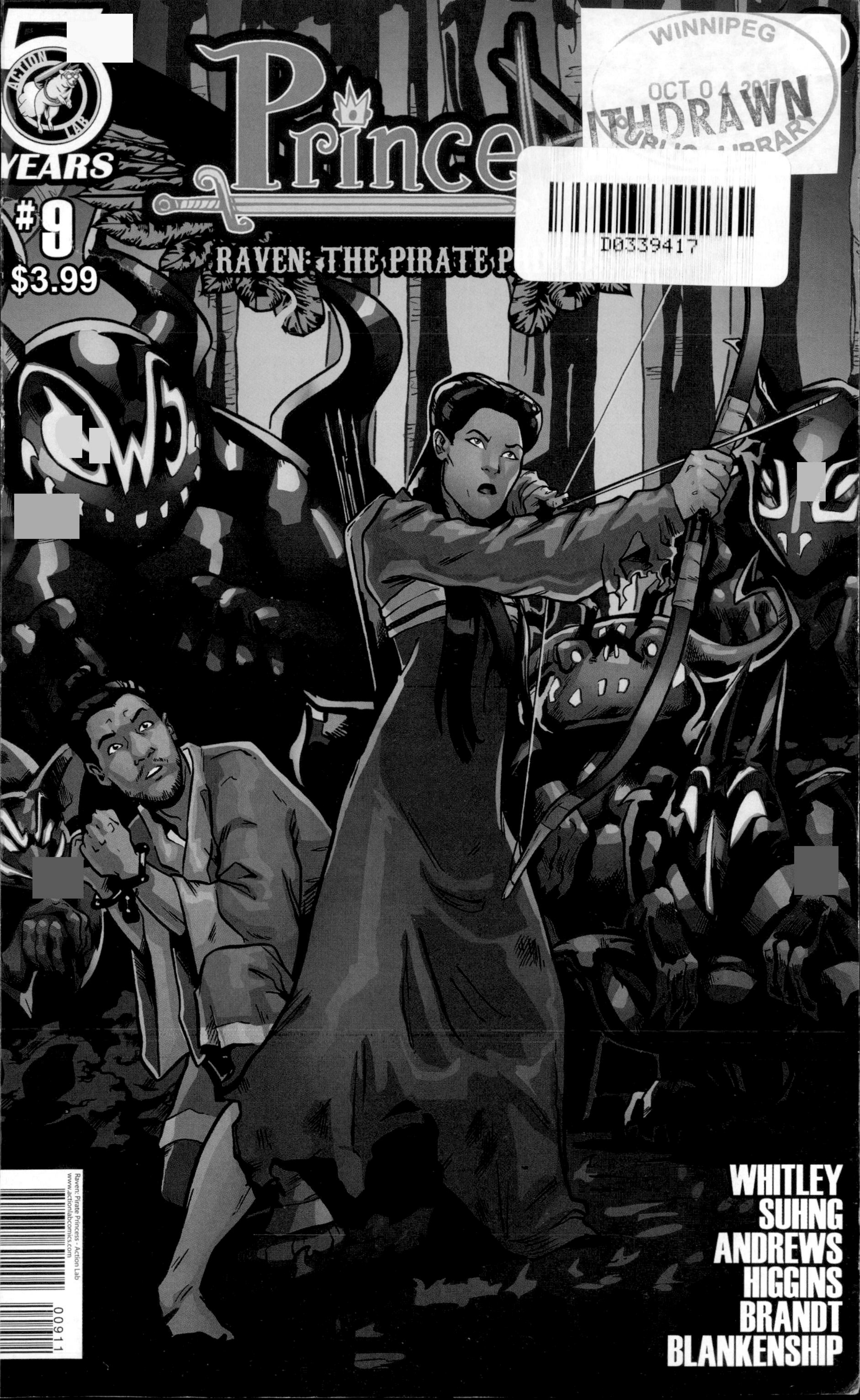

5 YEARS
ACTION LAB
Prince
RAVEN: THE PIRATE P
#9
$3.99
WHITLEY
SUHNG
ANDREWS
HIGGINS
BRANDT
BLANKENSHIP
Raven: Pirate Princess - Action Lab
www.actionlabcomics.com
00911

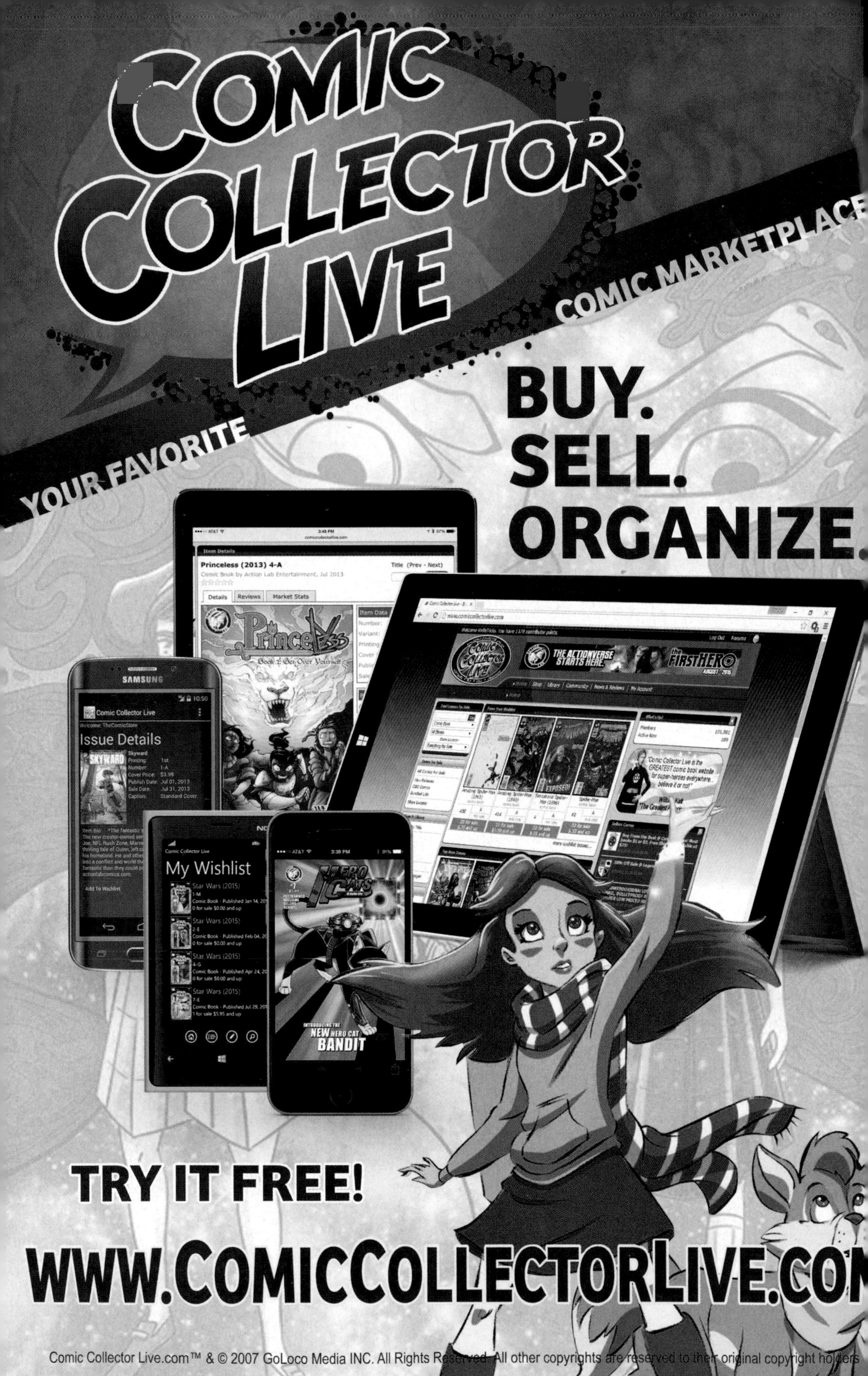

COMIC COLLECTOR LIVE
YOUR FAVORITE COMIC MARKETPLACE
BUY.
SELL.
ORGANIZE.
TRY IT FREE!
WWW.COMICCOLLECTORLIVE.COM

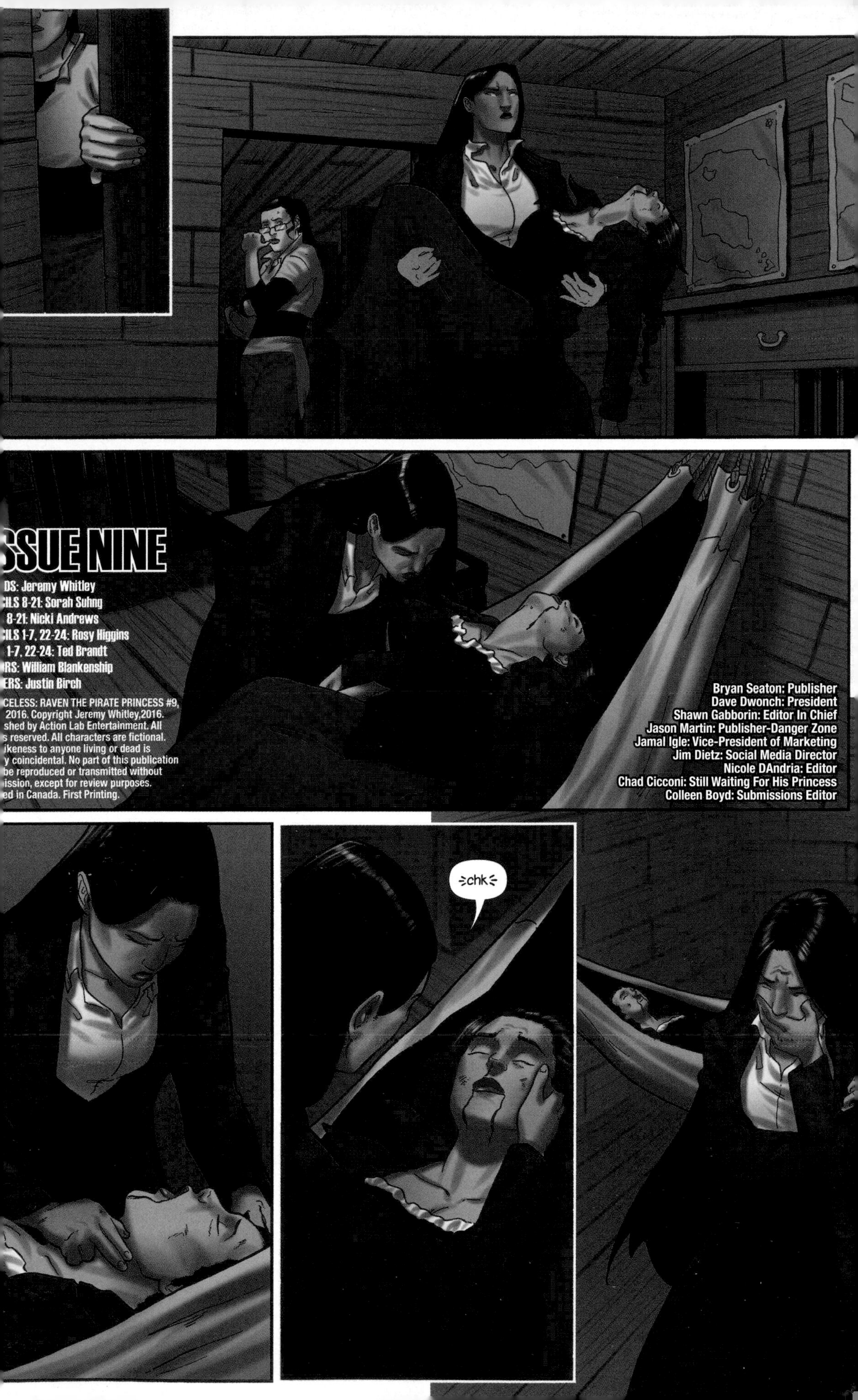
SSUE NINE
DS: Jeremy Whitley
CILS 8-21: Sorah Suhng
8-21: Nicki Andrews
CILS 1-7, 22-24: Rosy Higgins
1-7, 22-24: Ted Brandt
RS: William Blankenship
ERS: Justin Birch
CELESS: RAVEN THE PIRATE PRINCESS #9, 2016. Copyright Jeremy Whitley,2016. shed by Action Lab Entertainment. All s reserved. All characters are fictional. ikeness to anyone living or dead is y coincidental. No part of this publication be reproduced or transmitted without ission, except for review purposes. ed in Canada. First Printing.
Bryan Seaton: Publisher
Dave Dwonch: President
Shawn Gabborin: Editor In Chief
Jason Martin: Publisher-Danger Zone
Jamal Igle: Vice-President of Marketing
Jim Dietz: Social Media Director
Nicole DAndria: Editor
Chad Cicconi: Still Waiting For His Princess
Colleen Boyd: Submissions Editor
chk

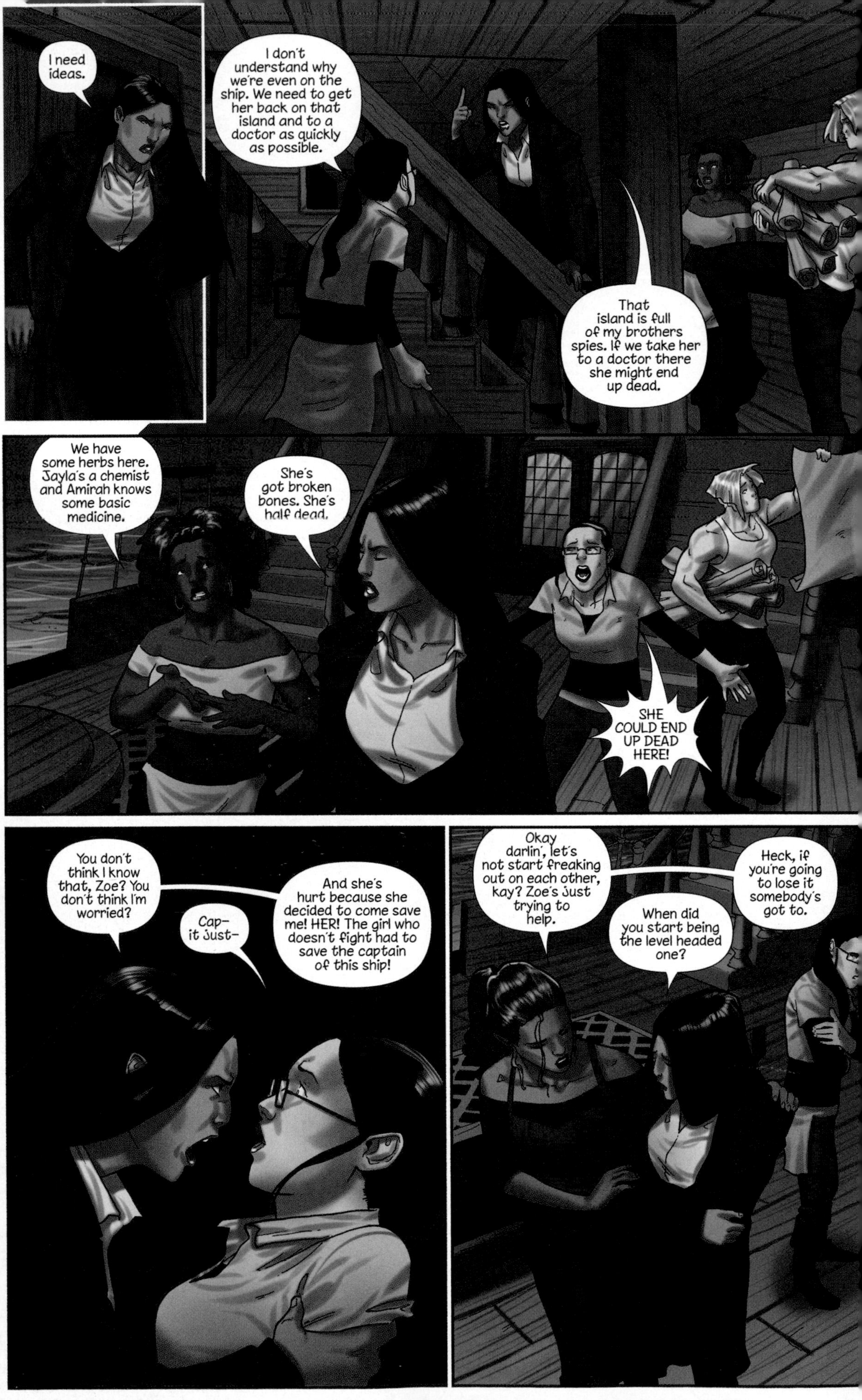
I need ideas.
I don't understand why we're even on the ship. We need to get her back on that island and to a doctor as quickly as possible.
That island is full of my brothers spies. If we take her to a doctor there she might end up dead.
We have some herbs here. Jayla's a chemist and Amirah knows some basic medicine.
She's got broken bones. She's half dead.
SHE COULD END UP DEAD HERE!
You don't think I know that, Zoe? You don't think I'm worried?
Cap- it just-
And she's hurt because she decided to come save me! HER! The girl who doesn't fight had to save the captain of this ship!
Okay darlin', let's not start freaking out on each other, kay? Zoe's just trying to help.
Heck, if you're going to lose it somebody's got to.
When did you start being the level headed one?

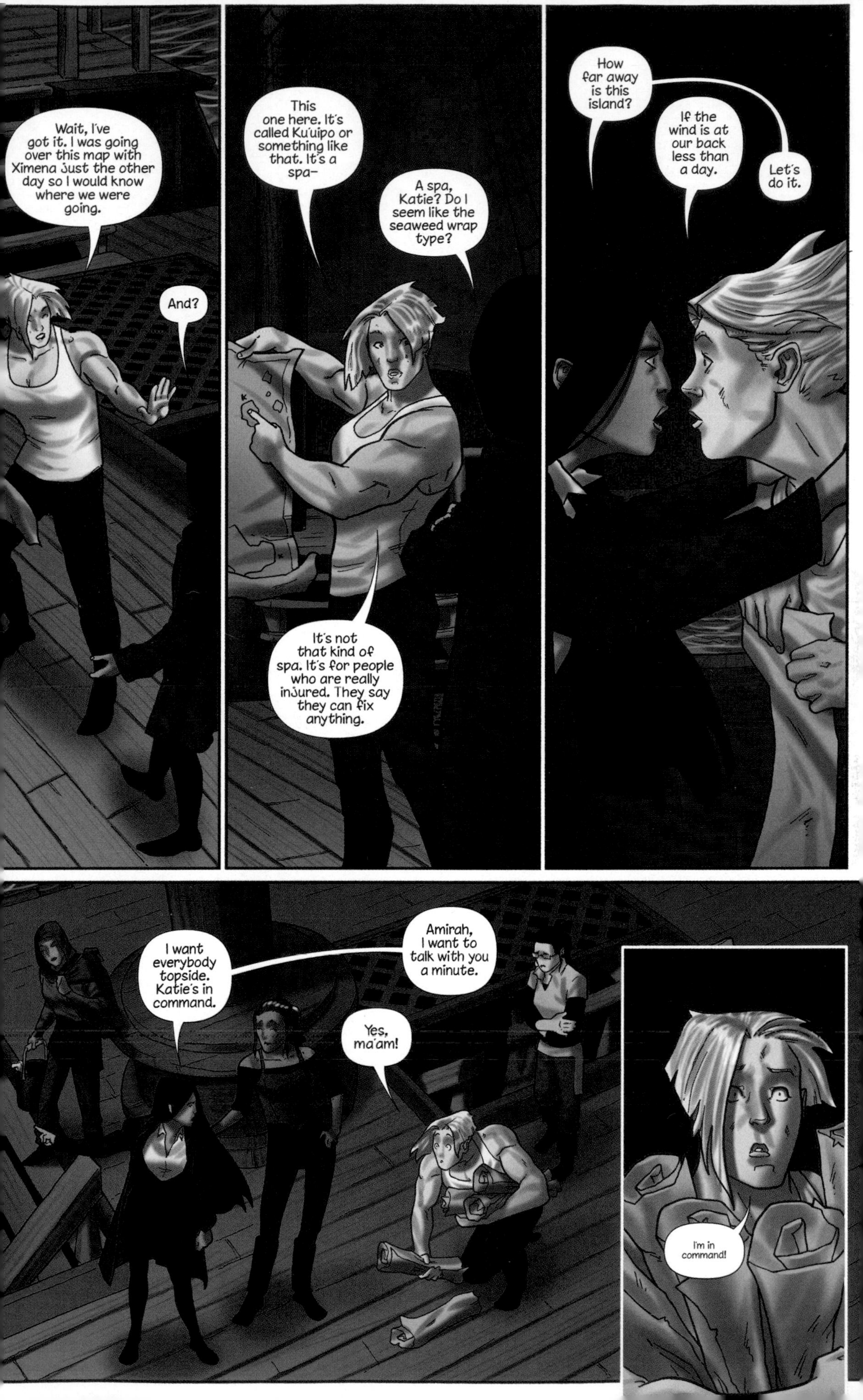
Wait, I've got it. I was going over this map with Ximena just the other day so I would know where we were going.
And?
This one here. It's called Ku'uipo or something like that. It's a spa–
A spa, Katie? Do I seem like the seaweed wrap type?
It's not that kind of spa. It's for people who are really injured. They say they can fix anything.
How far away is this island?
If the wind is at our back less than a day.
Let's do it.
I want everybody topside. Katie's in command.
Amirah, I want to talk with you a minute.
Yes, ma'am!
I'm in command!

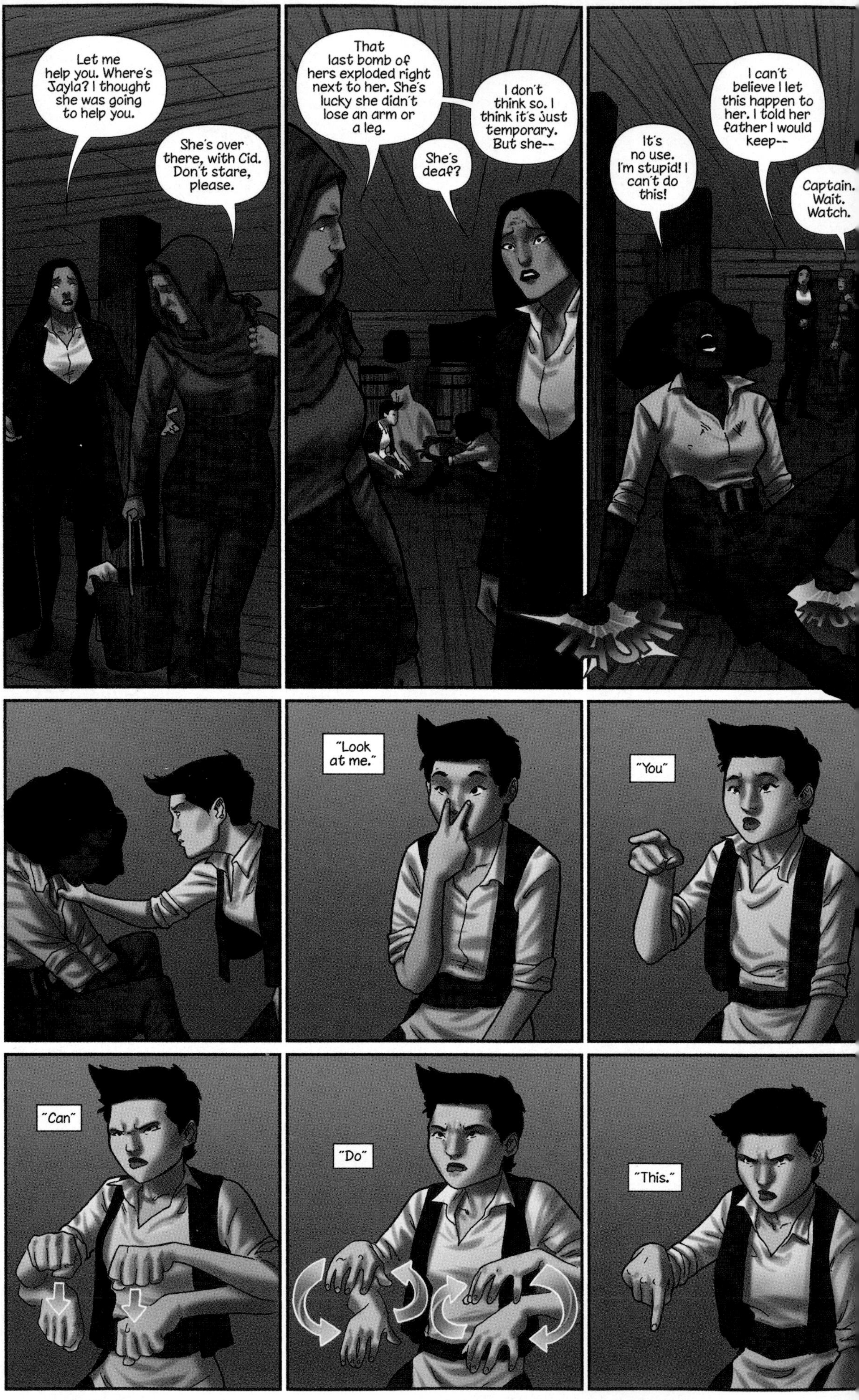

Let me help you. Where's Jayla? I thought she was going to help you.
She's over there, with Cid. Don't stare, please.
That last bomb of hers exploded right next to her. She's lucky she didn't lose an arm or a leg.
She's deaf?
I don't think so. I think it's just temporary. But she--
It's no use. I'm stupid! I can't do this!
I can't believe I let this happen to her. I told her father I would keep--
Captain. Wait. Watch.
THUMP
"Look at me."
"You"
"Can"
"Do"
"This."

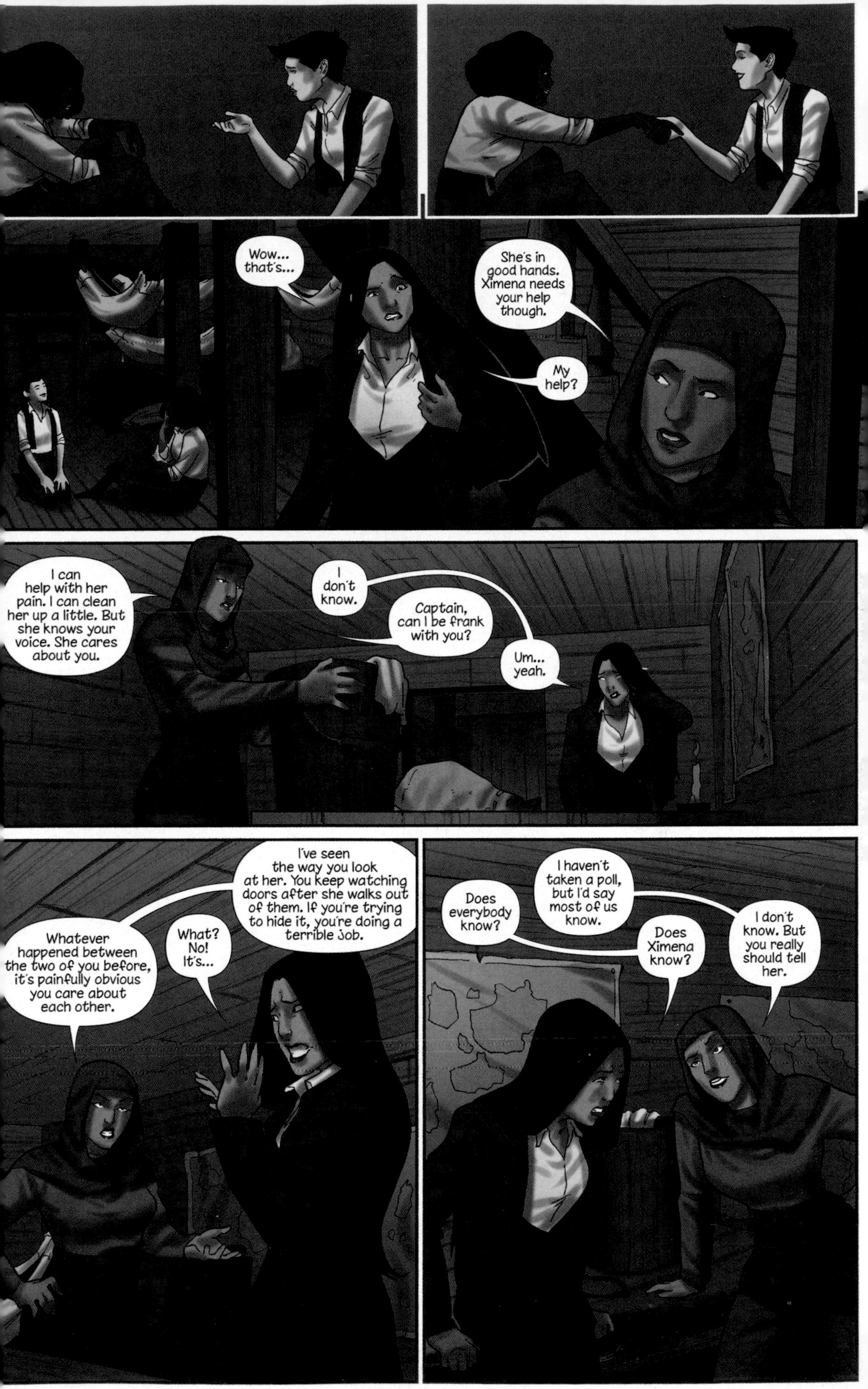
Wow... that's...
She's in good hands. Ximena needs your help though.
My help?
I can help with her pain. I can clean her up a little. But she knows your voice. She cares about you.
I don't know.
Captain, can I be frank with you?
Um... yeah.
Whatever happened between the two of you before, it's painfully obvious you care about each other.
What? No! It's...
I've seen the way you look at her. You keep watching doors after she walks out of them. If you're trying to hide it, you're doing a terrible job.
Does everybody know?
I haven't taken a poll, but I'd say most of us know.
Does Ximena know?
I don't know. But you really should tell her.

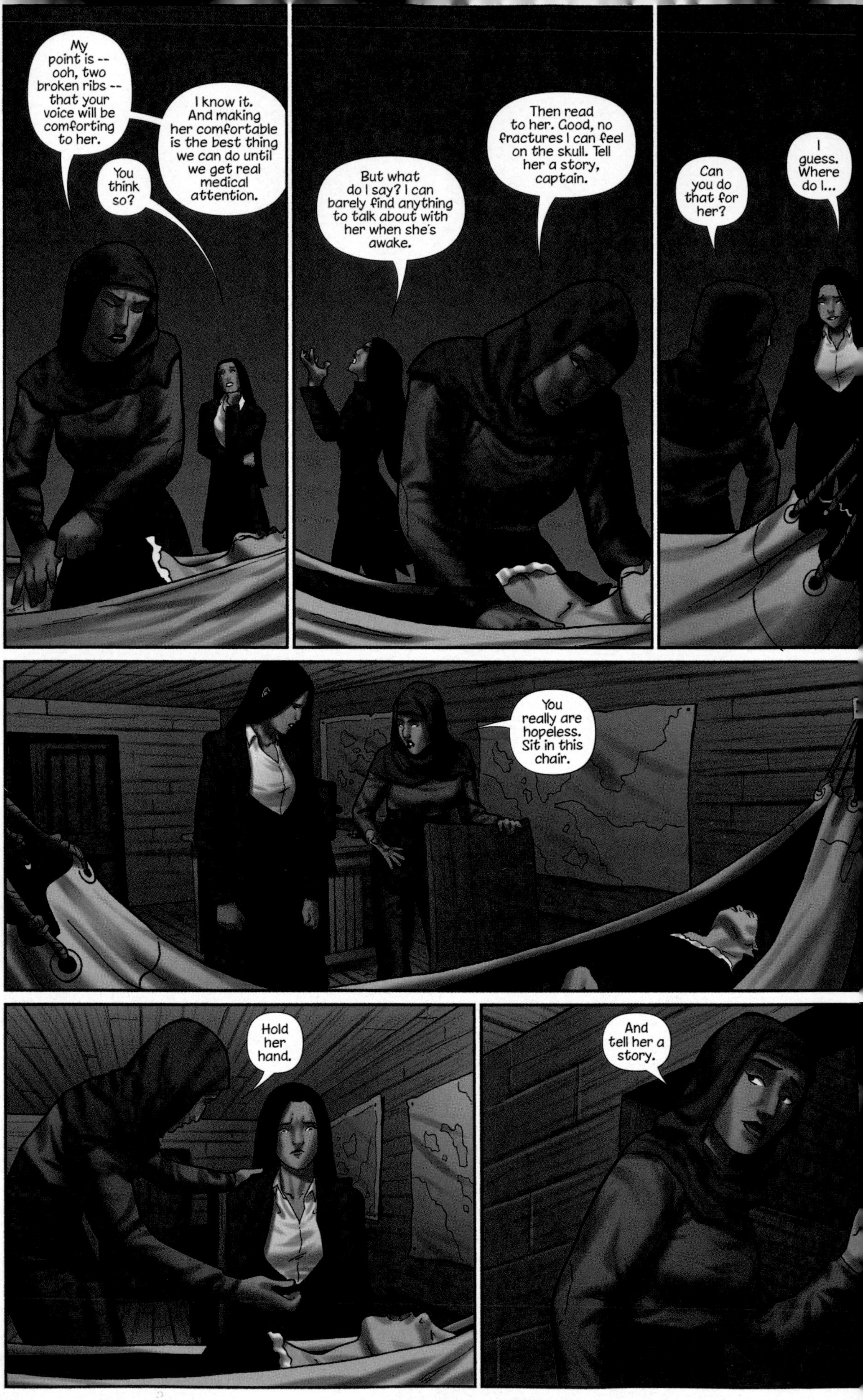
My point is -- ooh, two broken ribs -- that your voice will be comforting to her.
You think so?
I know it. And making her comfortable is the best thing we can do until we get real medical attention.
But what do I say? I can barely find anything to talk about with her when she's awake.
Then read to her. Good, no fractures I can feel on the skull. Tell her a story, captain.
Can you do that for her?
I guess. Where do I...
You really are hopeless. Sit in this chair.
Hold her hand.
And tell her a story.

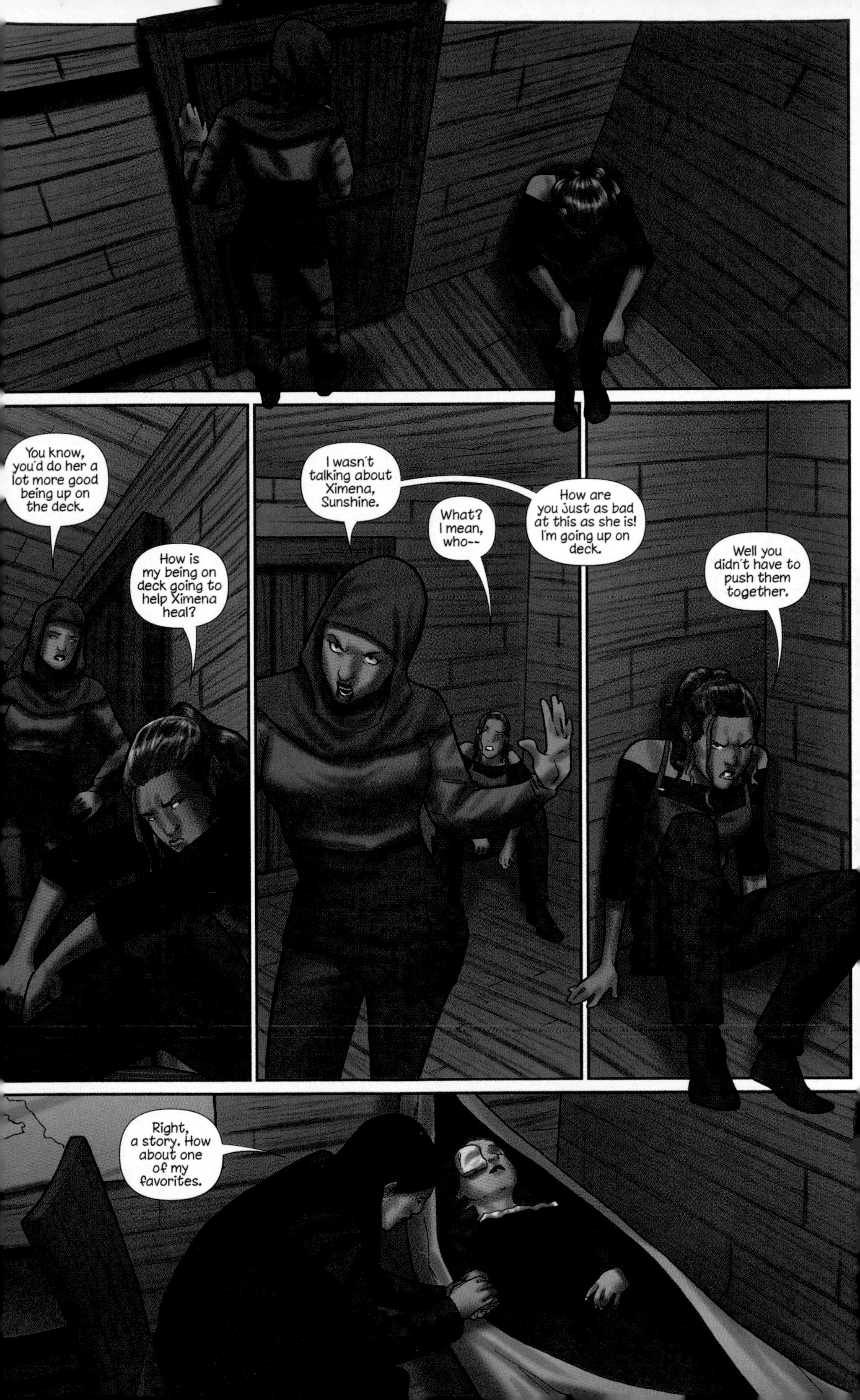
You know, you'd do her a lot more good being up on the deck.
How is my being on deck going to help Ximena heal?
I wasn't talking about Ximena, Sunshine.
What? I mean, who--
How are you just as bad at this as she is! I'm going up on deck.
Well you didn't have to push them together.
Right, a story. How about one of my favorites.

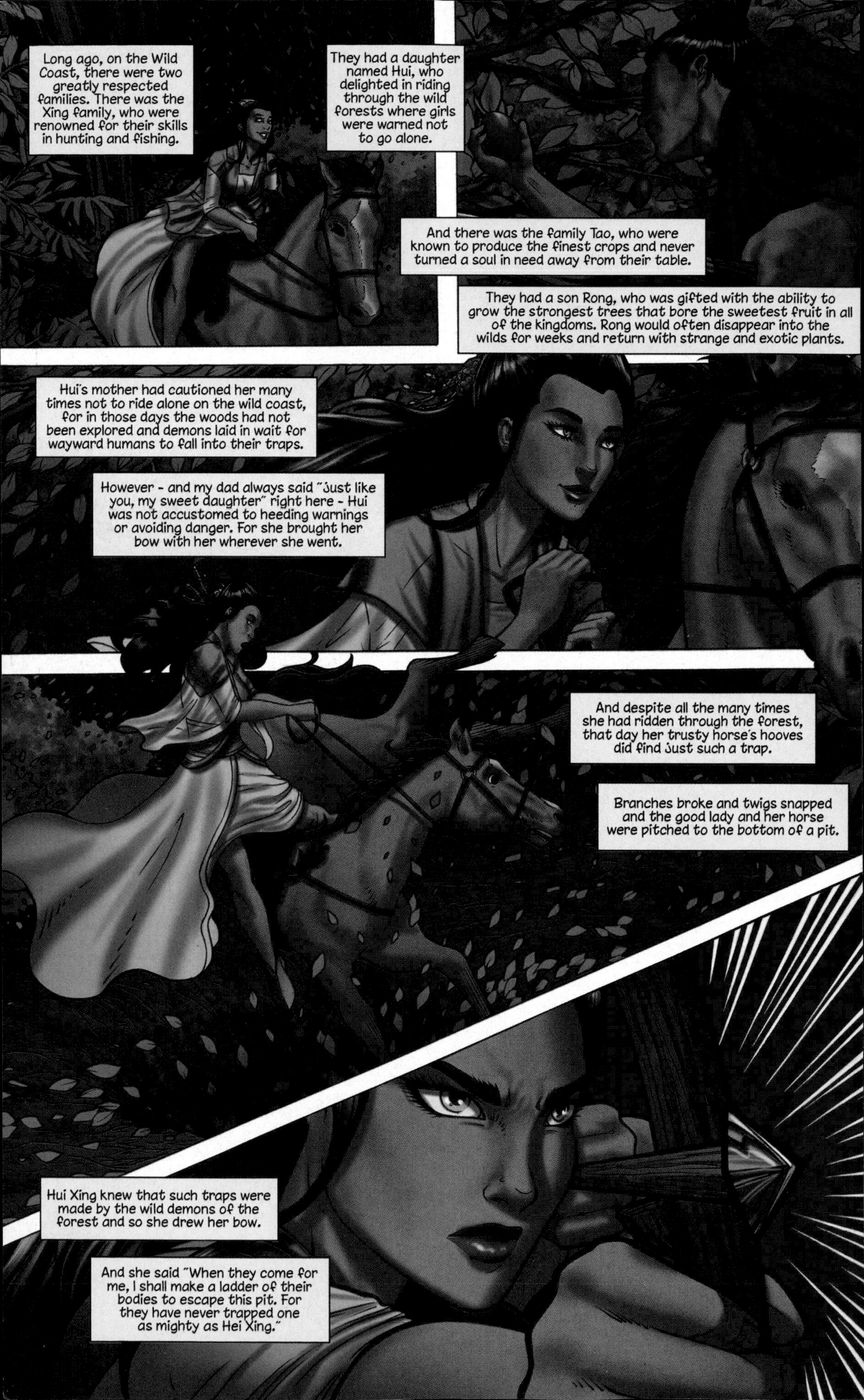
Long ago, on the Wild Coast, there were two greatly respected families. There was the Xing family, who were renowned for their skills in hunting and fishing.
They had a daughter named Hui, who delighted in riding through the wild forests where girls were warned not to go alone.
And there was the family Tao, who were known to produce the finest crops and never turned a soul in need away from their table.
They had a son Rong, who was gifted with the ability to grow the strongest trees that bore the sweetest fruit in all of the kingdoms. Rong would often disappear into the wilds for weeks and return with strange and exotic plants.
Hui's mother had cautioned her many times not to ride alone on the wild coast, for in those days the woods had not been explored and demons laid in wait for wayward humans to fall into their traps.
However - and my dad always said "Just like you, my sweet daughter" right here - Hui was not accustomed to heeding warnings or avoiding danger. For she brought her bow with her wherever she went.
And despite all the many times she had ridden through the forest, that day her trusty horse's hooves did find just such a trap.
Branches broke and twigs snapped and the good lady and her horse were pitched to the bottom of a pit.
Hui Xing knew that such traps were made by the wild demons of the forest and so she drew her bow.
And she said "When they come for me, I shall make a ladder of their bodies to escape this pit. For they have never trapped one as mighty as Hei Xing."

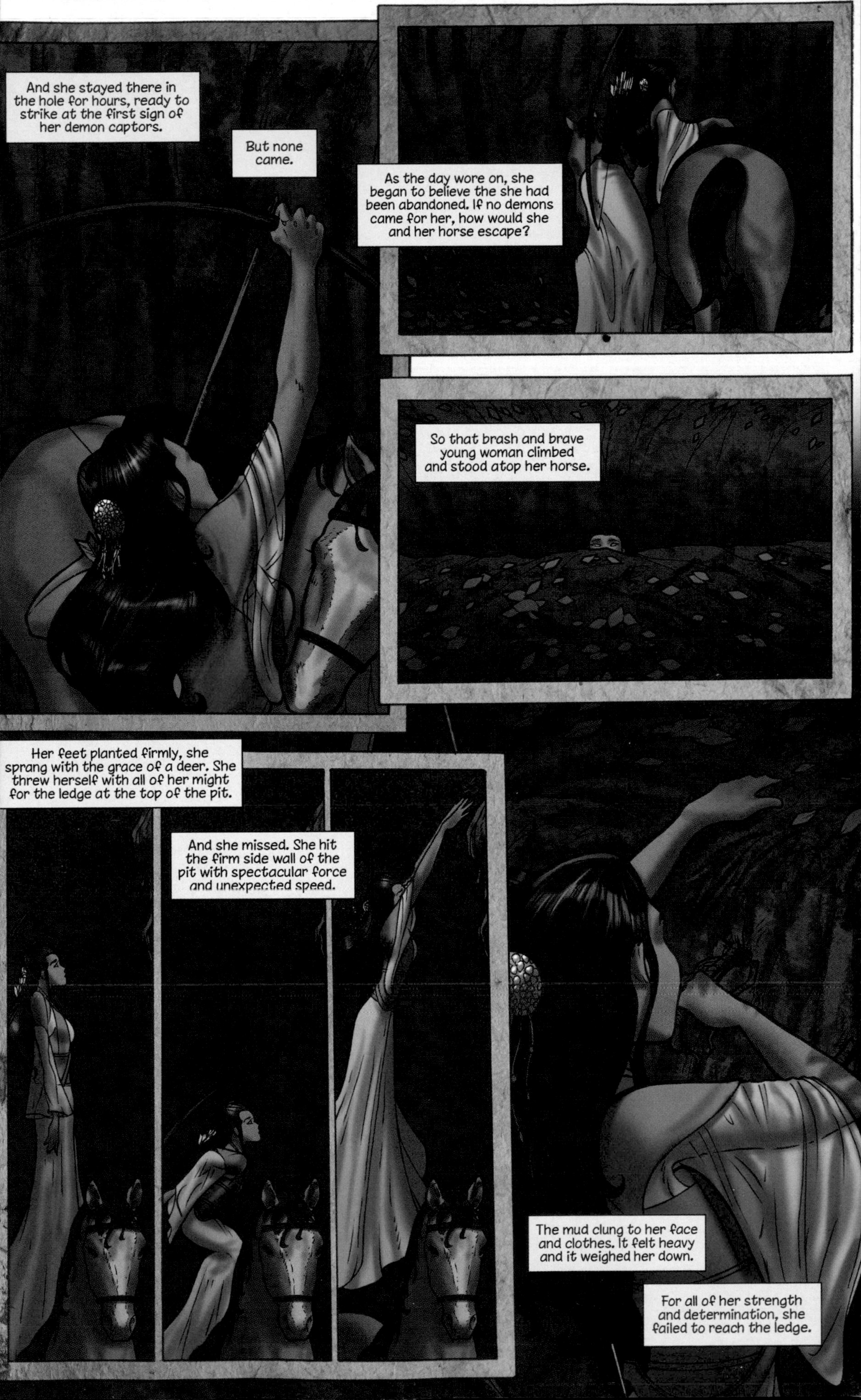
And she stayed there in the hole for hours, ready to strike at the first sign of her demon captors.
But none came.
As the day wore on, she began to believe the she had been abandoned. If no demons came for her, how would she and her horse escape?
So that brash and brave young woman climbed and stood atop her horse.
Her feet planted firmly, she sprang with the grace of a deer. She threw herself with all of her might for the ledge at the top of the pit.
And she missed. She hit the firm side wall of the pit with spectacular force and unexpected speed.
The mud clung to her face and clothes. It felt heavy and it weighed her down.
For all of her strength and determination, she failed to reach the ledge.

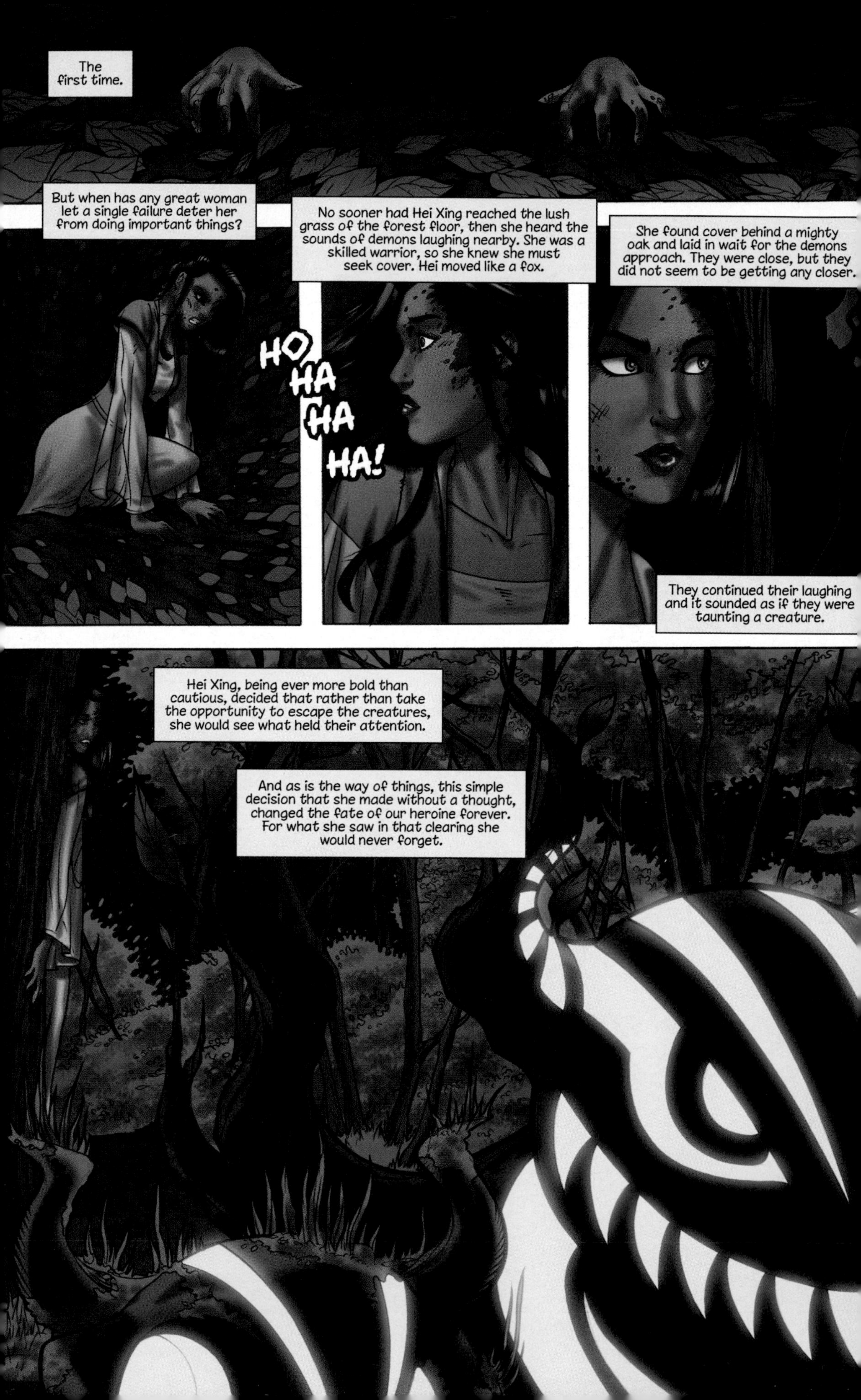
The first time.
But when has any great woman let a single failure deter her from doing important things?
No sooner had Hei Xing reached the lush grass of the forest floor, then she heard the sounds of demons laughing nearby. She was a skilled warrior, so she knew she must seek cover. Hei moved like a fox.
HO HA HA HA!
She found cover behind a mighty oak and laid in wait for the demons approach. They were close, but they did not seem to be getting any closer.
They continued their laughing and it sounded as if they were taunting a creature.
Hei Xing, being ever more bold than cautious, decided that rather than take the opportunity to escape the creatures, she would see what held their attention.
And as is the way of things, this simple decision that she made without a thought, changed the fate of our heroine forever. For what she saw in that clearing she would never forget.

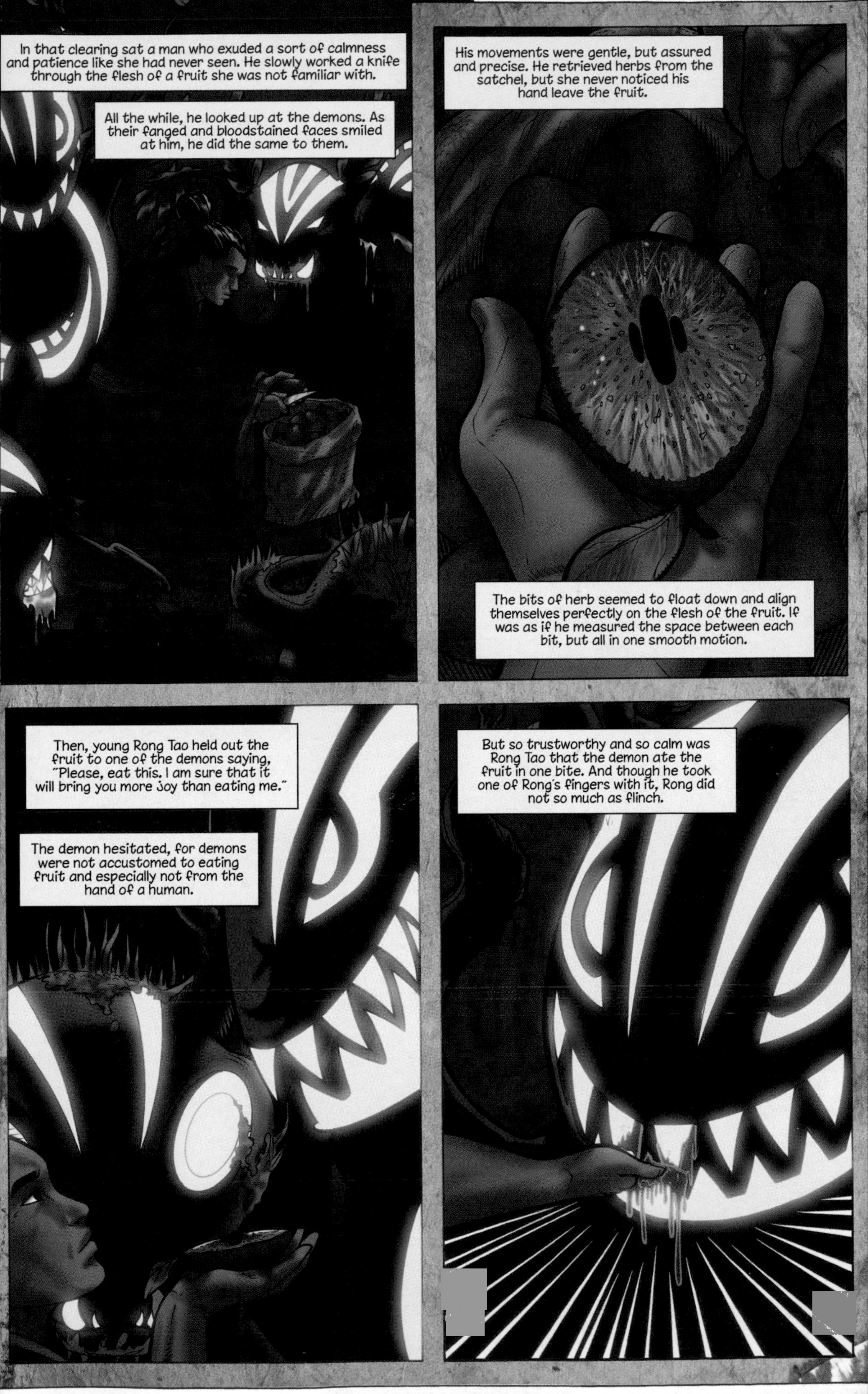
In that clearing sat a man who exuded a sort of calmness and patience like she had never seen. He slowly worked a knife through the flesh of a fruit she was not familiar with.
All the while, he looked up at the demons. As their fanged and bloodstained faces smiled at him, he did the same to them.
His movements were gentle, but assured and precise. He retrieved herbs from the satchel, but she never noticed his hand leave the fruit.
The bits of herb seemed to float down and align themselves perfectly on the flesh of the fruit. If was as if he measured the space between each bit, but all in one smooth motion.
Then, young Rong Tao held out the fruit to one of the demons saying, "Please, eat this. I am sure that it will bring you more joy than eating me."
The demon hesitated, for demons were not accustomed to eating fruit and especially not from the hand of a human.
But so trustworthy and so calm was Rong Tao that the demon ate the fruit in one bite. And though he took one of Rong's fingers with it, Rong did not so much as flinch.

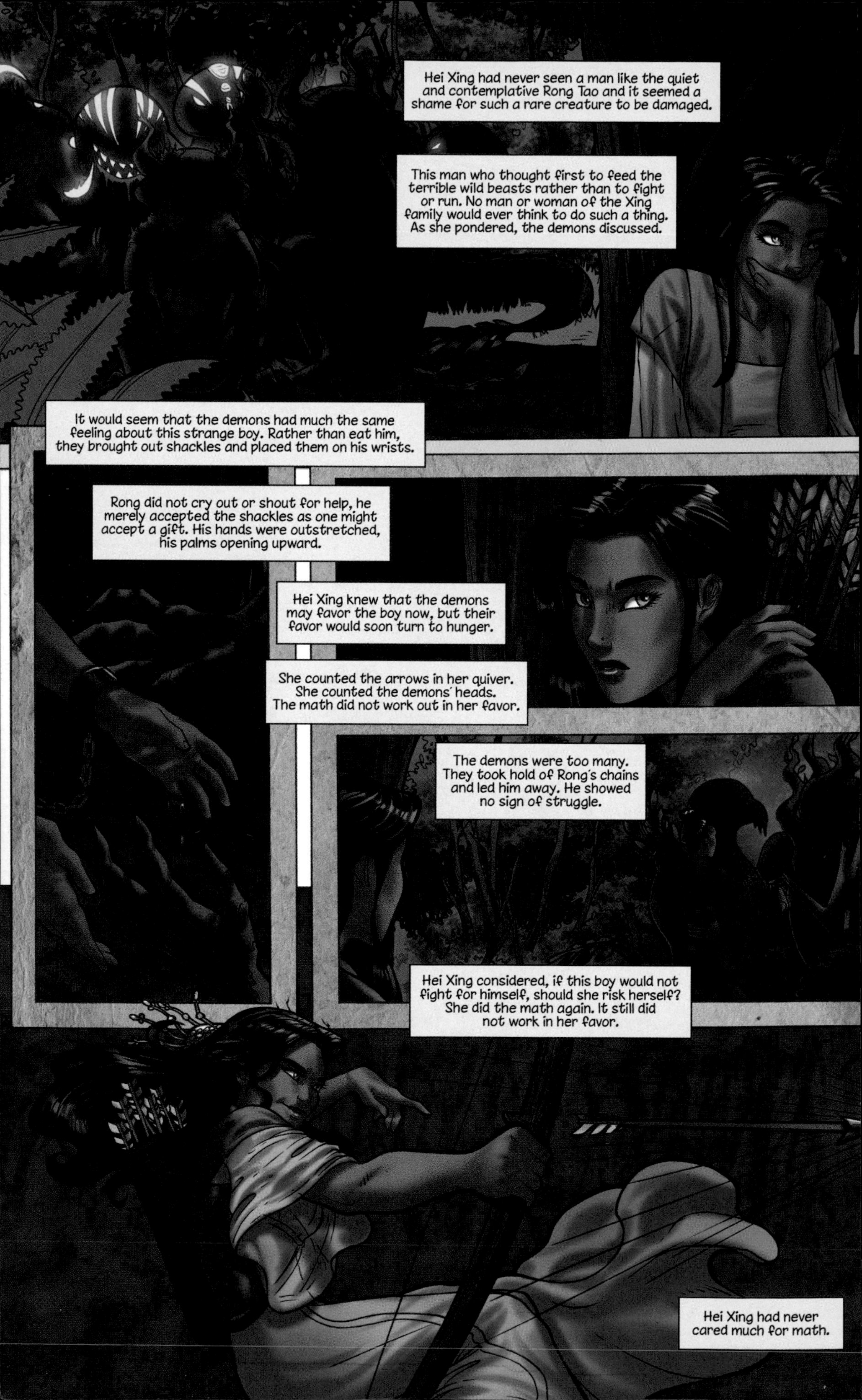

Hei Xing had never seen a man like the quiet and contemplative Rong Tao and it seemed a shame for such a rare creature to be damaged.
This man who thought first to feed the terrible wild beasts rather than to fight or run. No man or woman of the Xing family would ever think to do such a thing. As she pondered, the demons discussed.
It would seem that the demons had much the same feeling about this strange boy. Rather than eat him, they brought out shackles and placed them on his wrists.
Rong did not cry out or shout for help, he merely accepted the shackles as one might accept a gift. His hands were outstretched, his palms opening upward.
Hei Xing knew that the demons may favor the boy now, but their favor would soon turn to hunger.
She counted the arrows in her quiver. She counted the demons' heads. The math did not work out in her favor.
The demons were too many. They took hold of Rong's chains and led him away. He showed no sign of struggle.
Hei Xing considered, if this boy would not fight for himself, should she risk herself? She did the math again. It still did not work in her favor.
Hei Xing had never cared much for math.

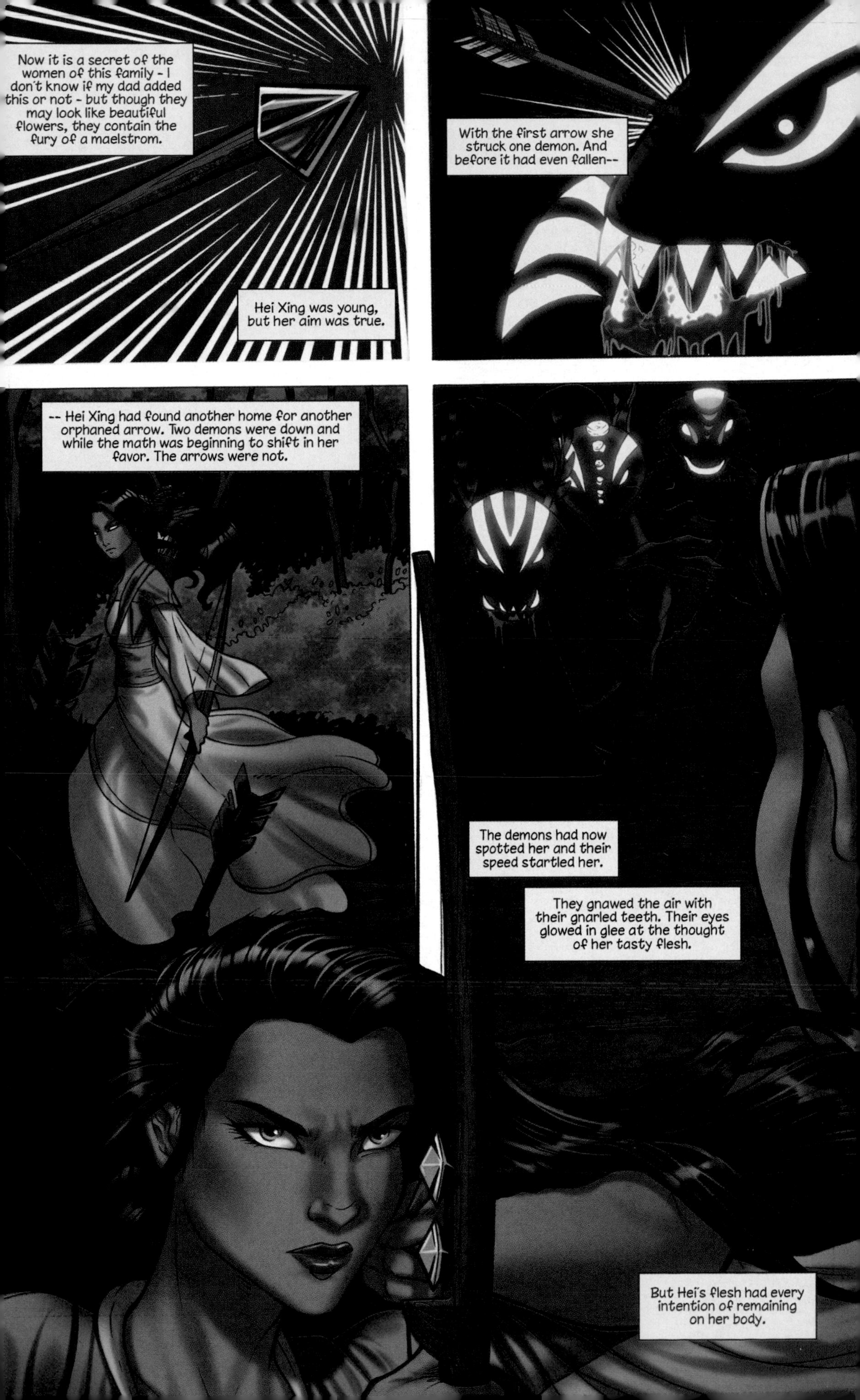
Now it is a secret of the women of this family - I don't know if my dad added this or not - but though they may look like beautiful flowers, they contain the fury of a maelstrom.
Hei Xing was young, but her aim was true.
With the first arrow she struck one demon. And before it had even fallen--
-- Hei Xing had found another home for another orphaned arrow. Two demons were down and while the math was beginning to shift in her favor. The arrows were not.
The demons had now spotted her and their speed startled her.
They gnawed the air with their gnarled teeth. Their eyes glowed in glee at the thought of her tasty flesh.
But Hei's flesh had every intention of remaining on her body.

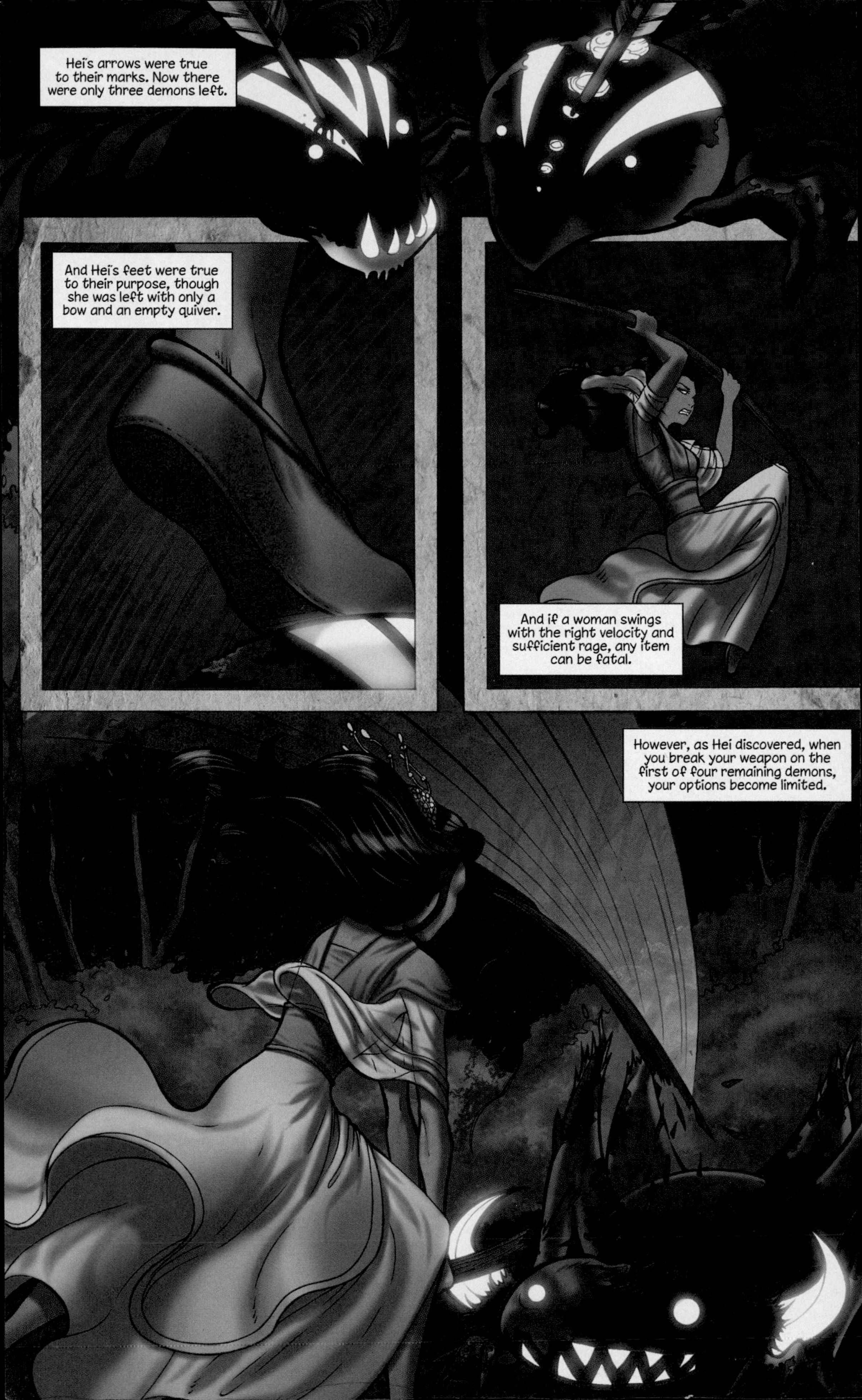
Hei's arrows were true to their marks. Now there were only three demons left.
And Hei's feet were true to their purpose, though she was left with only a bow and an empty quiver.
And if a woman swings with the right velocity and sufficient rage, any item can be fatal.
However, as Hei discovered, when you break your weapon on the first of four remaining demons, your options become limited.

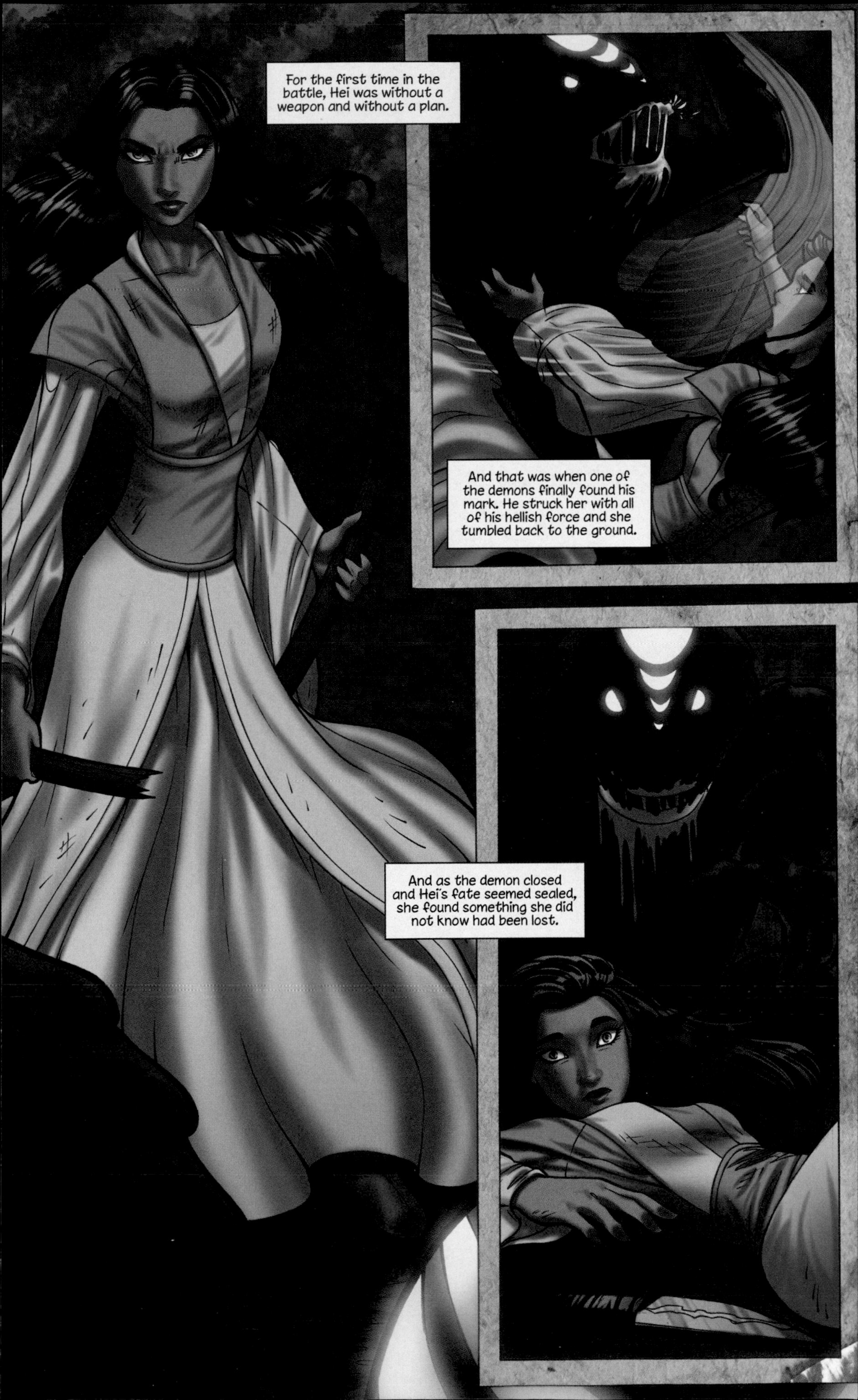
For the first time in the battle, Hei was without a weapon and without a plan.
And that was when one of the demons finally found his mark. He struck her with all of his hellish force and she tumbled back to the ground.
And as the demon closed and Hei's fate seemed sealed, she found something she did not know had been lost.

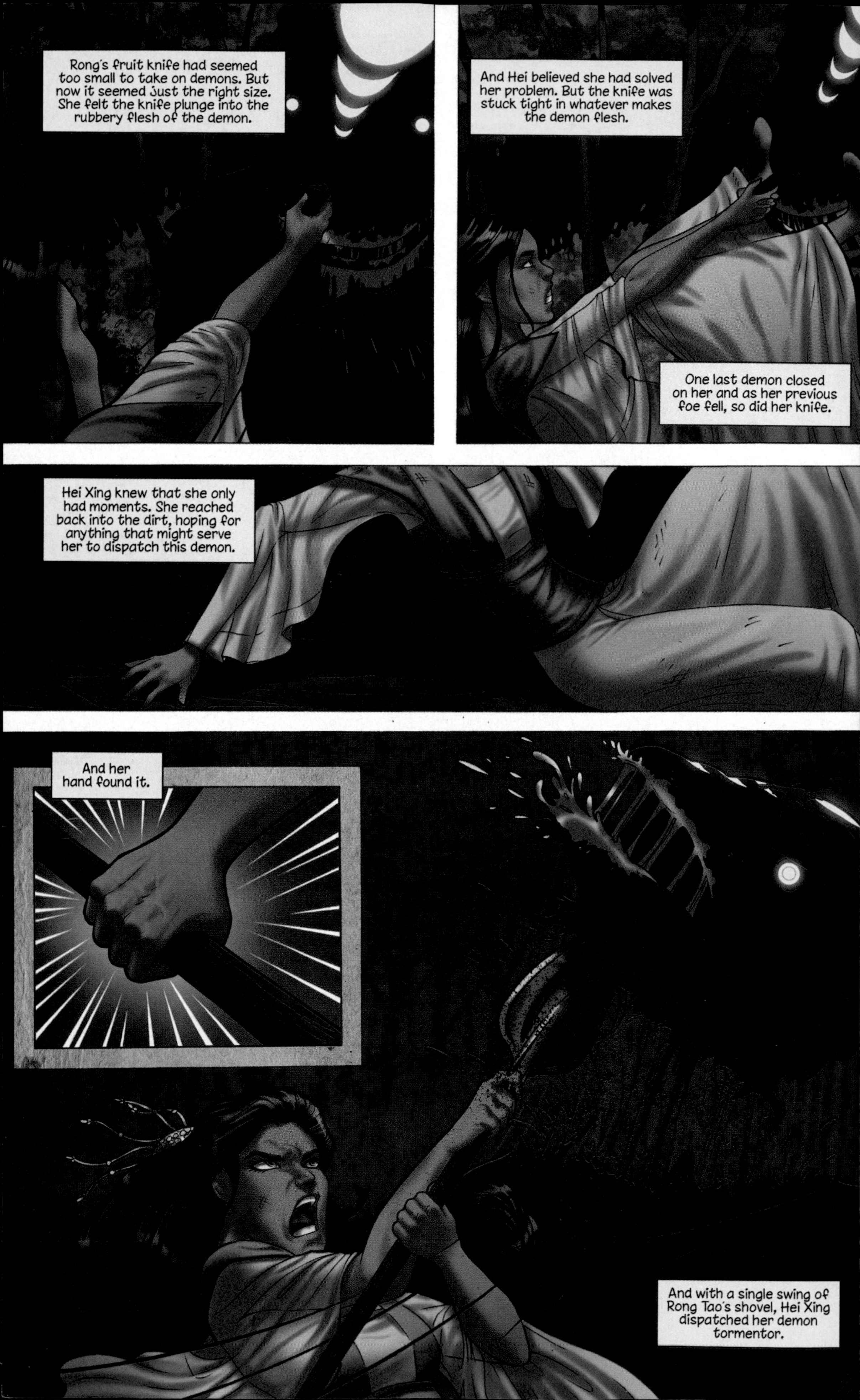
Rong's fruit knife had seemed too small to take on demons. But now it seemed just the right size. She felt the knife plunge into the rubbery flesh of the demon.
And Hei believed she had solved her problem. But the knife was stuck tight in whatever makes the demon flesh.
One last demon closed on her and as her previous foe fell, so did her knife.
Hei Xing knew that she only had moments. She reached back into the dirt, hoping for anything that might serve her to dispatch this demon.
And her hand found it.
And with a single swing of Rong Tao's shovel, Hei Xing dispatched her demon tormentor.

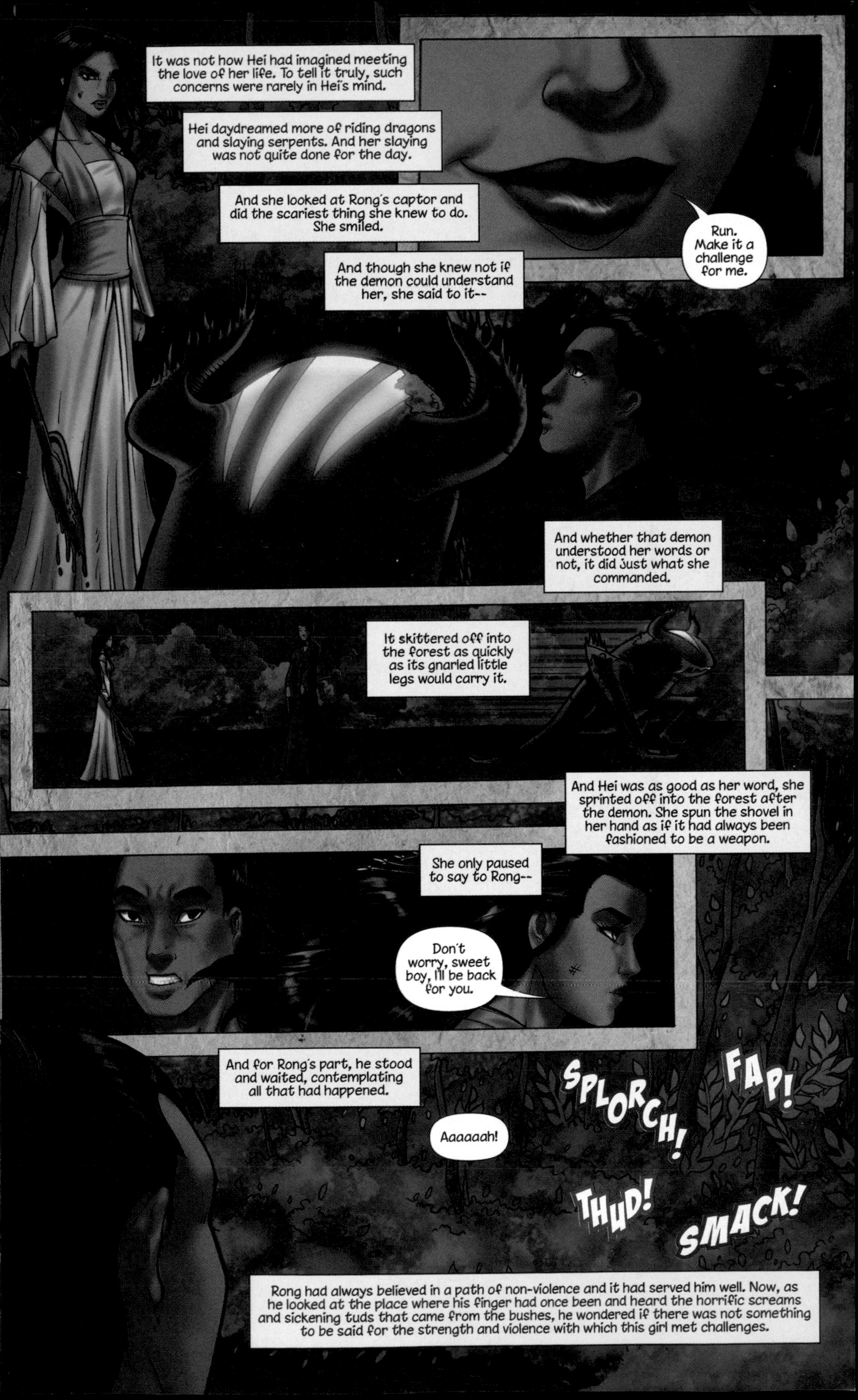
It was not how Hei had imagined meeting the love of her life. To tell it truly, such concerns were rarely in Hei's mind.
Hei daydreamed more of riding dragons and slaying serpents. And her slaying was not quite done for the day.
And she looked at Rong's captor and did the scariest thing she knew to do. She smiled.
And though she knew not if the demon could understand her, she said to it--
Run. Make it a challenge for me.
And whether that demon understood her words or not, it did just what she commanded.
It skittered off into the forest as quickly as its gnarled little legs would carry it.
And Hei was as good as her word, she sprinted off into the forest after the demon. She spun the shovel in her hand as if it had always been fashioned to be a weapon.
She only paused to say to Rong--
Don't worry, sweet boy, I'll be back for you.
And for Rong's part, he stood and waited, contemplating all that had happened.
SPLORCH!
FAP!
Aaaaaah!
THUD!
SMACK!
Rong had always believed in a path of non-violence and it had served him well. Now, as he looked at the place where his finger had once been and heard the horrific screams and sickening tuds that came from the bushes, he wondered if there was not something to be said for the strength and violence with which this girl met challenges.

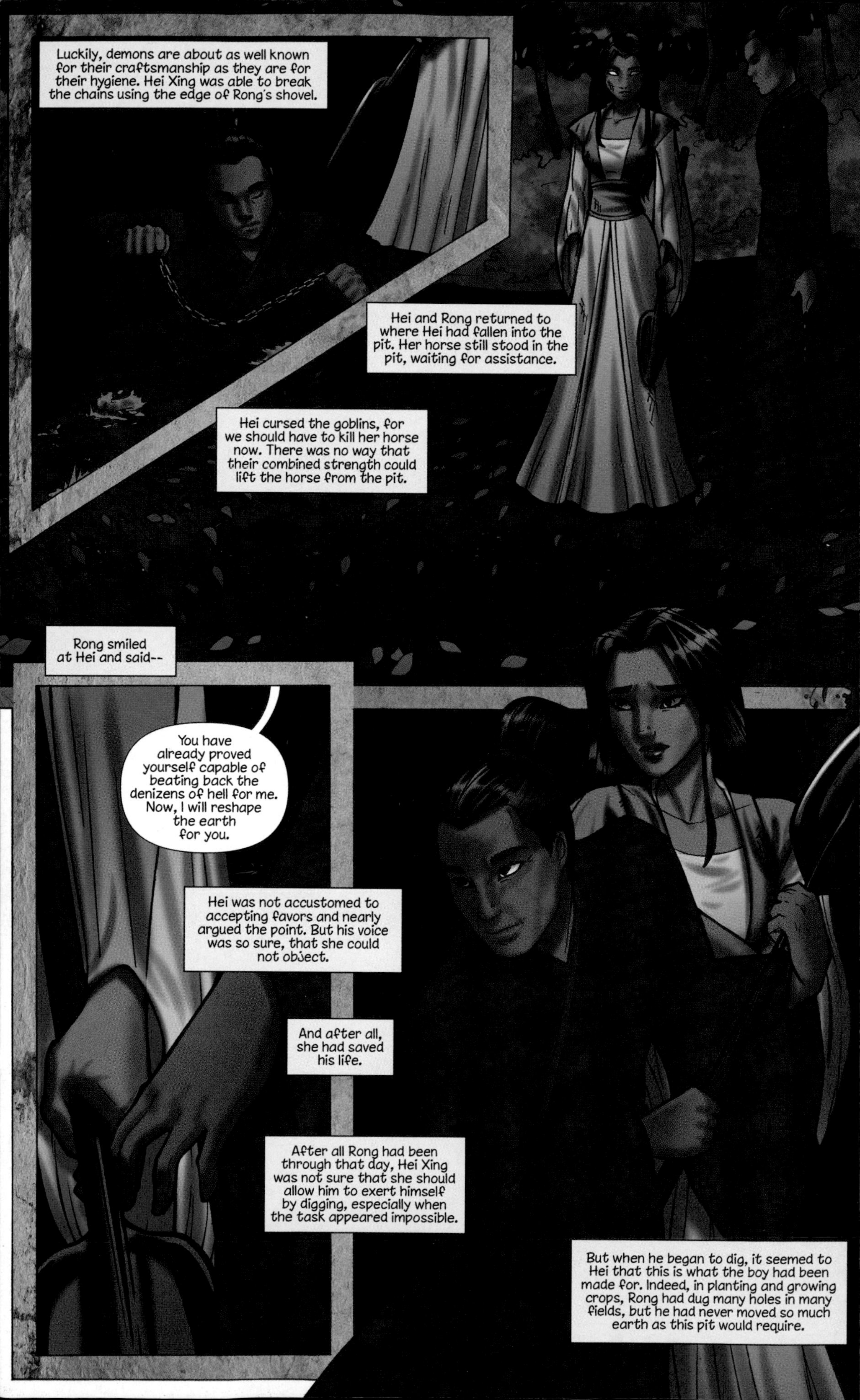
Luckily, demons are about as well known for their craftsmanship as they are for their hygiene. Hei Xing was able to break the chains using the edge of Rong's shovel.
Hei and Rong returned to where Hei had fallen into the pit. Her horse still stood in the pit, waiting for assistance.
Hei cursed the goblins, for we should have to kill her horse now. There was no way that their combined strength could lift the horse from the pit.
Rong smiled at Hei and said--
You have already proved yourself capable of beating back the denizens of hell for me. Now, I will reshape the earth for you.
Hei was not accustomed to accepting favors and nearly argued the point. But his voice was so sure, that she could not object.
And after all, she had saved his life.
After all Rong had been through that day, Hei Xing was not sure that she should allow him to exert himself by digging, especially when the task appeared impossible.
But when he began to dig, it seemed to Hei that this is what the boy had been made for. Indeed, in planting and growing crops, Rong had dug many holes in many fields, but he had never moved so much earth as this pit would require.

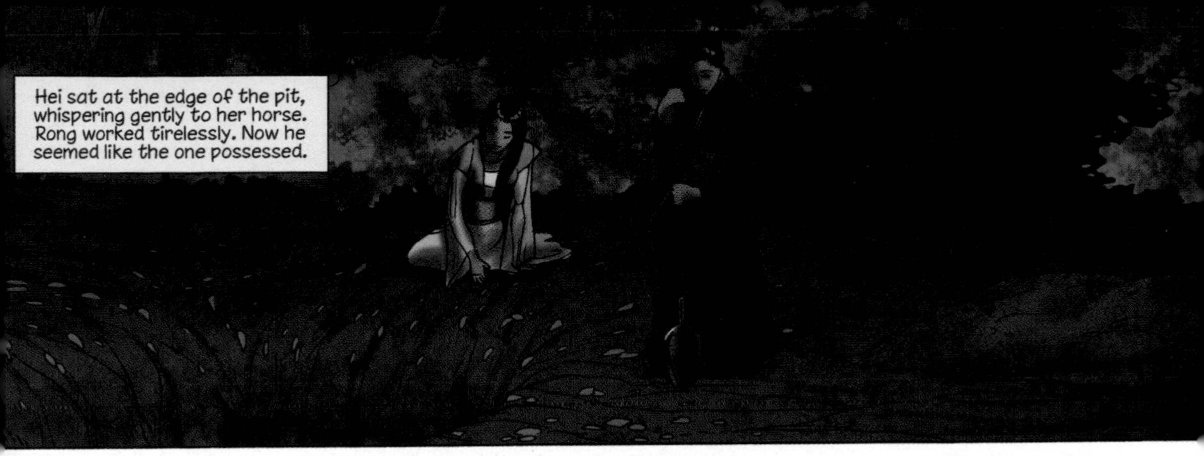
Hei sat at the edge of the pit, whispering gently to her horse. Rong worked tirelessly. Now he seemed like the one possessed.

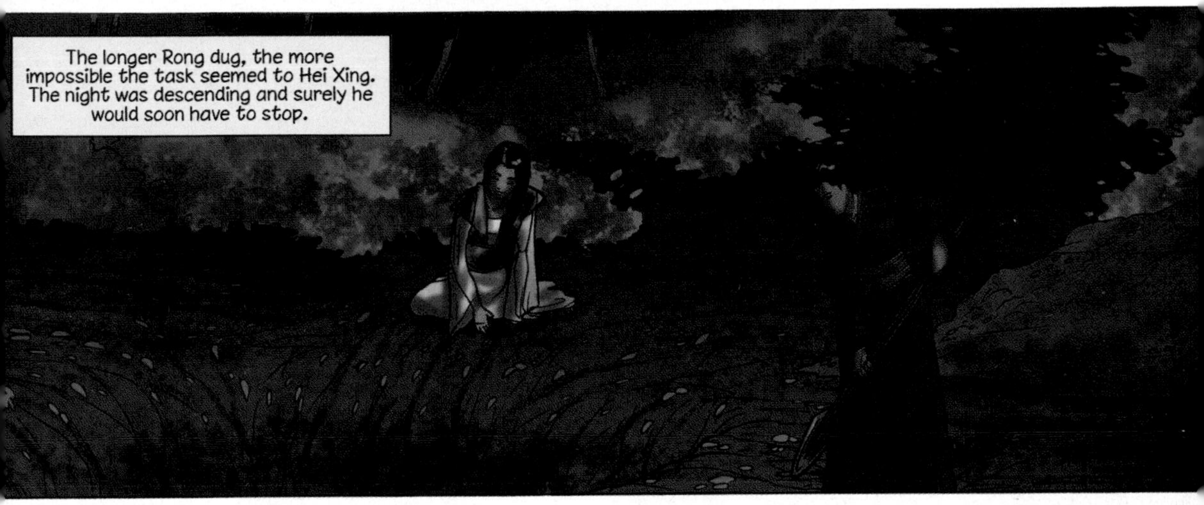
The longer Rong dug, the more impossible the task seemed to Hei Xing. The night was descending and surely he would soon have to stop.

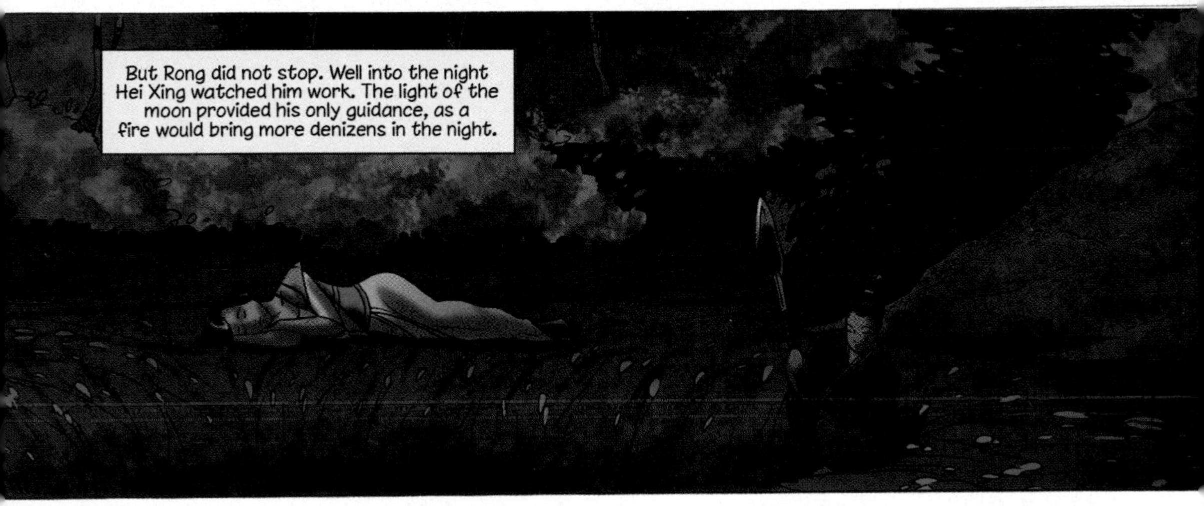
But Rong did not stop. Well into the night Hei Xing watched him work. The light of the moon provided his only guidance, as a fire would bring more denizens in the night.

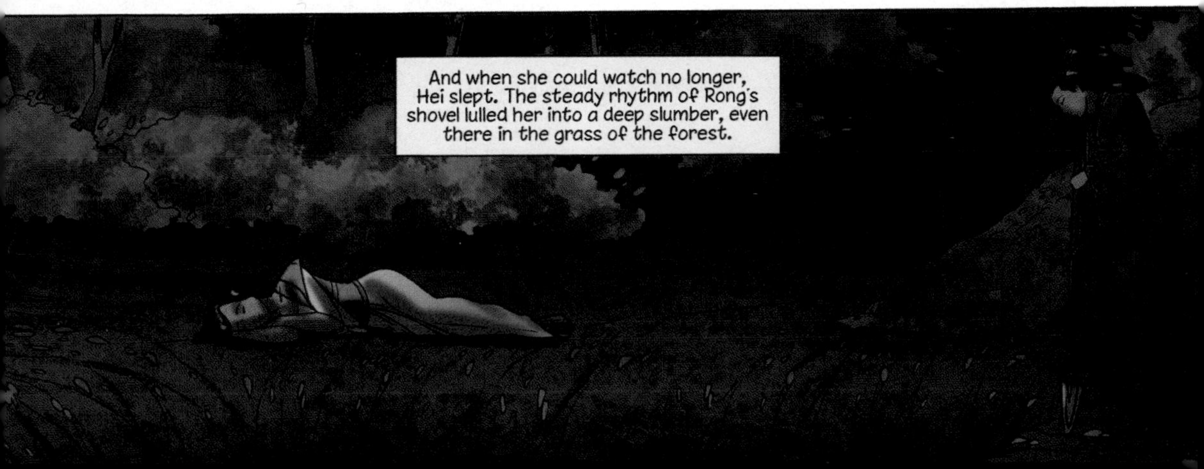
And when she could watch no longer, Hei slept. The steady rhythm of Rong's shovel lulled her into a deep slumber, even there in the grass of the forest.

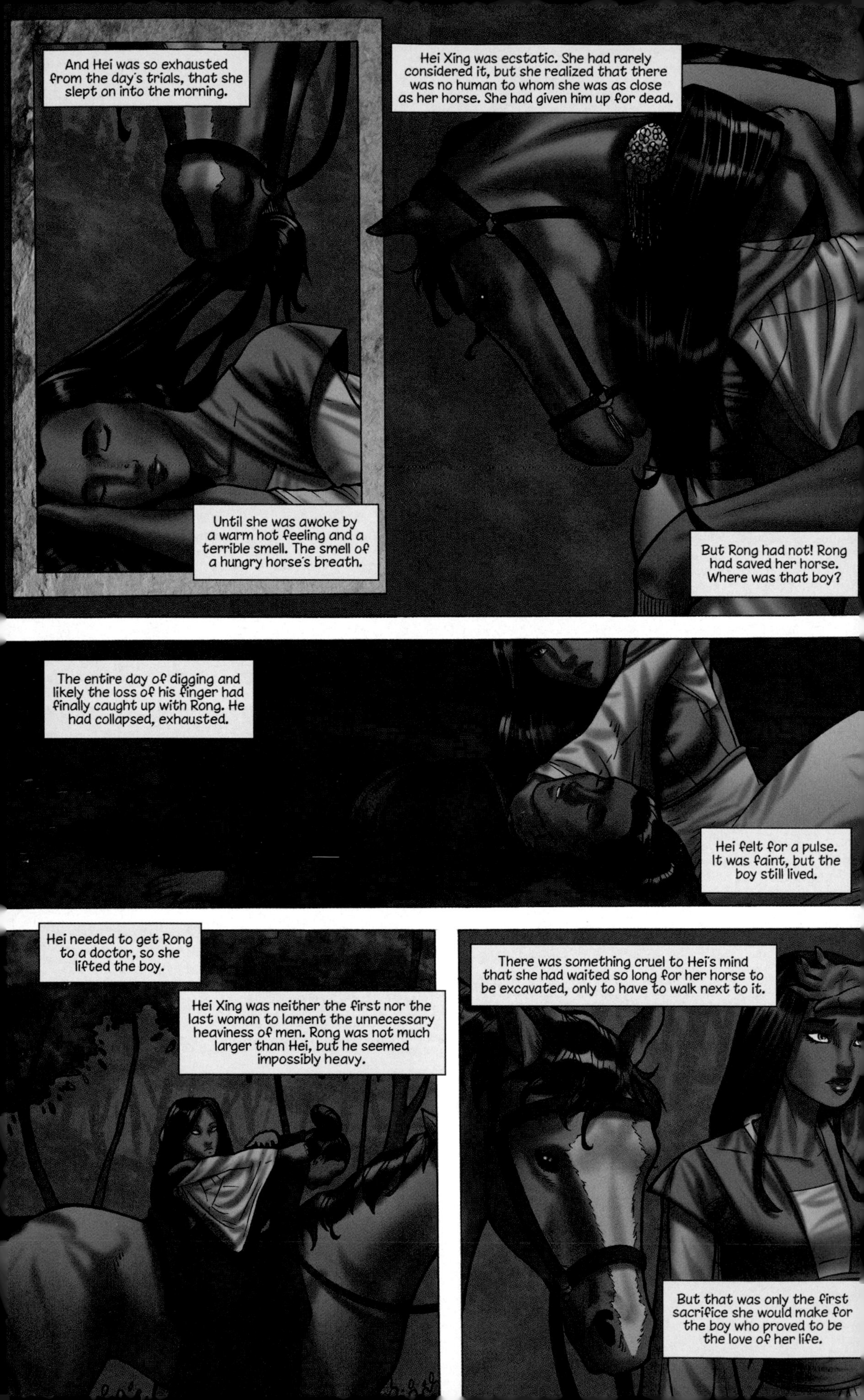
And Hei was so exhausted from the day's trials, that she slept on into the morning.
Until she was awoke by a warm hot feeling and a terrible smell. The smell of a hungry horse's breath.
Hei Xing was ecstatic. She had rarely considered it, but she realized that there was no human to whom she was as close as her horse. She had given him up for dead.
But Rong had not! Rong had saved her horse. Where was that boy?
The entire day of digging and likely the loss of his finger had finally caught up with Rong. He had collapsed, exhausted.
Hei felt for a pulse. It was faint, but the boy still lived.
Hei needed to get Rong to a doctor, so she lifted the boy.
Hei Xing was neither the first nor the last woman to lament the unnecessary heaviness of men. Rong was not much larger than Hei, but he seemed impossibly heavy.
There was something cruel to Hei's mind that she had waited so long for her horse to be excavated, only to have to walk next to it.
But that was only the first sacrifice she would make for the boy who proved to be the love of her life.

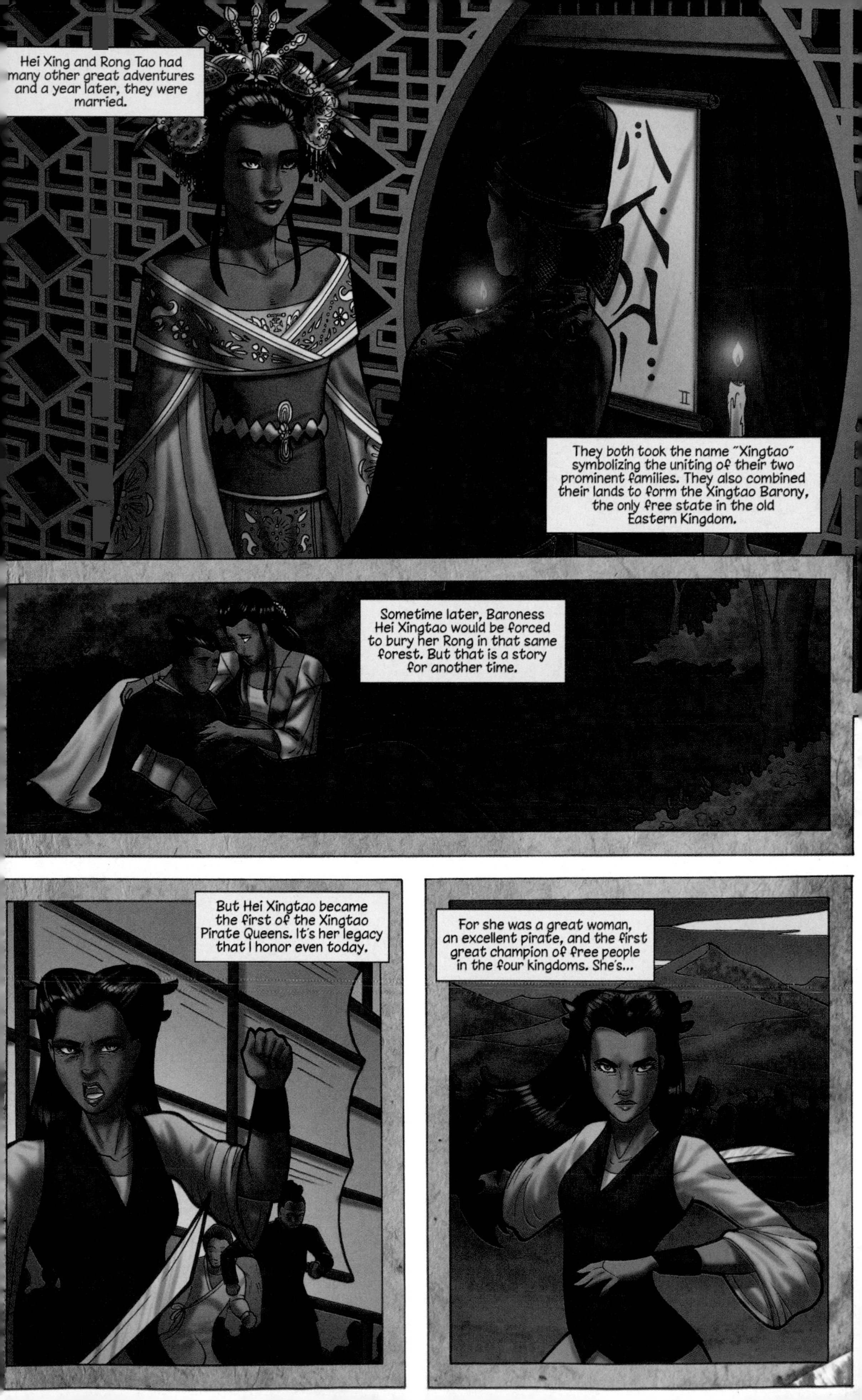
Hei Xing and Rong Tao had many other great adventures and a year later, they were married.
They both took the name "Xingtao" symbolizing the uniting of their two prominent families. They also combined their lands to form the Xingtao Barony, the only free state in the old Eastern Kingdom.
Sometime later, Baroness Hei Xingtao would be forced to bury her Rong in that same forest. But that is a story for another time.
But Hei Xingtao became the first of the Xingtao Pirate Queens. It's her legacy that I honor even today.
For she was a great woman, an excellent pirate, and the first great champion of free people in the four kingdoms. She's...

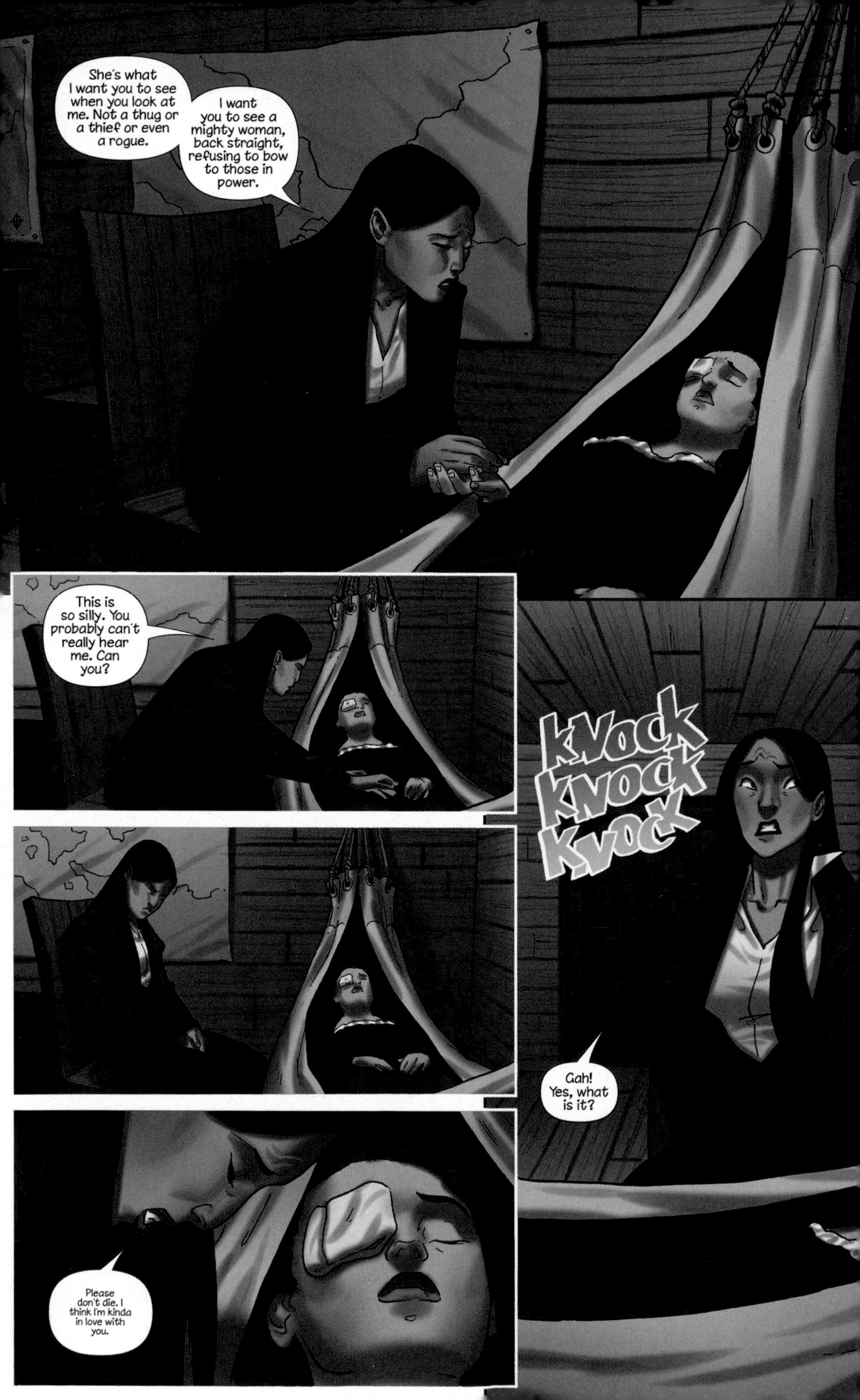
She's what I want you to see when you look at me. Not a thug or a thief or even a rogue.
I want you to see a mighty woman, back straight, refusing to bow to those in power.
This is so silly. You probably can't really hear me. Can you?
Please don't die. I think I'm kinda in love with you.
KNOCK KNOCK KNOCK
Gah! Yes, what is it?

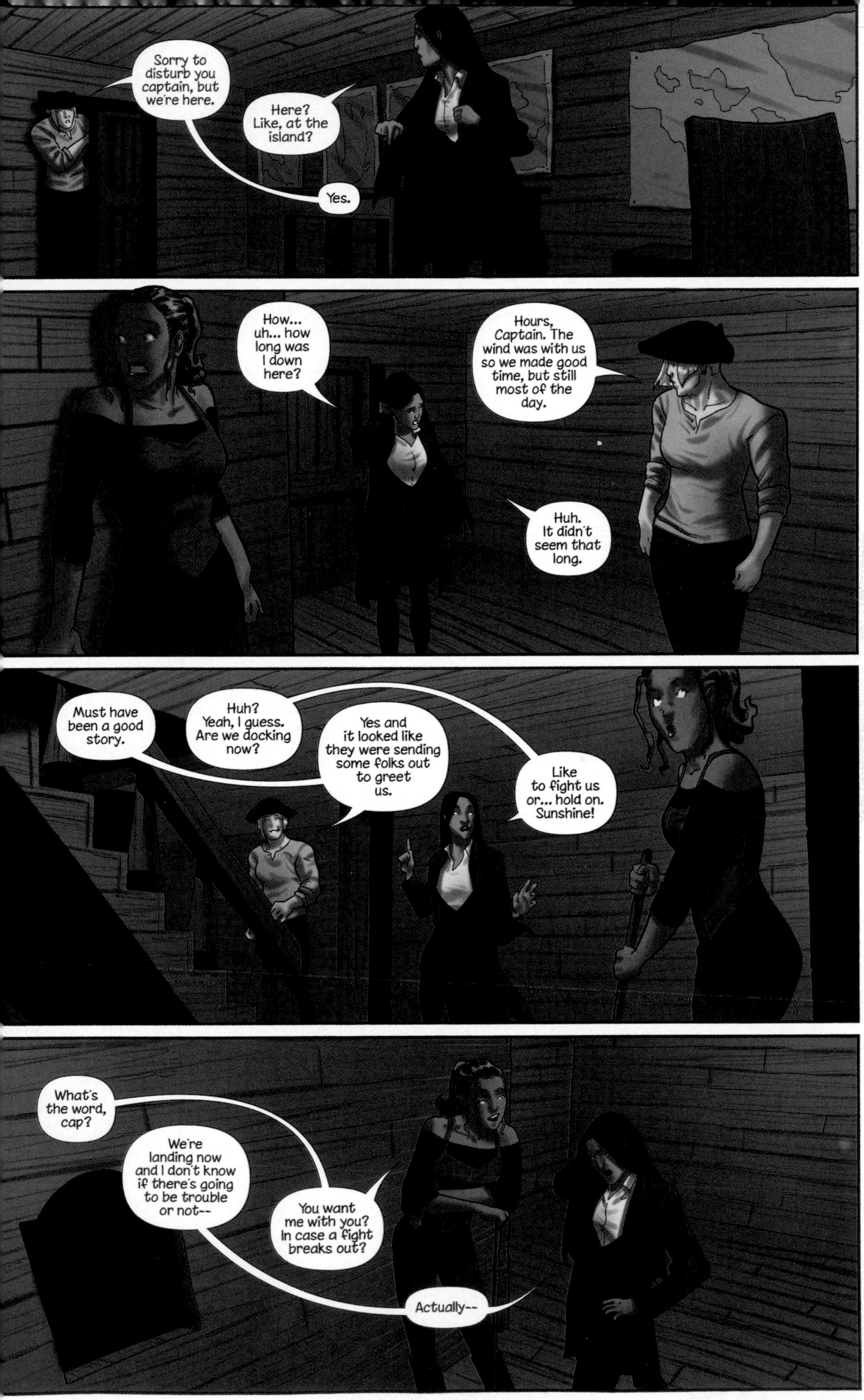
Sorry to disturb you captain, but we're here.
Here? Like, at the island?
Yes.
How... uh... how long was I down here?
Hours, Captain. The wind was with us so we made good time, but still most of the day.
Huh. It didn't seem that long.
Must have been a good story.
Huh? Yeah, I guess. Are we docking now?
Yes and it looked like they were sending some folks out to greet us.
Like to fight us or... hold on. Sunshine!
What's the word, cap?
We're landing now and I don't know if there's going to be trouble or not--
You want me with you? In case a fight breaks out?
Actually--

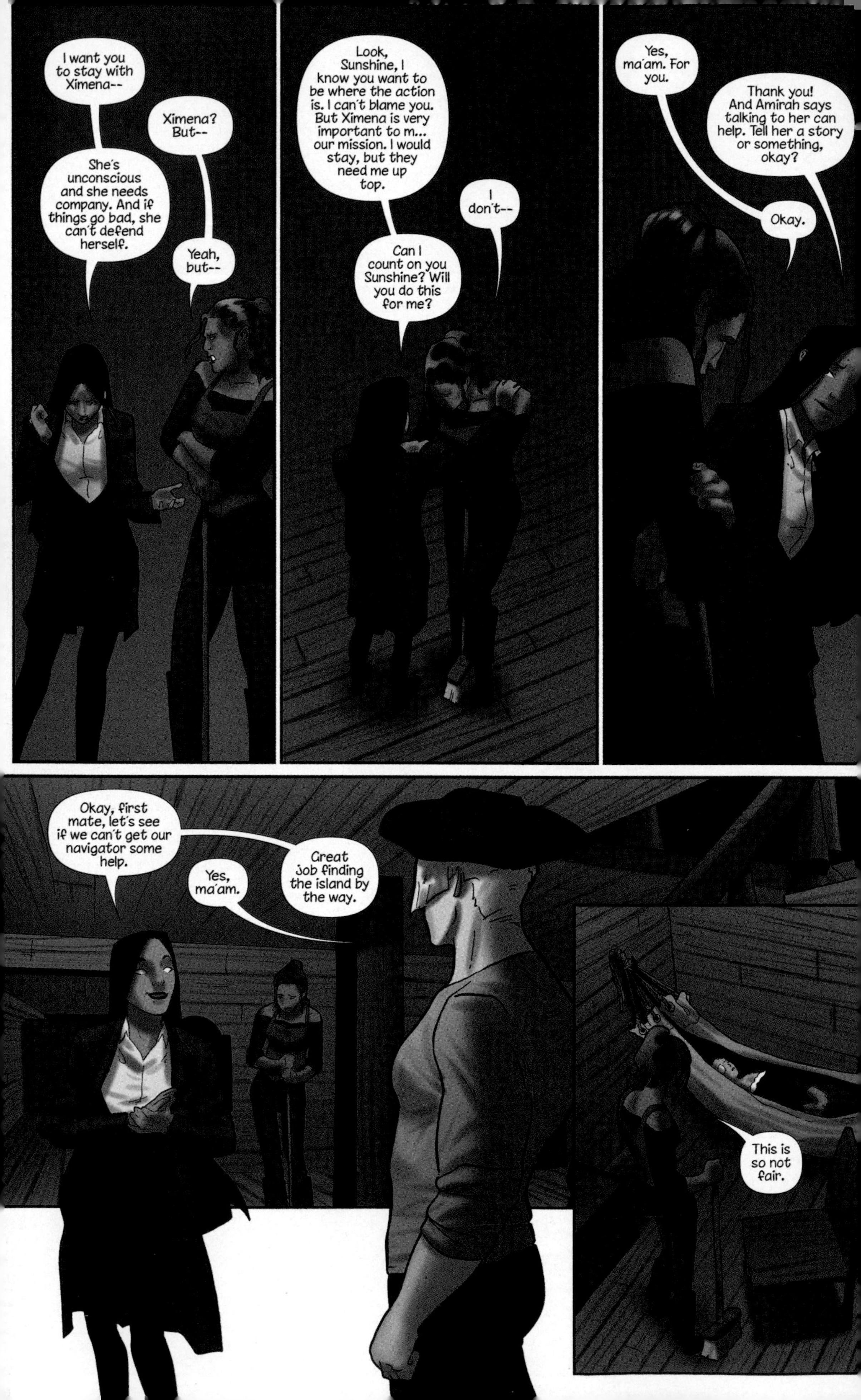
I want you to stay with Ximena--
Ximena? But--
She's unconscious and she needs company. And if things go bad, she can't defend herself.
Yeah, but--
Look, Sunshine, I know you want to be where the action is. I can't blame you. But Ximena is very important to m... our mission. I would stay, but they need me up top.
I don't--
Can I count on you Sunshine? Will you do this for me?
Yes, ma'am. For you.
Thank you! And Amirah says talking to her can help. Tell her a story or something, okay?
Okay.
Okay, first mate, let's see if we can't get our navigator some help.
Yes, ma'am.
Great job finding the island by the way.
This is so not fair.

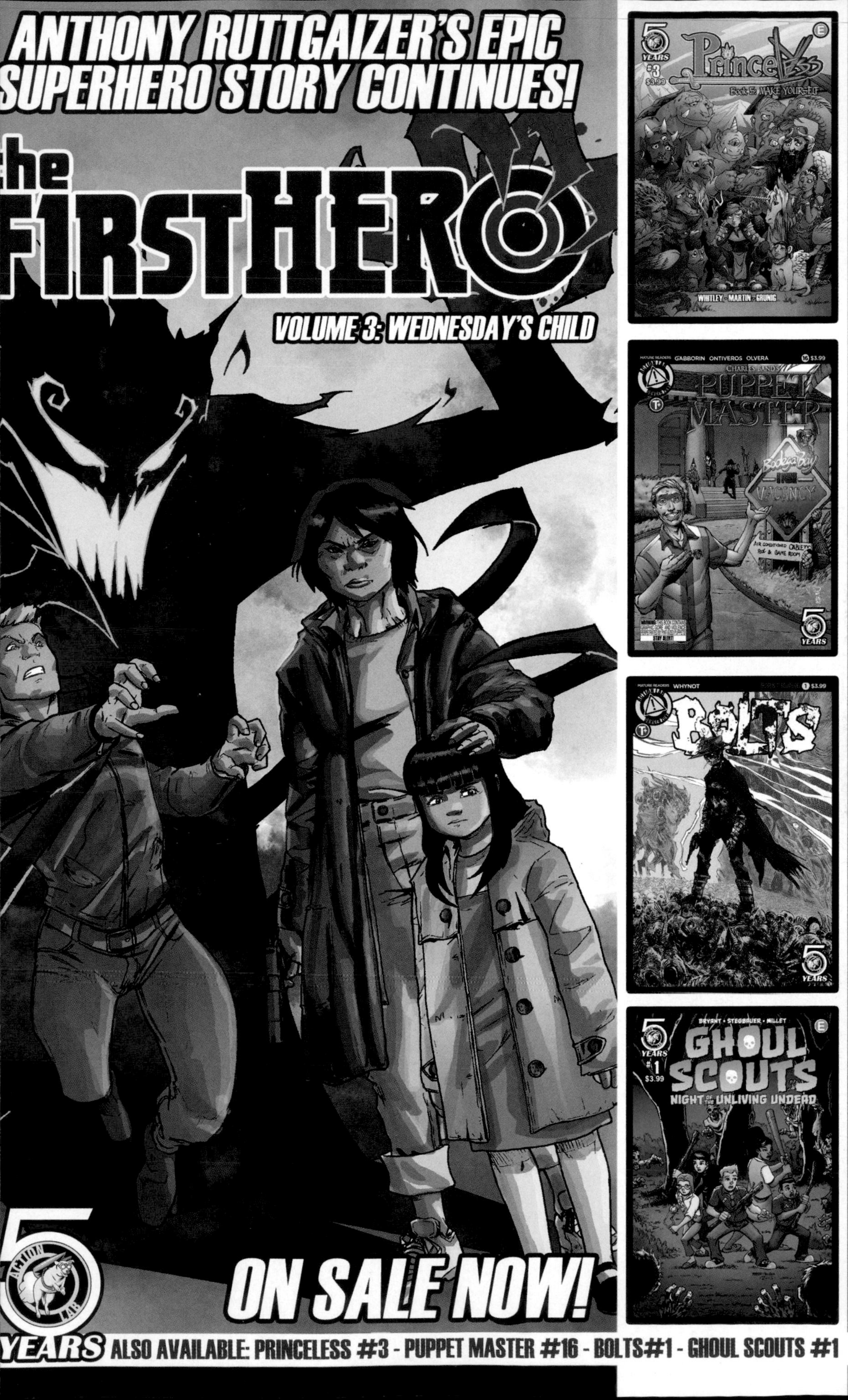
ANTHONY RUTTGAIZER'S EPIC SUPERHERO STORY CONTINUES!
the FIRST HERO
VOLUME 3: WEDNESDAY'S CHILD
ON SALE NOW!
5 YEARS
Princeless
#3
$3.99
WHITLEY MARTIN GRUNIG
MATURE READERS GABBORIN ONTIVEROS OLVERA 16 $3.99
CHARLES BAND'S
PUPPET MASTER
VACANCY
MATURE READERS WHYNOT 1 $3.99
BOLTS
BRYANT • STEGBAUER • MILLET
#1
$3.99
GHOUL SCOUTS
NIGHT OF THE UNLIVING UNDEAD
ALSO AVAILABLE: PRINCELESS #3 - PUPPET MASTER #16 - BOLTS#1 - GHOUL SCOUTS #1

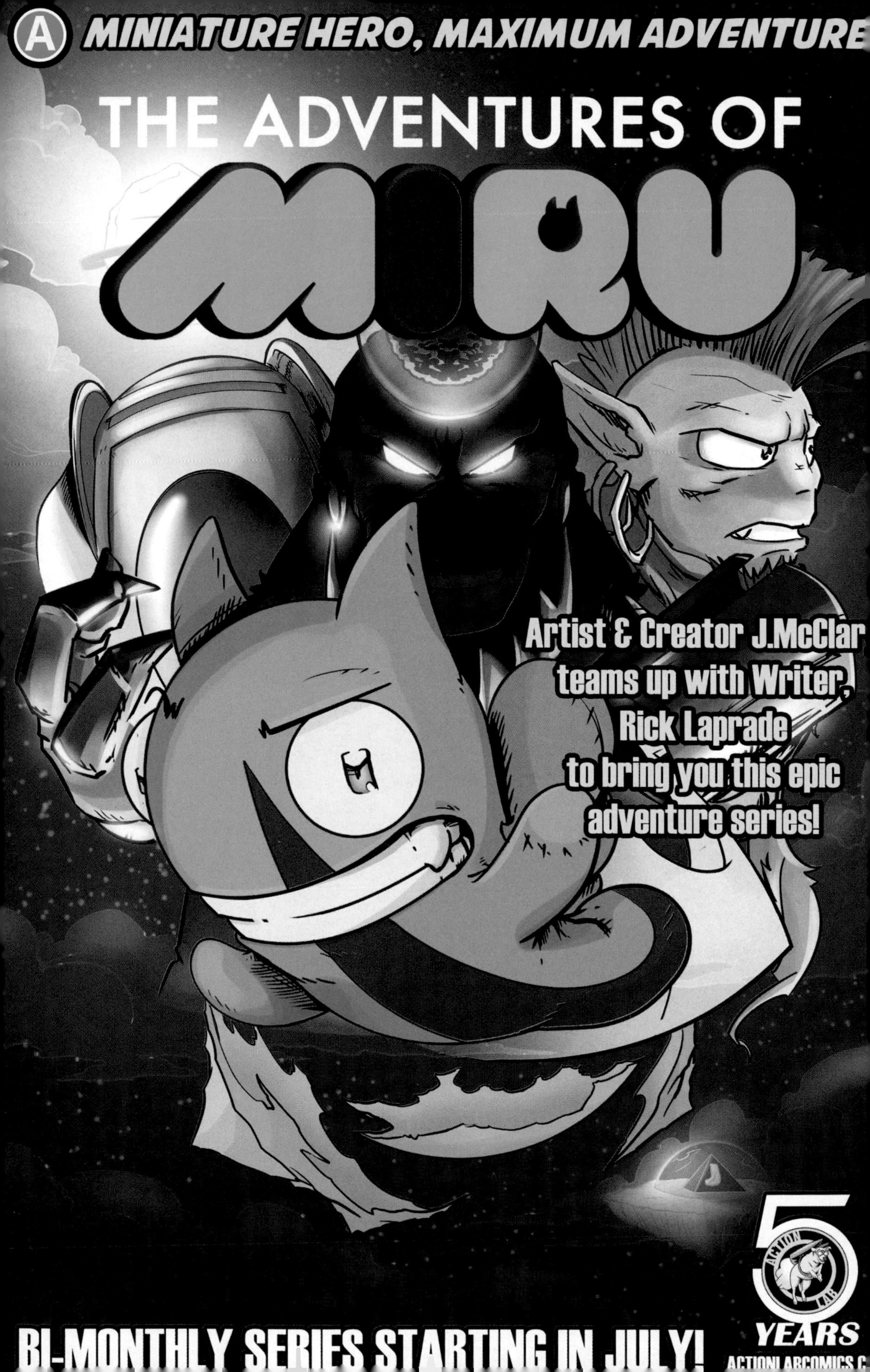
MINIATURE HERO, MAXIMUM ADVENTURE
THE ADVENTURES OF
MIRU
Artist & Creator J.McClar teams up with Writer, Rick Laprade to bring you this epic adventure series!
5 YEARS
BI-MONTHLY SERIES STARTING IN JULY!

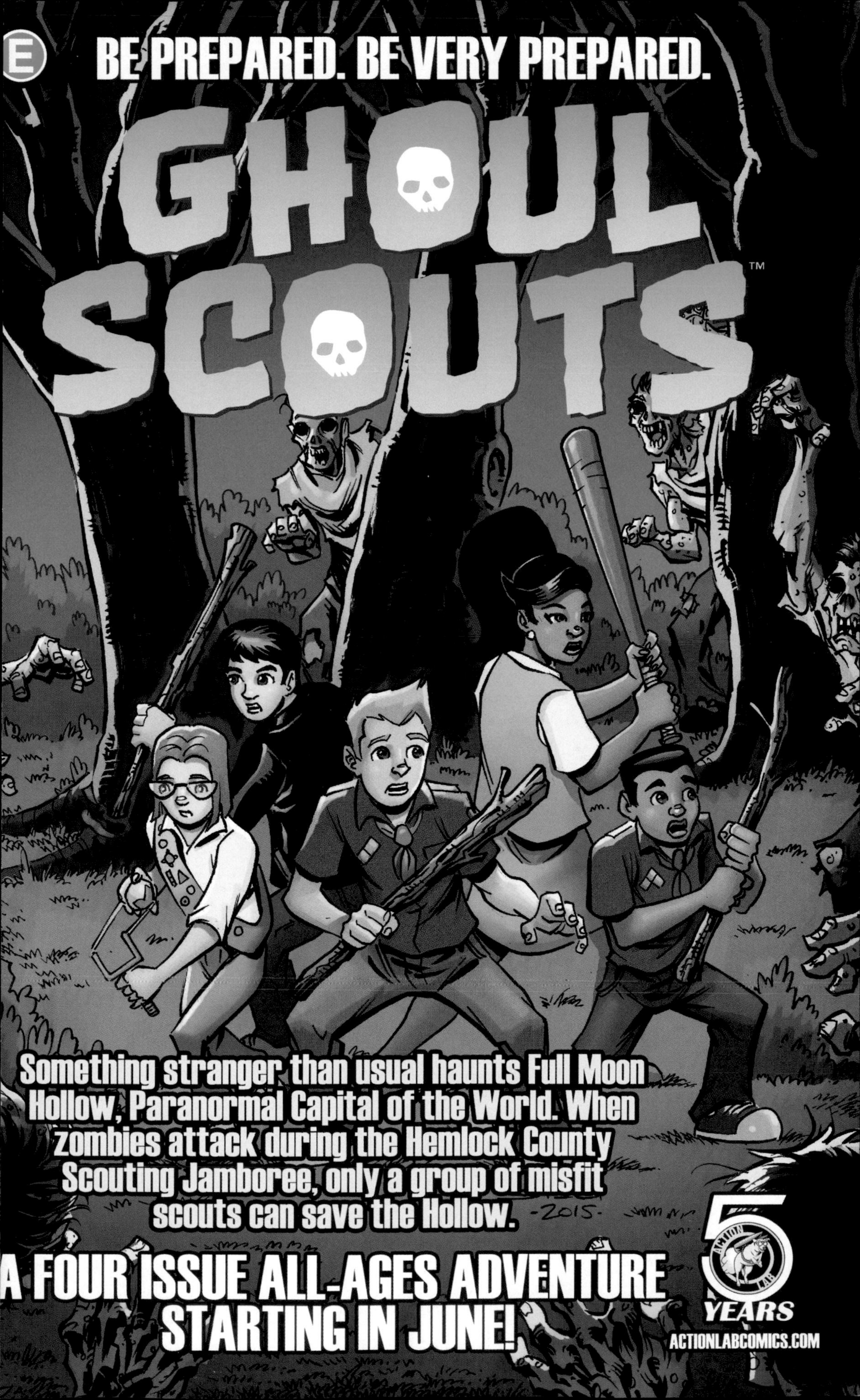
E
BE PREPARED. BE VERY PREPARED.
GHOUL SCOUTS™
Something stranger than usual haunts Full Moon Hollow, Paranormal Capital of the World. When zombies attack during the Hemlock County Scouting Jamboree, only a group of misfit scouts can save the Hollow.
-2015-
A FOUR ISSUE ALL-AGES ADVENTURE STARTING IN JUNE!
5 ACTION LAB YEARS
ACTIONLABCOMICS.COM

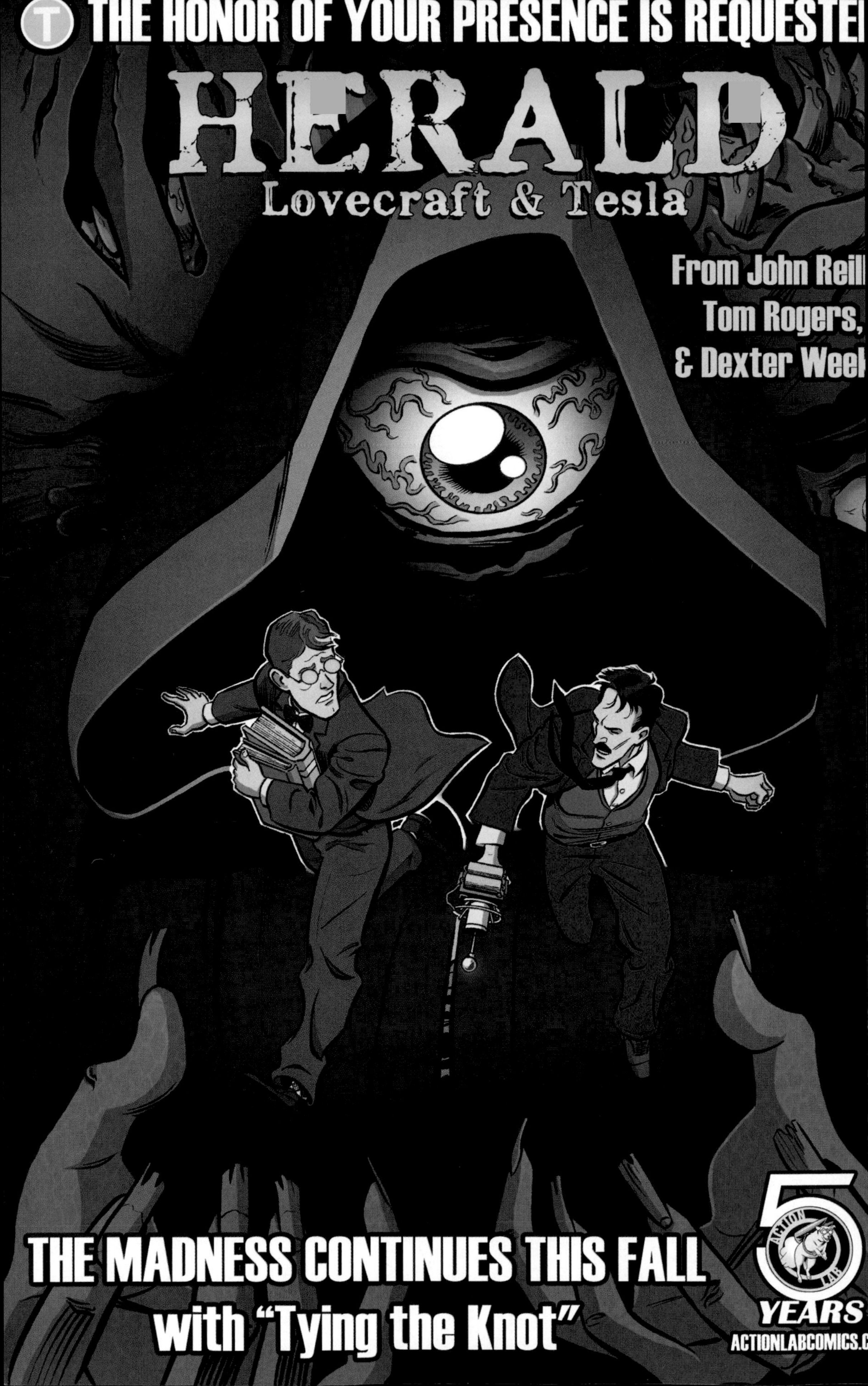
THE HONOR OF YOUR PRESENCE IS REQUESTE
HERALD
Lovecraft & Tesla
From John Reill
Tom Rogers,
& Dexter Week
THE MADNESS CONTINUES THIS FALL
with "Tying the Knot"
ACTION LAB
5 YEARS
ACTIONLABCOMICS.C

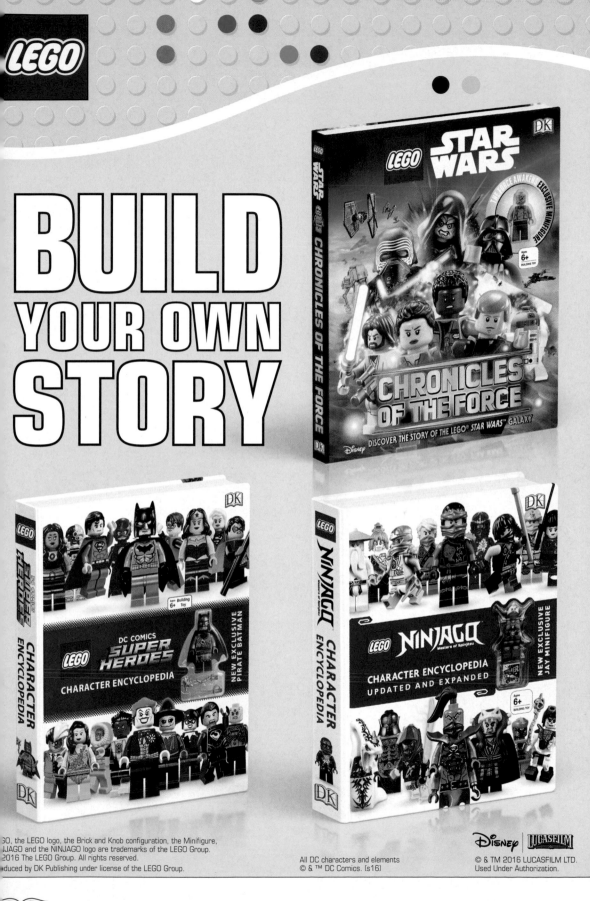

BUILD YOUR OWN STORY

LEGO STAR WARS
CHRONICLES OF THE FORCE
DISCOVER THE STORY OF THE LEGO® STAR WARS™ GALAXY

THE FORCE AWAKENS EXCLUSIVE MINIFIGURE

LEGO DC COMICS SUPER HEROES
CHARACTER ENCYCLOPEDIA
NEW EXCLUSIVE PIRATE BATMAN

LEGO NINJAGO Masters of Spinjitzu
CHARACTER ENCYCLOPEDIA
UPDATED AND EXPANDED
NEW EXCLUSIVE JAY MINIFIGURE

MARVEL
SUPER HEROES

BUILD SOMETHING
SUPER

LEGO.COM/MARVELSUPERHEROES

MARVEL
CAPTAIN AMERICA

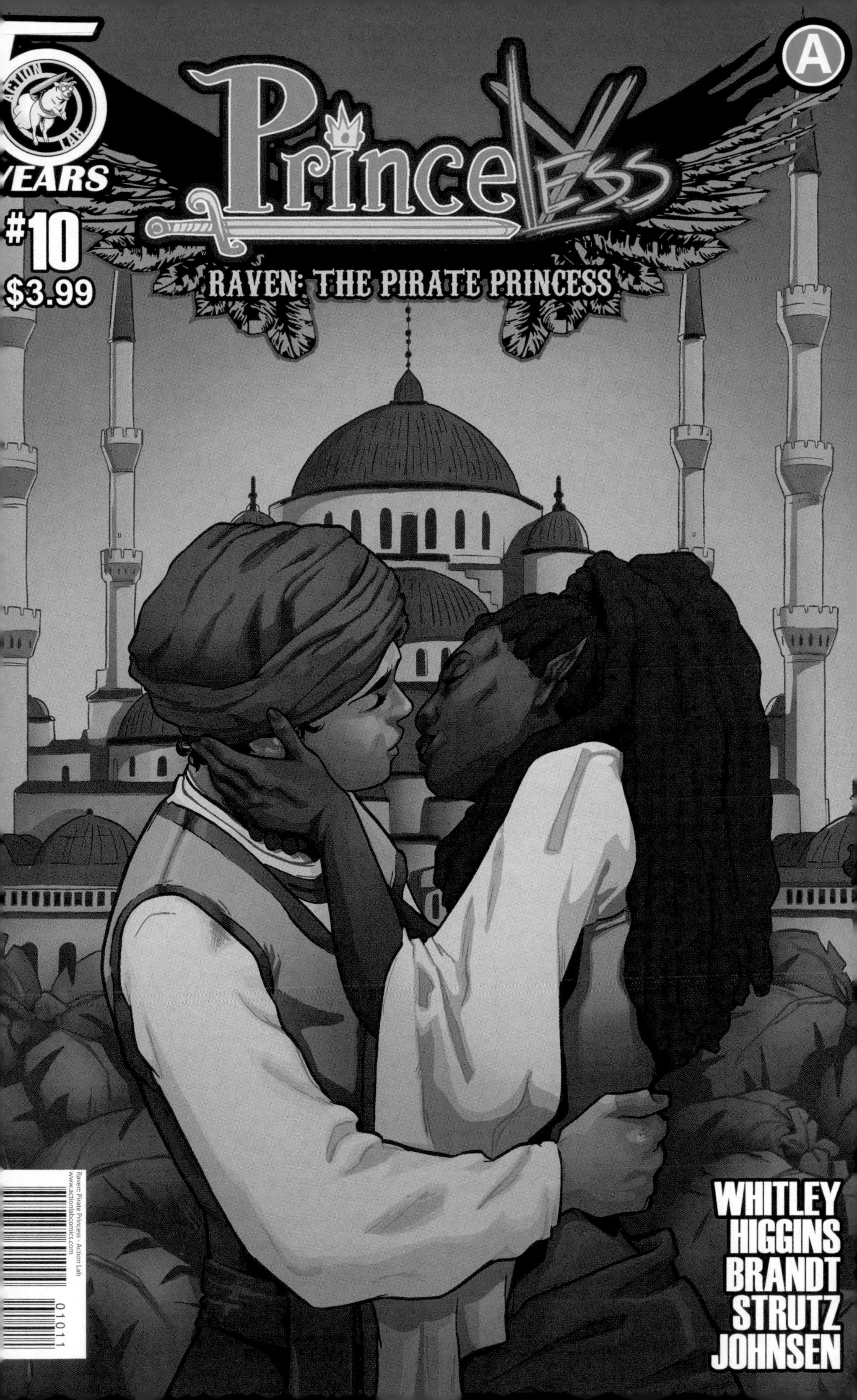
5 YEARS
ACTION LAB
Princeless
#10
$3.99
RAVEN: THE PIRATE PRINCESS
A
Raven: Pirate Princess - Action Lab
www.actionlabcomics.com
WHITLEY
HIGGINS
BRANDT
STRUTZ
JOHNSEN

FROM ALL-AGES TO MATURE READERS
ACTION LAB HAS YOU COVERED.

 **Appropriate for everyone.**

 **Appropriate for age 9 and up. Absent of profanity or adult content.**

Suggested for 12 and Up. Comics with this rating are comparable to a PG-13 movie rating. Recommended for our teen and young adult readers.

 **Appropriate for older teens. Similar to Teen, but featuring more mature themes and/or more graphic imagery.**

 **Contains extreme violence and some nudity. Basically the Rated-R of comics.**

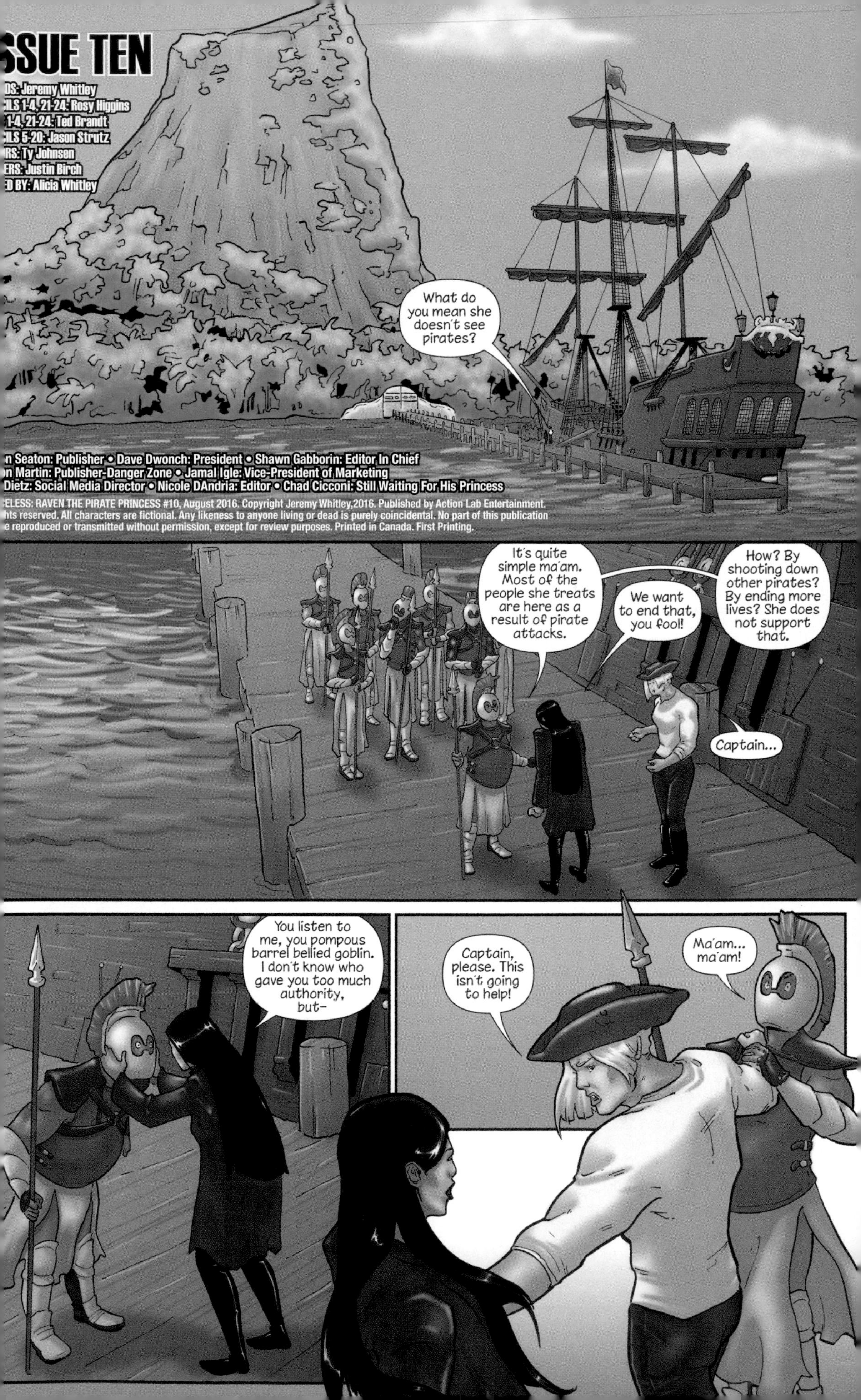
SSUE TEN
DS: Jeremy Whitley
CILS 1-4, 21-24: Rosy Higgins
1-4, 21-24: Ted Brandt
CILS 5-20: Jason Strutz
RS: Ty Johnsen
ERS: Justin Birch
ED BY: Alicia Whitley
What do you mean she doesn't see pirates?
n Seaton: Publisher • Dave Dwonch: President • Shawn Gabborin: Editor In Chief
on Martin: Publisher-Danger Zone • Jamal Igle: Vice-President of Marketing
Dietz: Social Media Director • Nicole DAndria: Editor • Chad Cicconi: Still Waiting For His Princess
ELESS: RAVEN THE PIRATE PRINCESS #10, August 2016. Copyright Jeremy Whitley,2016. Published by Action Lab Entertainment.
hts reserved. All characters are fictional. Any likeness to anyone living or dead is purely coincidental. No part of this publication
e reproduced or transmitted without permission, except for review purposes. Printed in Canada. First Printing.
It's quite simple ma'am. Most of the people she treats are here as a result of pirate attacks.
We want to end that, you fool!
How? By shooting down other pirates? By ending more lives? She does not support that.
Captain...
You listen to me, you pompous barrel bellied goblin. I don't know who gave you too much authority, but-
Captain, please. This isn't going to help!
Ma'am... ma'am!

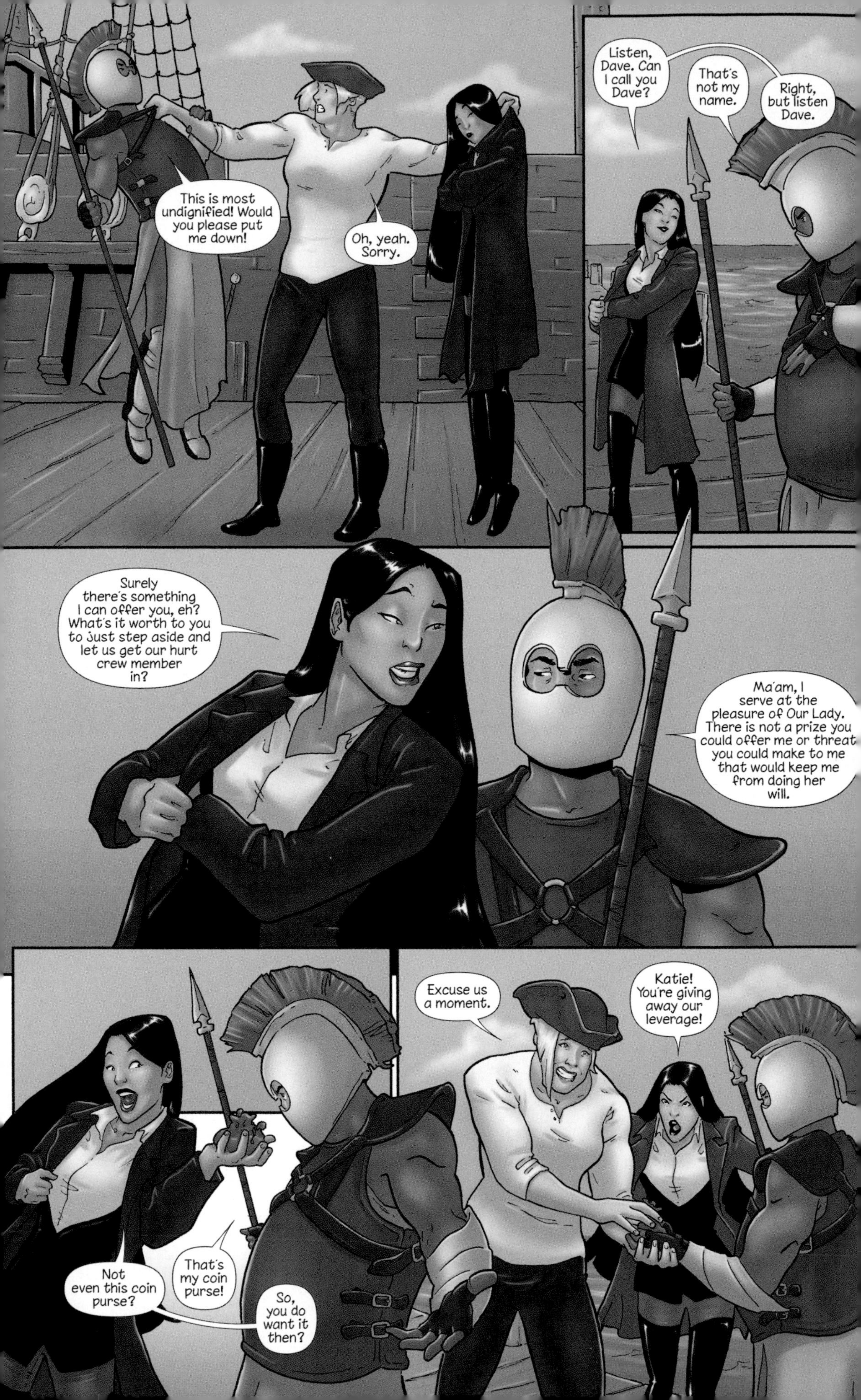
This is most undignified! Would you please put me down!
Oh, yeah. Sorry.
Listen, Dave. Can I call you Dave?
That's not my name.
Right, but listen Dave.
Surely there's something I can offer you, eh? What's it worth to you to just step aside and let us get our hurt crew member in?
Ma'am, I serve at the pleasure of Our Lady. There is not a prize you could offer me or threat you could make to me that would keep me from doing her will.
Not even this coin purse?
That's my coin purse!
So, you do want it then?
Excuse us a moment.
Katie! You're giving away our leverage!

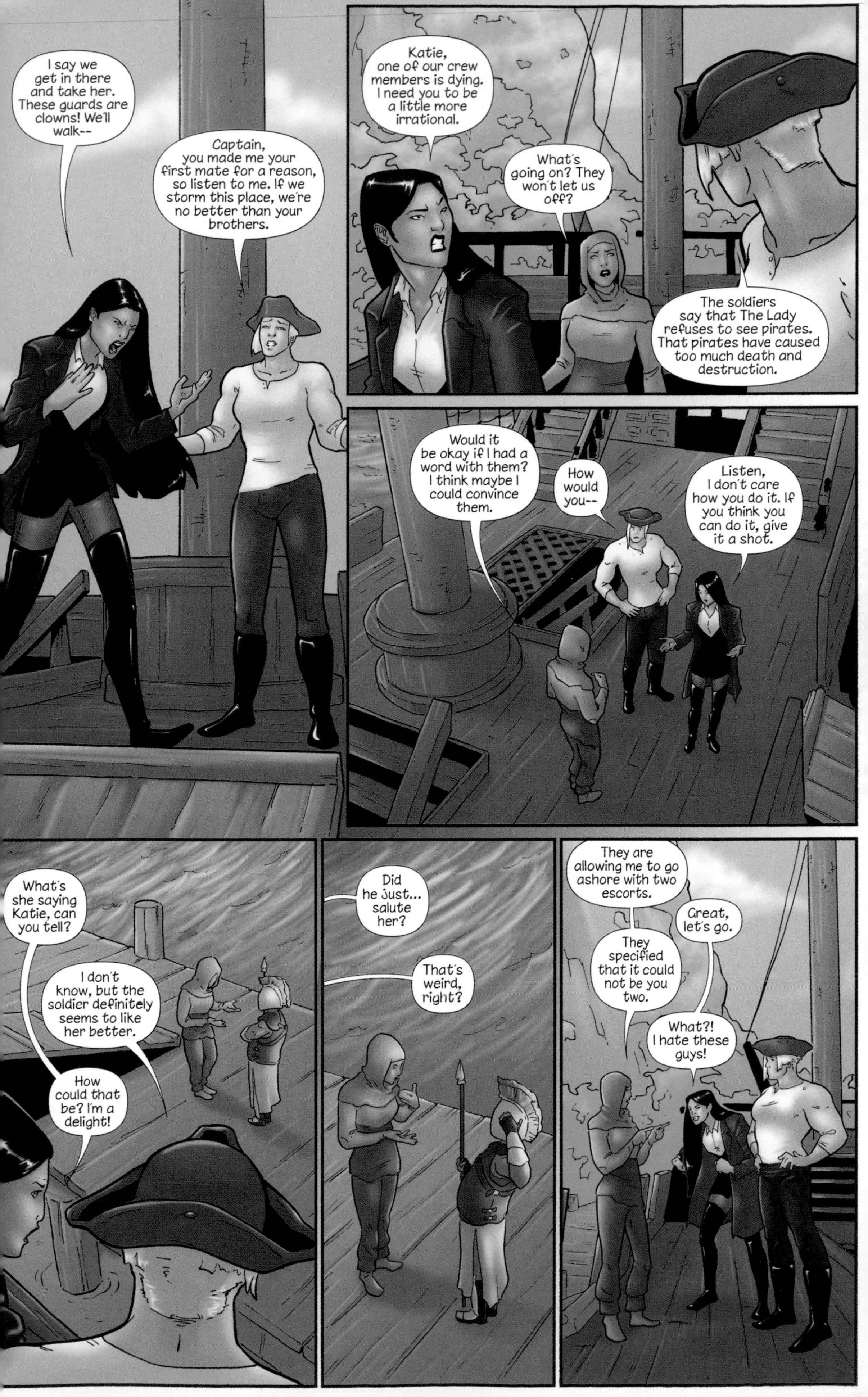
I say we get in there and take her. These guards are clowns! We'll walk--
Captain, you made me your first mate for a reason, so listen to me. If we storm this place, we're no better than your brothers.
Katie, one of our crew members is dying. I need you to be a little more irrational.
What's going on? They won't let us off?
The soldiers say that The Lady refuses to see pirates. That pirates have caused too much death and destruction.
Would it be okay if I had a word with them? I think maybe I could convince them.
How would you--
Listen, I don't care how you do it. If you think you can do it, give it a shot.
What's she saying Katie, can you tell?
I don't know, but the soldier definitely seems to like her better.
How could that be? I'm a delight!
Did he just... salute her?
That's weird, right?
They are allowing me to go ashore with two escorts.
They specified that it could not be you two.
Great, let's go.
What?! I hate these guys!

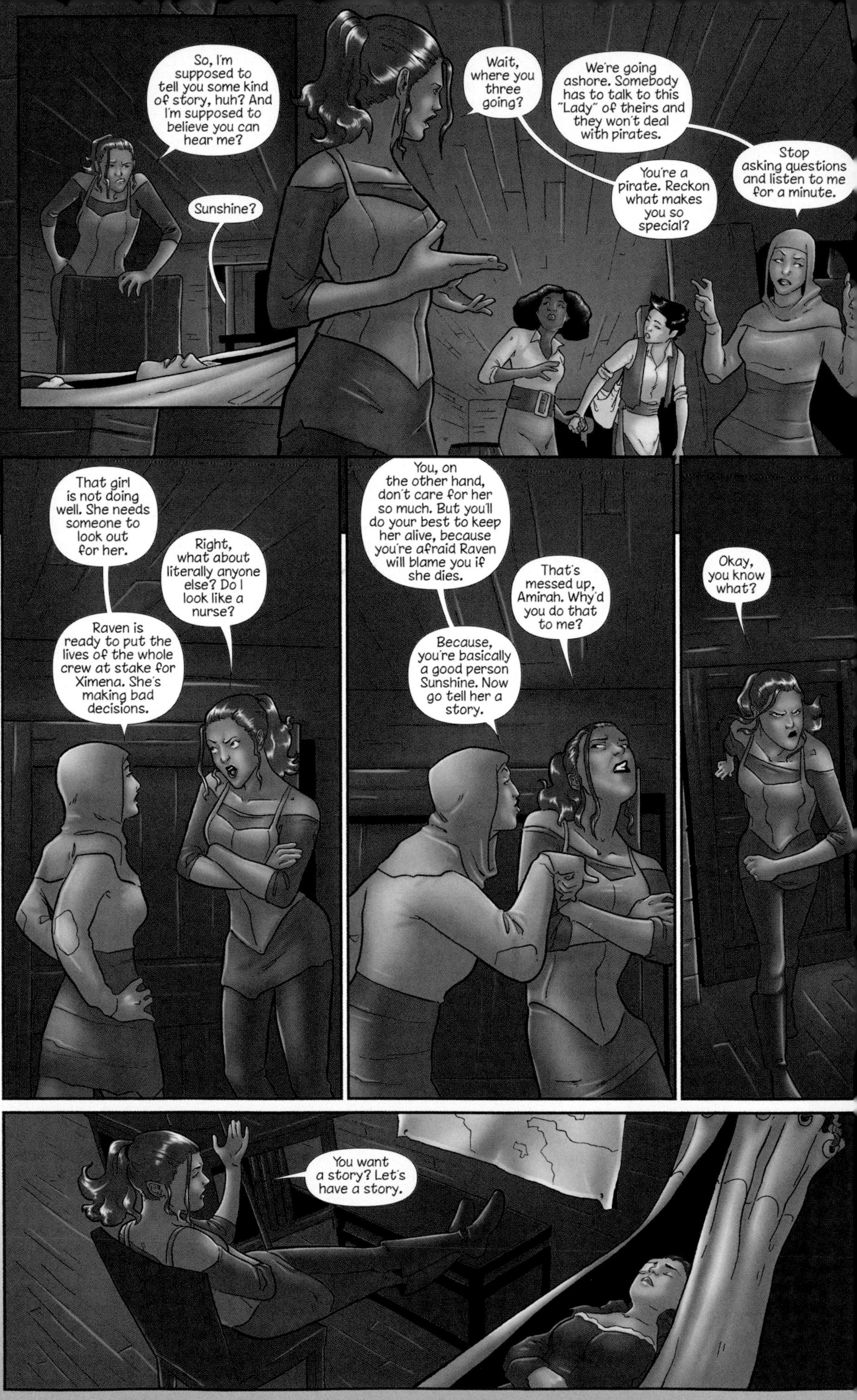
So, I'm supposed to tell you some kind of story, huh? And I'm supposed to believe you can hear me?
Sunshine?
Wait, where you three going?
We're going ashore. Somebody has to talk to this "Lady" of theirs and they won't deal with pirates.
You're a pirate. Reckon what makes you so special?
Stop asking questions and listen to me for a minute.
That girl is not doing well. She needs someone to look out for her.
Raven is ready to put the lives of the whole crew at stake for Ximena. She's making bad decisions.
Right, what about literally anyone else? Do I look like a nurse?
You, on the other hand, don't care for her so much. But you'll do your best to keep her alive, because you're afraid Raven will blame you if she dies.
Because, you're basically a good person Sunshine. Now go tell her a story.
That's messed up, Amirah. Why'd you do that to me?
Okay, you know what?
You want a story? Let's have a story.

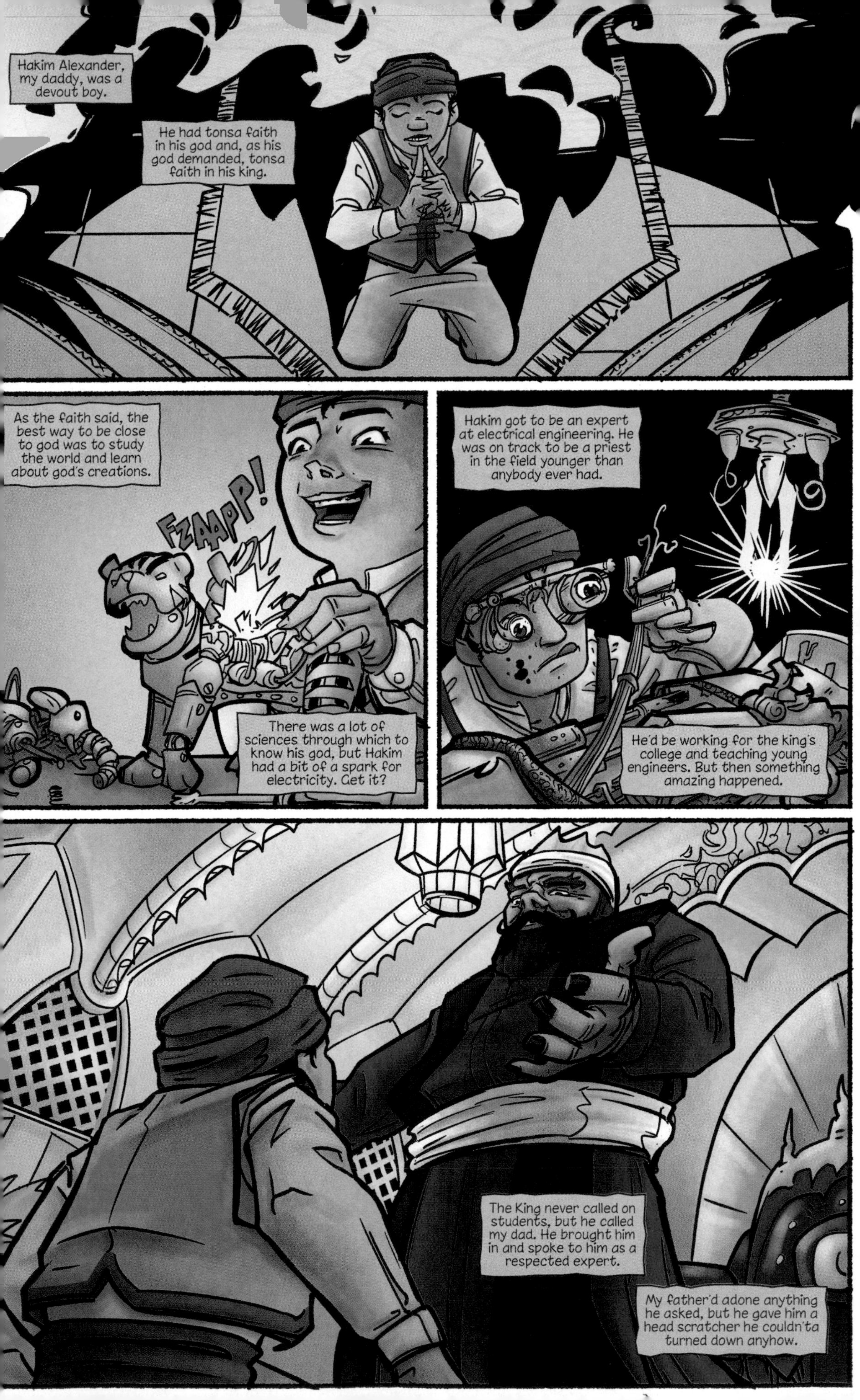

Hakim Alexander, my daddy, was a devout boy.
He had tonsa faith in his god and, as his god demanded, tonsa faith in his king.
As the faith said, the best way to be close to god was to study the world and learn about god's creations.
FZAAPP!
There was a lot of sciences through which to know his god, but Hakim had a bit of a spark for electricity. Get it?
Hakim got to be an expert at electrical engineering. He was on track to be a priest in the field younger than anybody ever had.
He'd be working for the king's college and teaching young engineers. But then something amazing happened.
The King never called on students, but he called my dad. He brought him in and spoke to him as a respected expert.
My father'd adone anything he asked, but he gave him a head scratcher he couldn'ta turned down anyhow.

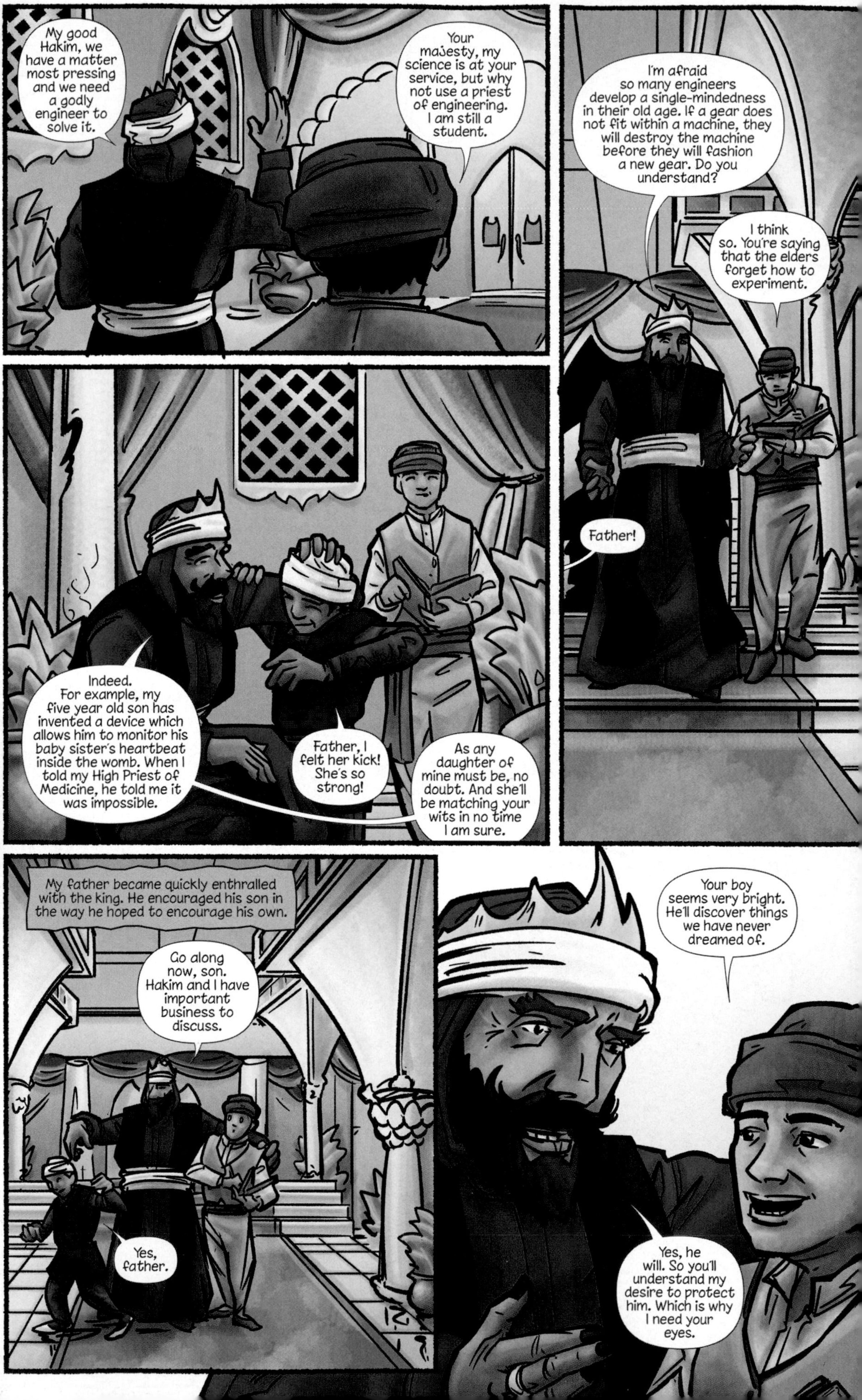
My good Hakim, we have a matter most pressing and we need a godly engineer to solve it.
Your majesty, my science is at your service, but why not use a priest of engineering. I am still a student.
I'm afraid so many engineers develop a single-mindedness in their old age. If a gear does not fit within a machine, they will destroy the machine before they will fashion a new gear. Do you understand?
I think so. You're saying that the elders forget how to experiment.
Father!
Indeed. For example, my five year old son has invented a device which allows him to monitor his baby sister's heartbeat inside the womb. When I told my High Priest of Medicine, he told me it was impossible.
Father, I felt her kick! She's so strong!
As any daughter of mine must be, no doubt. And she'll be matching your wits in no time I am sure.
My father became quickly enthralled with the king. He encouraged his son in the way he hoped to encourage his own.
Go along now, son. Hakim and I have important business to discuss.
Yes, father.
Your boy seems very bright. He'll discover things we have never dreamed of.
Yes, he will. So you'll understand my desire to protect him. Which is why I need your eyes.

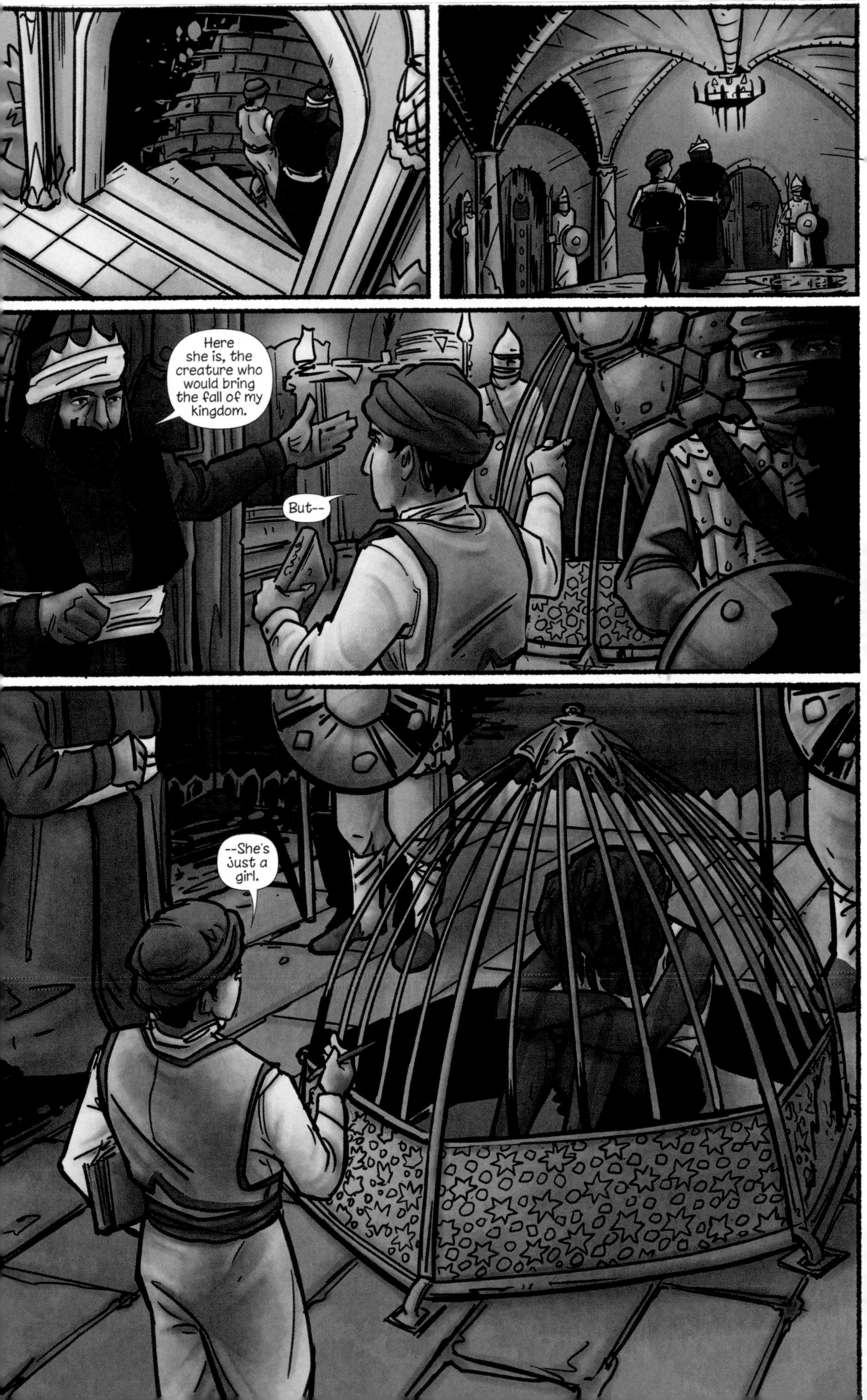
Here she is, the creature who would bring the fall of my kingdom.
But--
--She's just a girl.

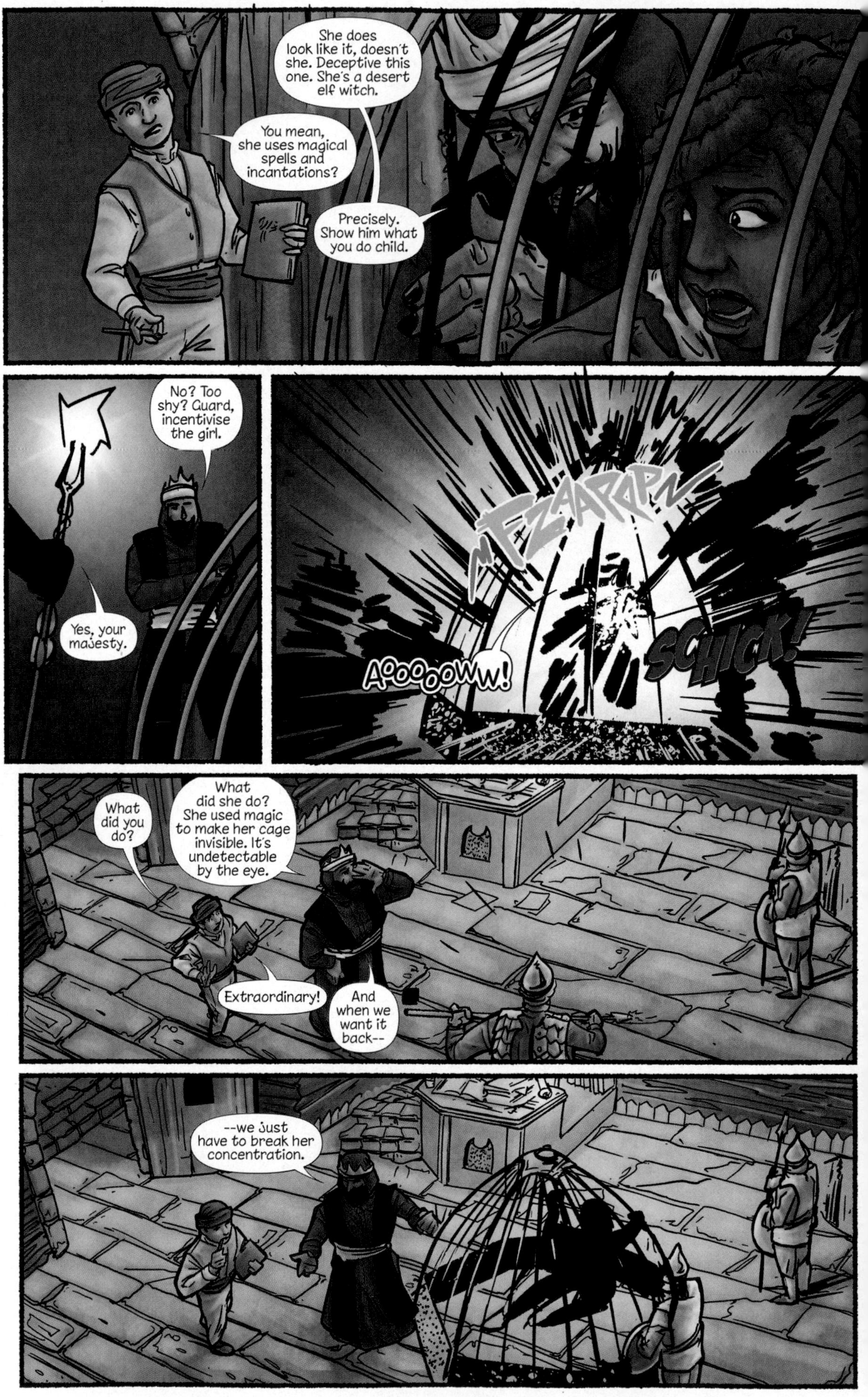
She does look like it, doesn't she. Deceptive this one. She's a desert elf witch.
You mean, she uses magical spells and incantations?
Precisely. Show him what you do child.
No? Too shy? Guard, incentivise the girl.
Yes, your majesty.
FZAAPOPN
AOOOOOWW!
SCHICK!
What did you do?
What did she do? She used magic to make her cage invisible. It's undetectable by the eye.
Extraordinary!
And when we want it back--
--we just have to break her concentration.

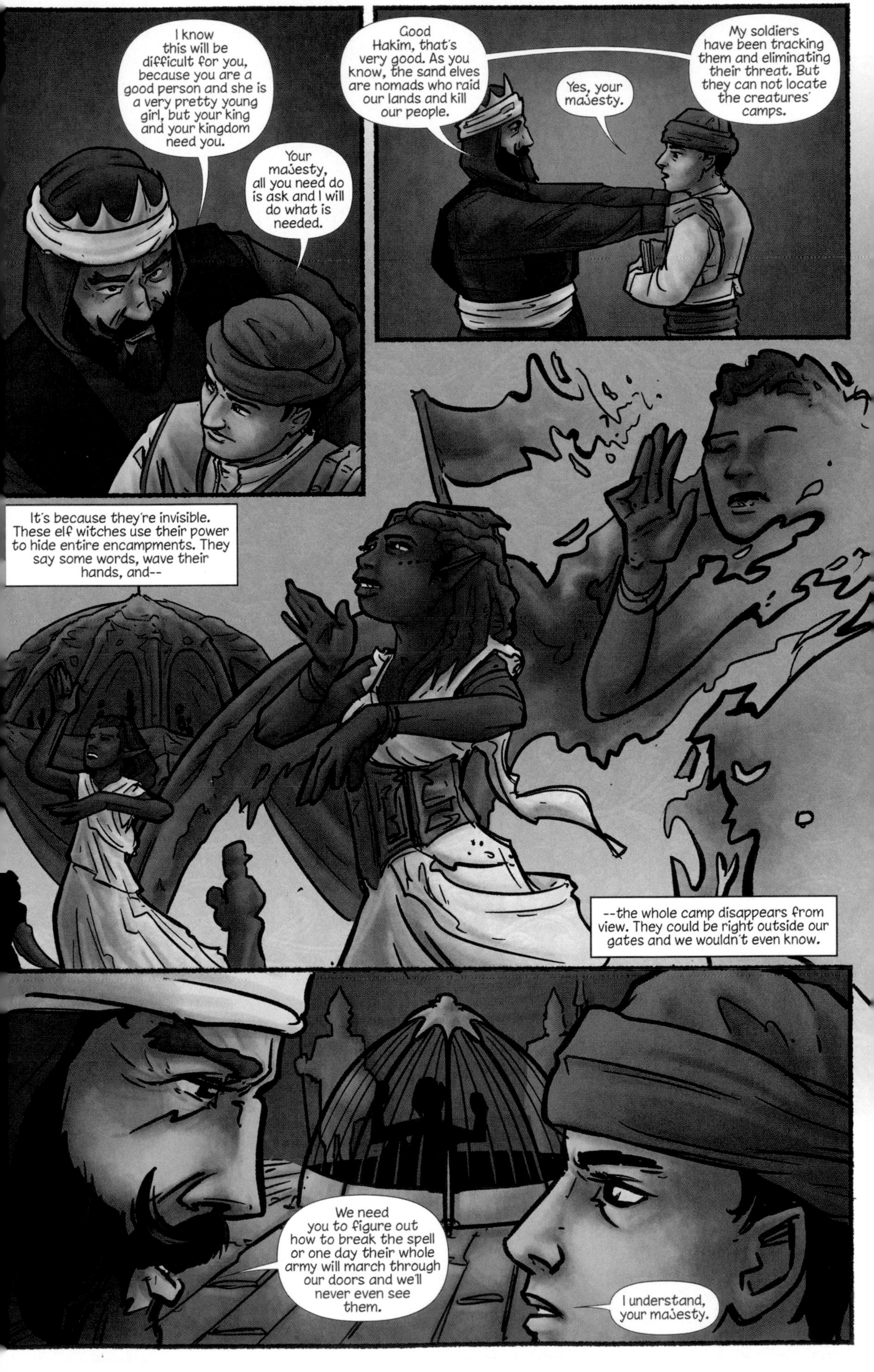
I know this will be difficult for you, because you are a good person and she is a very pretty young girl, but your king and your kingdom need you.
Your majesty, all you need do is ask and I will do what is needed.
Good Hakim, that's very good. As you know, the sand elves are nomads who raid our lands and kill our people.
Yes, your majesty.
My soldiers have been tracking them and eliminating their threat. But they can not locate the creatures' camps.
It's because they're invisible. These elf witches use their power to hide entire encampments. They say some words, wave their hands, and--
--the whole camp disappears from view. They could be right outside our gates and we wouldn't even know.
We need you to figure out how to break the spell or one day their whole army will march through our doors and we'll never even see them.
I understand, your majesty.

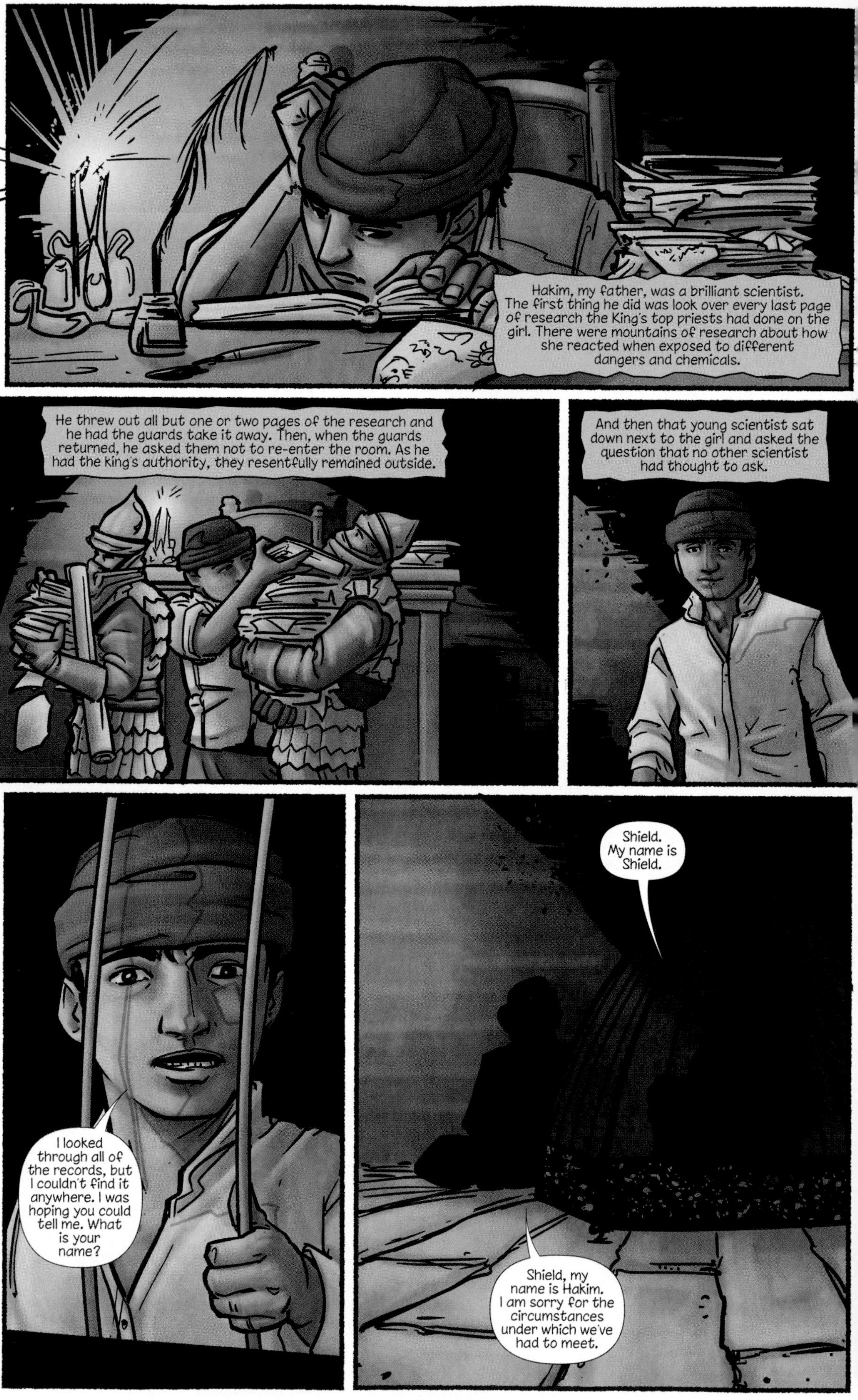
Hakim, my father, was a brilliant scientist. The first thing he did was look over every last page of research the King's top priests had done on the girl. There were mountains of research about how she reacted when exposed to different dangers and chemicals.
He threw out all but one or two pages of the research and he had the guards take it away. Then, when the guards returned, he asked them not to re-enter the room. As he had the king's authority, they resentfully remained outside.
And then that young scientist sat down next to the girl and asked the question that no other scientist had thought to ask.
I looked through all of the records, but I couldn't find it anywhere. I was hoping you could tell me. What is your name?
Shield. My name is Shield.
Shield, my name is Hakim. I am sorry for the circumstances under which we've had to meet.

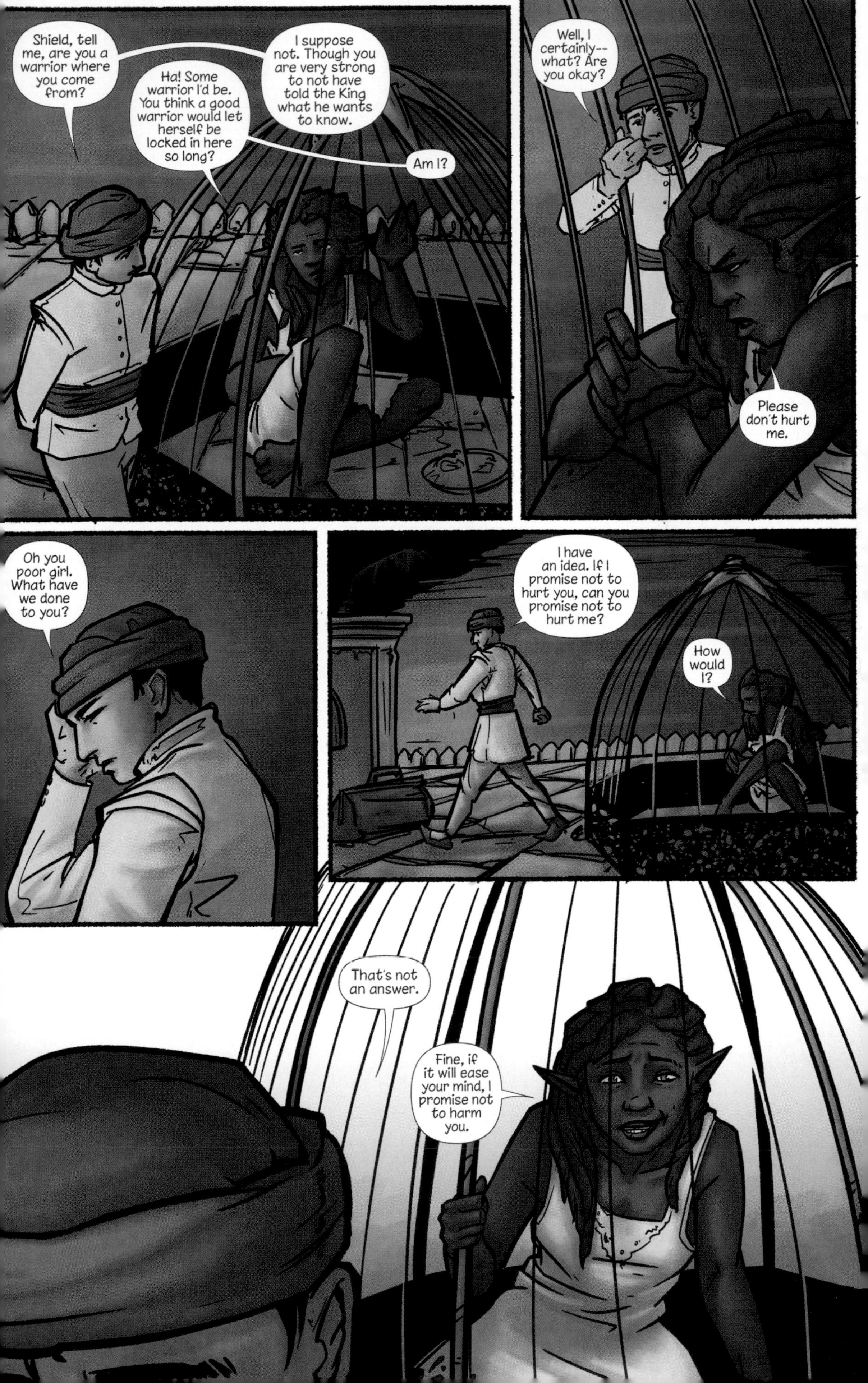
Shield, tell me, are you a warrior where you come from?
Ha! Some warrior I'd be. You think a good warrior would let herself be locked in here so long?
I suppose not. Though you are very strong to not have told the King what he wants to know.
Am I?
Well, I certainly-- what? Are you okay?
Please don't hurt me.
Oh you poor girl. What have we done to you?
I have an idea. If I promise not to hurt you, can you promise not to hurt me?
How would I?
That's not an answer.
Fine, if it will ease your mind, I promise not to harm you.

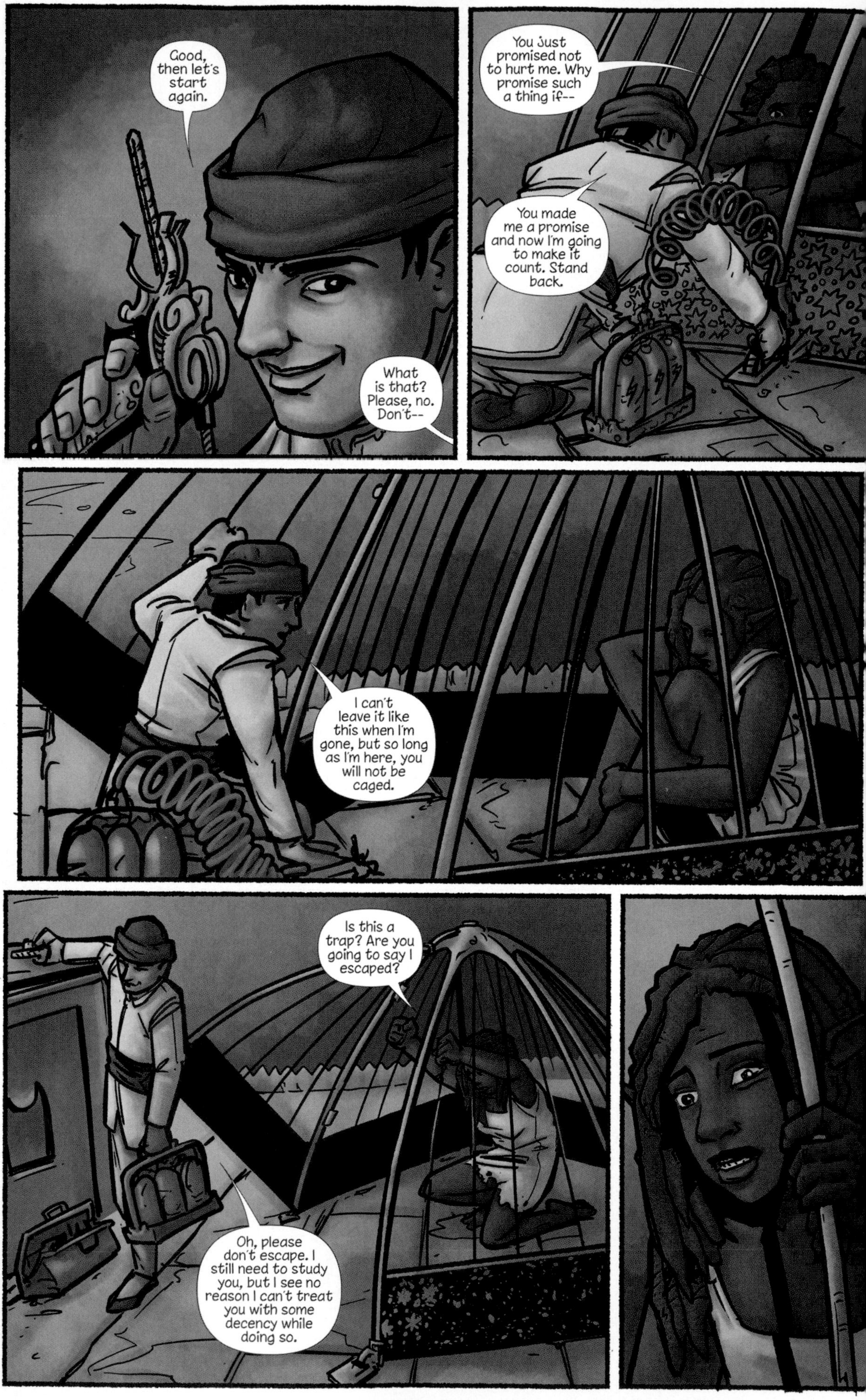
Good, then let's start again.
What is that? Please, no. Don't--
You just promised not to hurt me. Why promise such a thing if--
You made me a promise and now I'm going to make it count. Stand back.
I can't leave it like this when I'm gone, but so long as I'm here, you will not be caged.
Is this a trap? Are you going to say I escaped?
Oh, please don't escape. I still need to study you, but I see no reason I can't treat you with some decency while doing so.

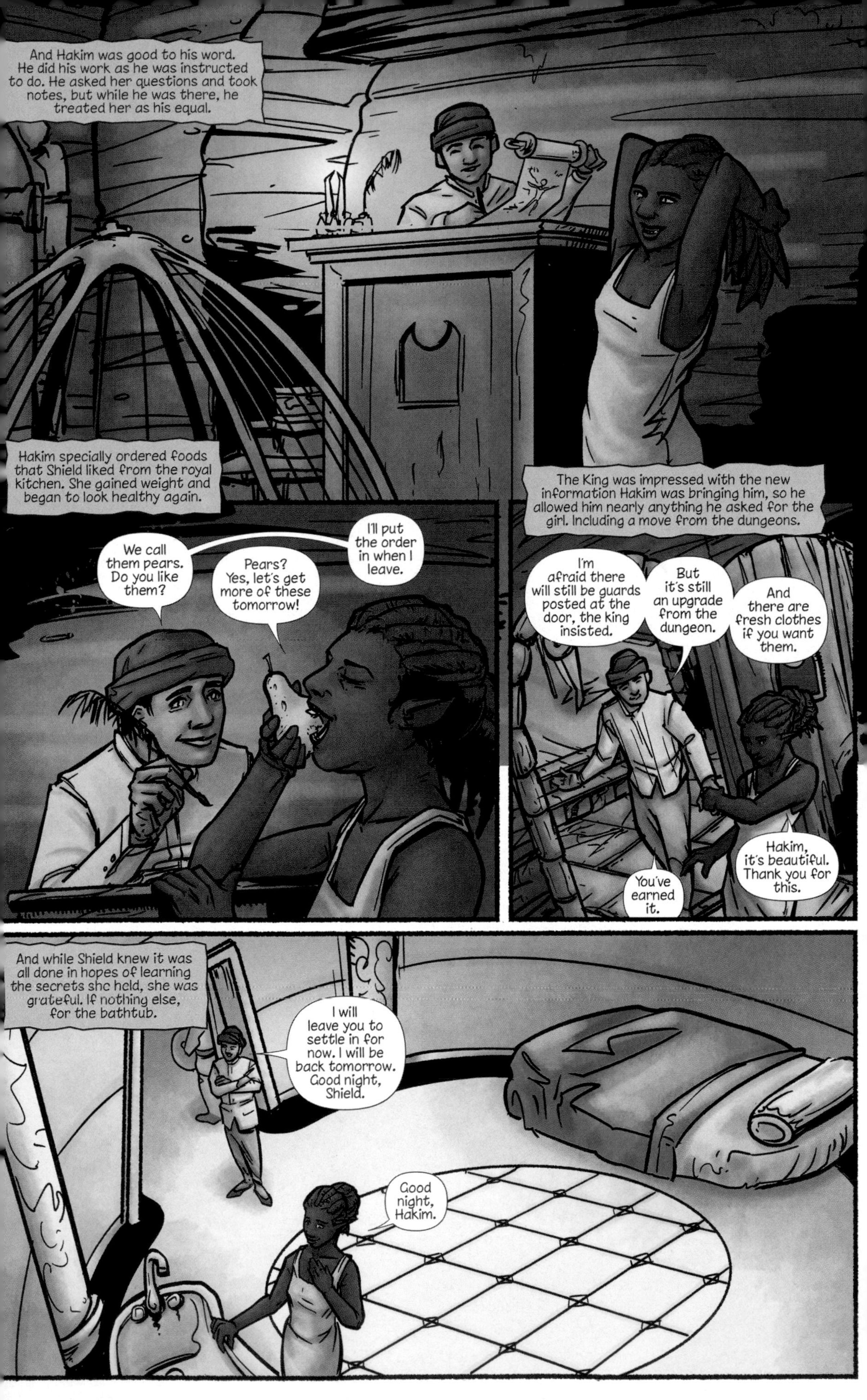

And Hakim was good to his word. He did his work as he was instructed to do. He asked her questions and took notes, but while he was there, he treated her as his equal.
Hakim specially ordered foods that Shield liked from the royal kitchen. She gained weight and began to look healthy again.
We call them pears. Do you like them?
Pears? Yes, let's get more of these tomorrow!
I'll put the order in when I leave.
The King was impressed with the new information Hakim was bringing him, so he allowed him nearly anything he asked for the girl. Including a move from the dungeons.
I'm afraid there will still be guards posted at the door, the king insisted.
But it's still an upgrade from the dungeon.
And there are fresh clothes if you want them.
Hakim, it's beautiful. Thank you for this.
You've earned it.
And while Shield knew it was all done in hopes of learning the secrets she held, she was grateful. If nothing else, for the bathtub.
I will leave you to settle in for now. I will be back tomorrow. Good night, Shield.
Good night, Hakim.

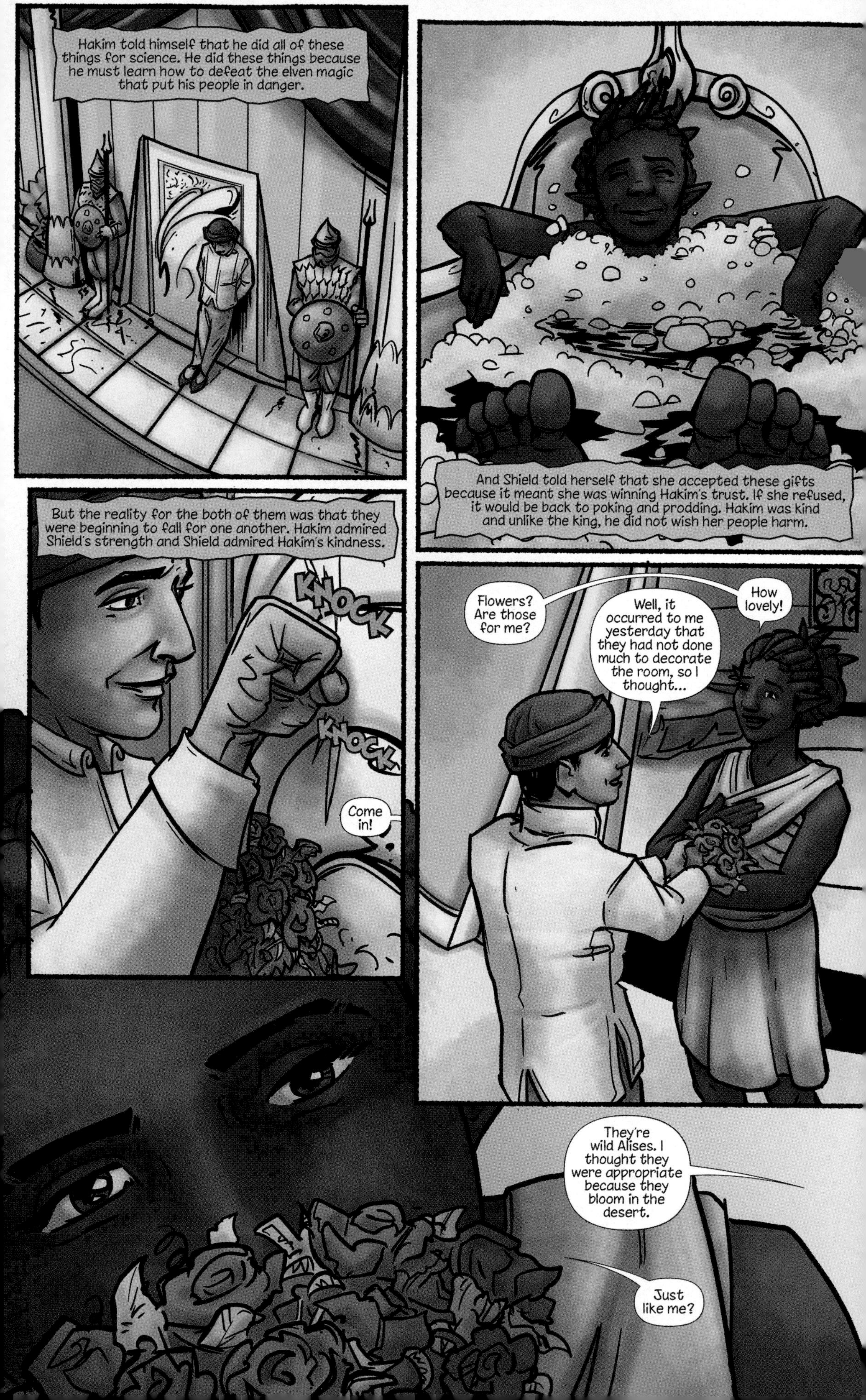
Hakim told himself that he did all of these things for science. He did these things because he must learn how to defeat the elven magic that put his people in danger.
And Shield told herself that she accepted these gifts because it meant she was winning Hakim's trust. If she refused, it would be back to poking and prodding. Hakim was kind and unlike the king, he did not wish her people harm.
But the reality for the both of them was that they were beginning to fall for one another. Hakim admired Shield's strength and Shield admired Hakim's kindness.
KNOCK
KNOCK
Come in!
Flowers? Are those for me?
Well, it occurred to me yesterday that they had not done much to decorate the room, so I thought...
How lovely!
They're wild Alises. I thought they were appropriate because they bloom in the desert.
Just like me?

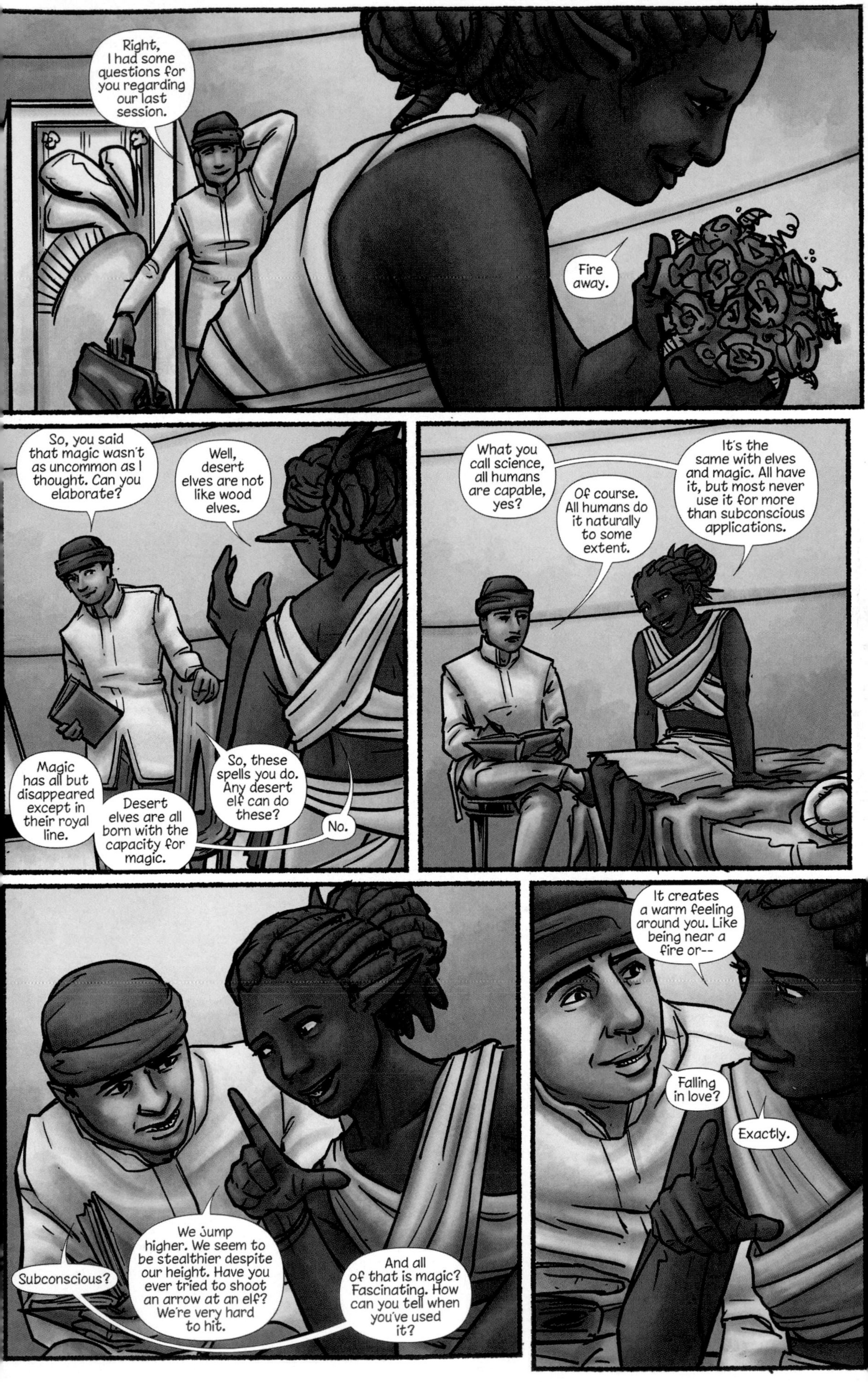
Right, I had some questions for you regarding our last session.
Fire away.
So, you said that magic wasn't as uncommon as I thought. Can you elaborate?
Well, desert elves are not like wood elves.
Magic has all but disappeared except in their royal line.
Desert elves are all born with the capacity for magic.
So, these spells you do. Any desert elf can do these?
No.
What you call science, all humans are capable, yes?
Of course. All humans do it naturally to some extent.
It's the same with elves and magic. All have it, but most never use it for more than subconscious applications.
Subconscious?
We jump higher. We seem to be stealthier despite our height. Have you ever tried to shoot an arrow at an elf? We're very hard to hit.
And all of that is magic? Fascinating. How can you tell when you've used it?
It creates a warm feeling around you. Like being near a fire or--
Falling in love?
Exactly.

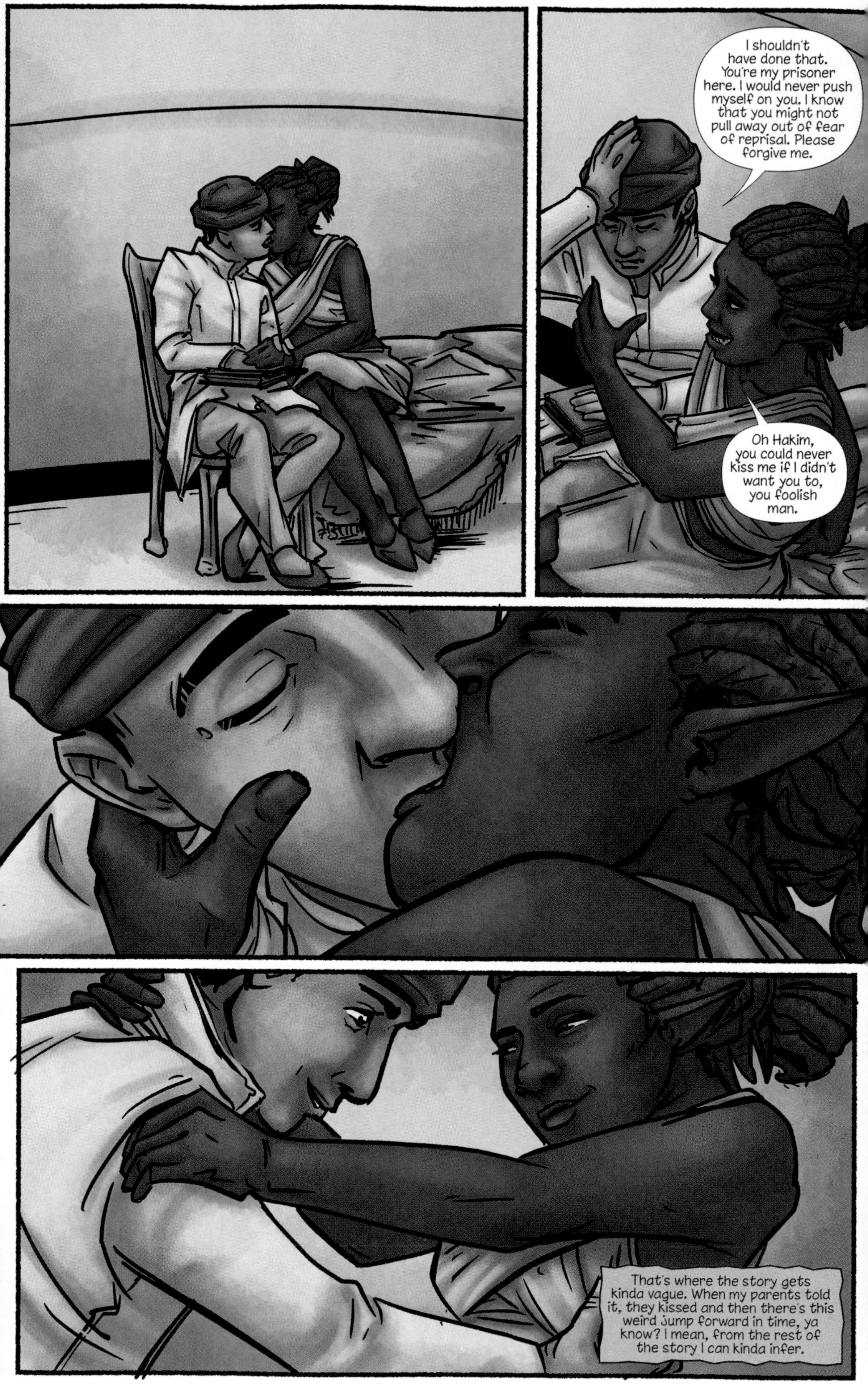
I shouldn't have done that. You're my prisoner here. I would never push myself on you. I know that you might not pull away out of fear of reprisal. Please forgive me.
Oh Hakim, you could never kiss me if I didn't want you to, you foolish man.
That's where the story gets kinda vague. When my parents told it, they kissed and then there's this weird jump forward in time, ya know? I mean, from the rest of the story I can kinda infer.

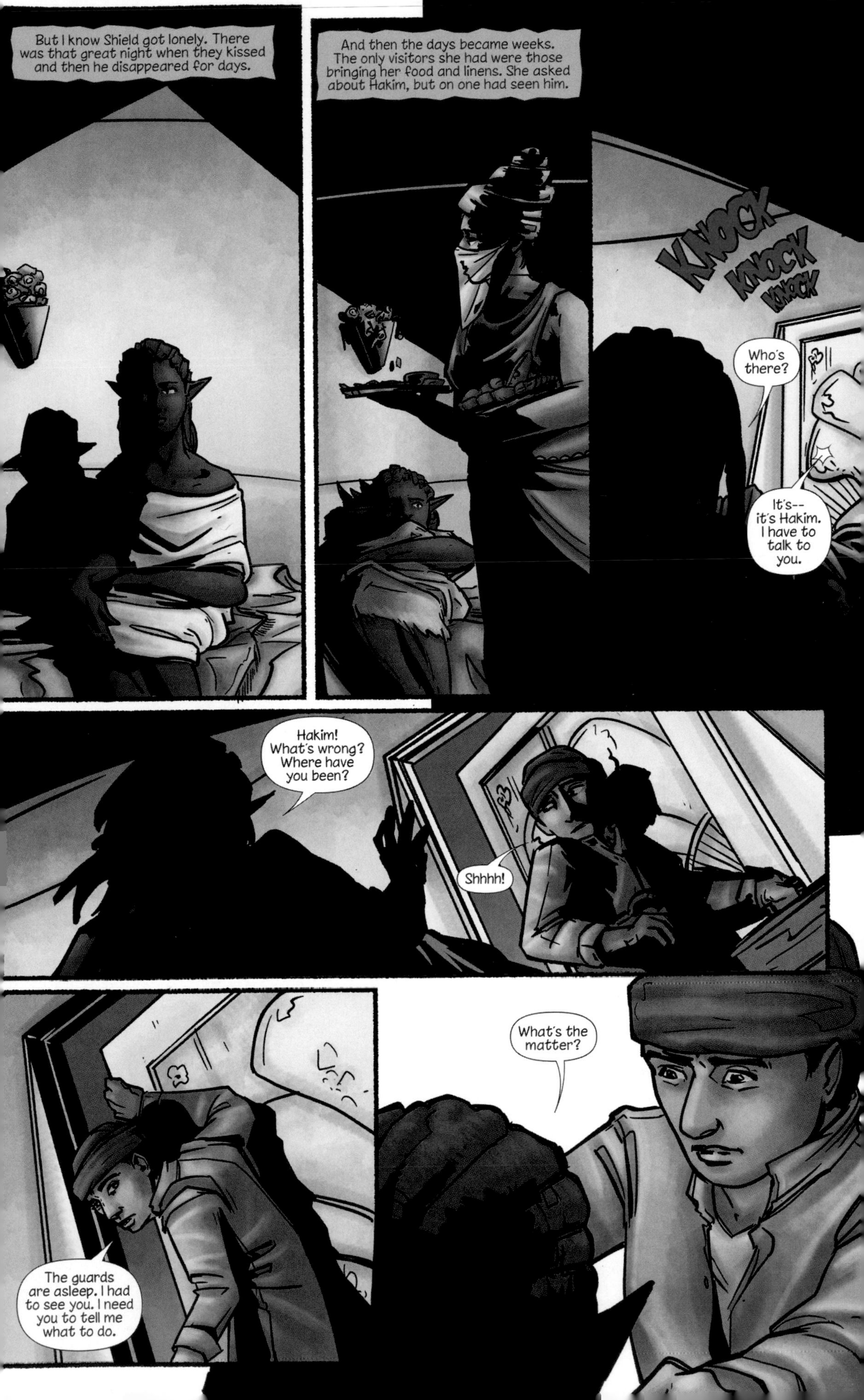
But I know Shield got lonely. There was that great night when they kissed and then he disappeared for days.
And then the days became weeks. The only visitors she had were those bringing her food and linens. She asked about Hakim, but on one had seen him.
KNOCK KNOCK KNOCK
Who's there?
It's-- it's Hakim. I have to talk to you.
Hakim! What's wrong? Where have you been?
Shhhh!
What's the matter?
The guards are asleep. I had to see you. I need you to tell me what to do.

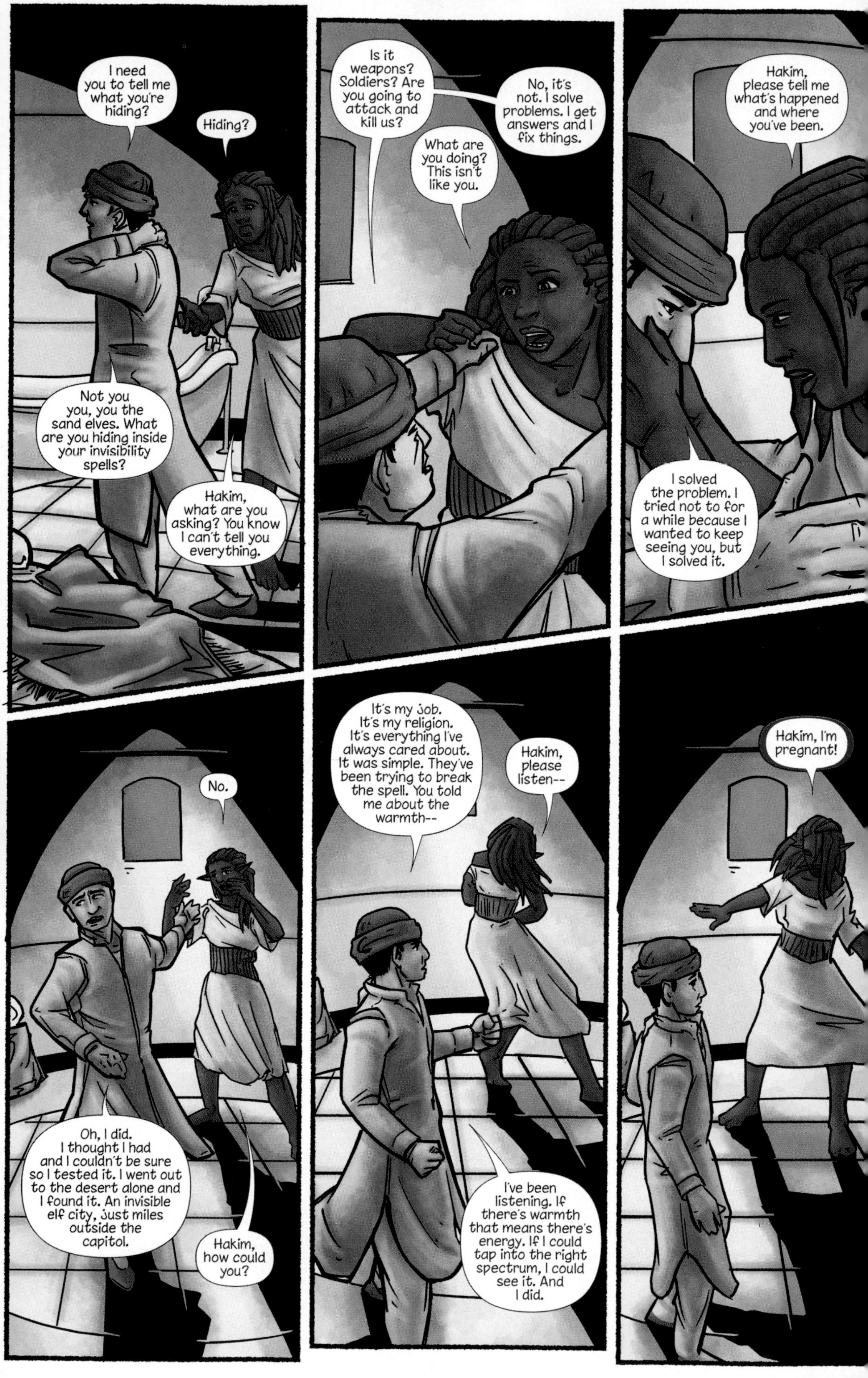
I need you to tell me what you're hiding?
Hiding?
Not you you, you the sand elves. What are you hiding inside your invisibility spells?
Hakim, what are you asking? You know I can't tell you everything.
Is it weapons? Soldiers? Are you going to attack and kill us?
No, it's not. I solve problems. I get answers and I fix things.
What are you doing? This isn't like you.
Hakim, please tell me what's happened and where you've been.
I solved the problem. I tried not to for a while because I wanted to keep seeing you, but I solved it.
No.
Oh, I did. I thought I had and I couldn't be sure so I tested it. I went out to the desert alone and I found it. An invisible elf city, just miles outside the capitol.
Hakim, how could you?
It's my job. It's my religion. It's everything I've always cared about. It was simple. They've been trying to break the spell. You told me about the warmth--
Hakim, please listen--
I've been listening. If there's warmth that means there's energy. If I could tap into the right spectrum, I could see it. And I did.
Hakim, I'm pregnant!

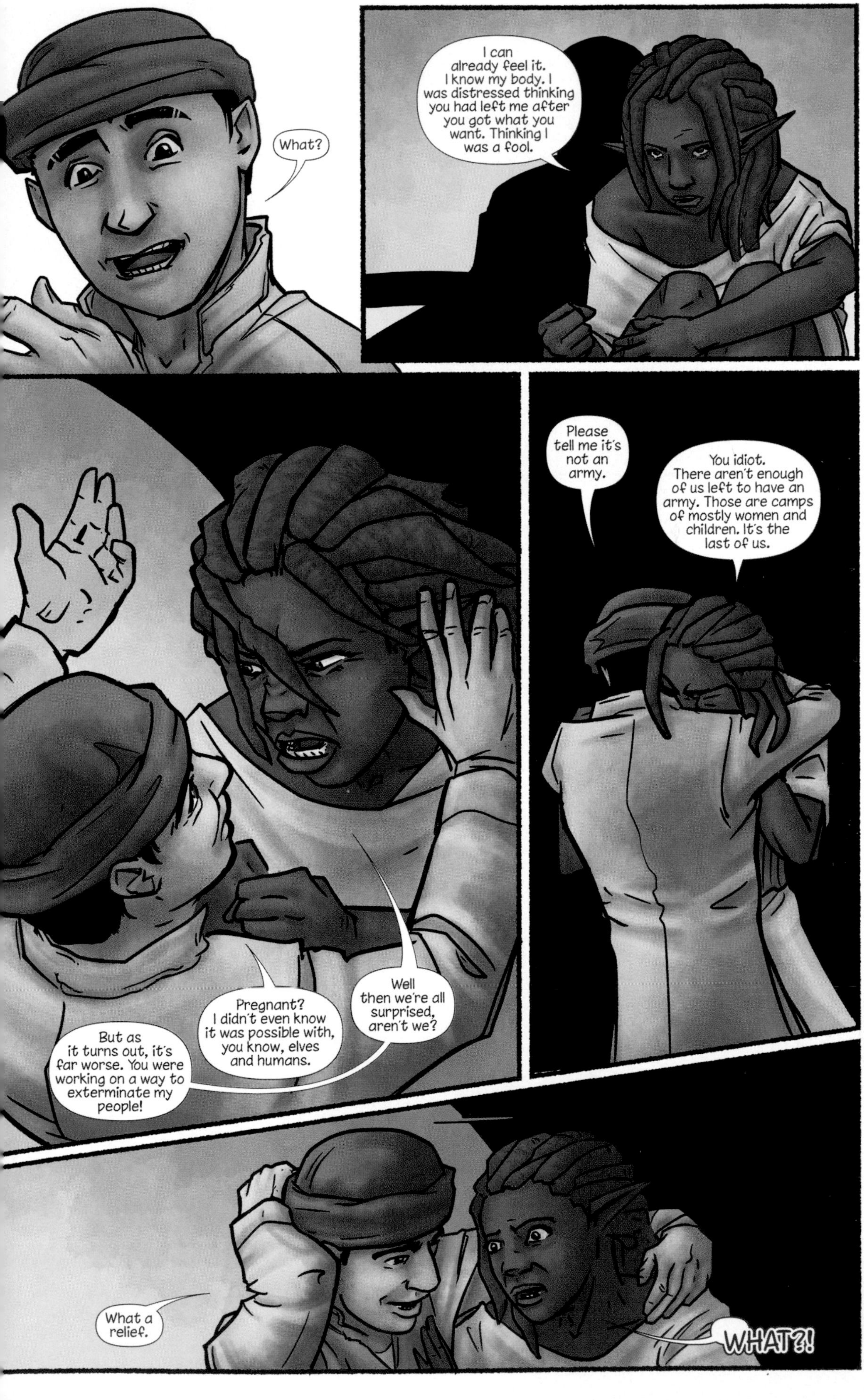
What?
I can already feel it. I know my body. I was distressed thinking you had left me after you got what you want. Thinking I was a fool.
Pregnant? I didn't even know it was possible with, you know, elves and humans.
Well then we're all surprised, aren't we?
But as it turns out, it's far worse. You were working on a way to exterminate my people!
Please tell me it's not an army.
You idiot. There aren't enough of us left to have an army. Those are camps of mostly women and children. It's the last of us.
What a relief.
WHAT?!

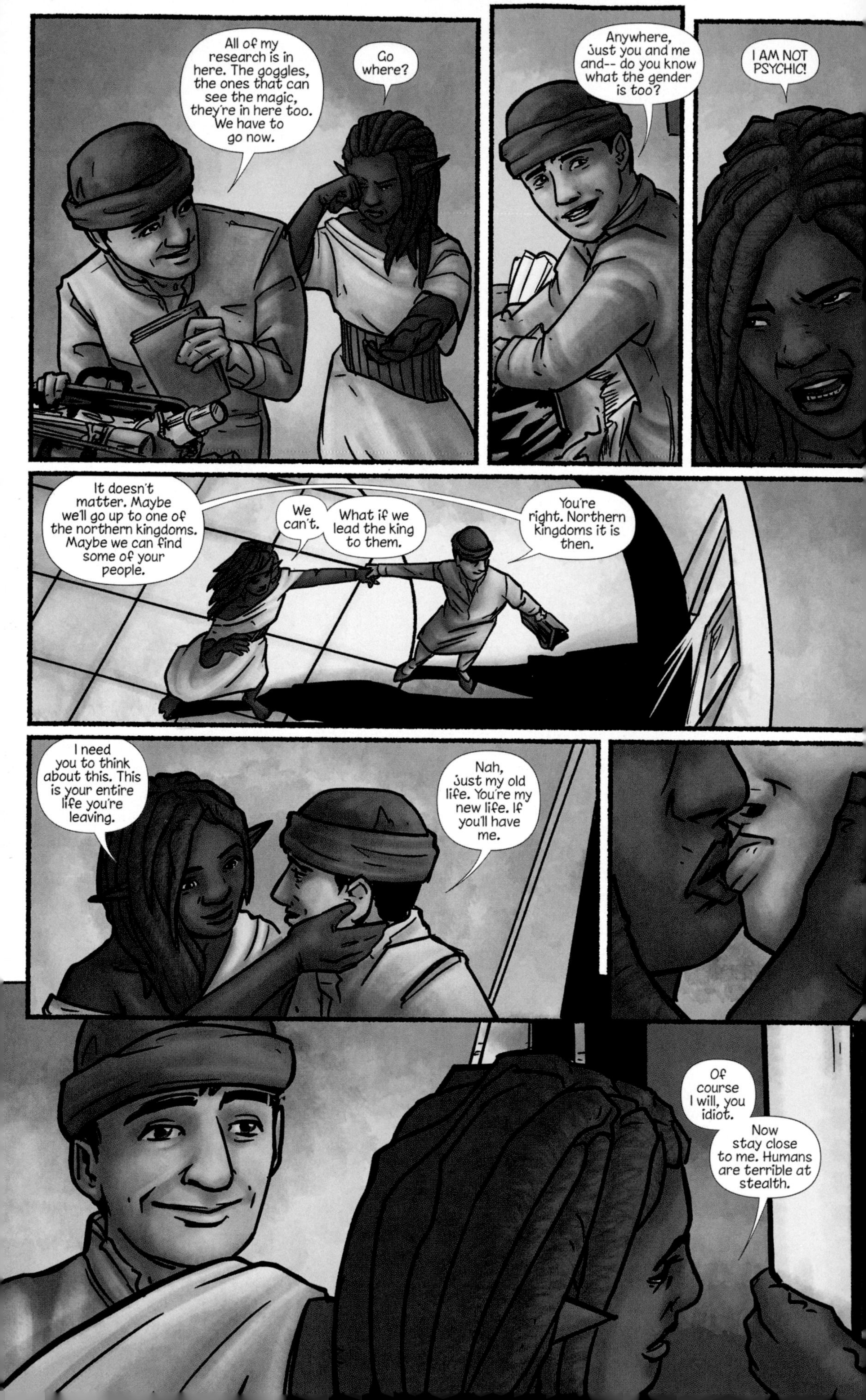
All of my research is in here. The goggles, the ones that can see the magic, they're in here too. We have to go now.
Go where?
Anywhere, just you and me and-- do you know what the gender is too?
I AM NOT PSYCHIC!
It doesn't matter. Maybe we'll go up to one of the northern kingdoms. Maybe we can find some of your people.
We can't.
What if we lead the king to them.
You're right. Northern kingdoms it is then.
I need you to think about this. This is your entire life you're leaving.
Nah, just my old life. You're my new life. If you'll have me.
Of course I will, you idiot.
Now stay close to me. Humans are terrible at stealth.

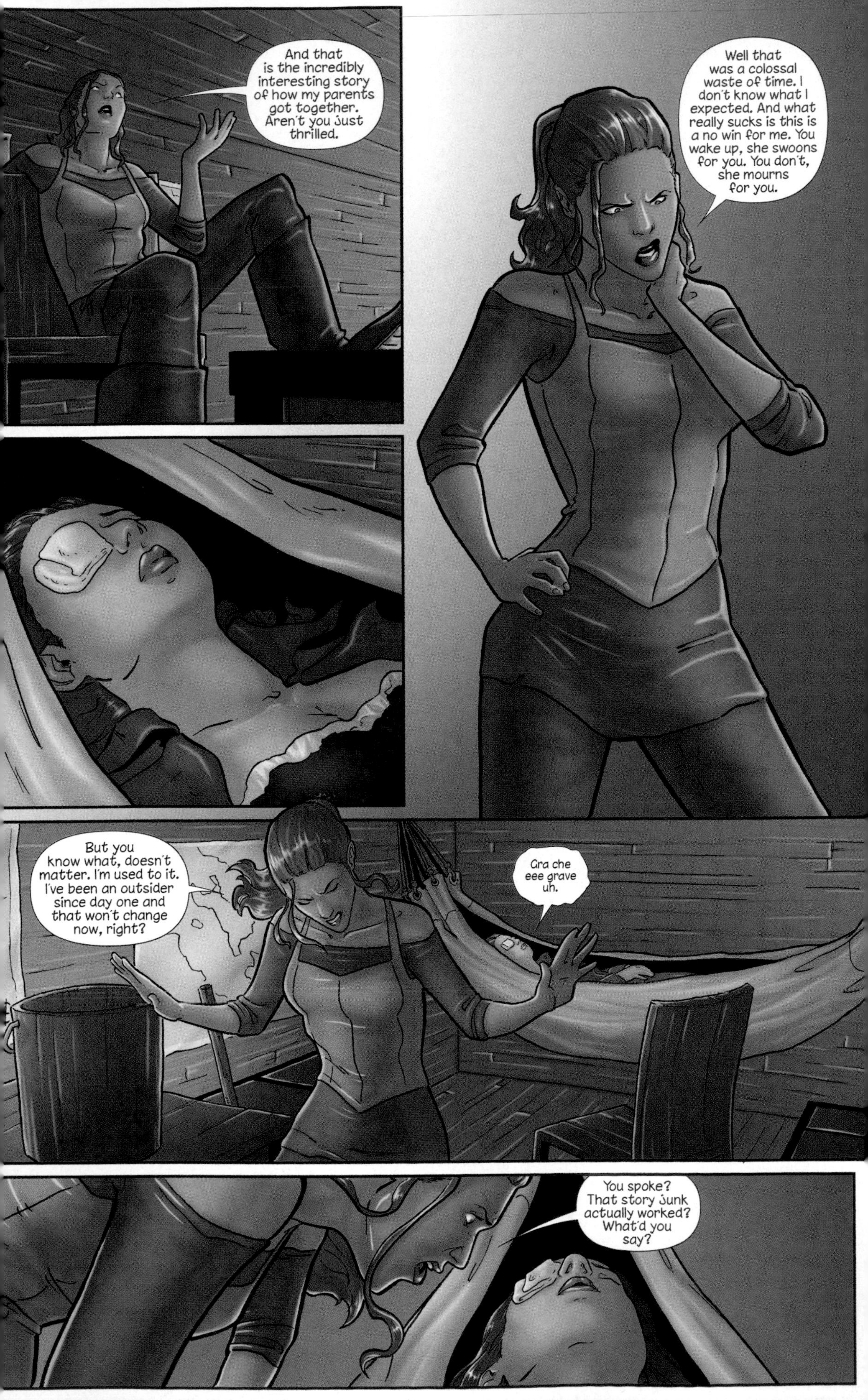
And that is the incredibly interesting story of how my parents got together. Aren't you just thrilled.
Well that was a colossal waste of time. I don't know what I expected. And what really sucks is this is a no win for me. You wake up, she swoons for you. You don't, she mourns for you.
But you know what, doesn't matter. I'm used to it. I've been an outsider since day one and that won't change now, right?
Gra che eee grave uh.
You spoke? That story junk actually worked? What'd you say?

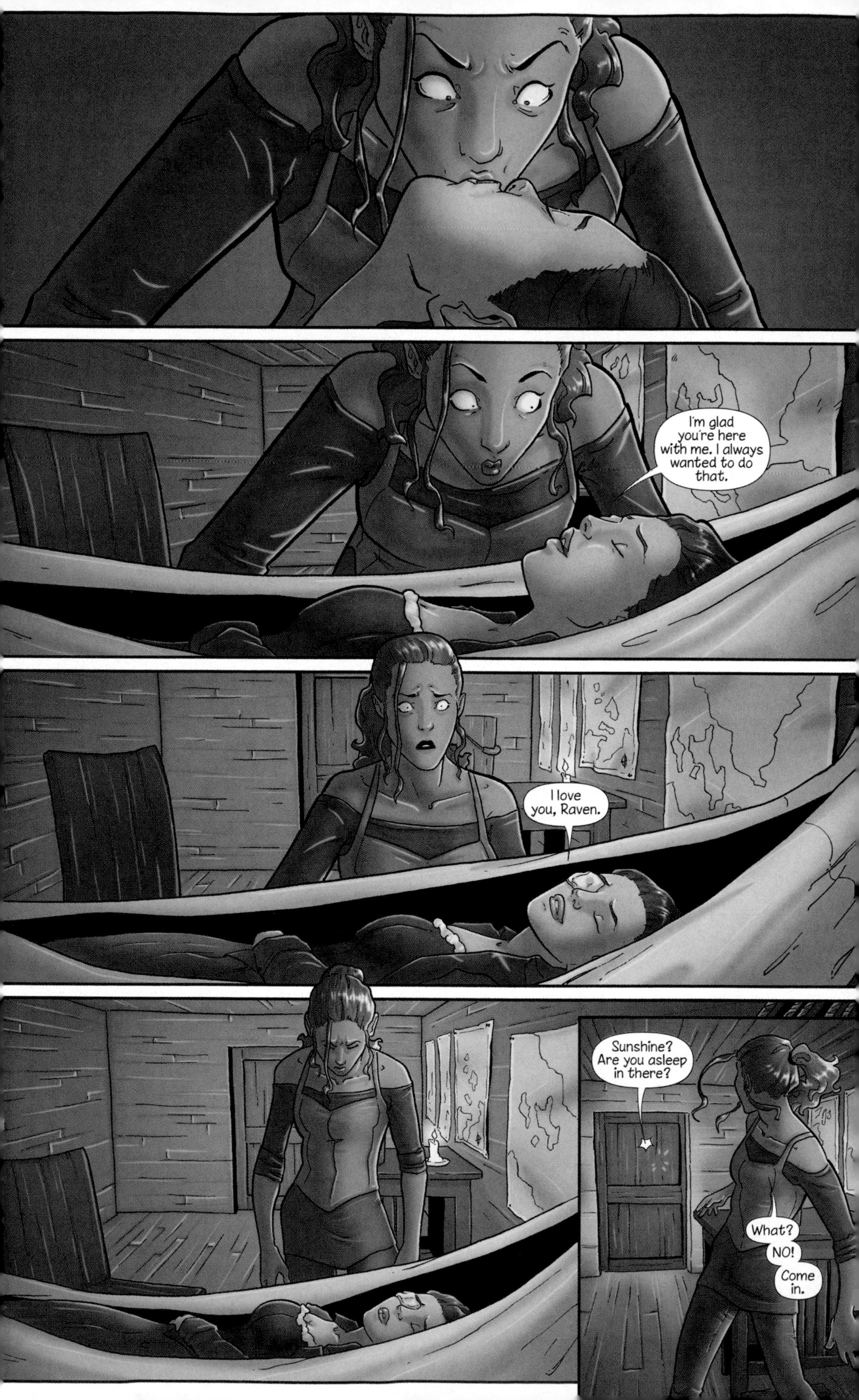
I'm glad you're here with me. I always wanted to do that.
I love you, Raven.
Sunshine? Are you asleep in there?
What?
NO!
Come in.

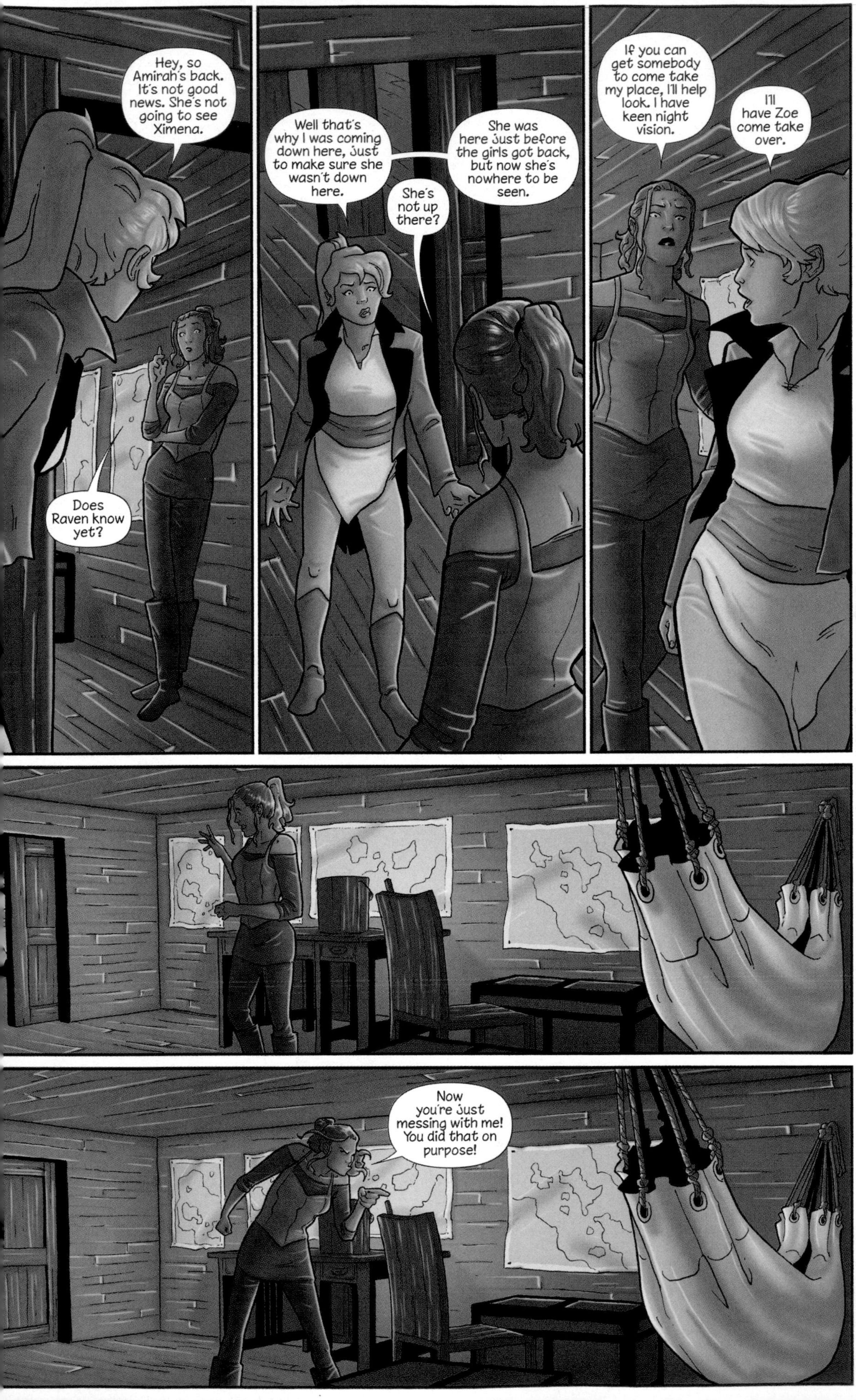
Hey, so Amirah's back. It's not good news. She's not going to see Ximena.
Does Raven know yet?
Well that's why I was coming down here, just to make sure she wasn't down here.
She was here just before the girls got back, but now she's nowhere to be seen.
She's not up there?
If you can get somebody to come take my place, I'll help look. I have keen night vision.
I'll have Zoe come take over.
Now you're just messing with me! You did that on purpose!

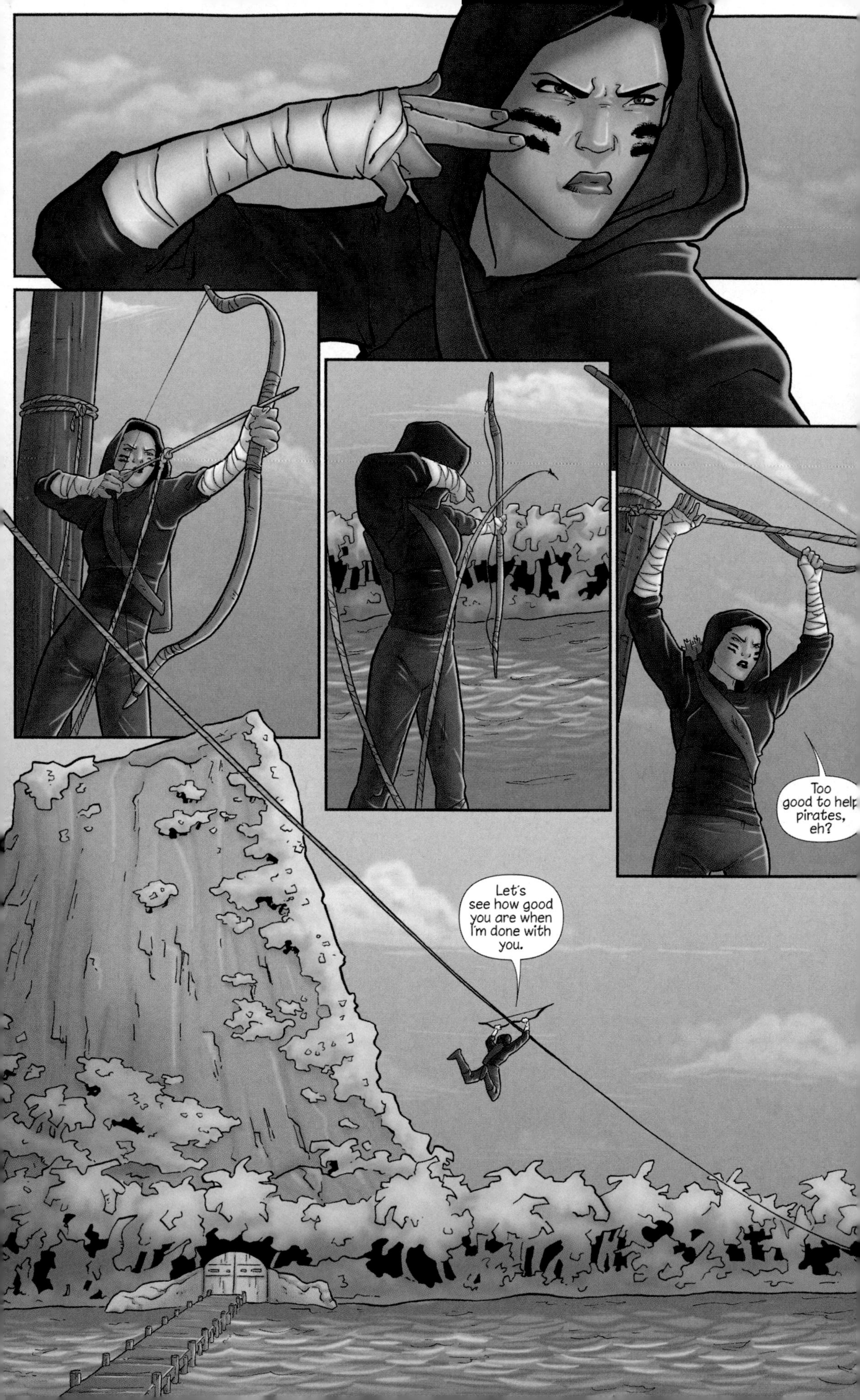
Too good to help pirates, eh?
Let's see how good you are when I'm done with you.

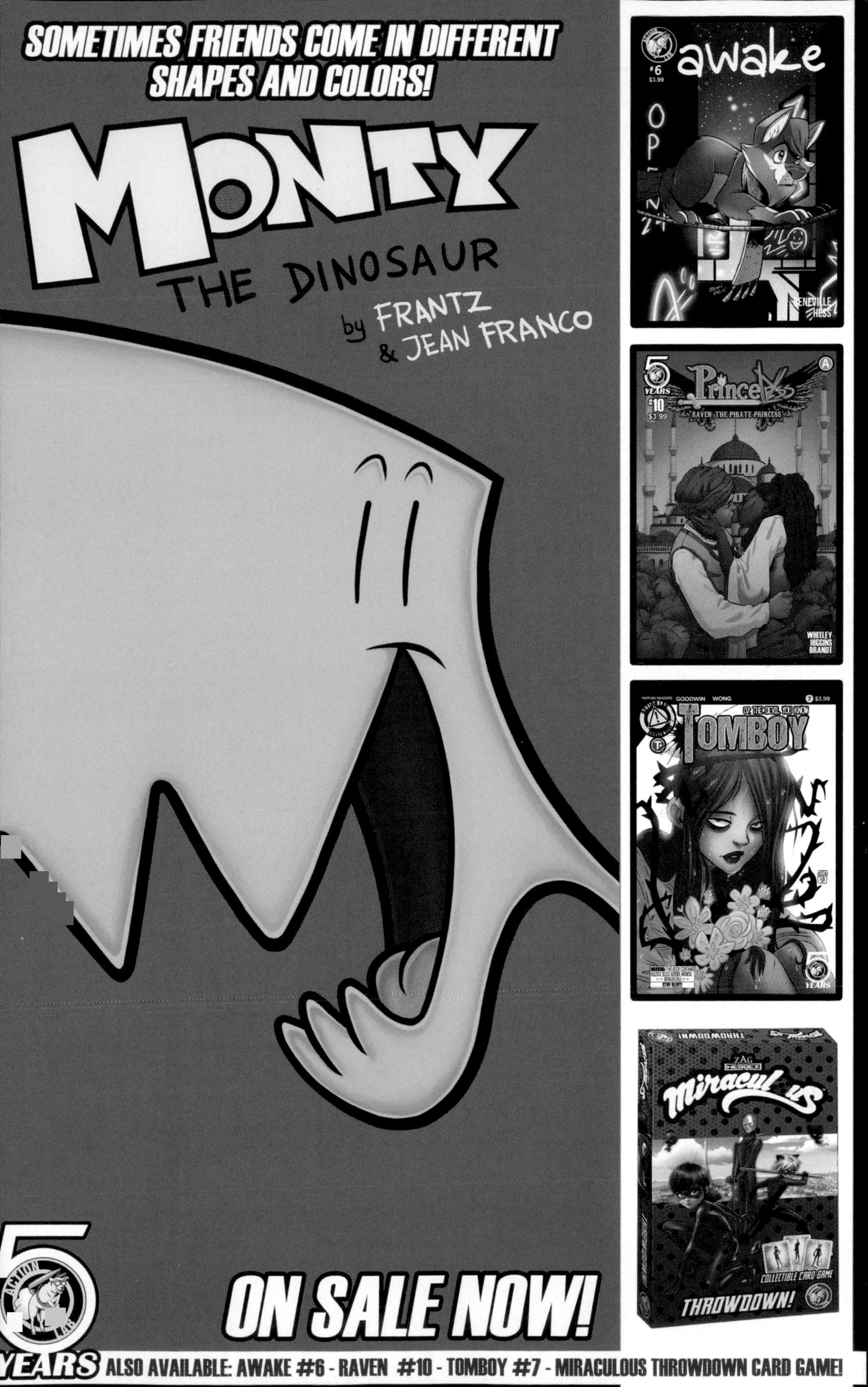
SOMETIMES FRIENDS COME IN DIFFERENT SHAPES AND COLORS!
MONTY
THE DINOSAUR
by FRANTZ & JEAN FRANCO
ON SALE NOW!
5 YEARS
ALSO AVAILABLE: AWAKE #6 - RAVEN #10 - TOMBOY #7 - MIRACULOUS THROWDOWN CARD GAME!
awake
#6
$3.99
NEVILLE HESS
Princeless
#10
$3.99
RAVEN THE PIRATE PRINCESS
WHITLEY HIGGINS BRANDT
GOODWIN WONG
$3.99
OR THE DEVIL YOU KNOW
TOMBOY
miraculous
COLLECTIBLE CARD GAME
THROWDOWN!

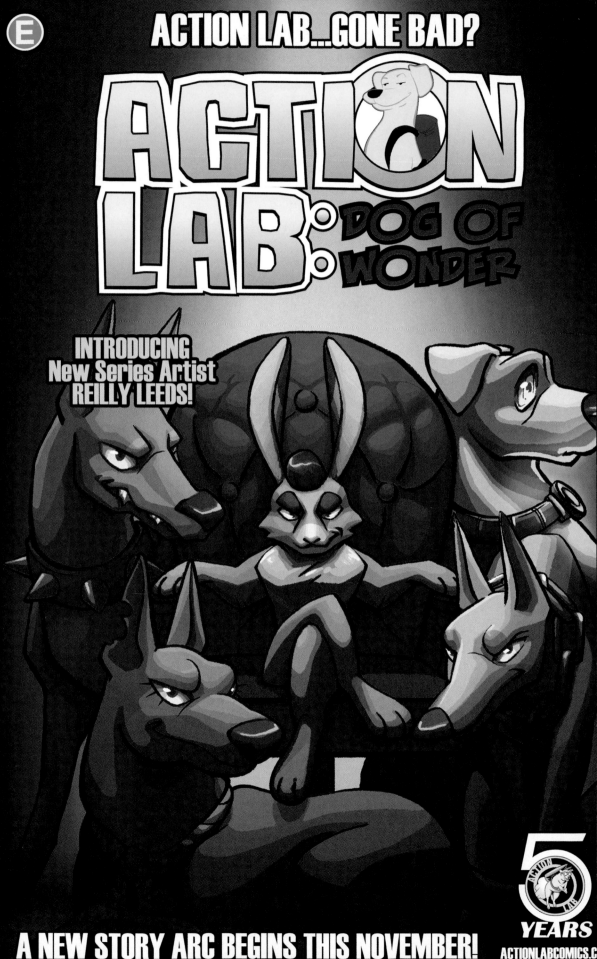

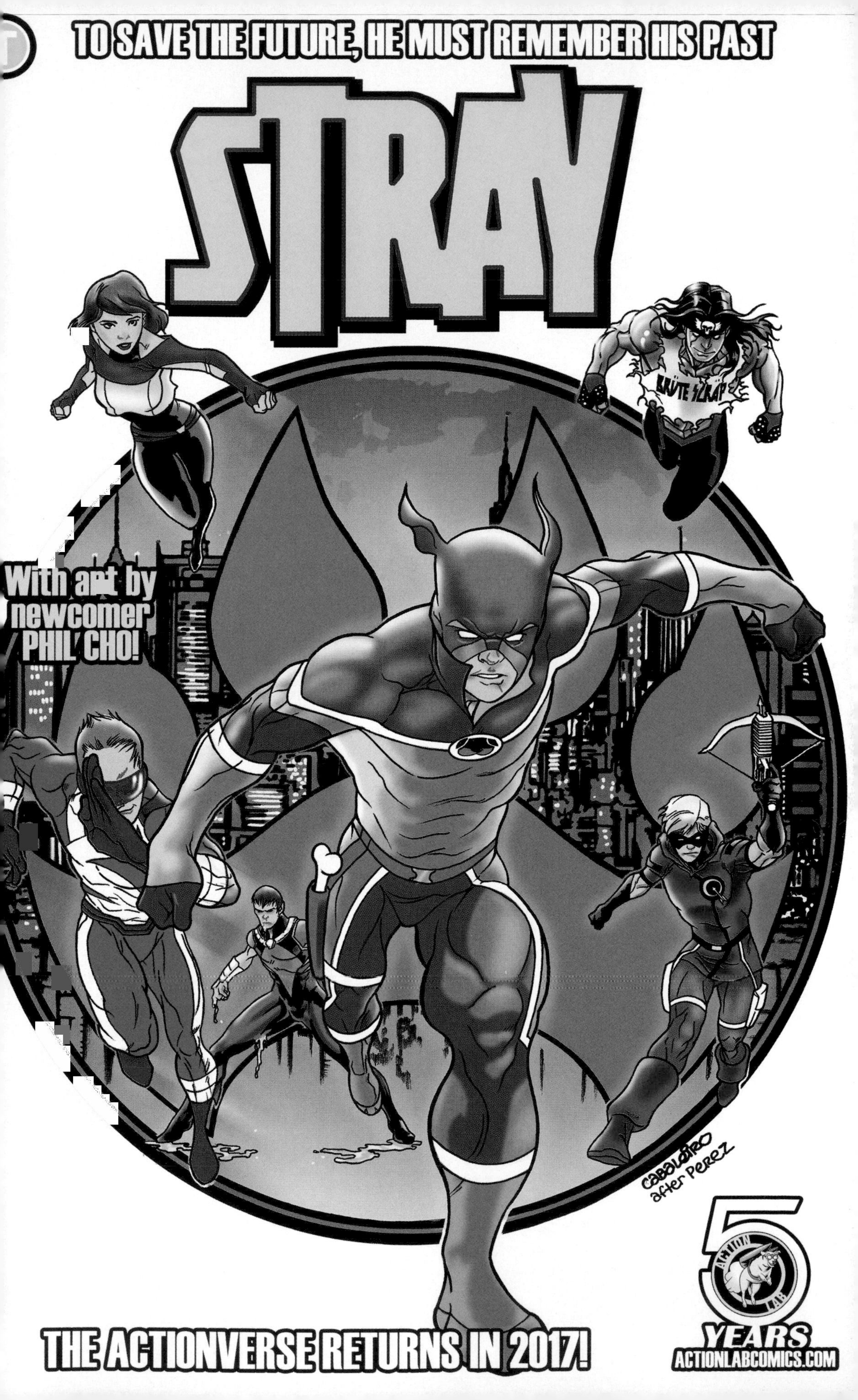
TO SAVE THE FUTURE, HE MUST REMEMBER HIS PAST
STRAY
With art by newcomer PHIL CHO!
THE ACTIONVERSE RETURNS IN 2017!
5 YEARS
ACTIONLABCOMICS.COM

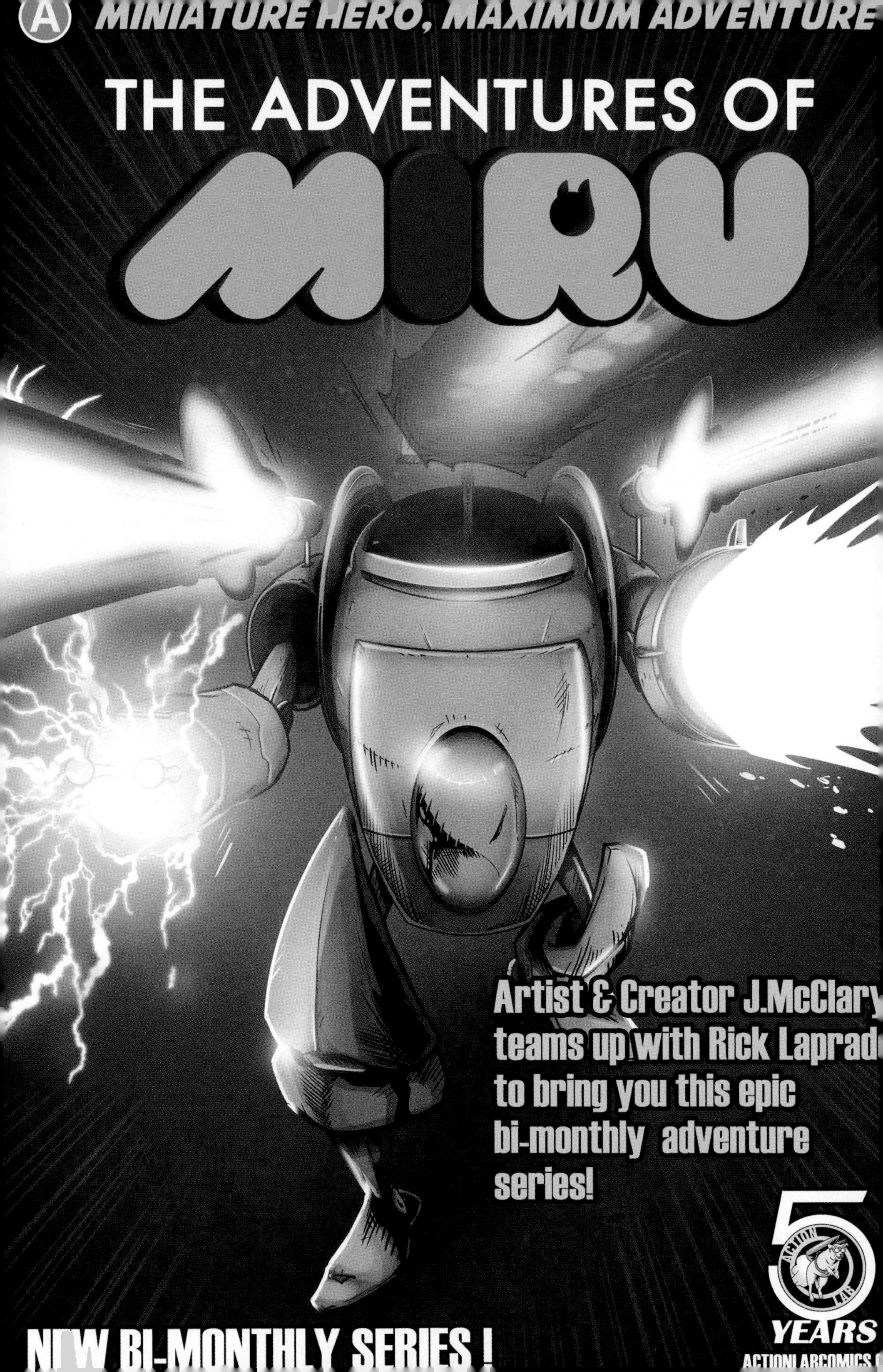
MINIATURE HERO, MAXIMUM ADVENTURE
THE ADVENTURES OF
MIRU
Artist & Creator J.McClary
teams up with Rick Laprad
to bring you this epic
bi-monthly adventure
series!
5 YEARS
ACTIONLABCOMICS
NEW BI-MONTHLY SERIES !

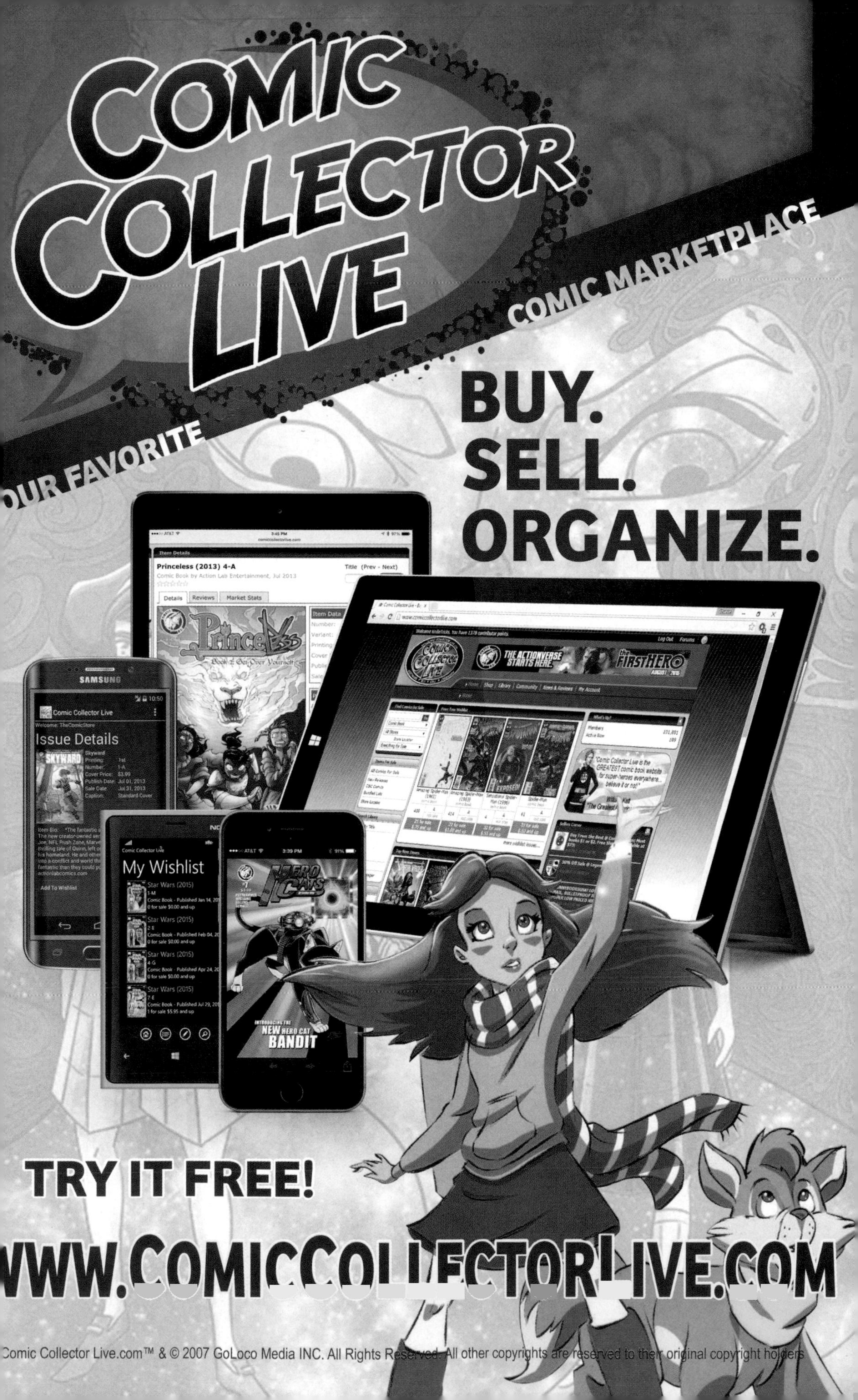
COMIC COLLECTOR LIVE
YOUR FAVORITE COMIC MARKETPLACE
BUY.
SELL.
ORGANIZE.
TRY IT FREE!
WWW.COMICCOLLECTORLIVE.COM
Comic Collector Live.com™ & © 2007 GoLoco Media INC. All Rights Reserved. All other copyrights are reserved to their original copyright holders

Meet the new class

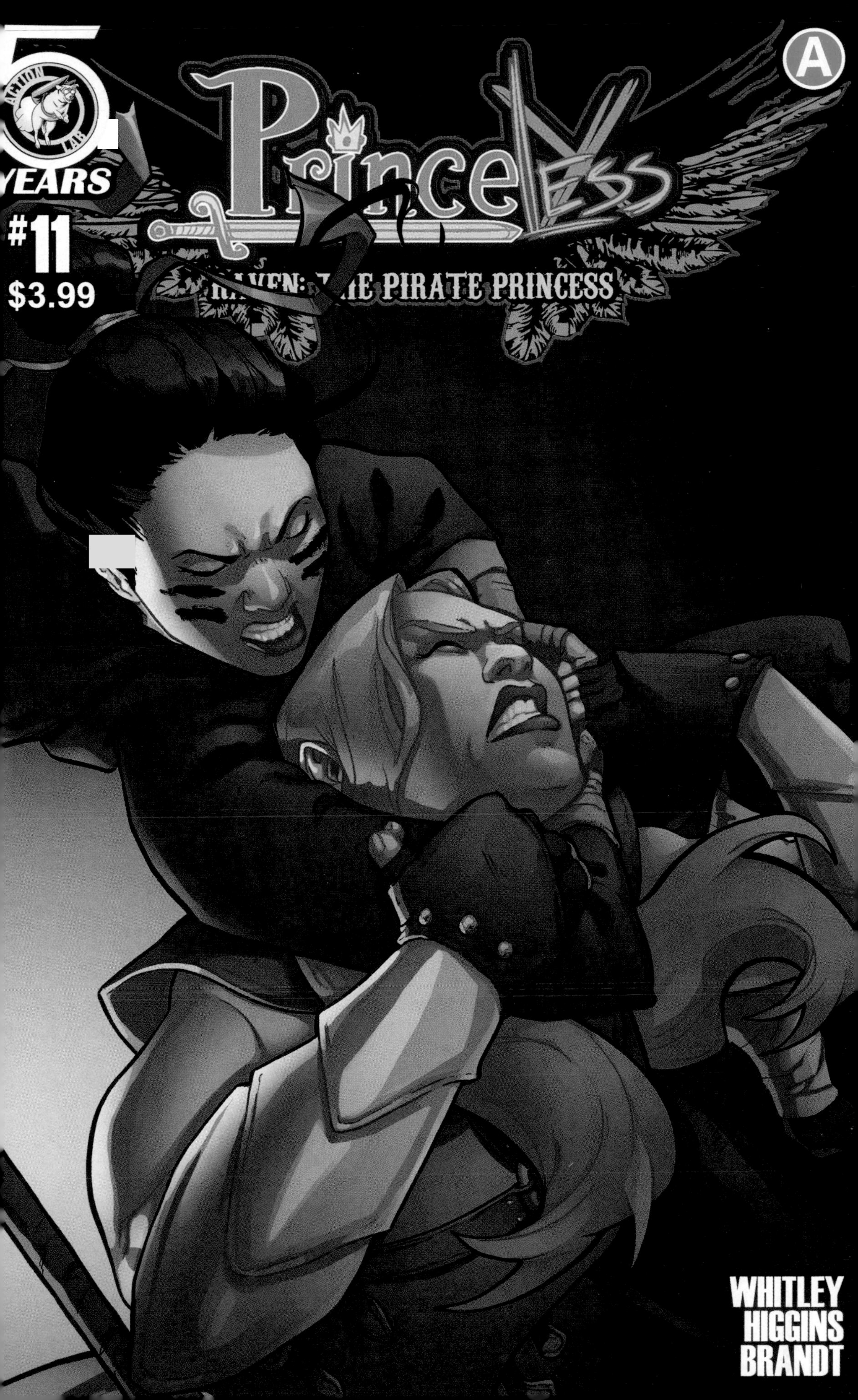

5 YEARS
ACTION LAB
#11
$3.99
Princeless
PIRATE PRINCESS
A
WHITLEY
HIGGINS
BRANDT

FROM ALL-AGES TO MATURE READERS
ACTION LAB HAS YOU COVERED.

 **Appropriate for everyone.**

 **Appropriate for age 9 and up. Absent of profanity or adult content.**

Suggested for 12 and Up. Comics with this rating are comparable to a PG-13 movie rating. Recommended for our teen and young adult readers.

 **Appropriate for older teens. Similar to Teen, but featuring more mature themes and/or more graphic imagery.**

 **Contains extreme violence and some nudity. Basically the Rated-R of comics.**

 **FIND YOUR NEW FAVORITE COMICS.**

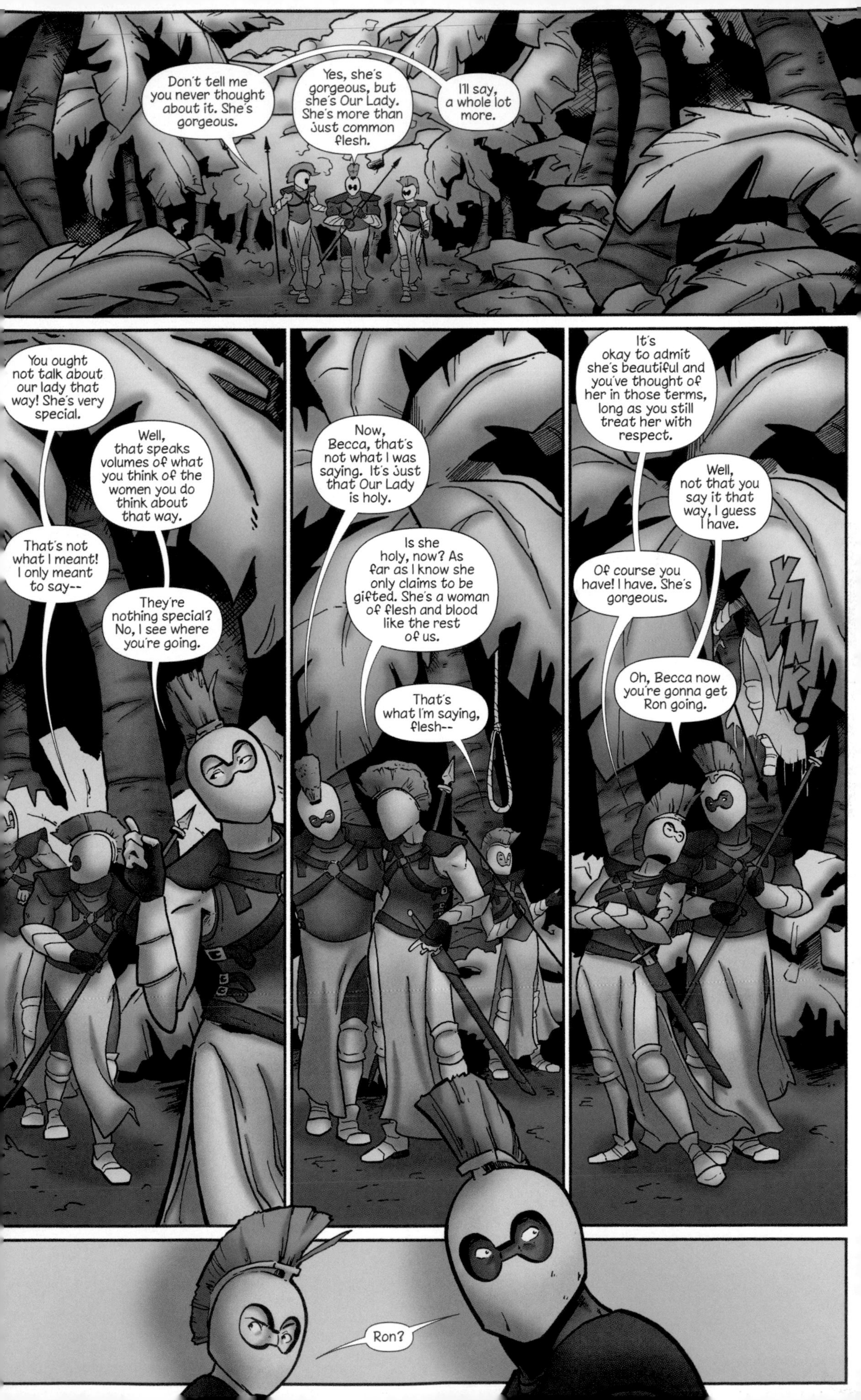
Don't tell me you never thought about it. She's gorgeous.
Yes, she's gorgeous, but she's Our Lady. She's more than just common flesh.
I'll say, a whole lot more.
You ought not talk about our lady that way! She's very special.
Well, that speaks volumes of what you think of the women you do think about that way.
That's not what I meant! I only meant to say--
They're nothing special? No, I see where you're going.
Now, Becca, that's not what I was saying. It's just that Our Lady is holy.
Is she holy, now? As far as I know she only claims to be gifted. She's a woman of flesh and blood like the rest of us.
That's what I'm saying, flesh--
It's okay to admit she's beautiful and you've thought of her in those terms, long as you still treat her with respect.
Well, not that you say it that way, I guess I have.
Of course you have! I have. She's gorgeous.
YANK!
Oh, Becca now you're gonna get Ron going.
Ron?

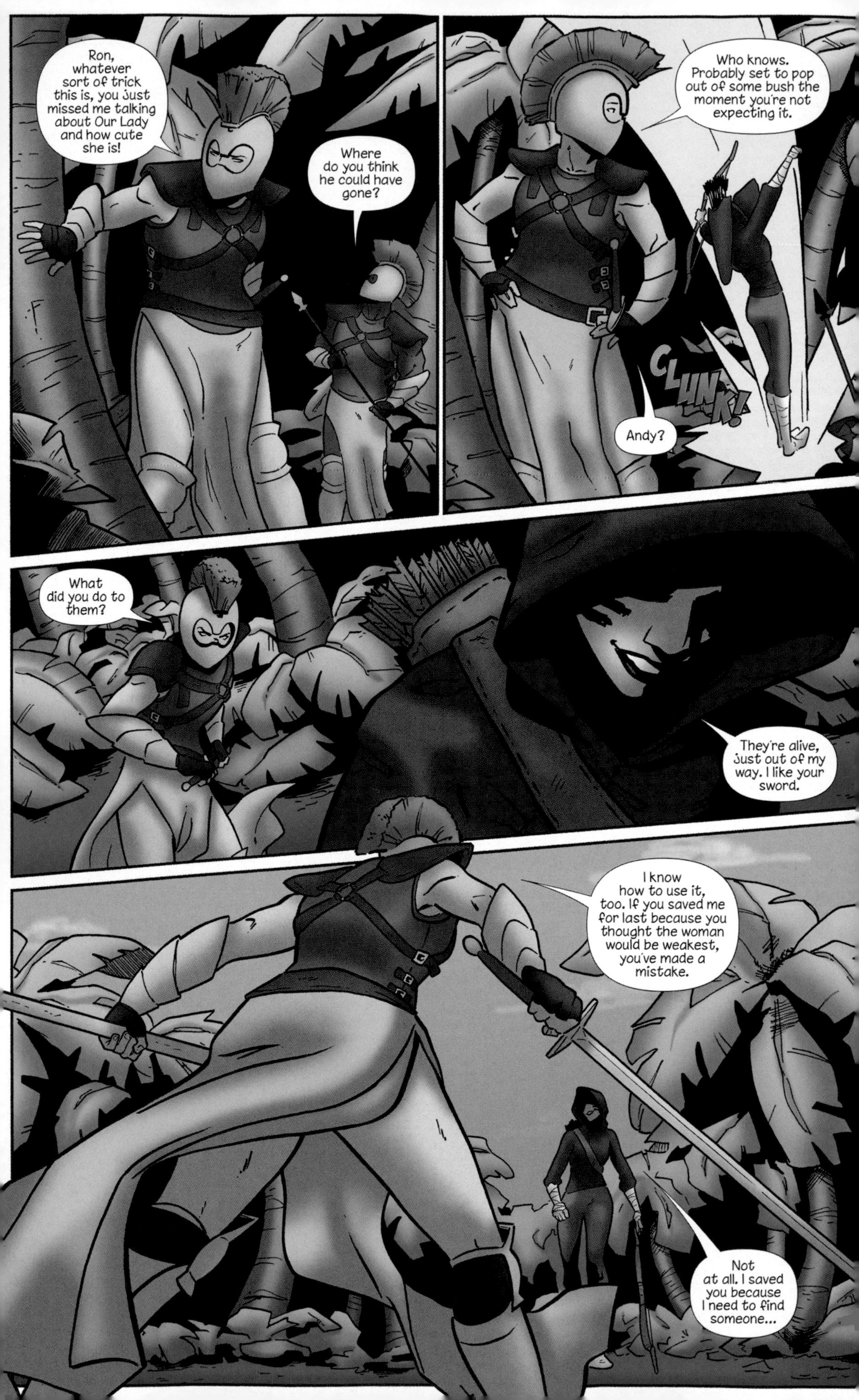
Ron, whatever sort of trick this is, you just missed me talking about Our Lady and how cute she is!
Where do you think he could have gone?
Who knows. Probably set to pop out of some bush the moment you're not expecting it.
CLUNK!
Andy?
What did you do to them?
They're alive, just out of my way. I like your sword.
I know how to use it, too. If you saved me for last because you thought the woman would be weakest, you've made a mistake.
Not at all. I saved you because I need to find someone...

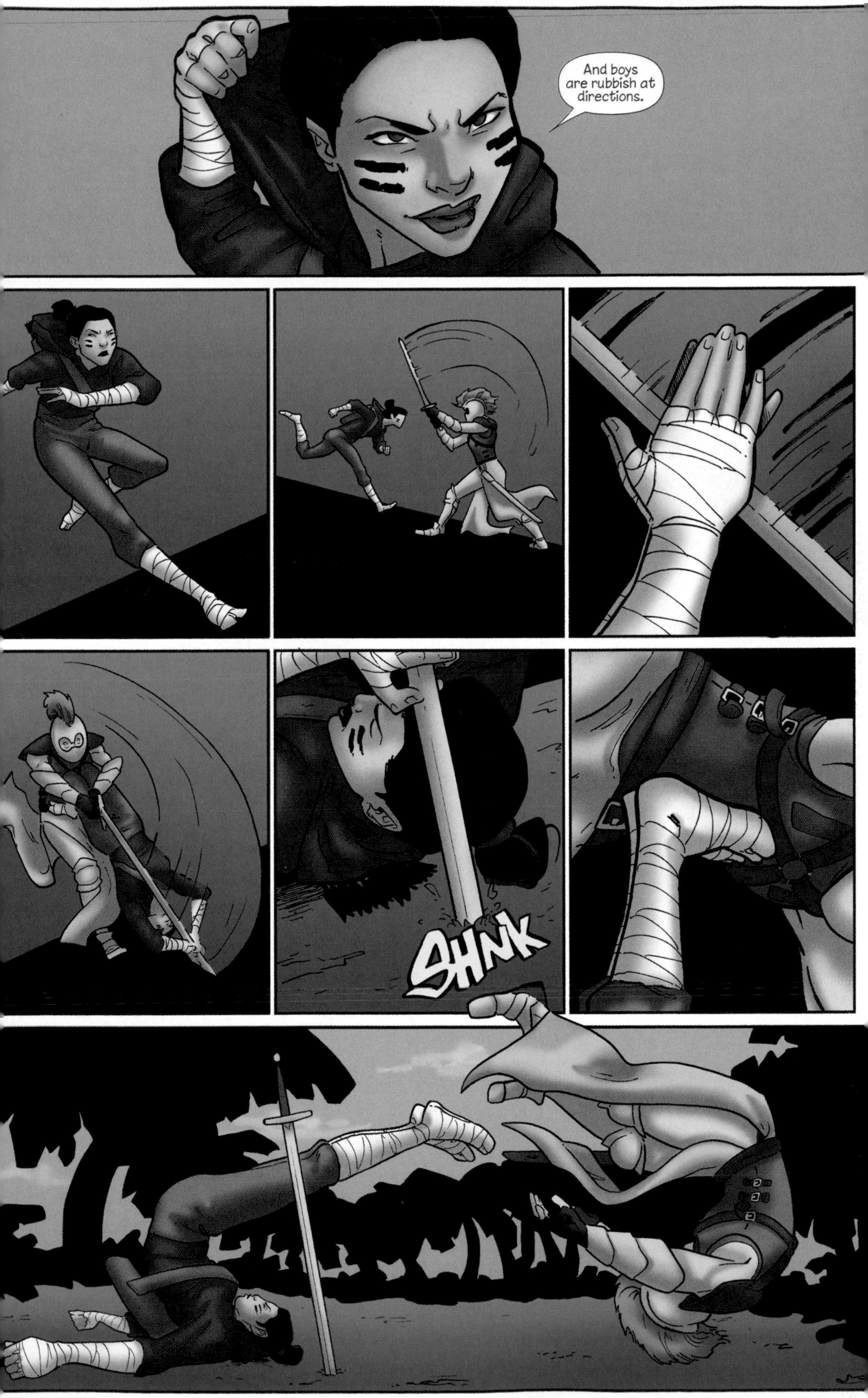
And boys are rubbish at directions.
SHNK

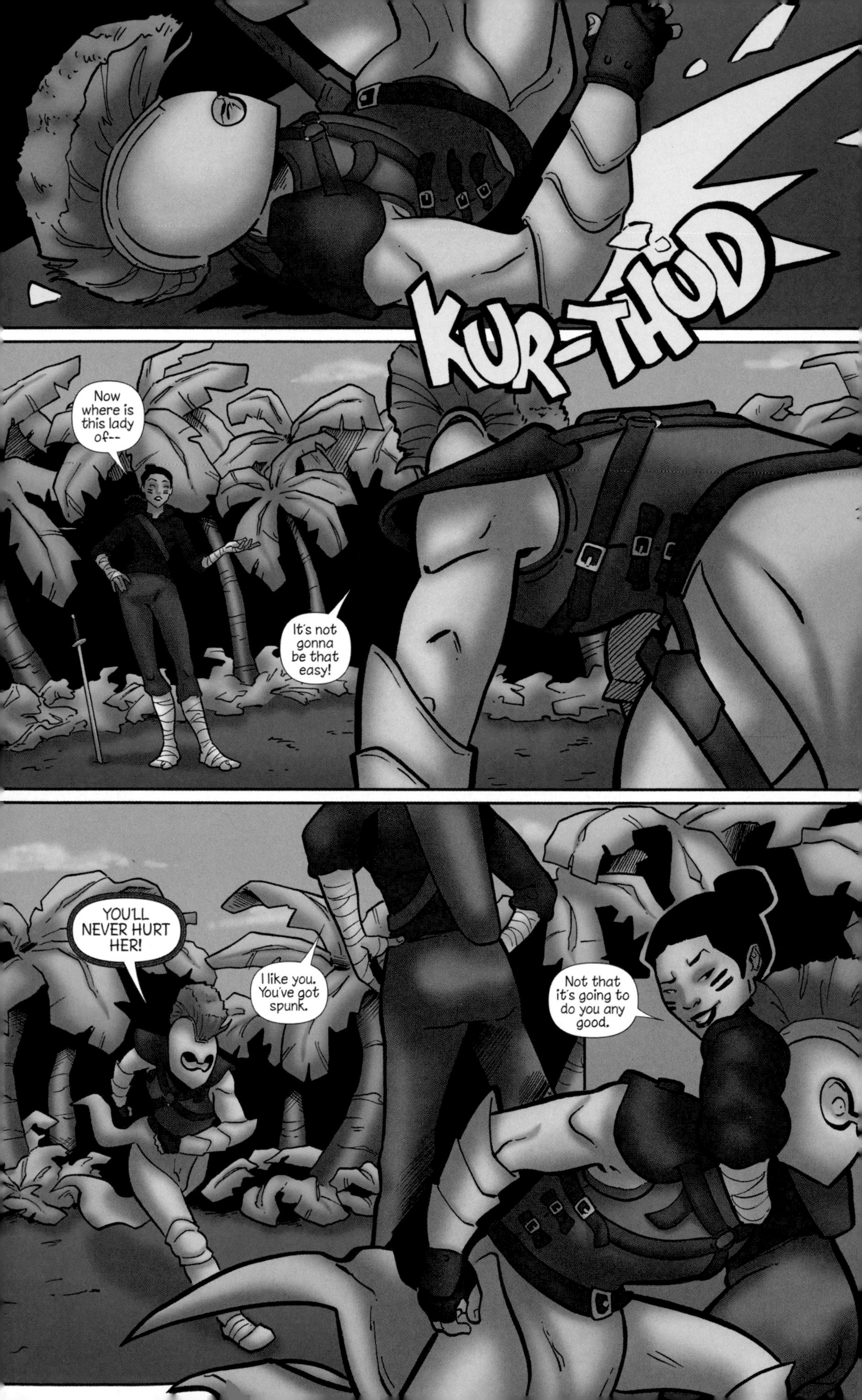
KUR-THUD
Now where is this lady of--
It's not gonna be that easy!
YOU'LL NEVER HURT HER!
I like you. You've got spunk.
Not that it's going to do you any good.

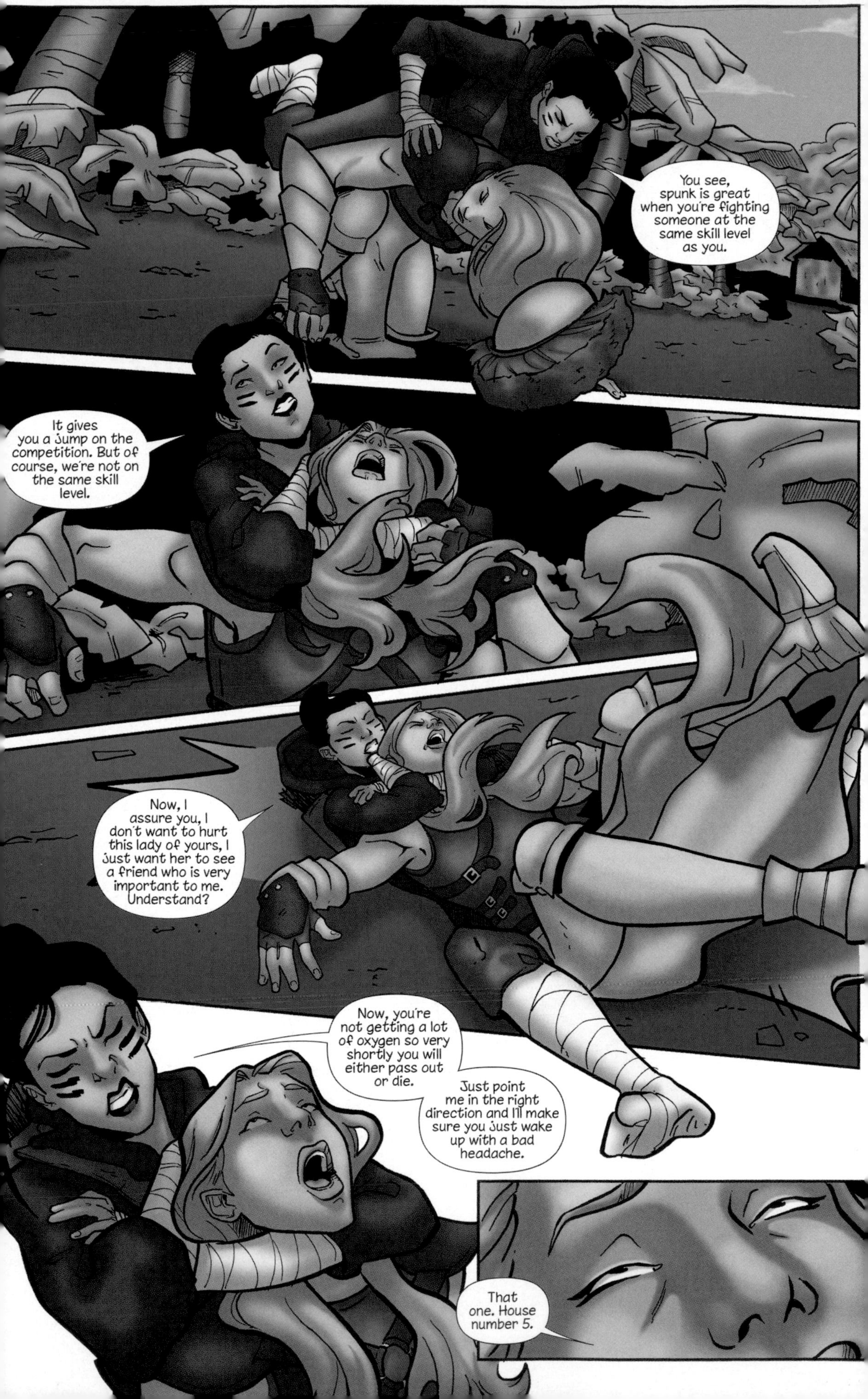
You see, spunk is great when you're fighting someone at the same skill level as you.
It gives you a jump on the competition. But of course, we're not on the same skill level.
Now, I assure you, I don't want to hurt this lady of yours, I just want her to see a friend who is very important to me. Understand?
Now, you're not getting a lot of oxygen so very shortly you will either pass out or die.
Just point me in the right direction and I'll make sure you just wake up with a bad headache.
That one. House number 5.

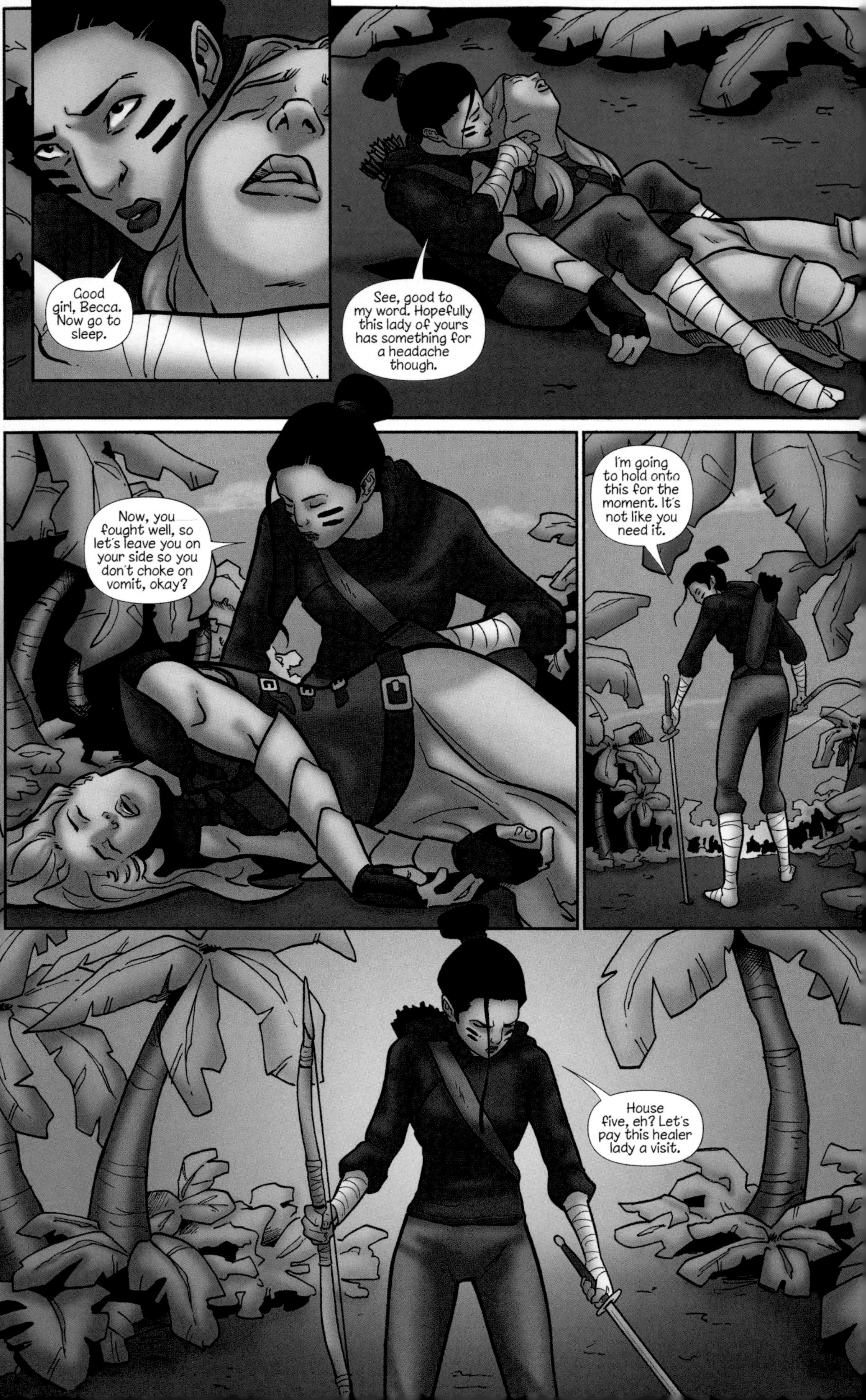
Good girl, Becca. Now go to sleep.
See, good to my word. Hopefully this lady of yours has something for a headache though.
Now, you fought well, so let's leave you on your side so you don't choke on vomit, okay?
I'm going to hold onto this for the moment. It's not like you need it.
House five, eh? Let's pay this healer lady a visit.

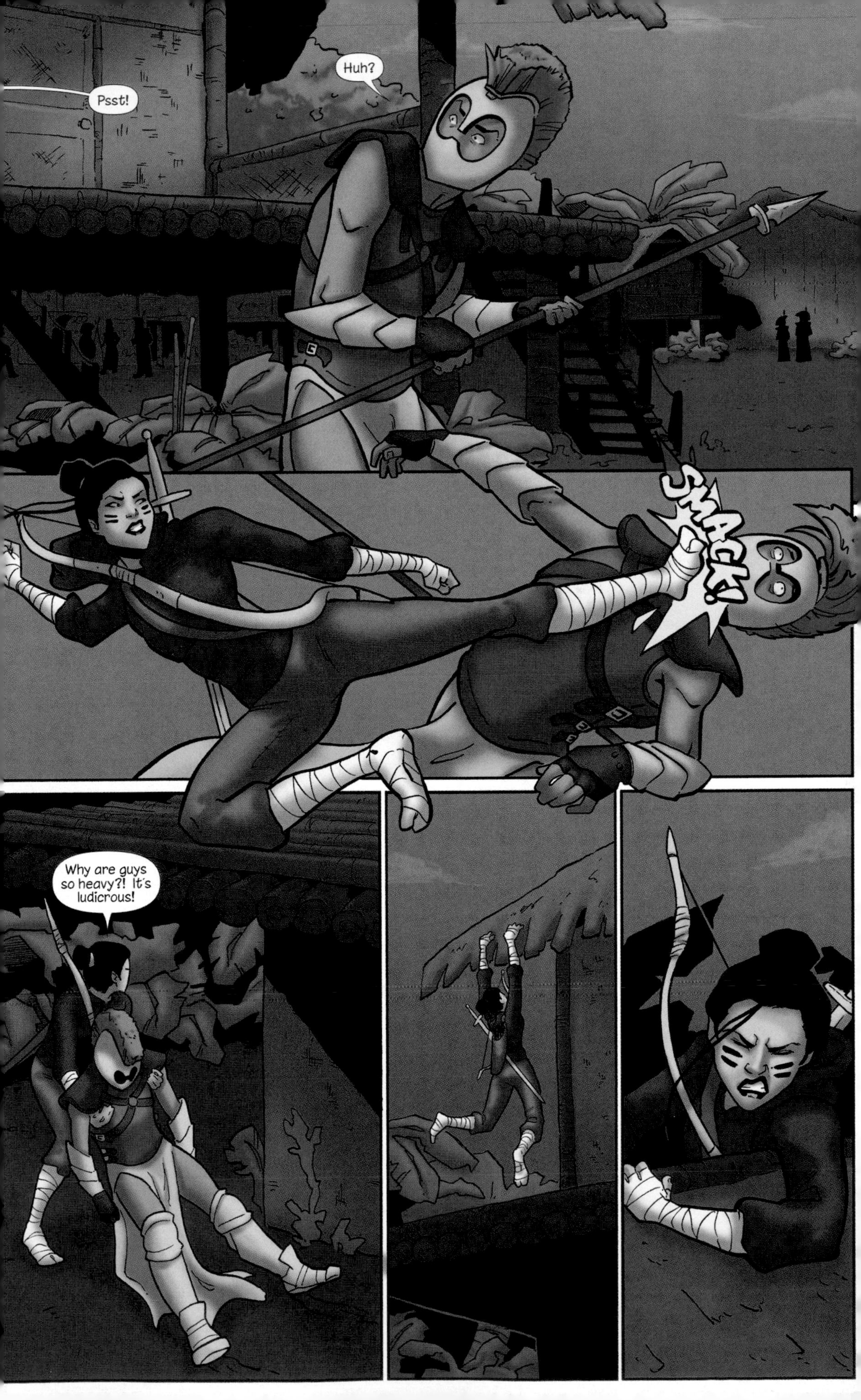
Psst!
Huh?
SMACK!
Why are guys so heavy?! It's ludicrous!

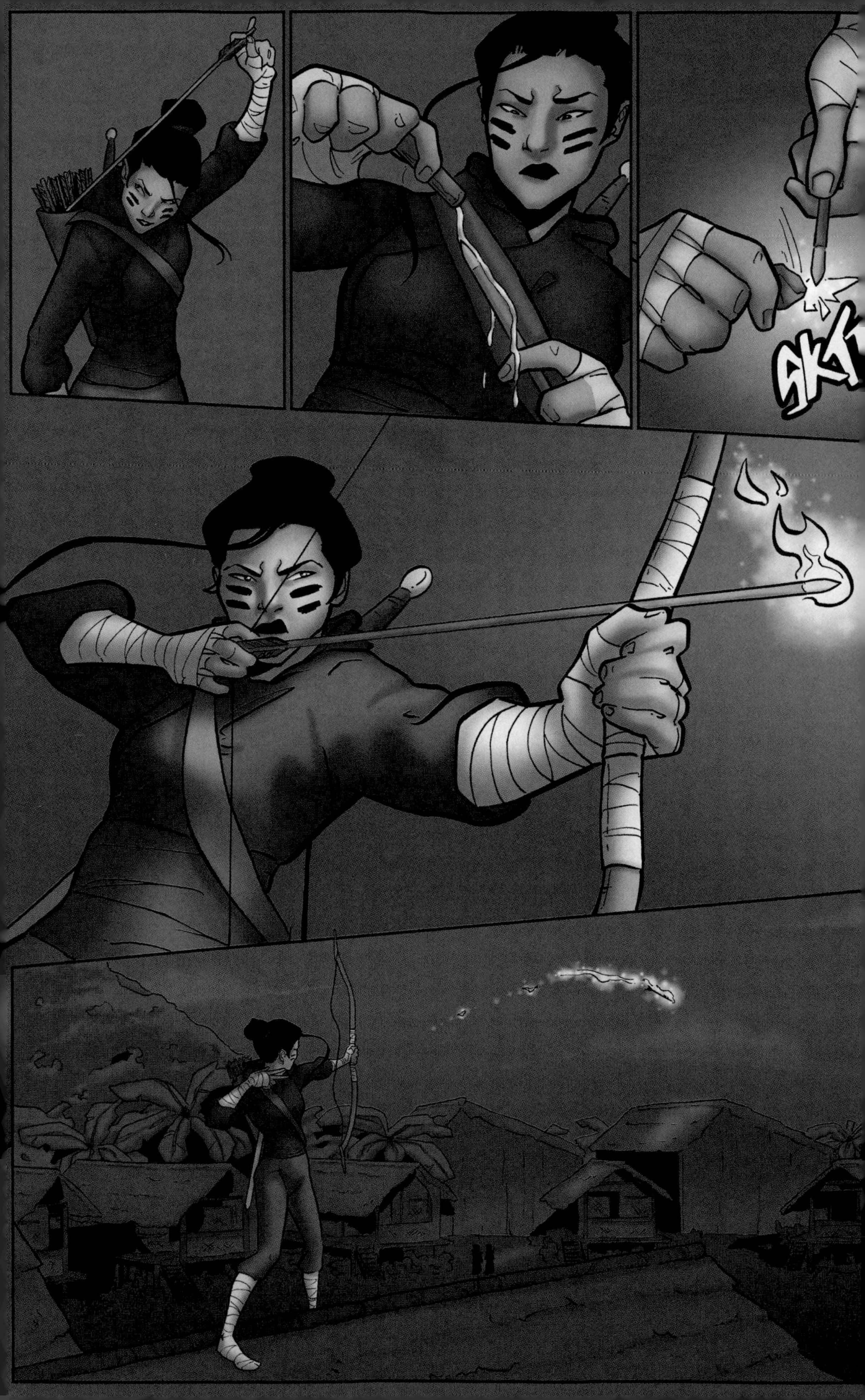
SKT

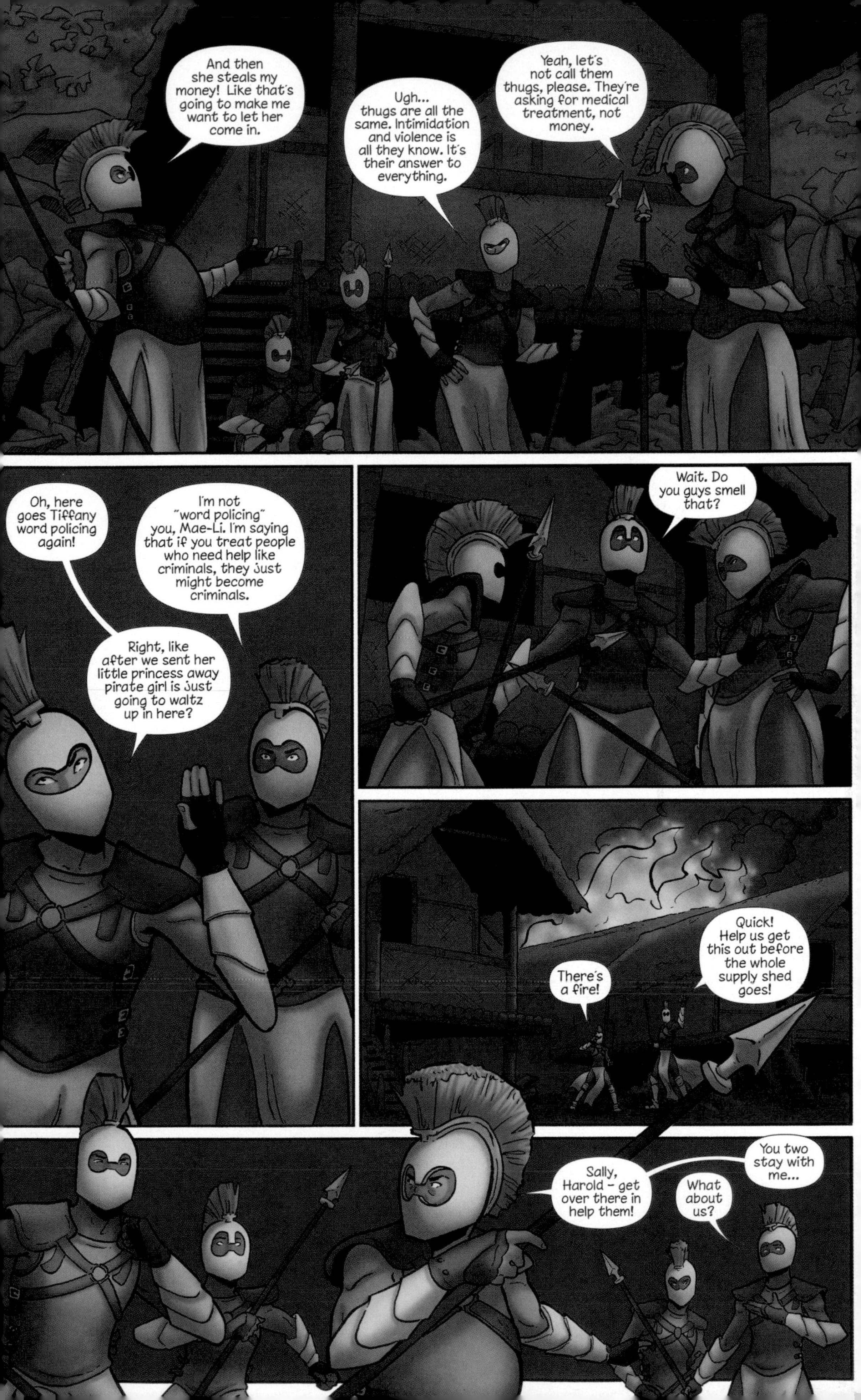
And then she steals my money! Like that's going to make me want to let her come in.
Ugh... thugs are all the same. Intimidation and violence is all they know. It's their answer to everything.
Yeah, let's not call them thugs, please. They're asking for medical treatment, not money.
Oh, here goes Tiffany word policing again!
I'm not "word policing" you, Mae-Li. I'm saying that if you treat people who need help like criminals, they just might become criminals.
Right, like after we sent her little princess away pirate girl is just going to waltz up in here?
Wait. Do you guys smell that?
There's a fire!
Quick! Help us get this out before the whole supply shed goes!
Sally, Harold – get over there in help them!
You two stay with me...
What about us?

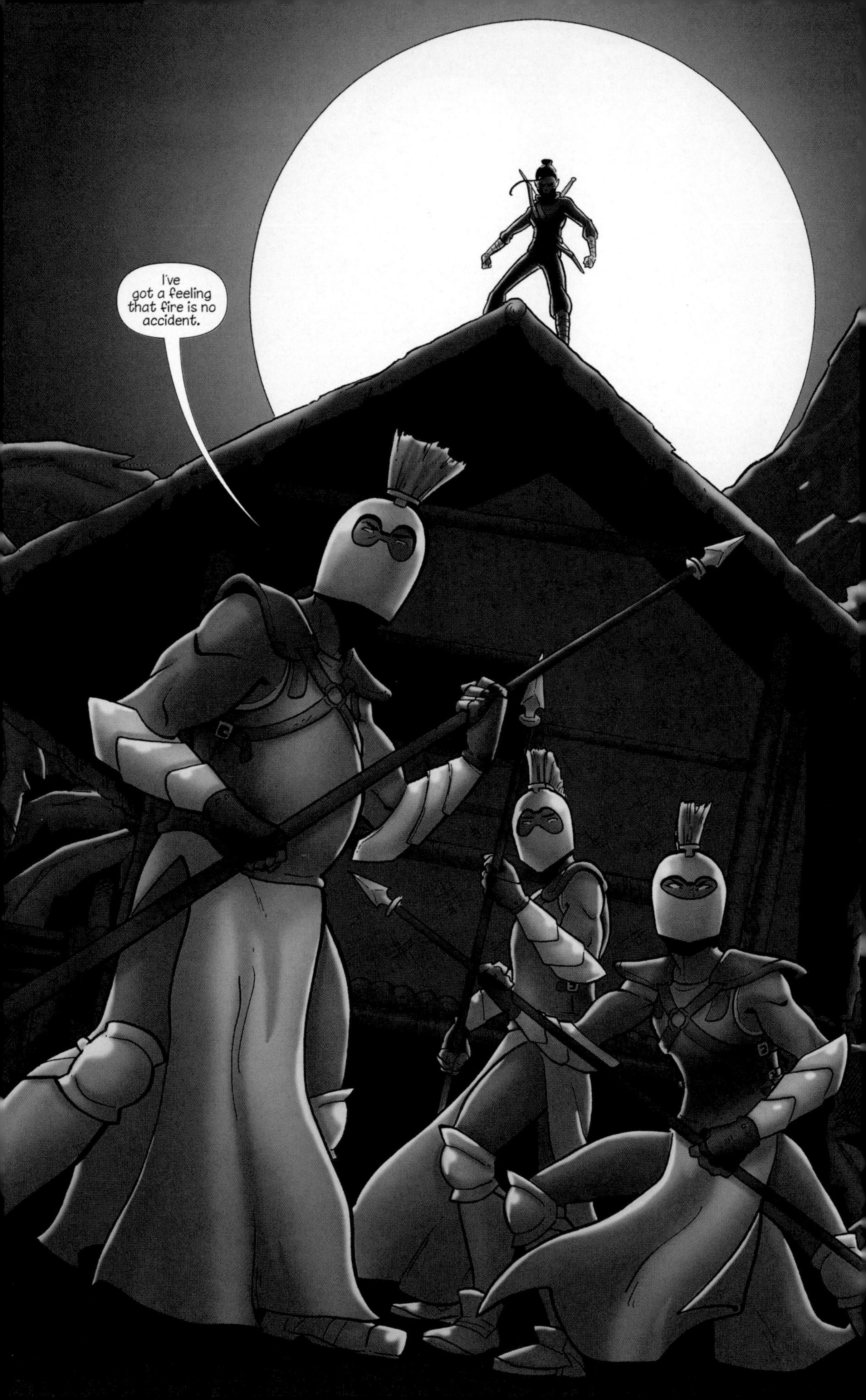
I've got a feeling that fire is no accident.

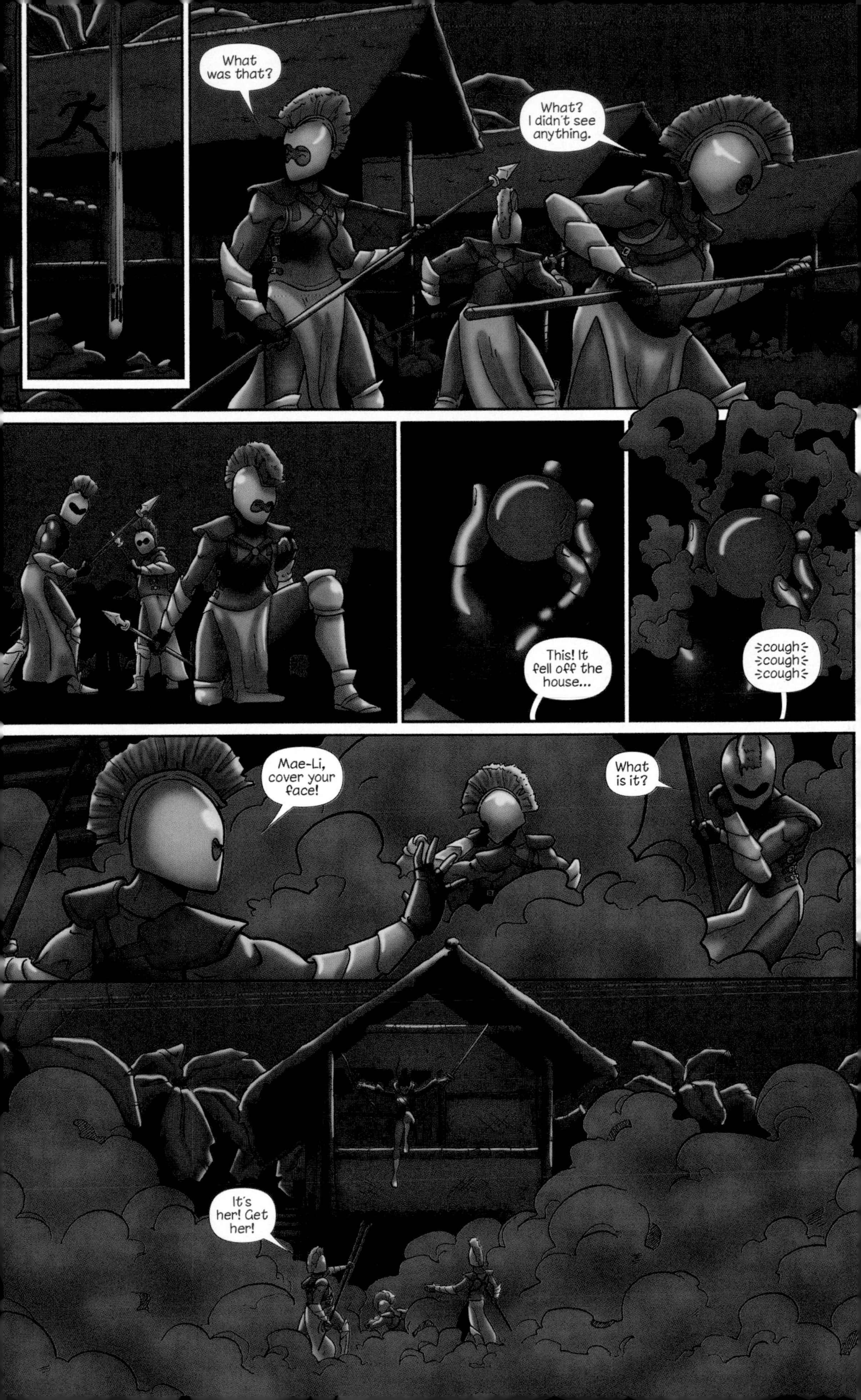
What was that?
What? I didn't see anything.
This! It fell off the house...
cough cough cough
Mae-Li, cover your face!
What is it?
It's her! Get her!

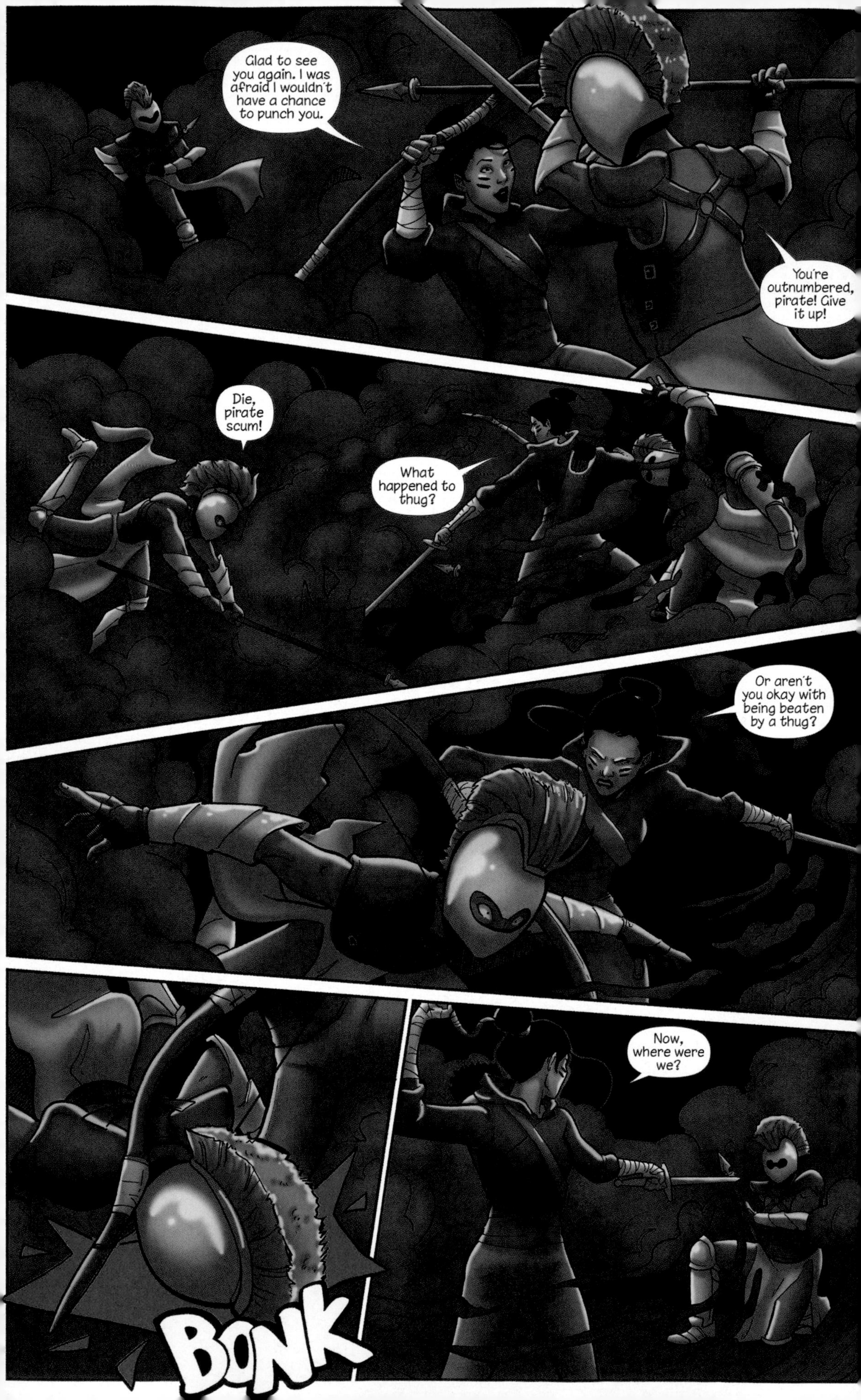
Glad to see you again. I was afraid I wouldn't have a chance to punch you.
You're outnumbered, pirate! Give it up!
Die, pirate scum!
What happened to thug?
Or aren't you okay with being beaten by a thug?
BONK
Now, where were we?

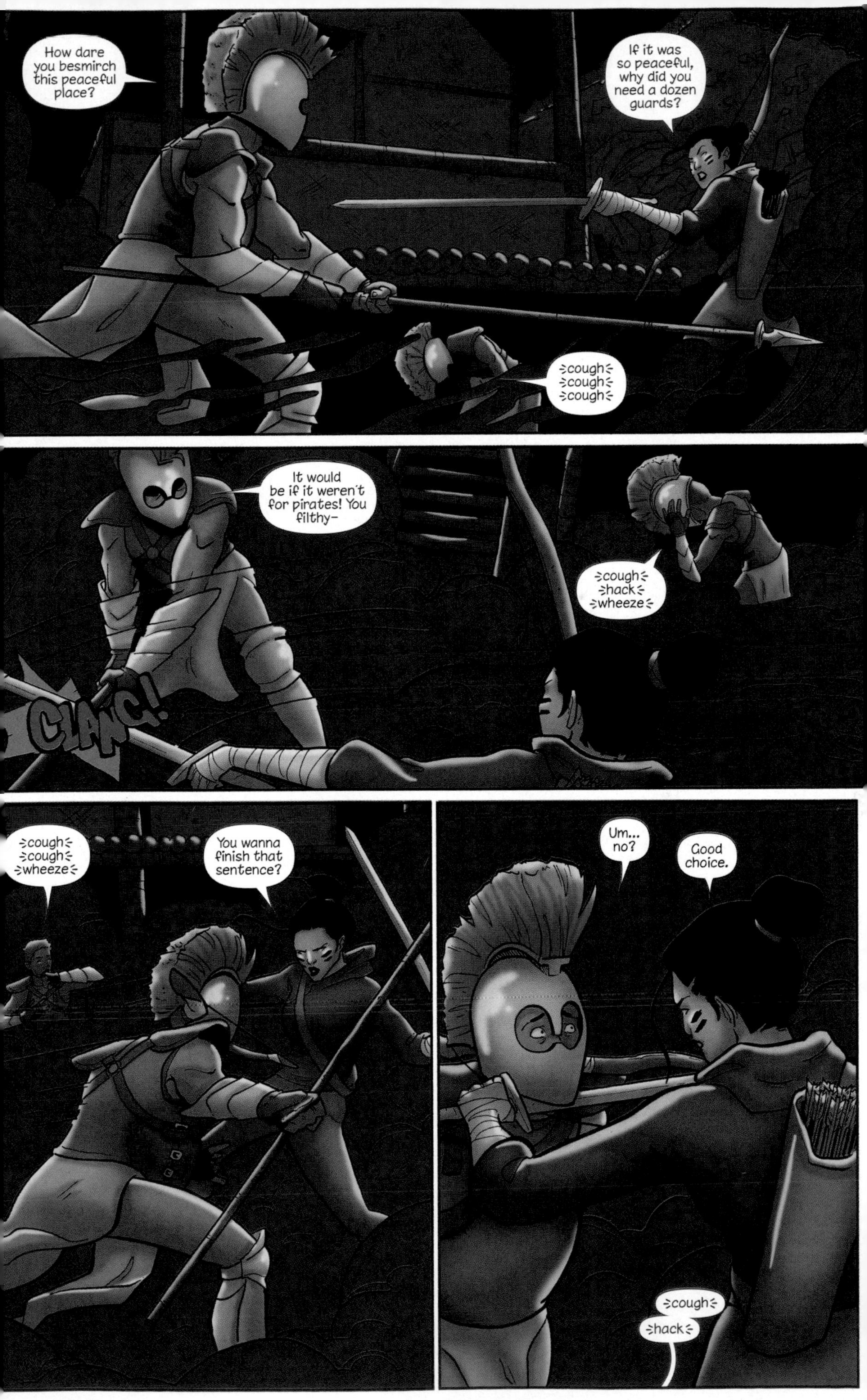
How dare you besmirch this peaceful place?
If it was so peaceful, why did you need a dozen guards?
cough cough cough
It would be if it weren't for pirates! You filthy–
cough hack wheeze
CLANG!
cough cough wheeze
You wanna finish that sentence?
Um... no?
Good choice.
cough
hack

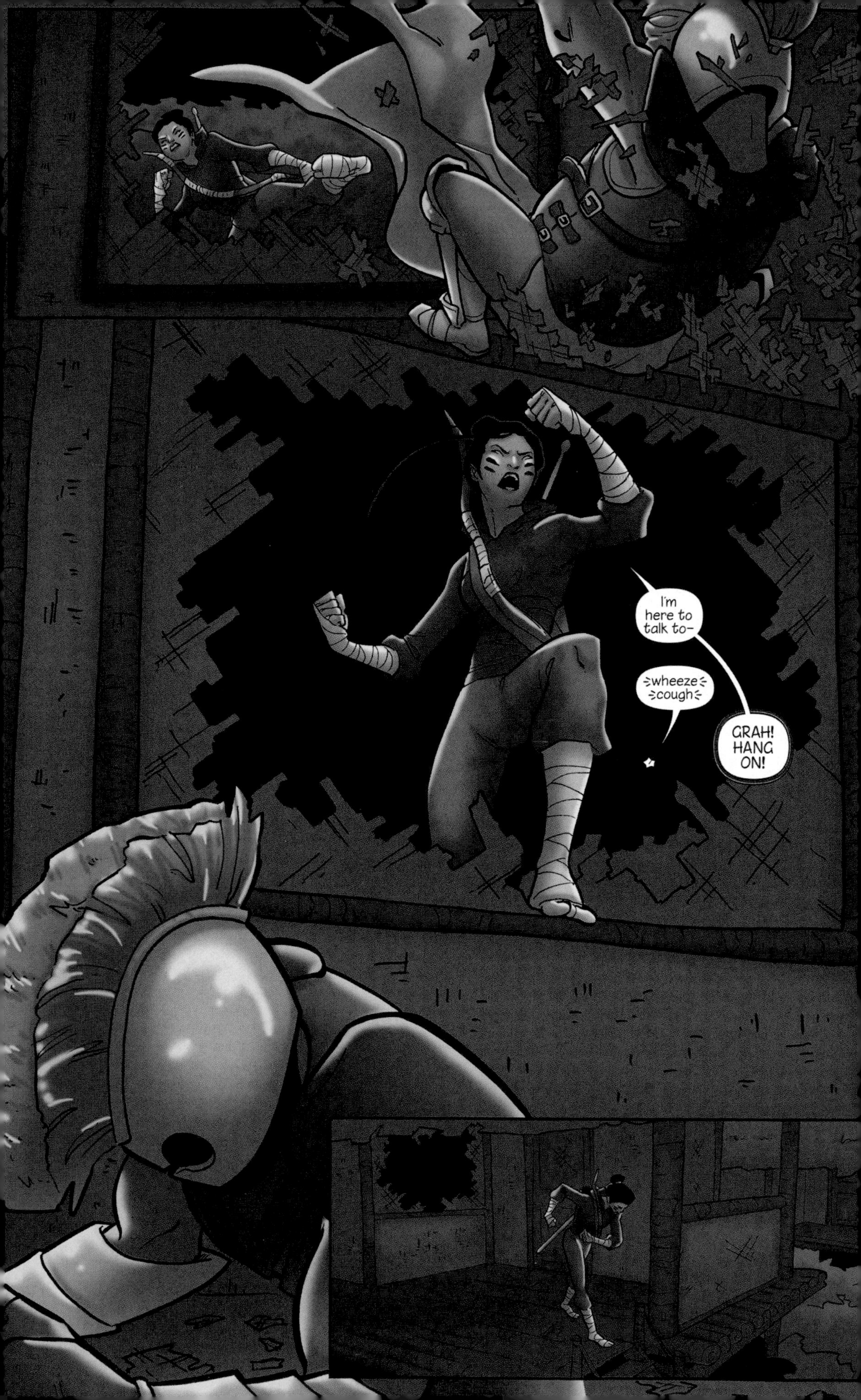
I'm here to talk to-
wheeze cough
GRAH! HANG ON!

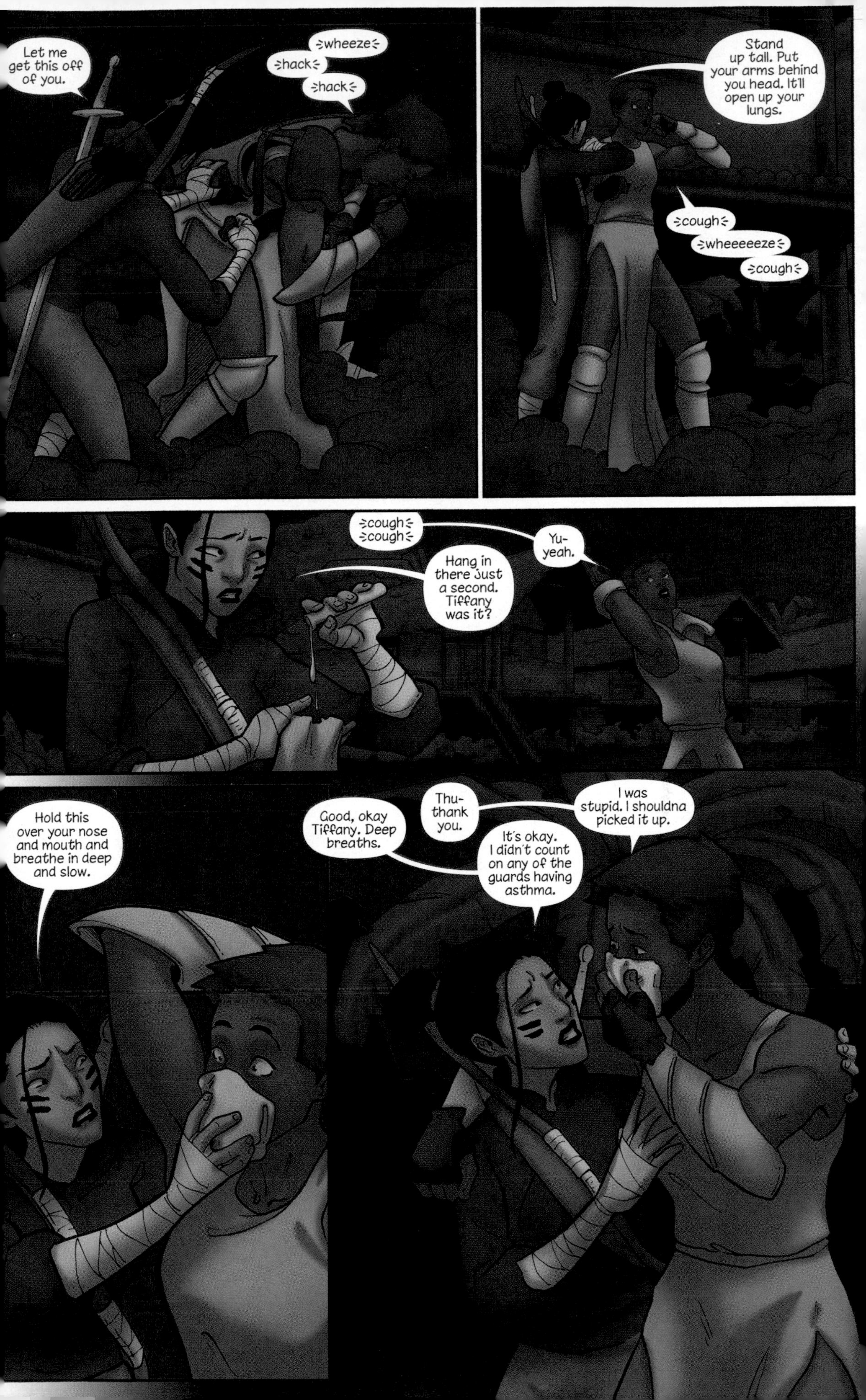
Let me get this off of you.
wheeze
hack
hack
Stand up tall. Put your arms behind you head. It'll open up your lungs.
cough
wheeeeeze
cough
cough
cough
Yu-yeah.
Hang in there just a second. Tiffany was it?
Hold this over your nose and mouth and breathe in deep and slow.
Good, okay Tiffany. Deep breaths.
Thu-thank you.
It's okay. I didn't count on any of the guards having asthma.
I was stupid. I shouldna picked it up.

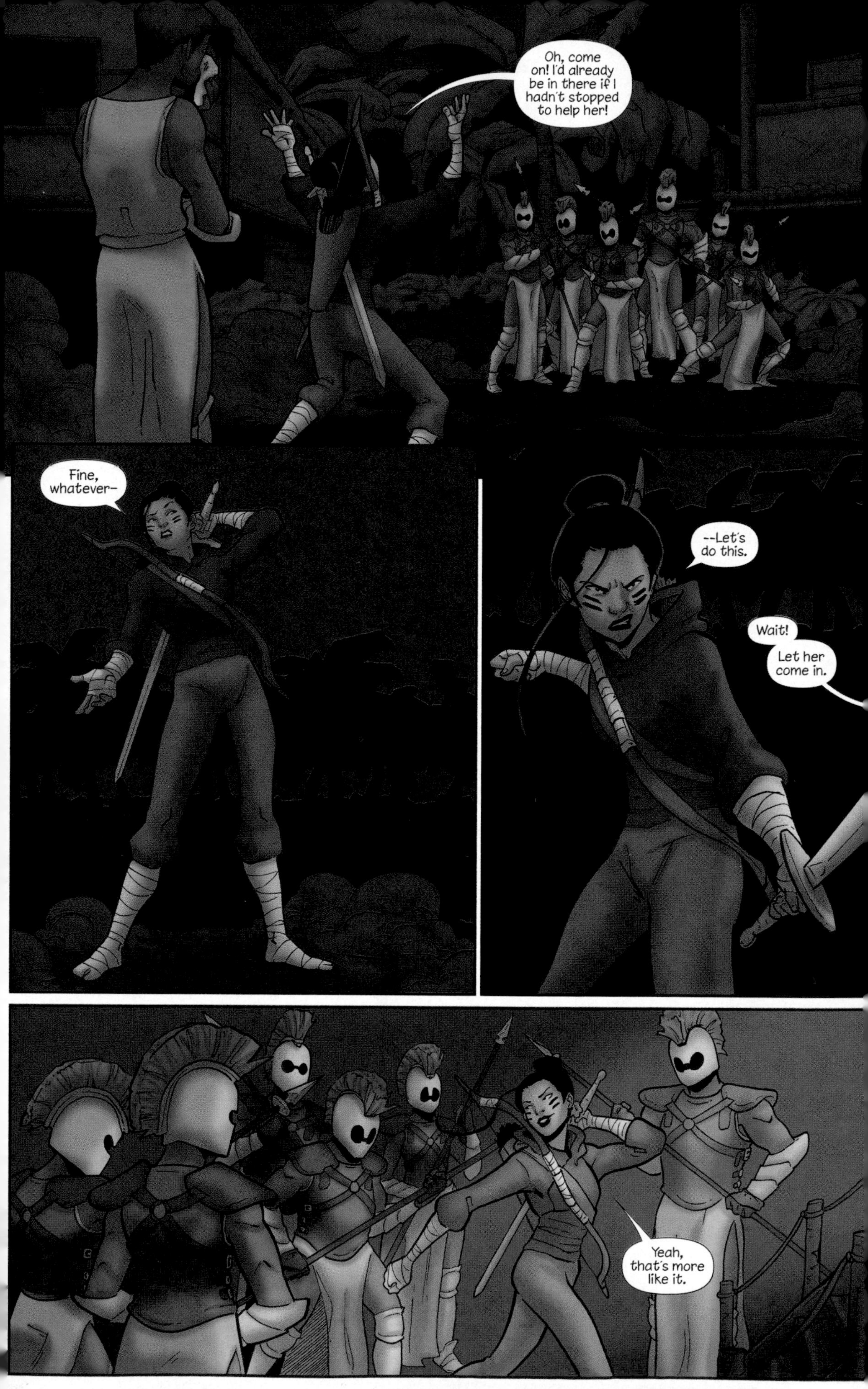
Oh, come on! I'd already be in there if I hadn't stopped to help her!
Fine, whatever-
--Let's do this.
Wait!
Let her come in.
Yeah, that's more like it.

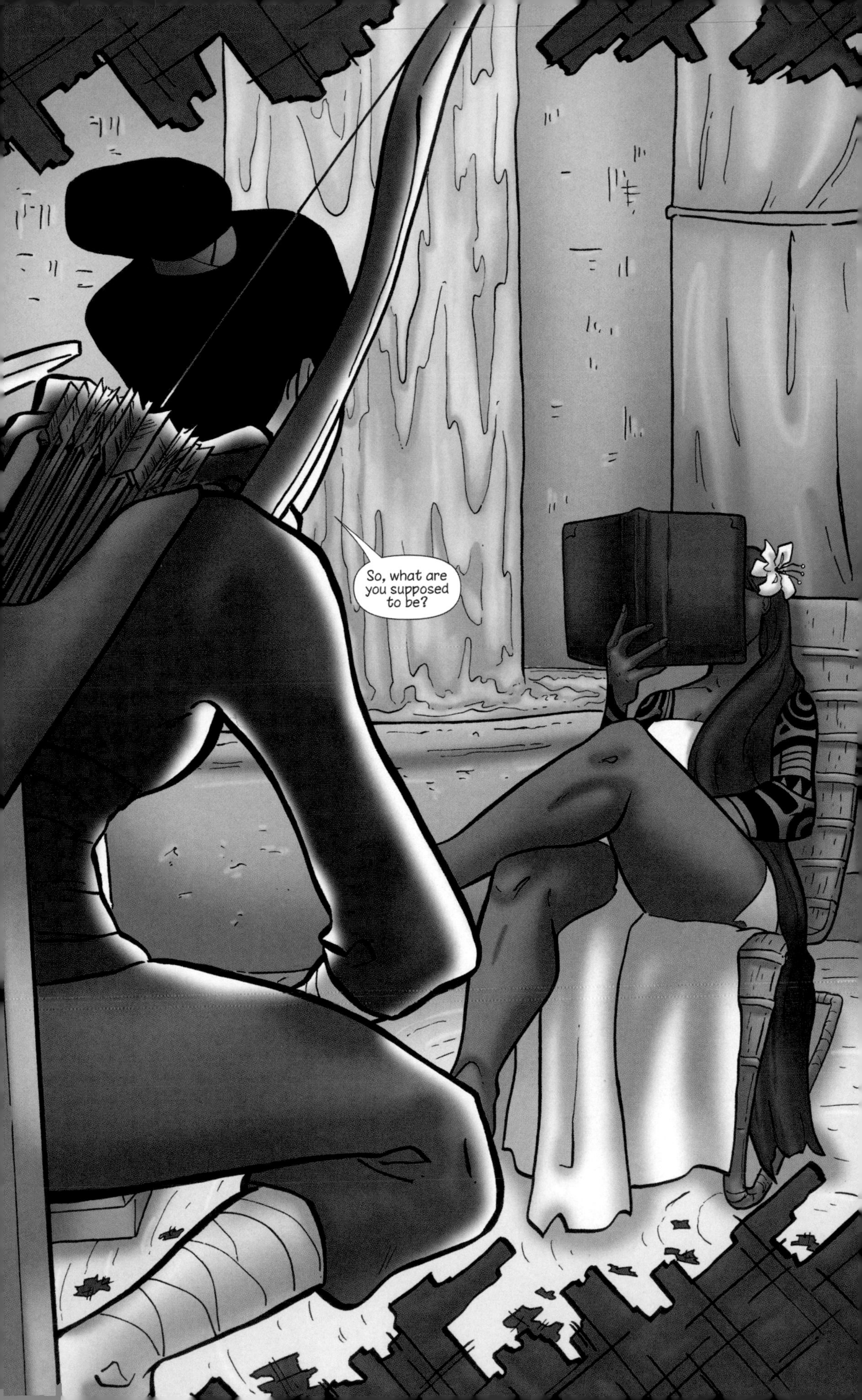
So, what are you supposed to be?

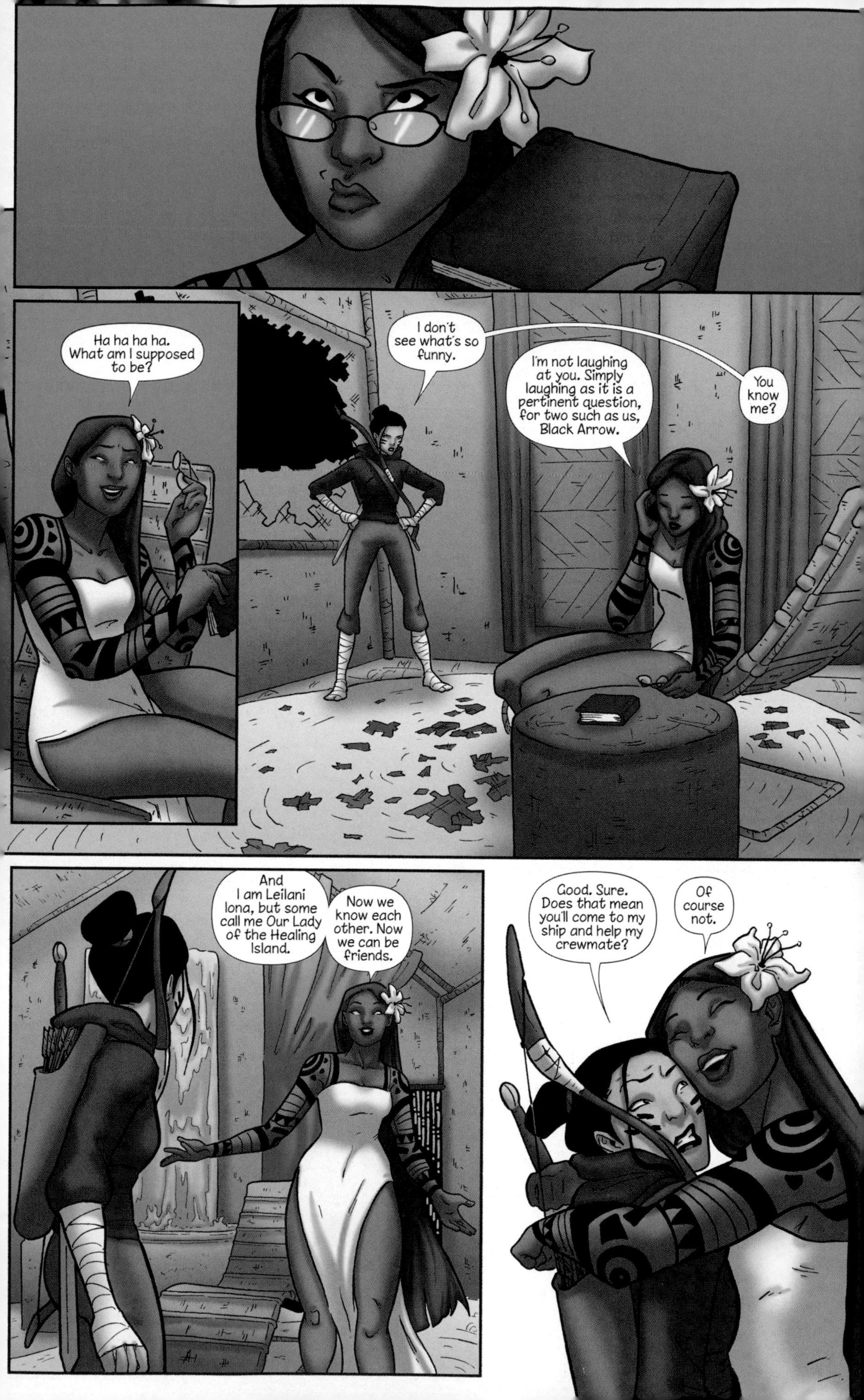
Ha ha ha ha. What am I supposed to be?
I don't see what's so funny.
I'm not laughing at you. Simply laughing as it is a pertinent question, for two such as us, Black Arrow.
You know me?
And I am Leilani Iona, but some call me Our Lady of the Healing Island.
Now we know each other. Now we can be friends.
Good. Sure. Does that mean you'll come to my ship and help my crewmate?
Of course not.

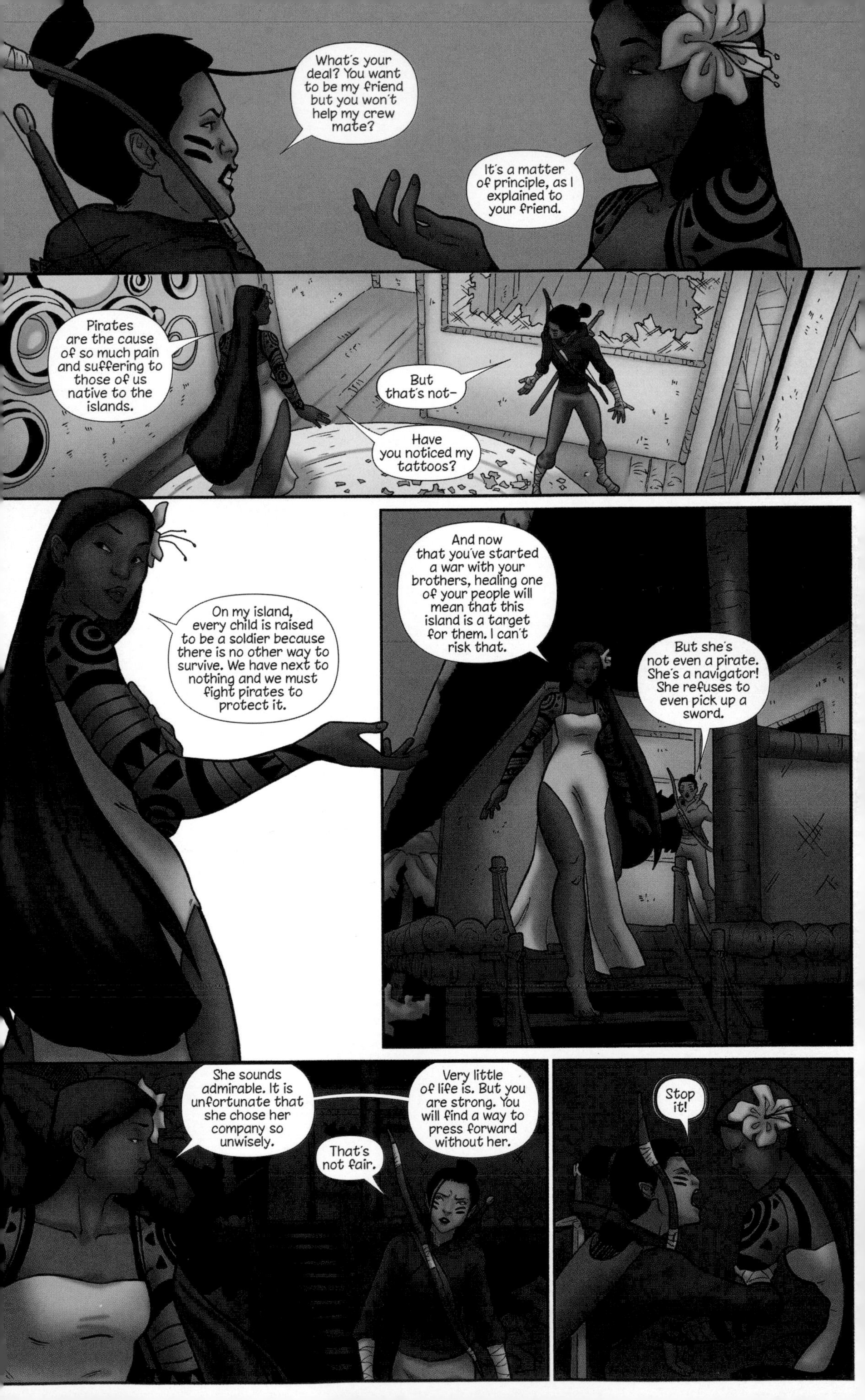
What's your deal? You want to be my friend but you won't help my crew mate?
It's a matter of principle, as I explained to your friend.
Pirates are the cause of so much pain and suffering to those of us native to the islands.
But that's not-
Have you noticed my tattoos?
On my island, every child is raised to be a soldier because there is no other way to survive. We have next to nothing and we must fight pirates to protect it.
And now that you've started a war with your brothers, healing one of your people will mean that this island is a target for them. I can't risk that.
But she's not even a pirate. She's a navigator! She refuses to even pick up a sword.
She sounds admirable. It is unfortunate that she chose her company so unwisely.
Very little of life is. But you are strong. You will find a way to press forward without her.
That's not fair.
Stop it!

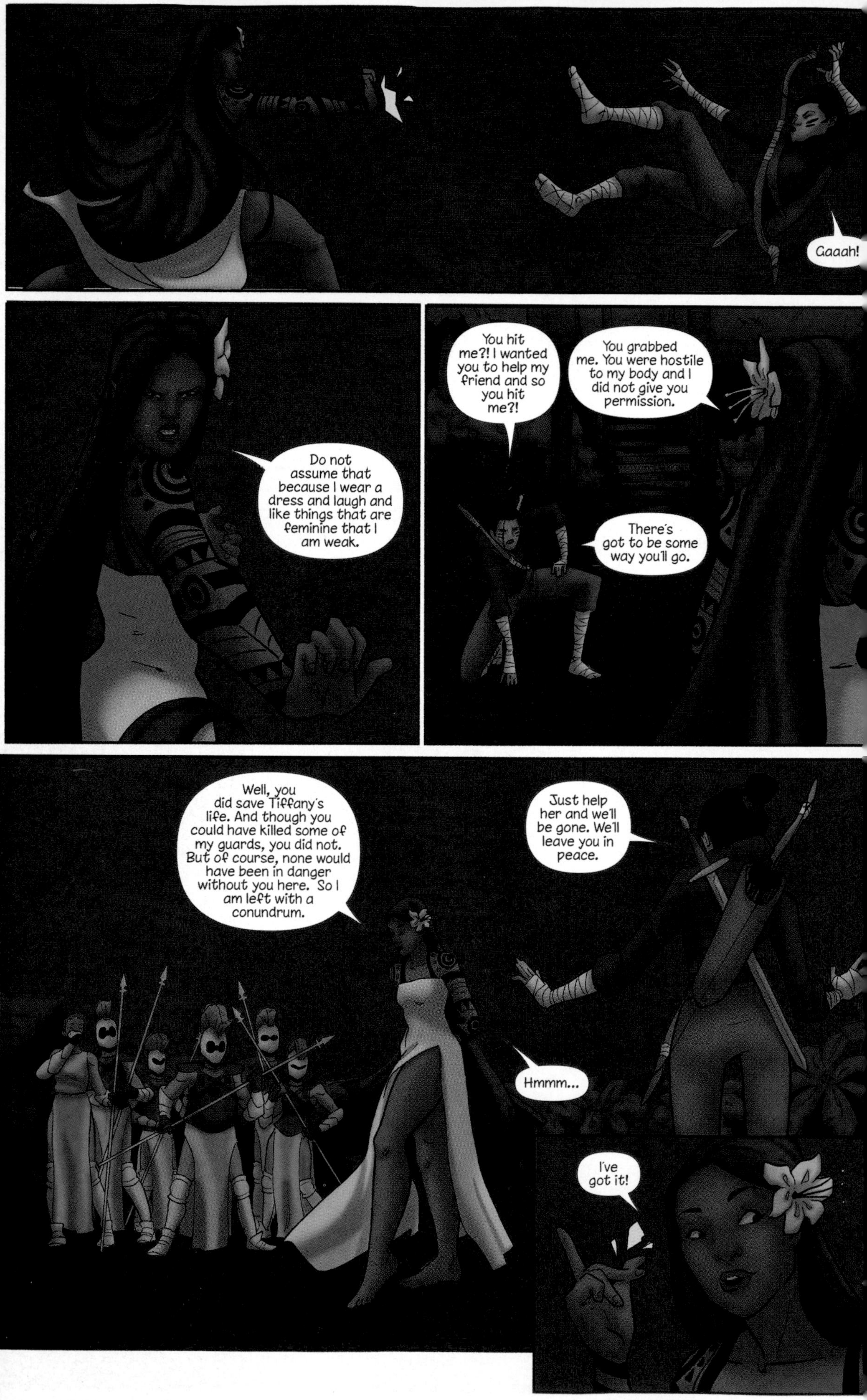
Gaaah!
Do not assume that because I wear a dress and laugh and like things that are feminine that I am weak.
You hit me?! I wanted you to help my friend and so you hit me?!
You grabbed me. You were hostile to my body and I did not give you permission.
There's got to be some way you'll go.
Well, you did save Tiffany's life. And though you could have killed some of my guards, you did not. But of course, none would have been in danger without you here. So I am left with a conundrum.
Just help her and we'll be gone. We'll leave you in peace.
Hmmm...
I've got it!

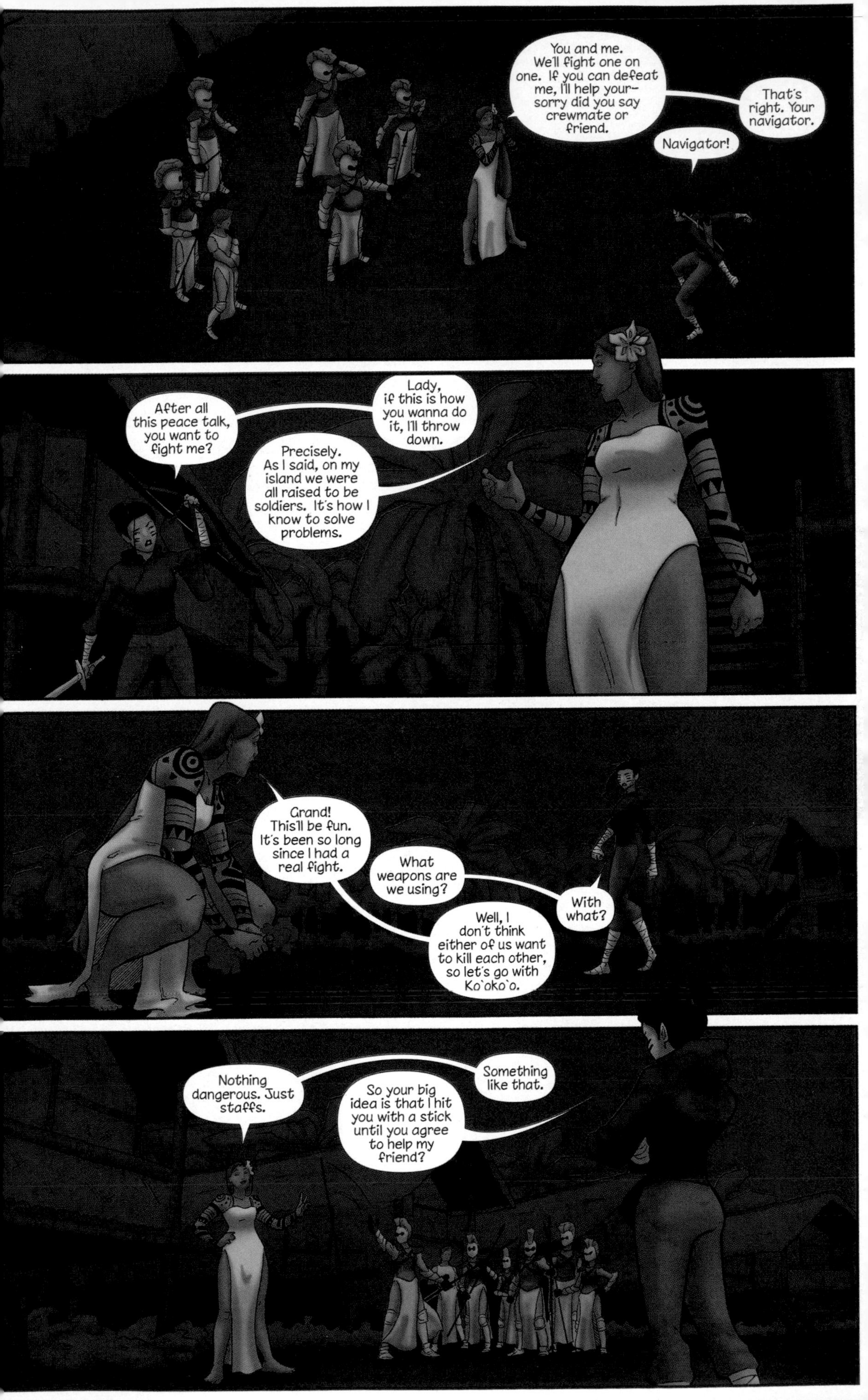
You and me. We'll fight one on one. If you can defeat me, I'll help your- sorry did you say crewmate or friend.
Navigator!
That's right. Your navigator.
After all this peace talk, you want to fight me?
Lady, if this is how you wanna do it, I'll throw down.
Precisely. As I said, on my island we were all raised to be soldiers. It's how I know to solve problems.
Grand! This'll be fun. It's been so long since I had a real fight.
With what?
What weapons are we using?
Well, I don't think either of us want to kill each other, so let's go with Ko`oko`o.
Nothing dangerous. Just staffs.
So your big idea is that I hit you with a stick until you agree to help my friend?
Something like that.

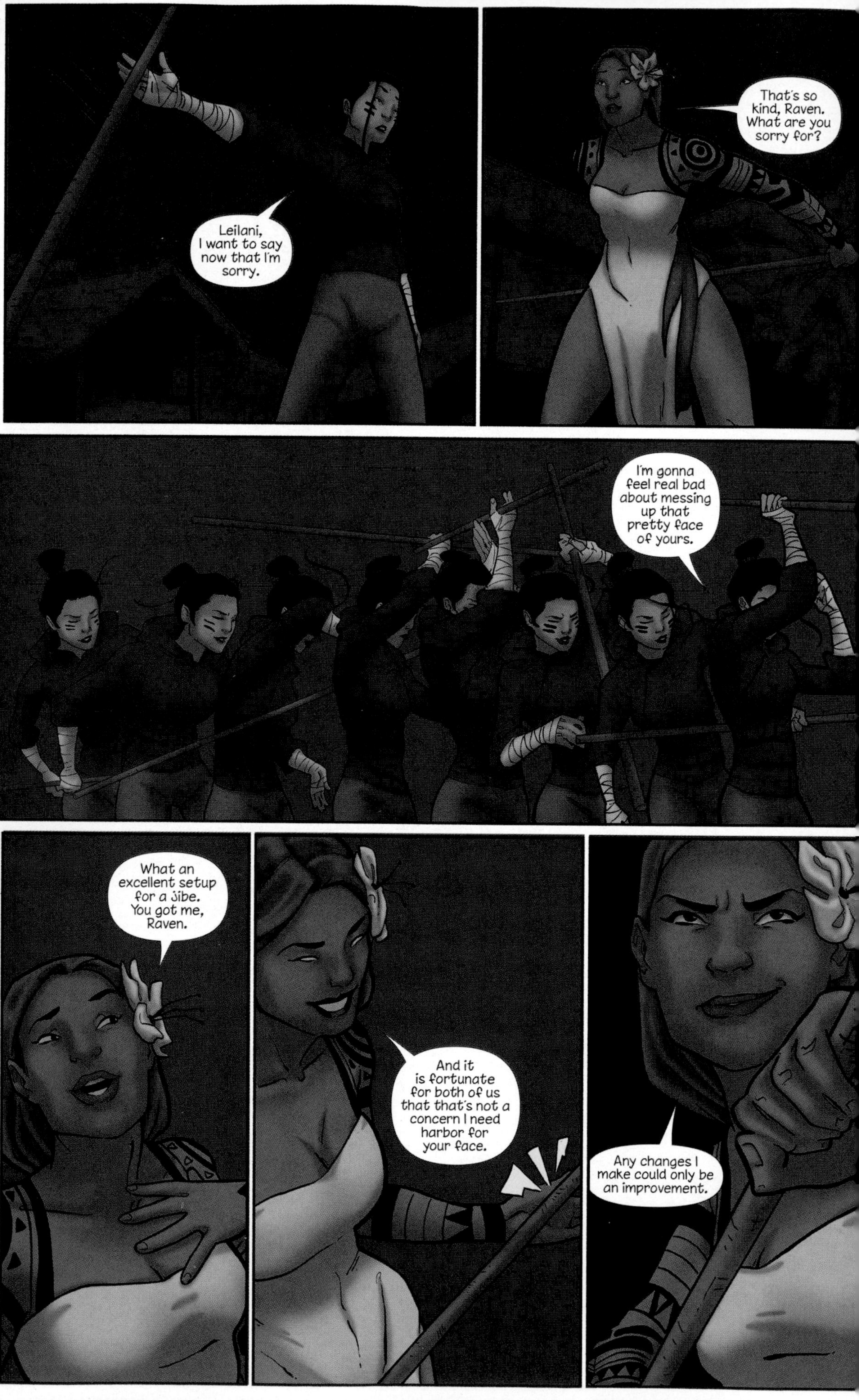
Leilani, I want to say now that I'm sorry.
That's so kind, Raven. What are you sorry for?
I'm gonna feel real bad about messing up that pretty face of yours.
What an excellent setup for a jibe. You got me, Raven.
And it is fortunate for both of us that that's not a concern I need harbor for your face.
Any changes I make could only be an improvement.

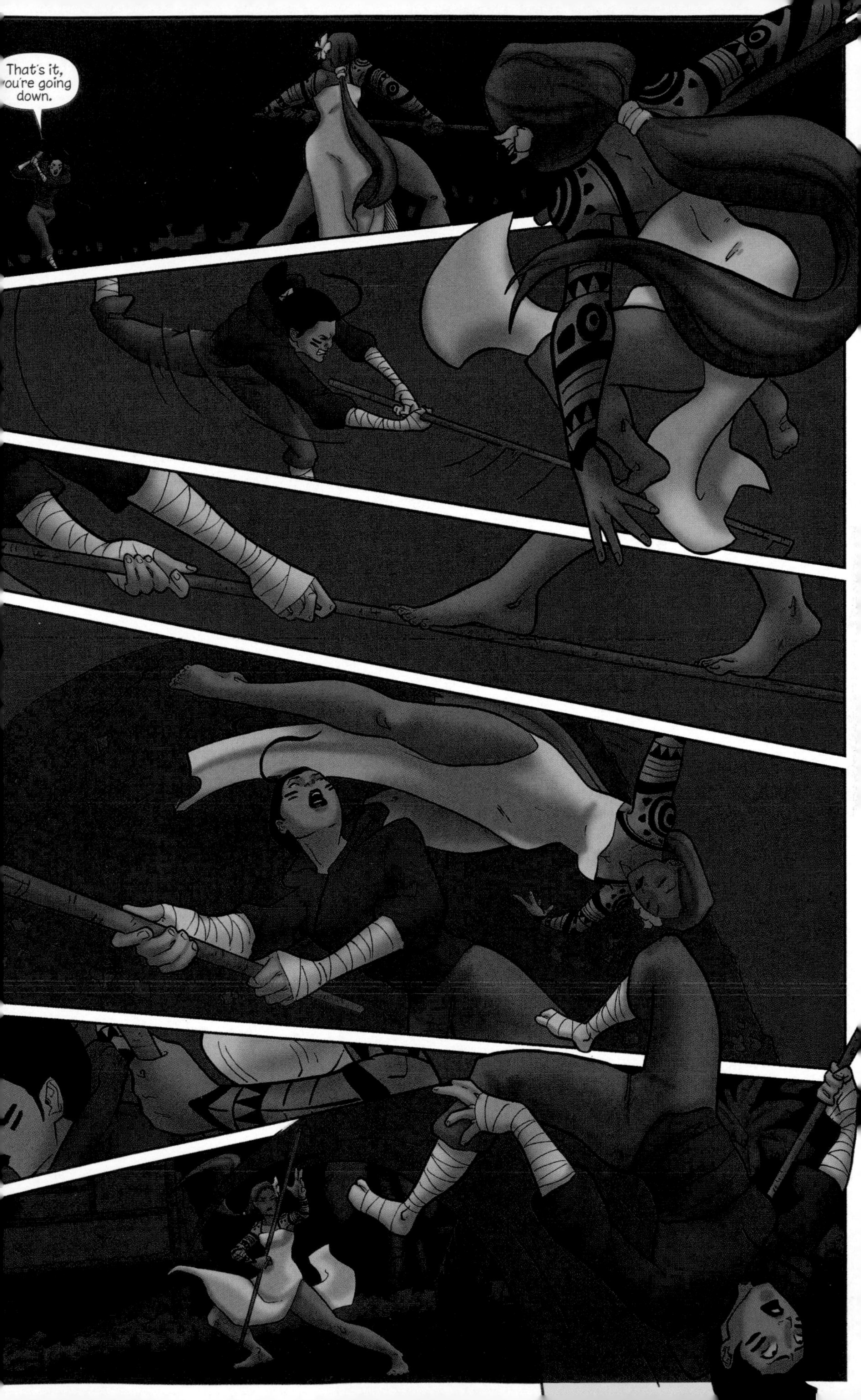
That's it, ou're going down.

ISSUE ELEVEN

WORDS: Jeremy Whitley
PENCILS: Rosy Higgins
INKS: Ted Brandt
COLORS: Ty Johnson
LETTERS: Justin Birch
EDITED BY: Alicia Whitley

You first.

Bryan Seaton: Publisher • Dave Dwonch: President • Shawn Gabborin: Editor In Chief • Jason Martin: Publisher-Danger Zone • Jamal Igle: Vice-President of Market
Jim Dietz: Social Media Director • Nicole DAndria: Editor • Chad Cicconi: Still Waiting For His Princess

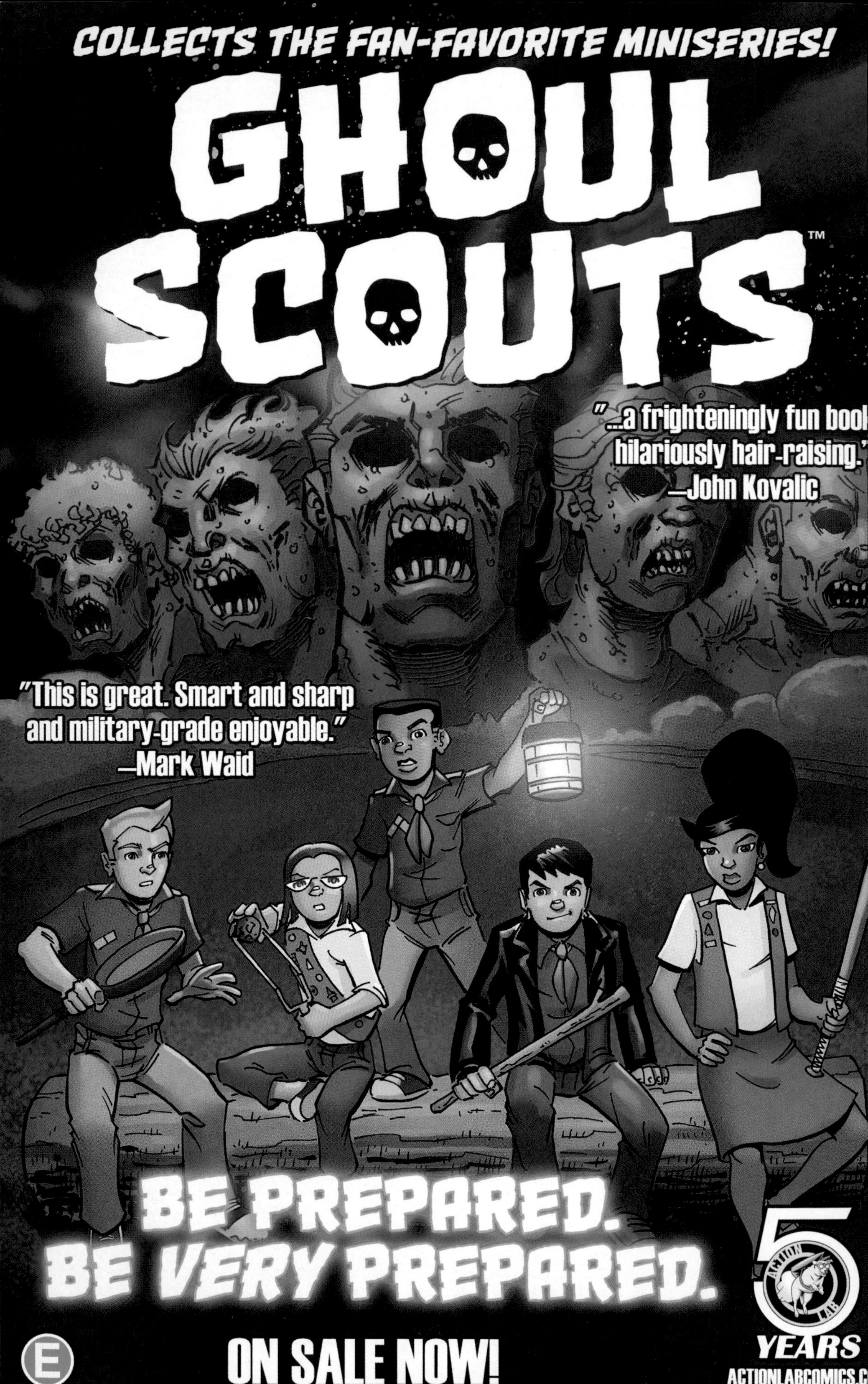

COLLECTS THE FAN-FAVORITE MINISERIES!
GHOUL SCOUTS™
"...a frighteningly fun book
hilariously hair-raising."
—John Kovalic
"This is great. Smart and sharp
and military-grade enjoyable."
—Mark Waid
BE PREPARED.
BE VERY PREPARED.
5 YEARS
E
ON SALE NOW!

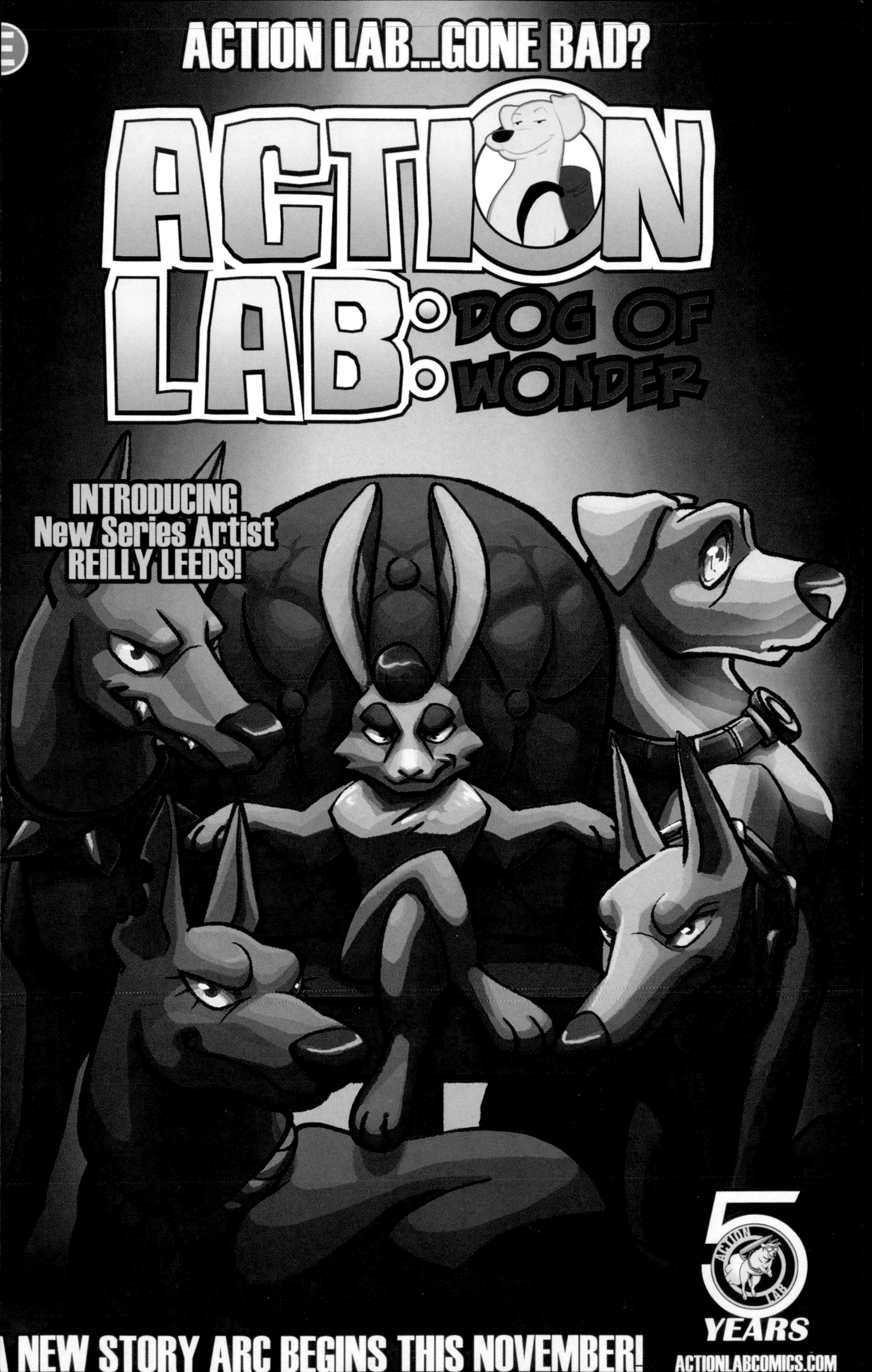
ACTION LAB...GONE BAD?
ACTION LAB: DOG OF WONDER
INTRODUCING
New Series Artist
REILLY LEEDS!
5 YEARS
A NEW STORY ARC BEGINS THIS NOVEMBER!
ACTIONLABCOMICS.COM

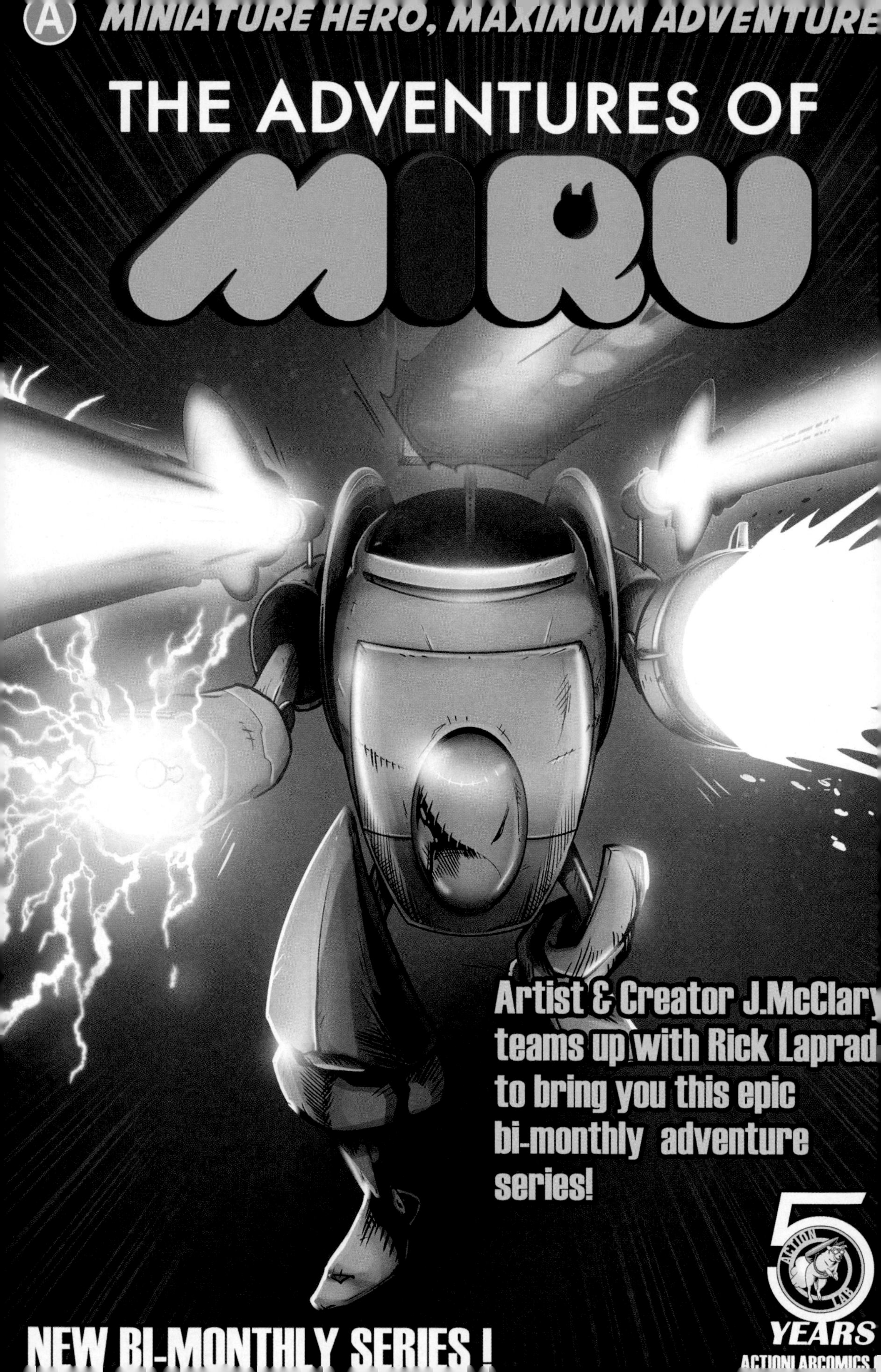
MINIATURE HERO, MAXIMUM ADVENTURE
THE ADVENTURES OF
MIRU
Artist & Creator J.McClary teams up with Rick Laprad to bring you this epic bi-monthly adventure series!
5 YEARS
NEW BI-MONTHLY SERIES !

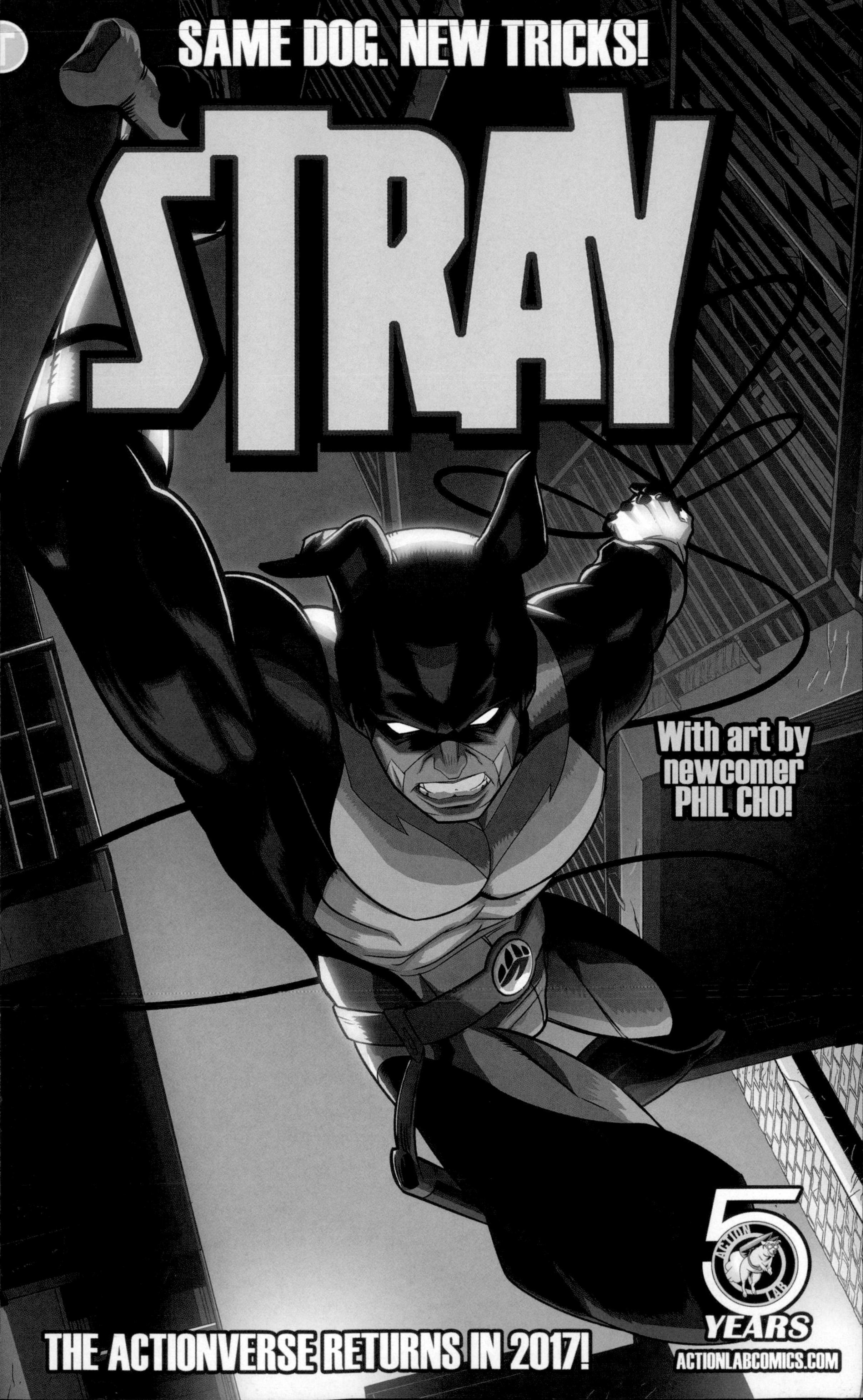

SAME DOG. NEW TRICKS!
STRAY
With art by newcomer PHIL CHO!
5 YEARS
ACTION LAB
THE ACTIONVERSE RETURNS IN 2017!
ACTIONLABCOMICS.COM

READ MORE NOW

ACTIONLABCOMICS.COM

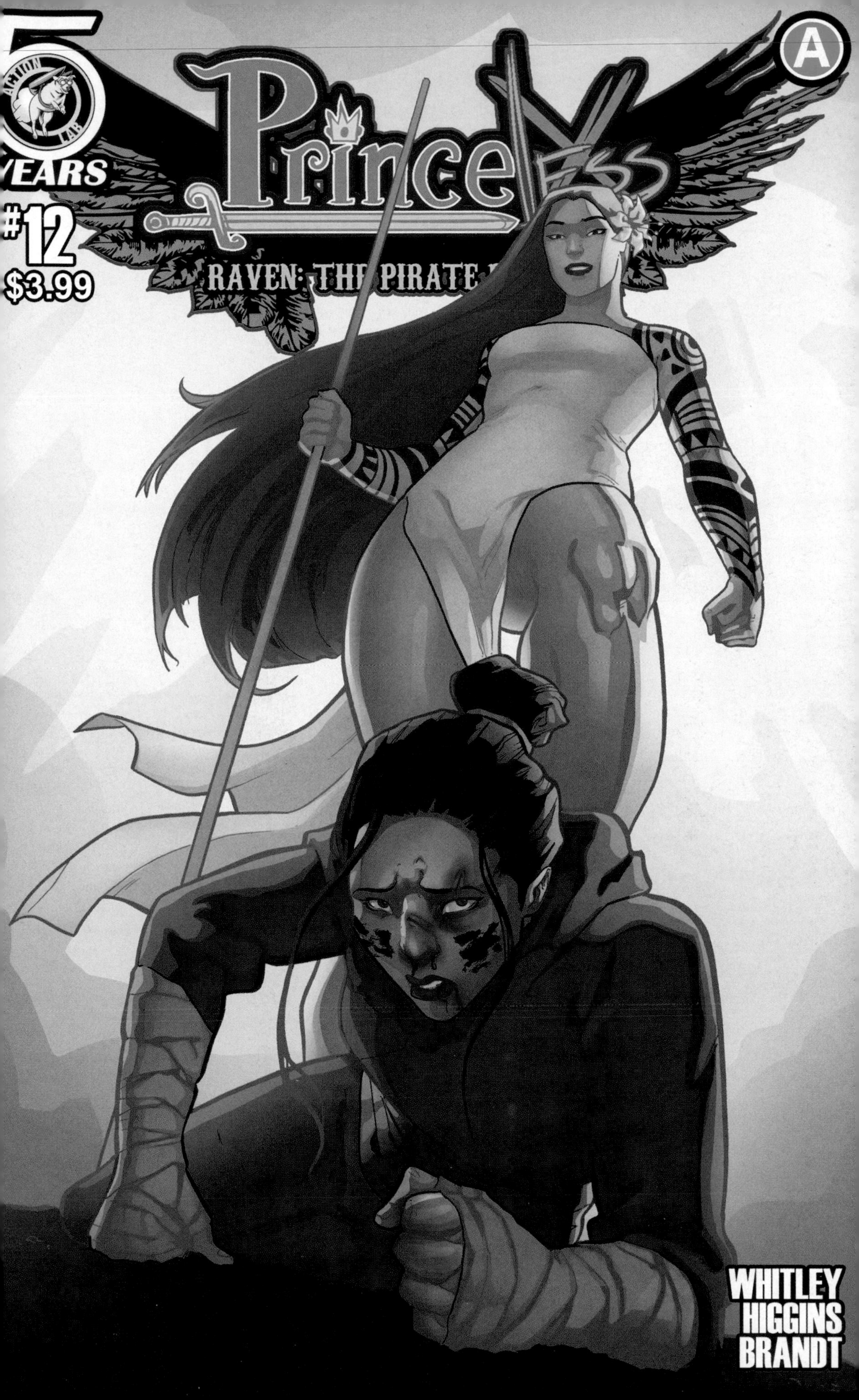
5 YEARS
#12
$3.99
Princeless
RAVEN: THE PIRATE
WHITLEY
HIGGINS
BRANDT

FROM ALL-AGES TO MATURE READERS ACTION LAB HAS YOU COVERED.

 **Appropriate for everyone.**

 **Appropriate for age 9 and up. Absent of profanity or adult content.**

 **Suggested for 12 and Up. Comics with this rating are comparable to a PG-13 movie rating. Recommended for our teen and young adult readers.**

 **Appropriate for older teens. Similar to Teen, but featuring more mature themes and/or more graphic imagery.**

 **Contains extreme violence and some nudity. Basically the Rated-R of comics.**

SSUE TWELVE

OS: Jeremy Whitley
ILS: Rosy Higgins
: Ted Brandt
RS: Ty Johnsen
ERS: Justin Birch
ED BY: Nicole D'Andria

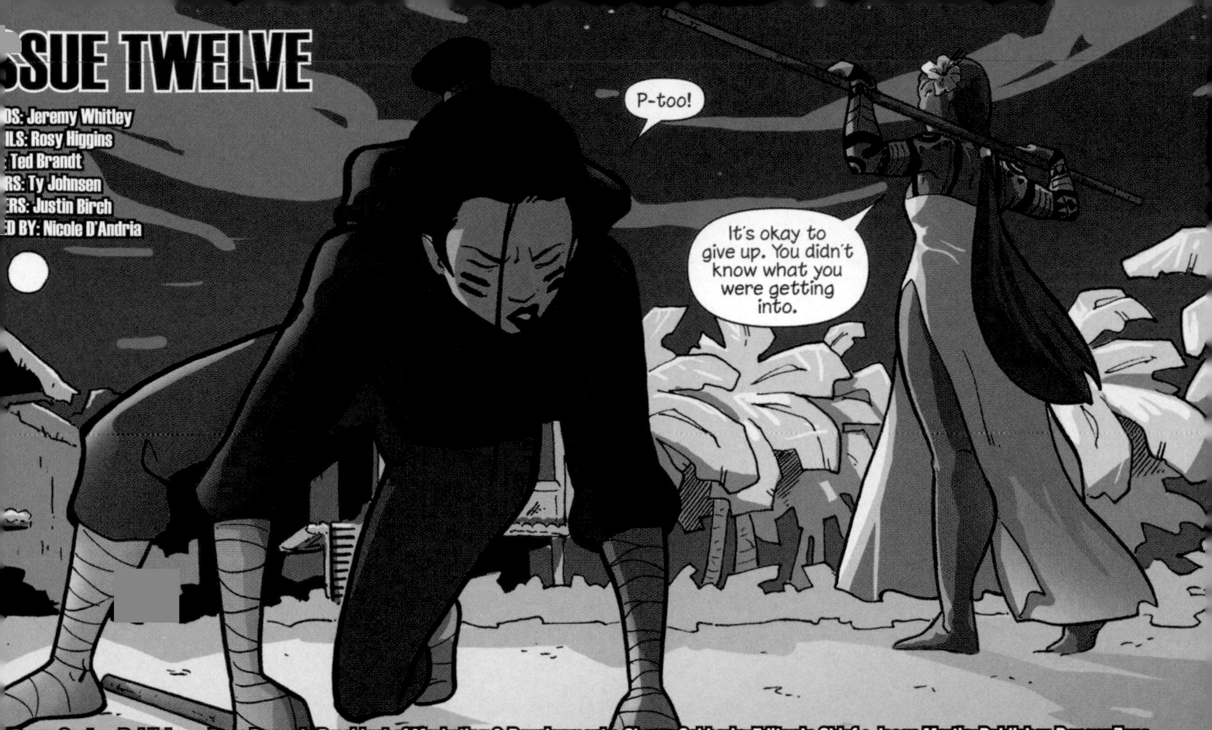
P-too!
It's okay to give up. You didn't know what you were getting into.

Bryan Seaton: Publisher • Dave Dwonch: President of Marketing & Development • Shawn Gabborin: Editor In Chief • Jason Martin: Publisher-Danger Zone
Nicole DAndria: Marketing Director/Editor • Jim Dietz: Social Media Manager • Scott Bradley: CFO • Chad Cicconi: Still Waiting For His Princess

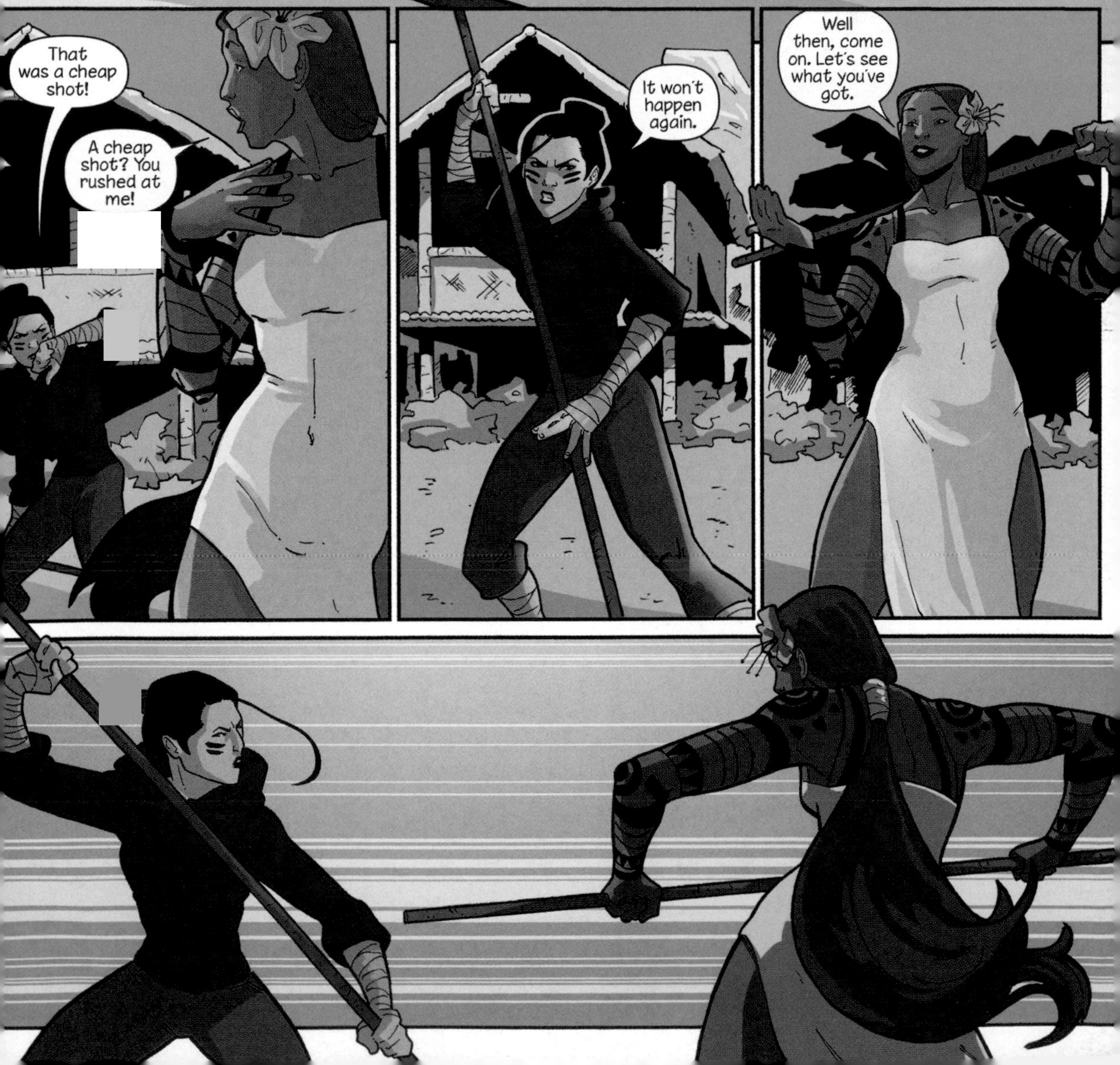
That was a cheap shot!
A cheap shot? You rushed at me!
It won't happen again.
Well then, come on. Let's see what you've got.

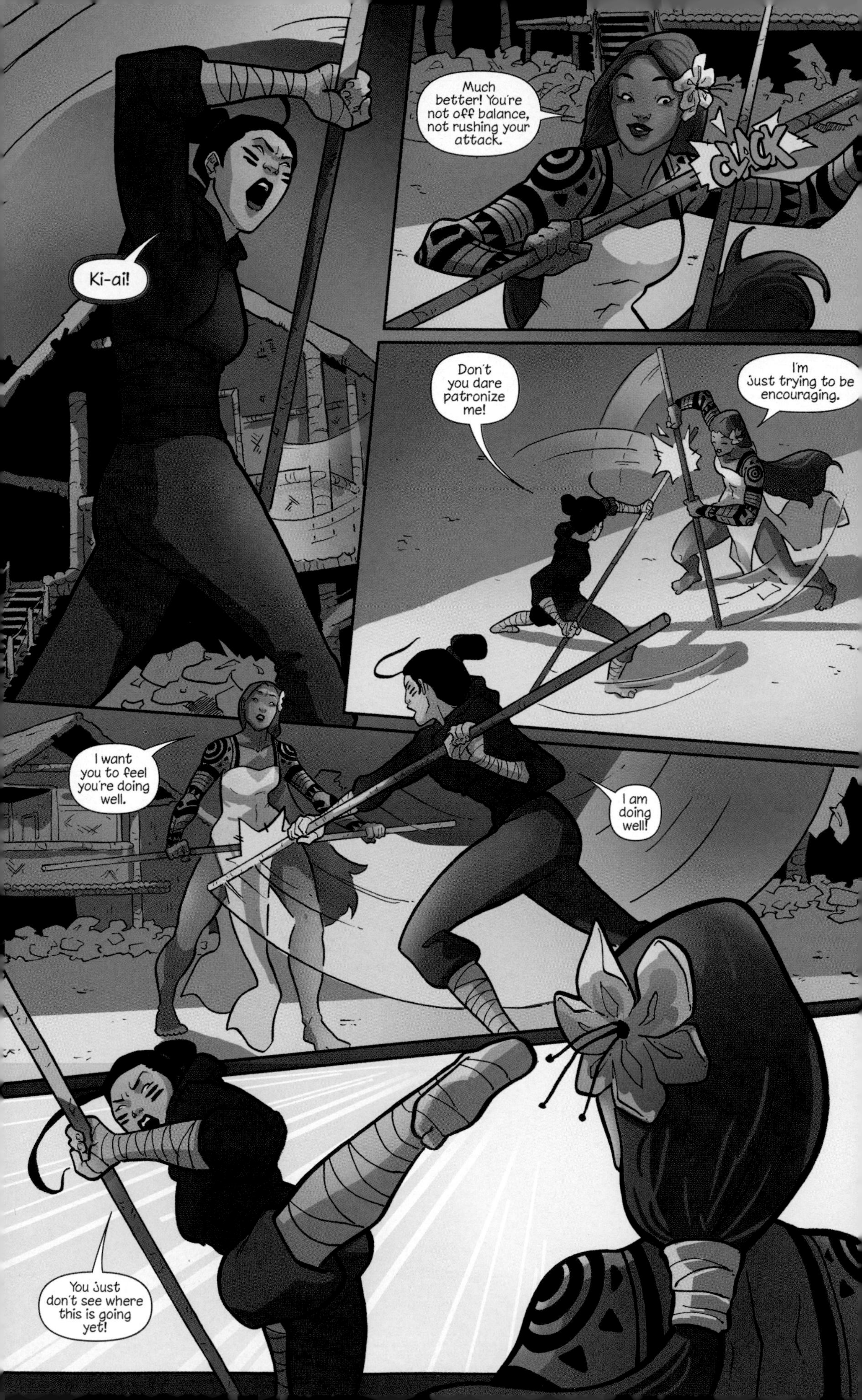
Ki-ai!
Much better! You're not off balance, not rushing your attack.
CLACK
Don't you dare patronize me!
I'm just trying to be encouraging.
I want you to feel you're doing well.
I am doing well!
You just don't see where this is going yet!

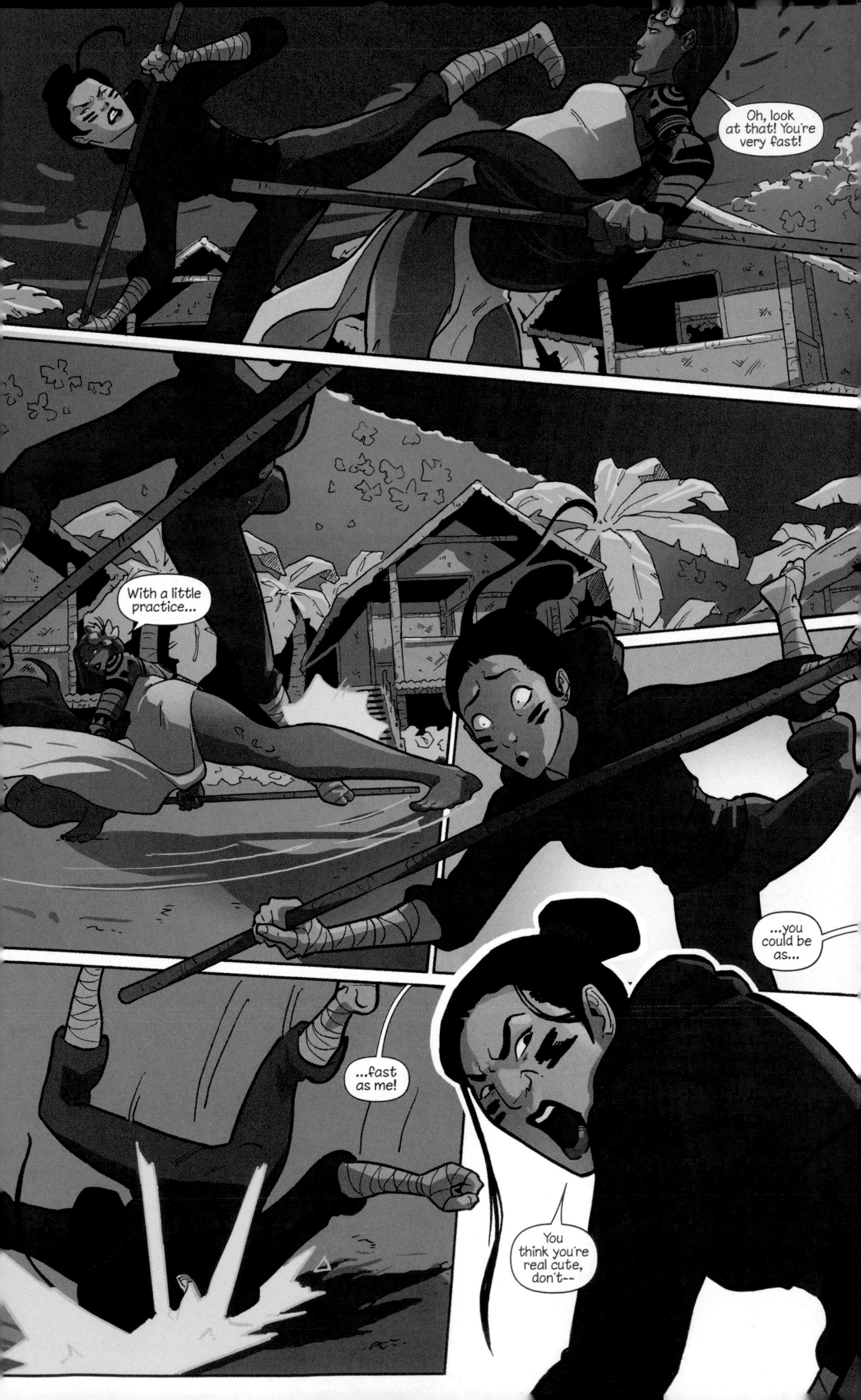
Oh, look at that! You're very fast!
With a little practice...
...you could be as...
...fast as me!
You think you're real cute, don't--

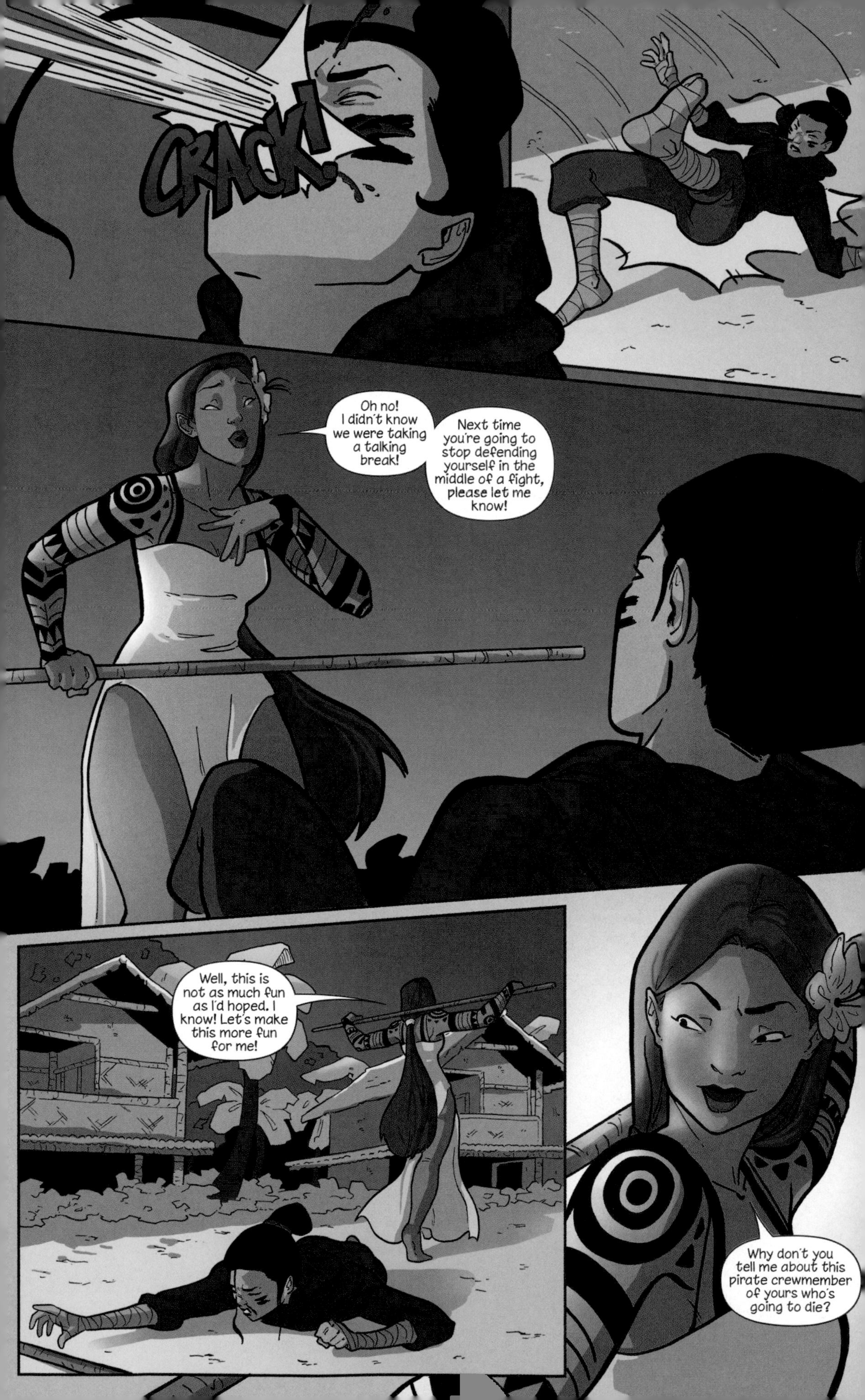
CRACK!
Oh no! I didn't know we were taking a talking break!
Next time you're going to stop defending yourself in the middle of a fight, please let me know!
Well, this is not as much fun as I'd hoped. I know! Let's make this more fun for me!
Why don't you tell me about this pirate crewmember of yours who's going to die?

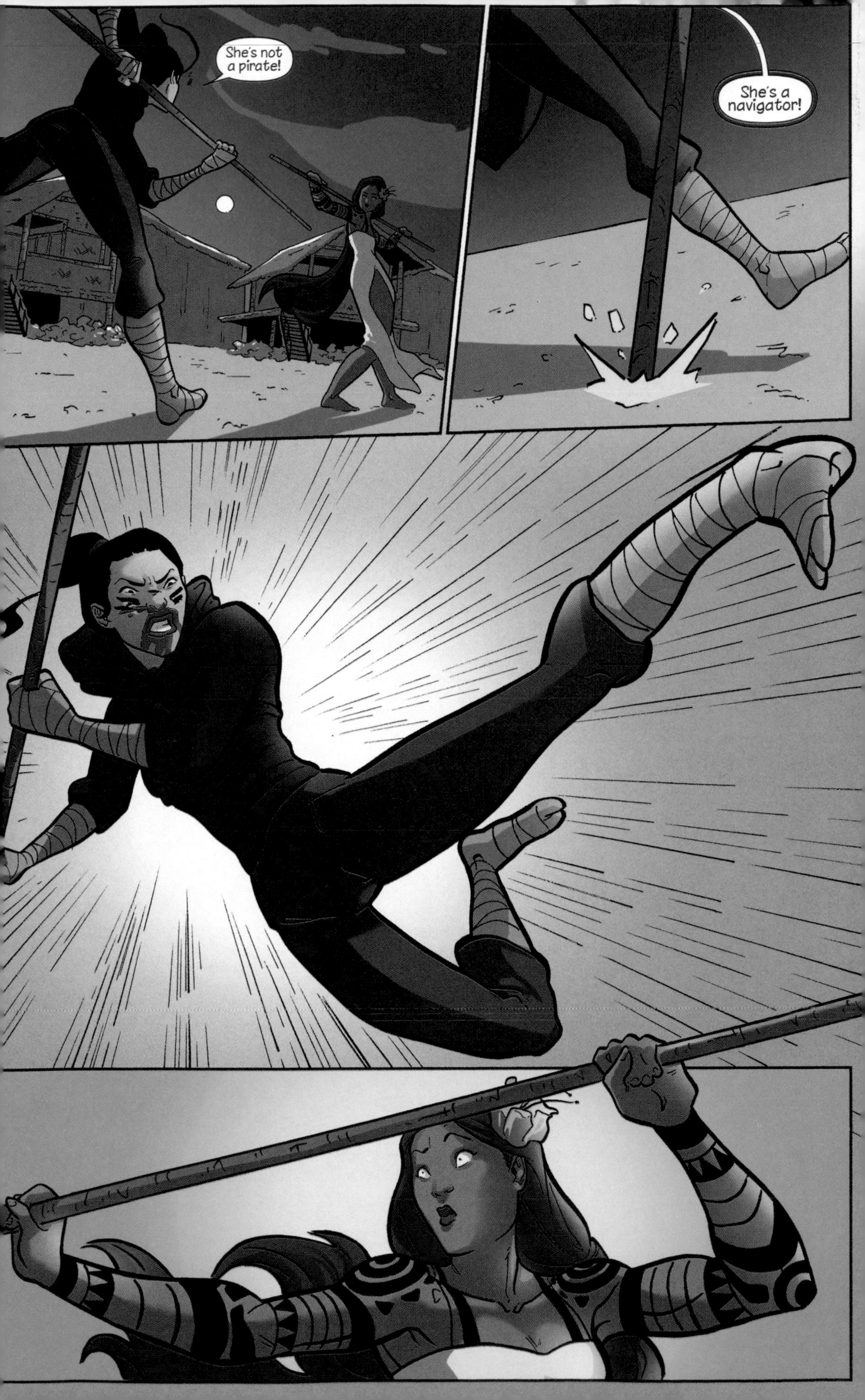
She's not a pirate!
She's a navigator!

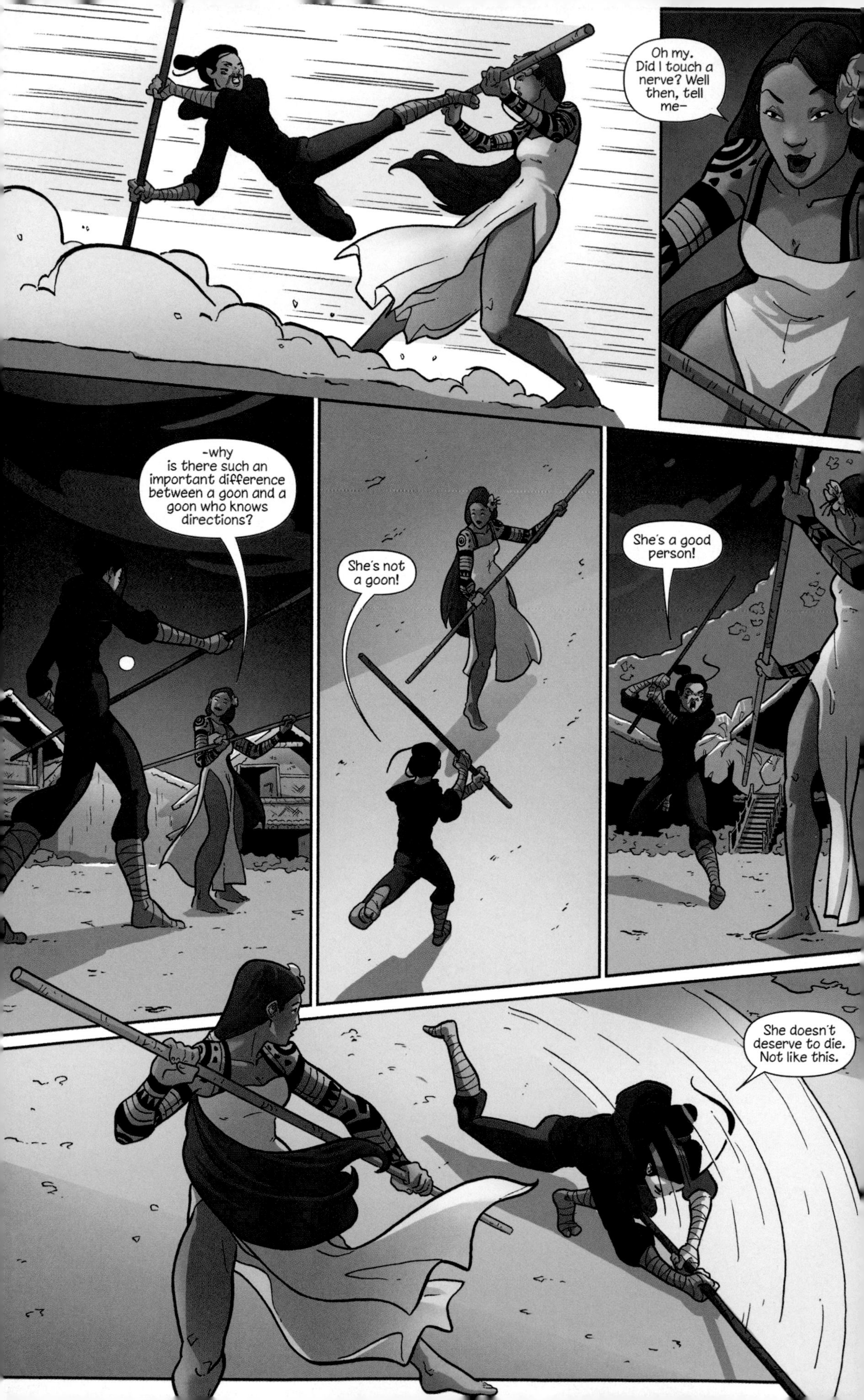
Oh my. Did I touch a nerve? Well then, tell me-
-why is there such an important difference between a goon and a goon who knows directions?
She's not a goon!
She's a good person!
She doesn't deserve to die. Not like this.

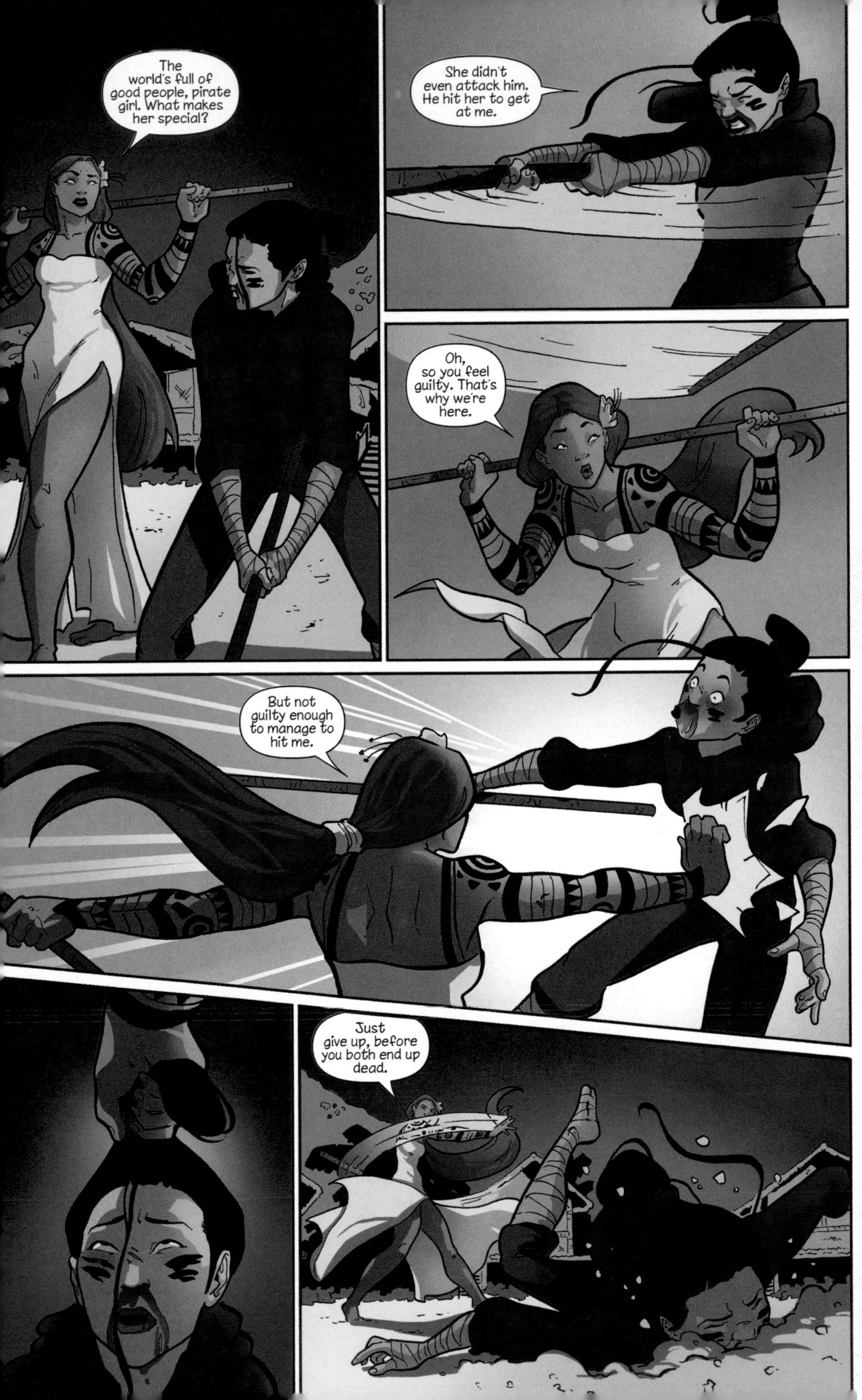
The world's full of good people, pirate girl. What makes her special?
She didn't even attack him. He hit her to get at me.
Oh, so you feel guilty. That's why we're here.
But not guilty enough to manage to hit me.
Just give up, before you both end up dead.

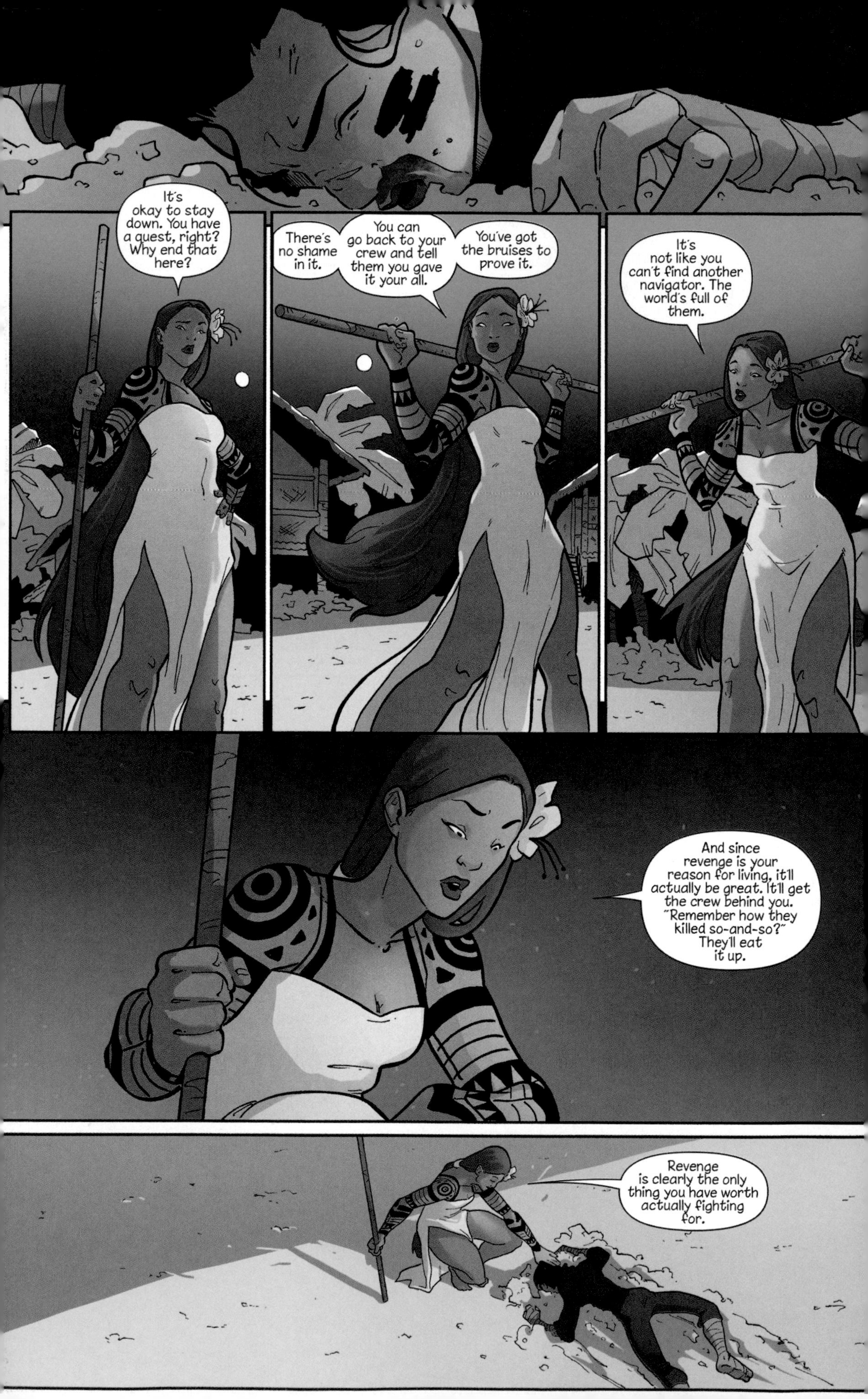
It's okay to stay down. You have a quest, right? Why end that here?
There's no shame in it.
You can go back to your crew and tell them you gave it your all.
You've got the bruises to prove it.
It's not like you can't find another navigator. The world's full of them.
And since revenge is your reason for living, it'll actually be great. It'll get the crew behind you. "Remember how they killed so-and-so?" They'll eat it up.
Revenge is clearly the only thing you have worth actually fighting for.

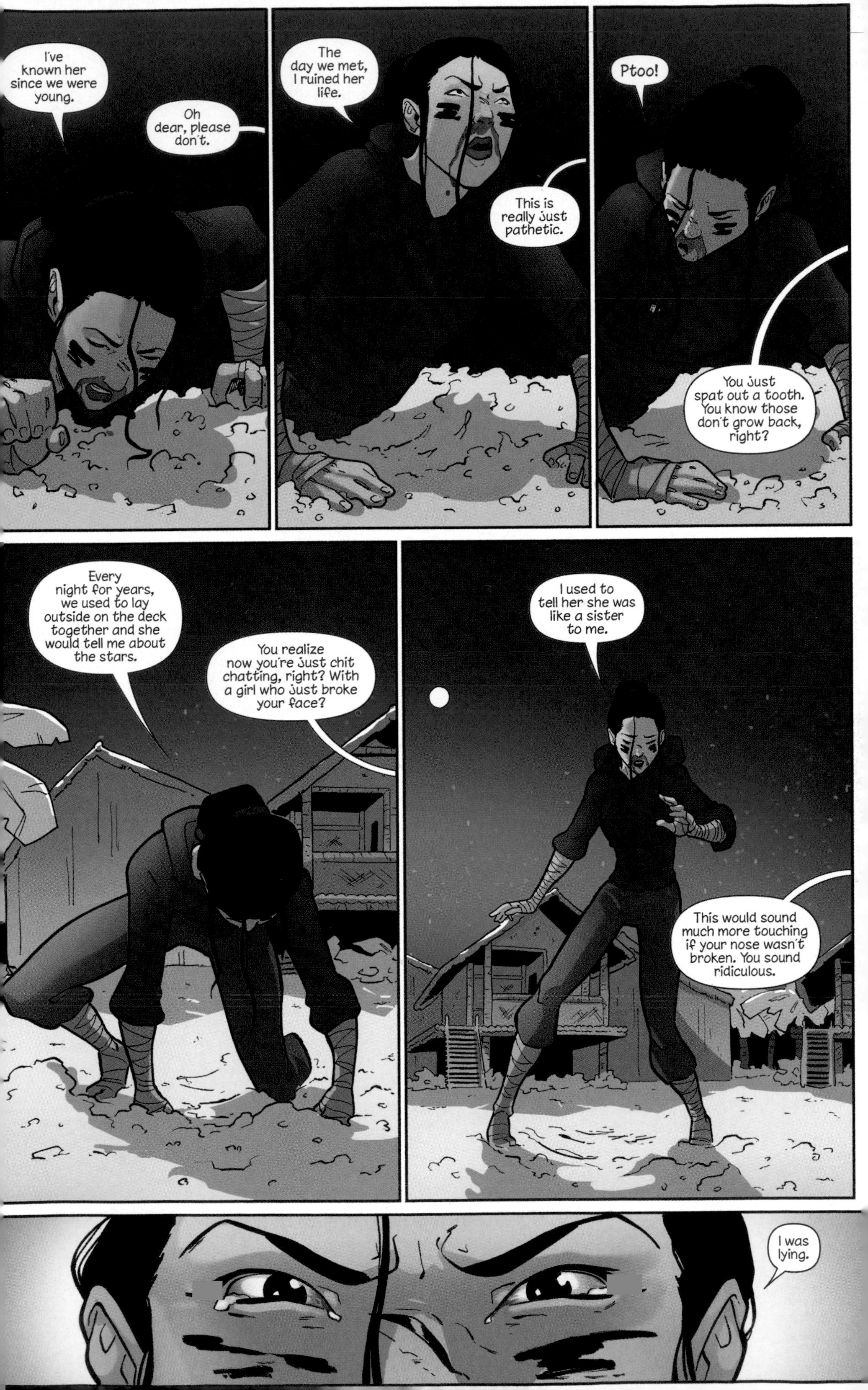
I've known her since we were young.
Oh dear, please don't.
The day we met, I ruined her life.
This is really just pathetic.
Ptoo!
You just spat out a tooth. You know those don't grow back, right?
Every night for years, we used to lay outside on the deck together and she would tell me about the stars.
You realize now you're just chit chatting, right? With a girl who just broke your face?
I used to tell her she was like a sister to me.
This would sound much more touching if your nose wasn't broken. You sound ridiculous.
I was lying.

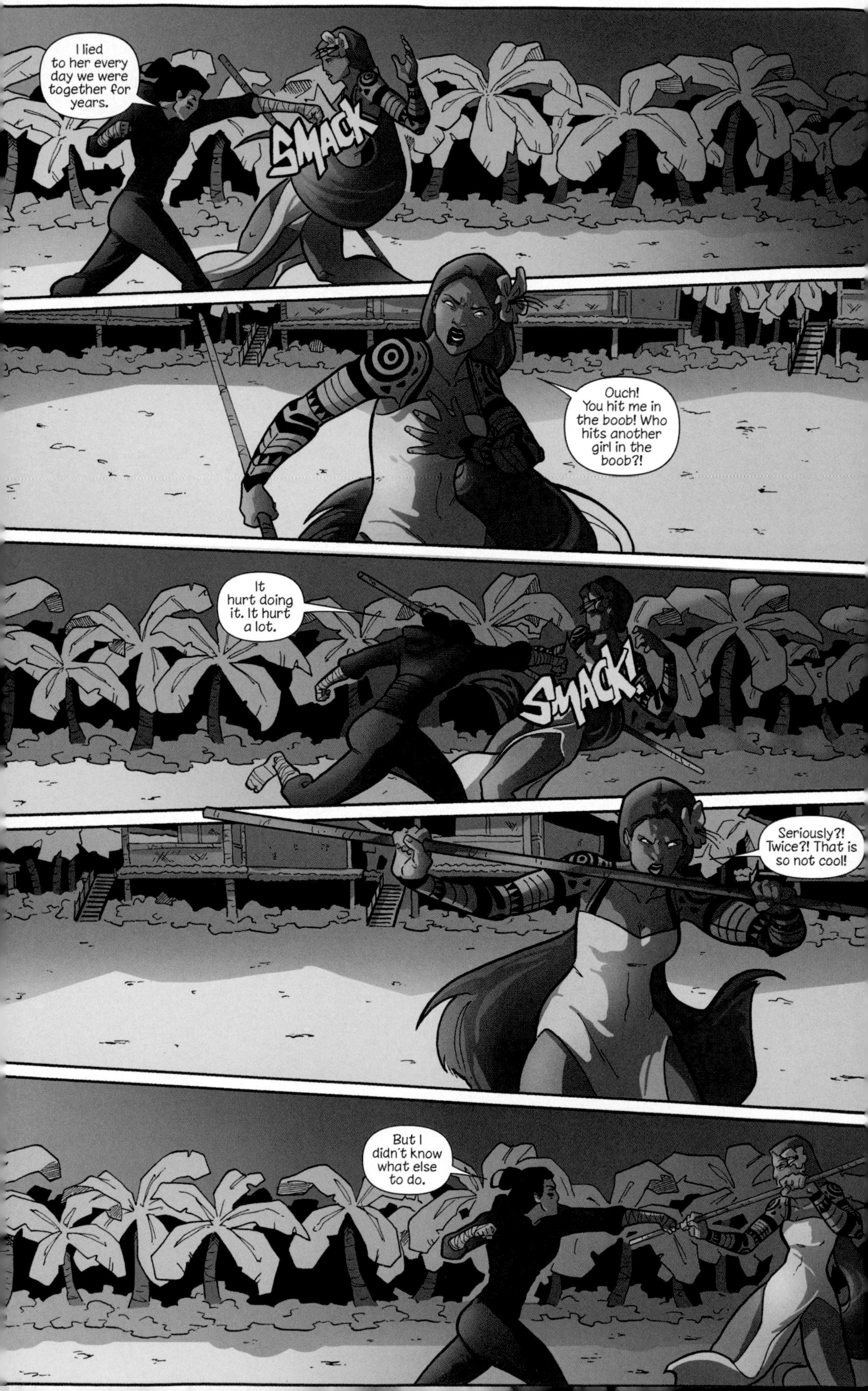
I lied to her every day we were together for years.
SMACK
Ouch! You hit me in the boob! Who hits another girl in the boob?!
It hurt doing it. It hurt a lot.
SMACK!
Seriously?! Twice?! That is so not cool!
But I didn't know what else to do.

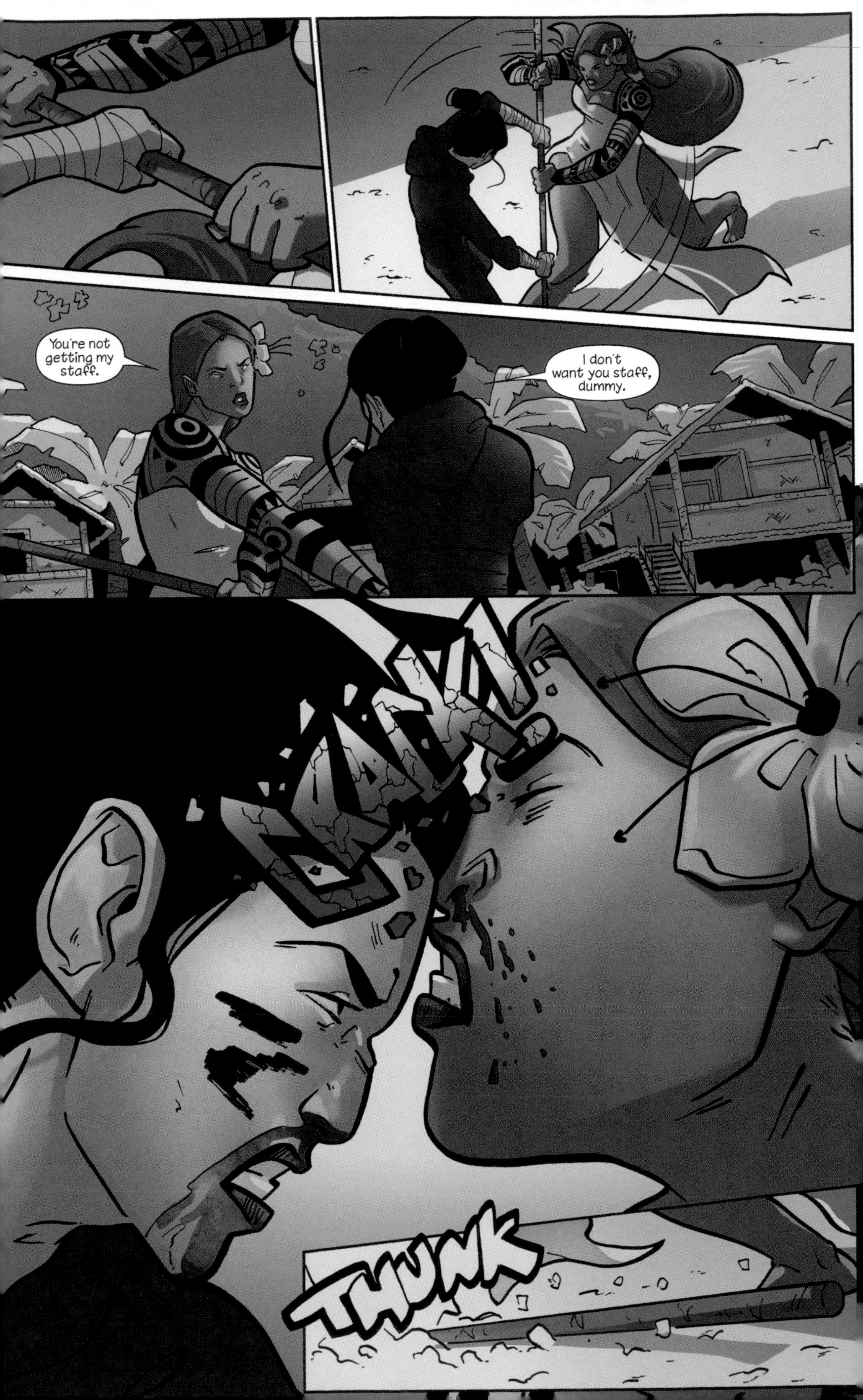
You're not getting my staff.
I don't want you staff, dummy.
THUNK

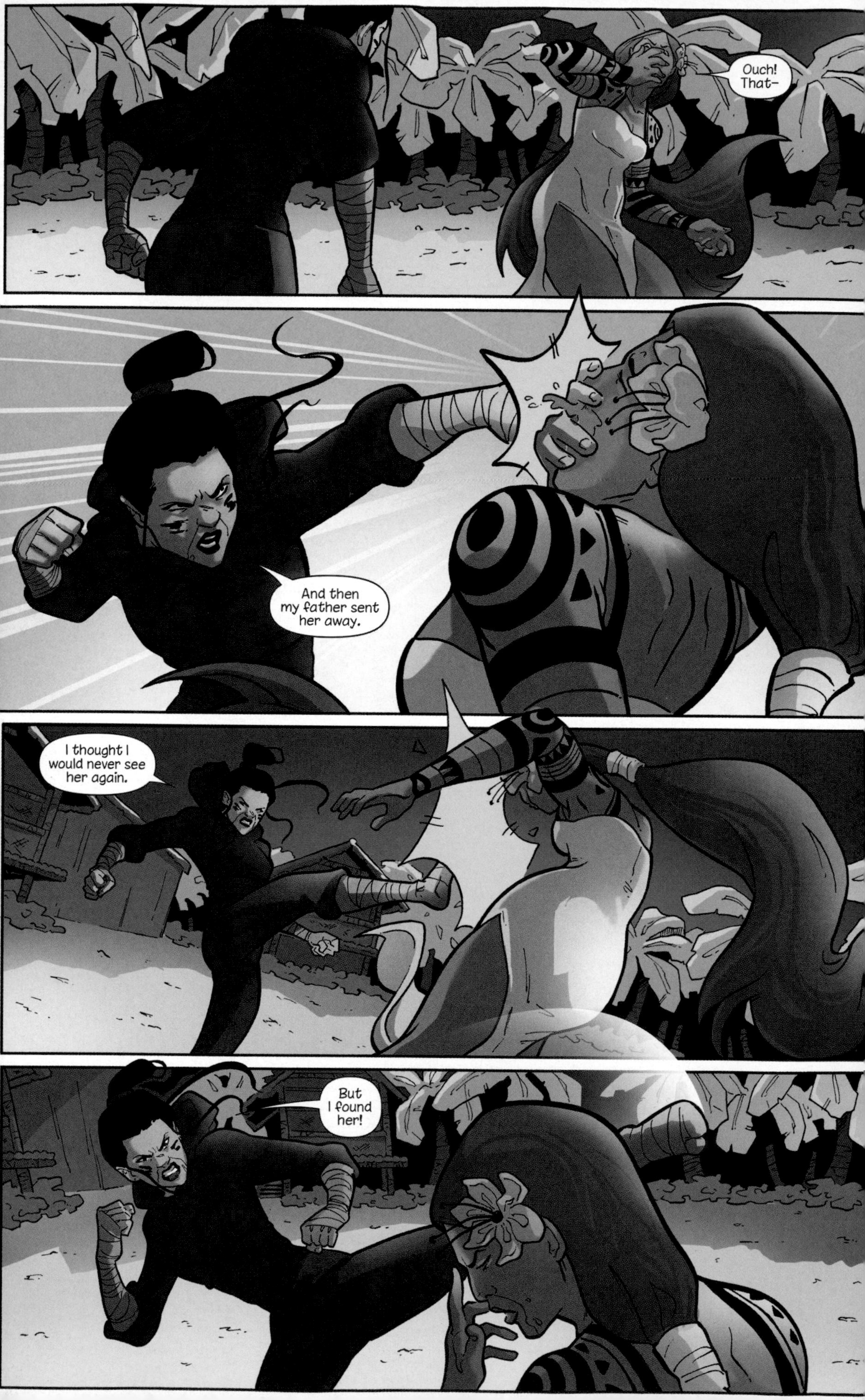
Ouch! That–
And then my father sent her away.
I thought I would never see her again.
But I found her!

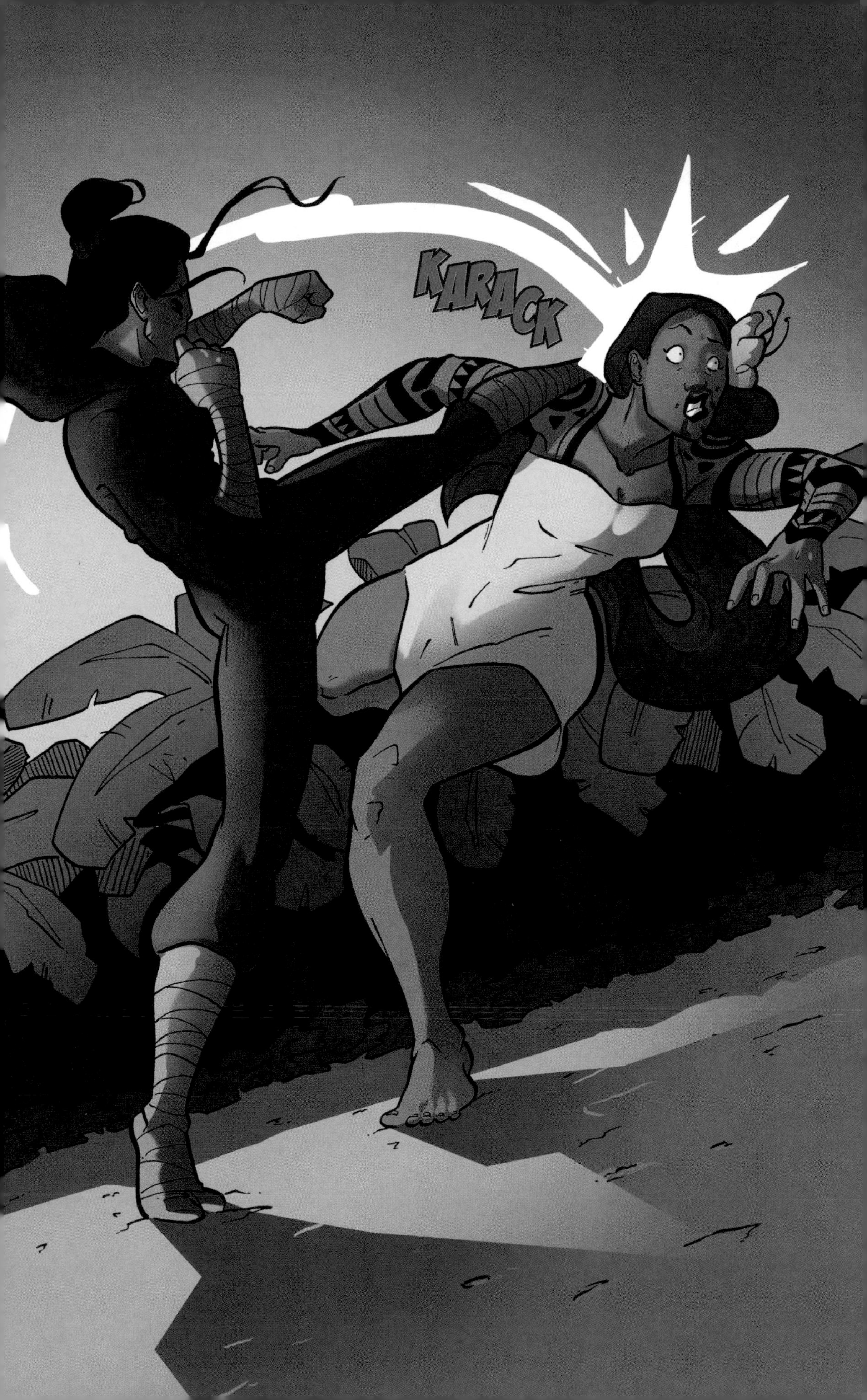
KARACK

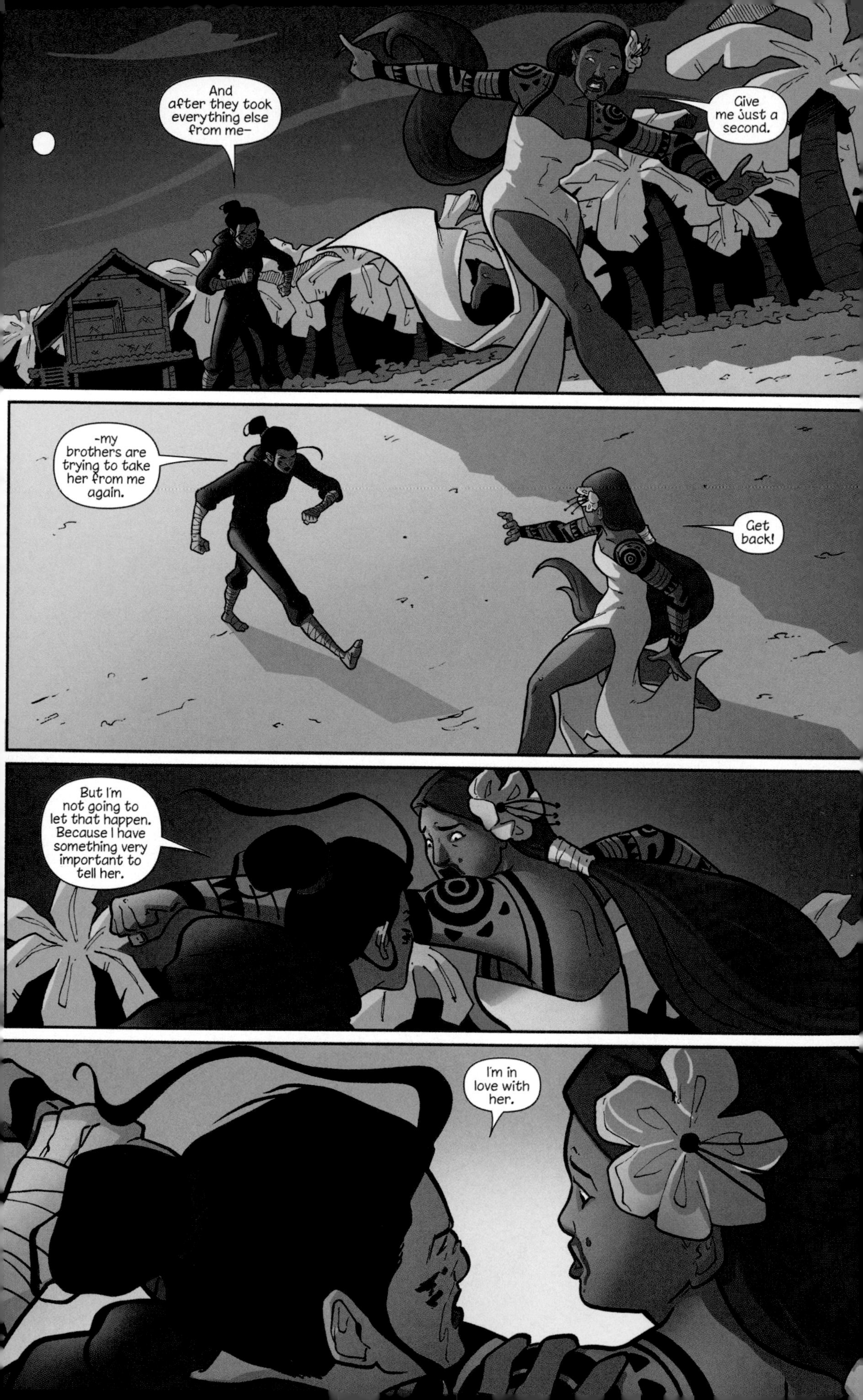
And after they took everything else from me–
Give me just a second.
-my brothers are trying to take her from me again.
Get back!
But I'm not going to let that happen. Because I have something very important to tell her.
I'm in love with her.

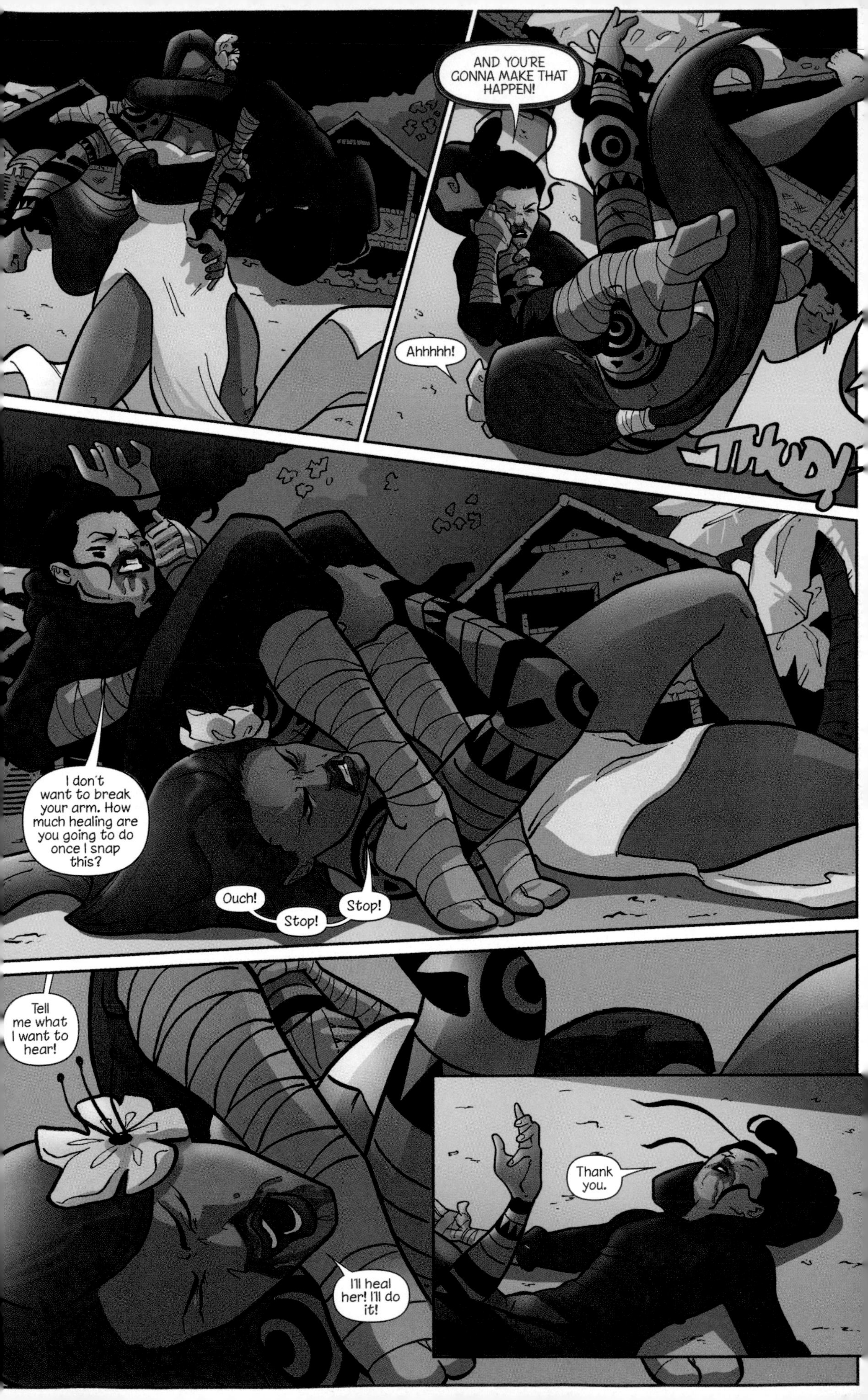
AND YOU'RE GONNA MAKE THAT HAPPEN!
Ahhhhh!
THUD!
I don't want to break your arm. How much healing are you going to do once I snap this?
Ouch!
Stop!
Stop!
Tell me what I want to hear!
I'll heal her! I'll do it!
Thank you.

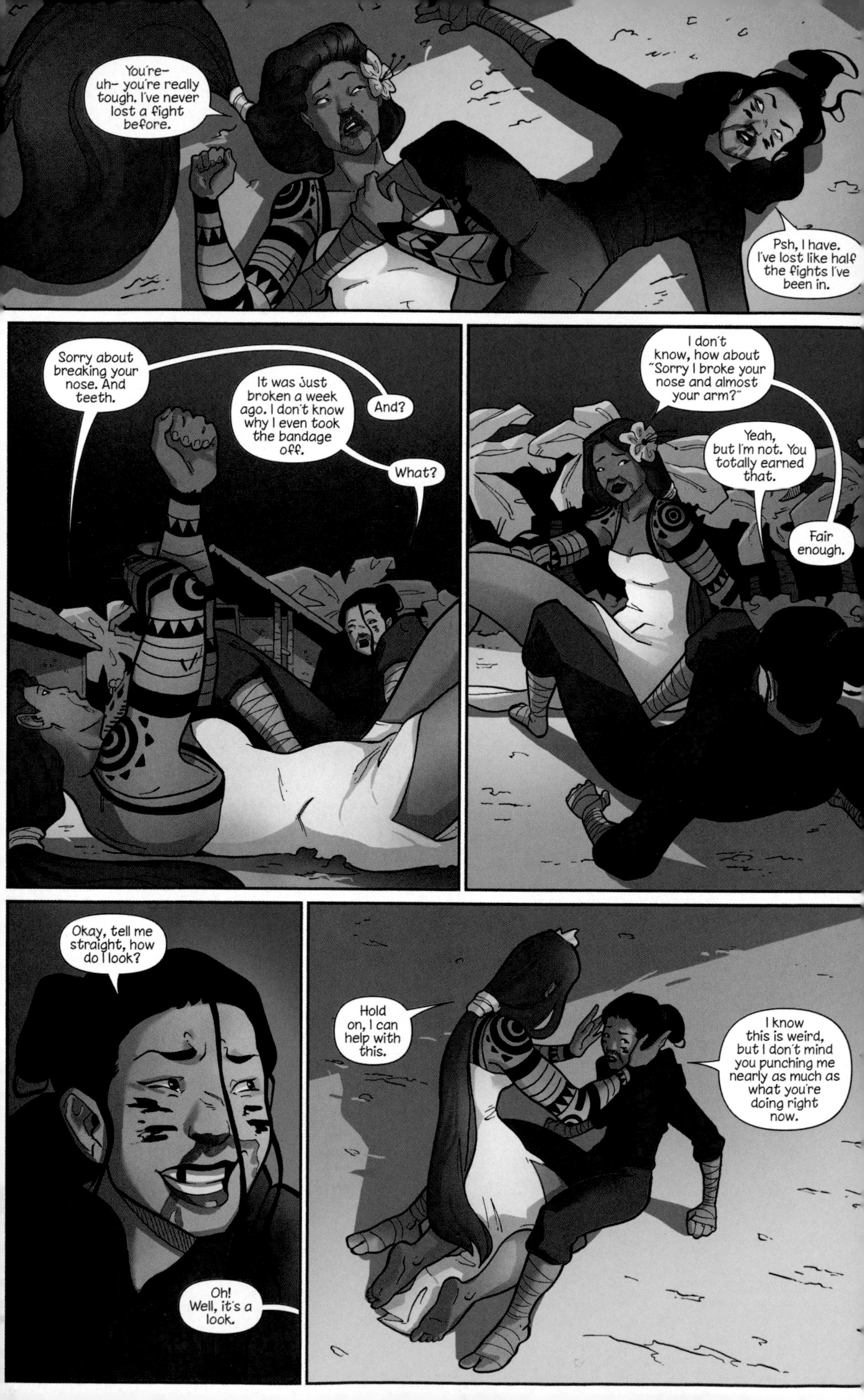
You're— uh— you're really tough. I've never lost a fight before.
Psh, I have. I've lost like half the fights I've been in.
Sorry about breaking your nose. And teeth.
It was just broken a week ago. I don't know why I even took the bandage off.
And?
What?
I don't know, how about "Sorry I broke your nose and almost your arm?"
Yeah, but I'm not. You totally earned that.
Fair enough.
Okay, tell me straight, how do I look?
Oh! Well, it's a look.
Hold on, I can help with this.
I know this is weird, but I don't mind you punching me nearly as much as what you're doing right now.

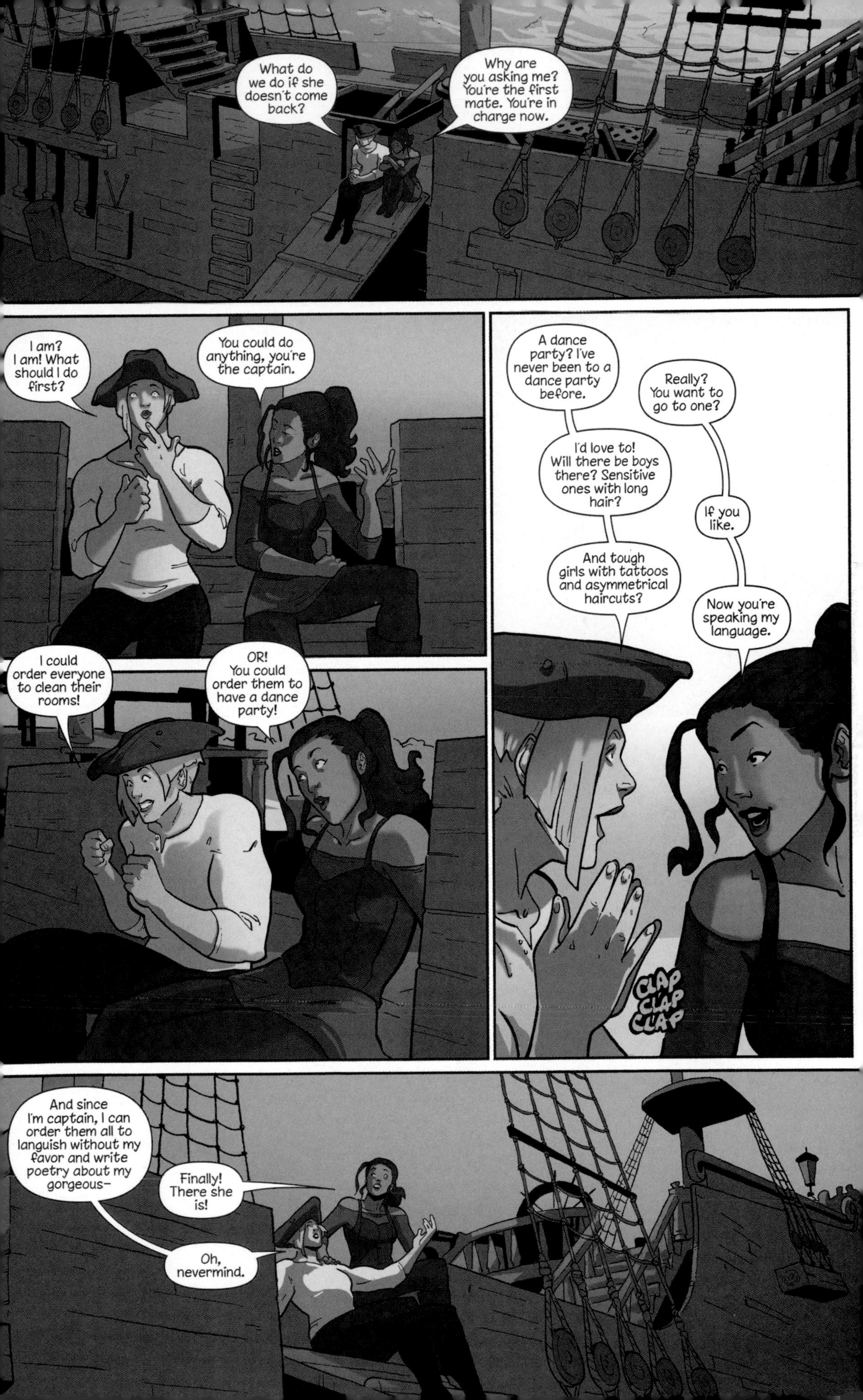
What do we do if she doesn't come back?
Why are you asking me? You're the first mate. You're in charge now.
I am? I am! What should I do first?
You could do anything, you're the captain.
I could order everyone to clean their rooms!
OR! You could order them to have a dance party!
A dance party? I've never been to a dance party before.
Really? You want to go to one?
I'd love to! Will there be boys there? Sensitive ones with long hair?
If you like.
And tough girls with tattoos and asymmetrical haircuts?
Now you're speaking my language.
CLAP CLAP CLAP
And since I'm captain, I can order them all to languish without my favor and write poetry about my gorgeous–
Finally! There she is!
Oh, nevermind.

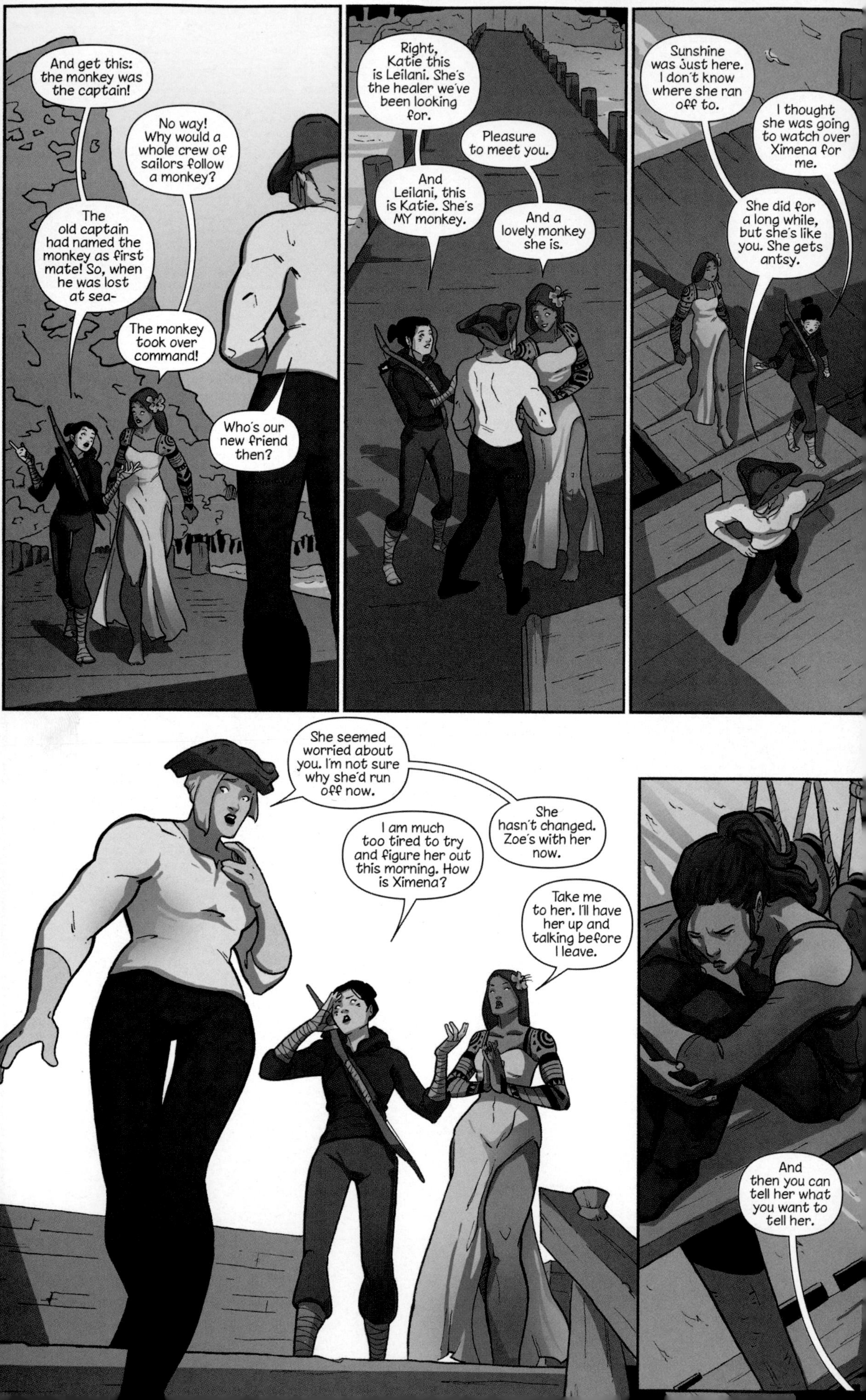

And get this: the monkey was the captain!
No way! Why would a whole crew of sailors follow a monkey?
The old captain had named the monkey as first mate! So, when he was lost at sea-
The monkey took over command!
Who's our new friend then?
Right, Katie this is Leilani. She's the healer we've been looking for.
Pleasure to meet you.
And Leilani, this is Katie. She's MY monkey.
And a lovely monkey she is.
Sunshine was just here. I don't know where she ran off to.
I thought she was going to watch over Ximena for me.
She did for a long while, but she's like you. She gets antsy.
She seemed worried about you. I'm not sure why she'd run off now.
She hasn't changed. Zoe's with her now.
I am much too tired to try and figure her out this morning. How is Ximena?
Take me to her. I'll have her up and talking before I leave.
And then you can tell her what you want to tell her.

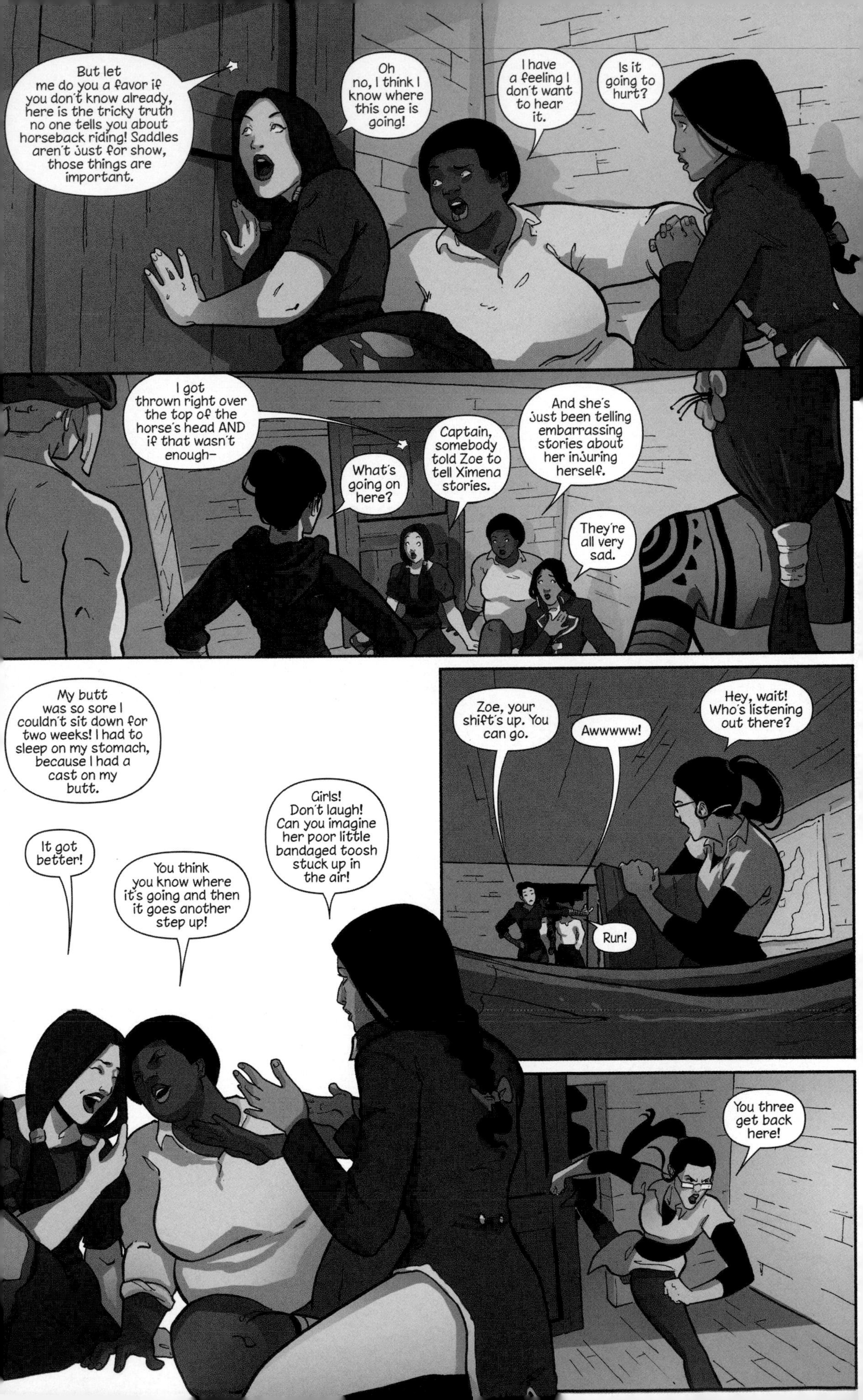
But let me do you a favor if you don't know already, here is the tricky truth no one tells you about horseback riding! Saddles aren't just for show, those things are important.
Oh no, I think I know where this one is going!
I have a feeling I don't want to hear it.
Is it going to hurt?
I got thrown right over the top of the horse's head AND if that wasn't enough–
What's going on here?
Captain, somebody told Zoe to tell Ximena stories.
And she's just been telling embarrassing stories about her injuring herself.
They're all very sad.
My butt was so sore I couldn't sit down for two weeks! I had to sleep on my stomach, because I had a cast on my butt.
It got better!
You think you know where it's going and then it goes another step up!
Girls! Don't laugh! Can you imagine her poor little bandaged toosh stuck up in the air!
Zoe, your shift's up. You can go.
Awwwww!
Hey, wait! Who's listening out there?
Run!
You three get back here!

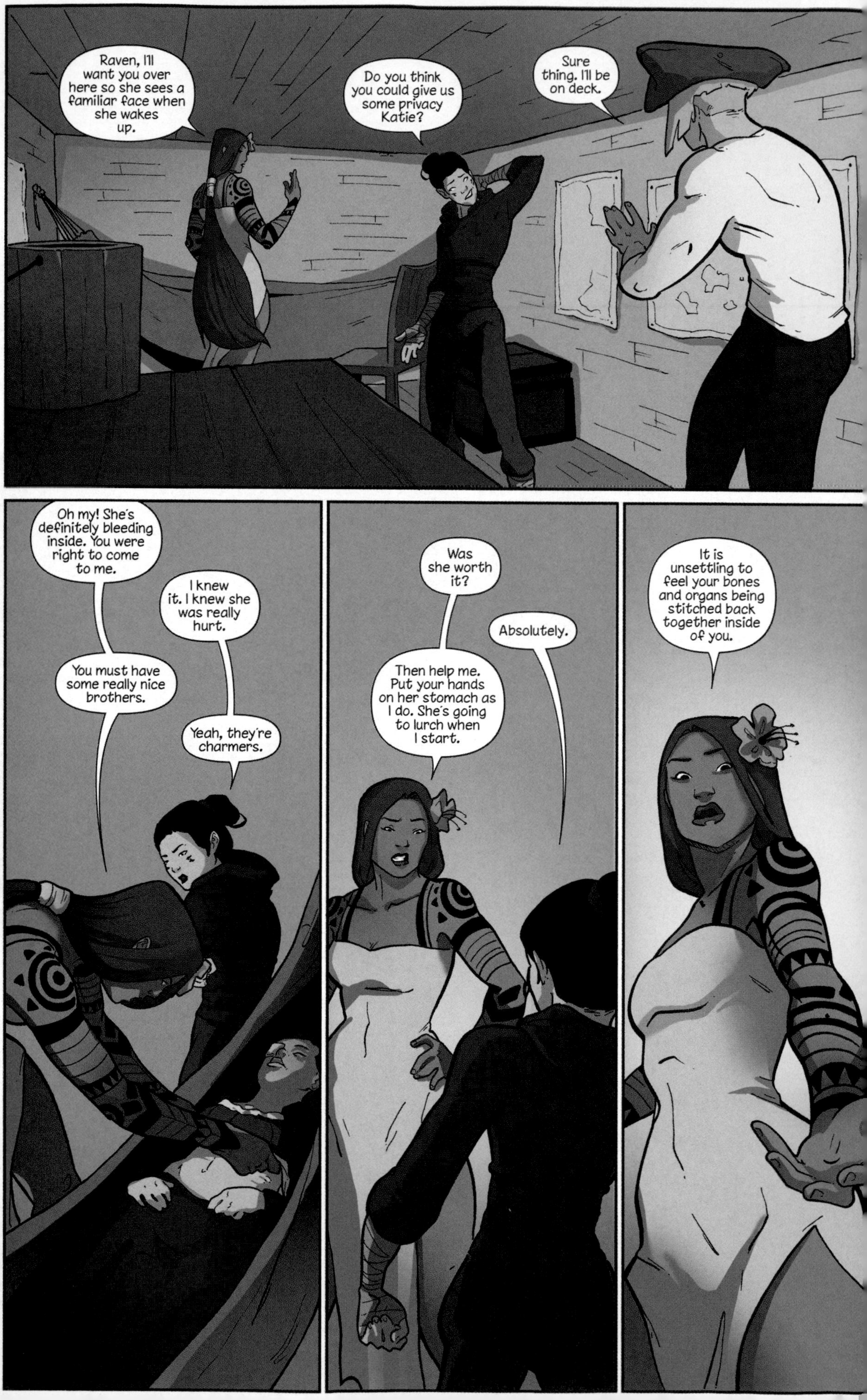
Raven, I'll want you over here so she sees a familiar face when she wakes up.
Do you think you could give us some privacy Katie?
Sure thing. I'll be on deck.
Oh my! She's definitely bleeding inside. You were right to come to me.
I knew it. I knew she was really hurt.
You must have some really nice brothers.
Yeah, they're charmers.
Was she worth it?
Absolutely.
Then help me. Put your hands on her stomach as I do. She's going to lurch when I start.
It is unsettling to feel your bones and organs being stitched back together inside of you.

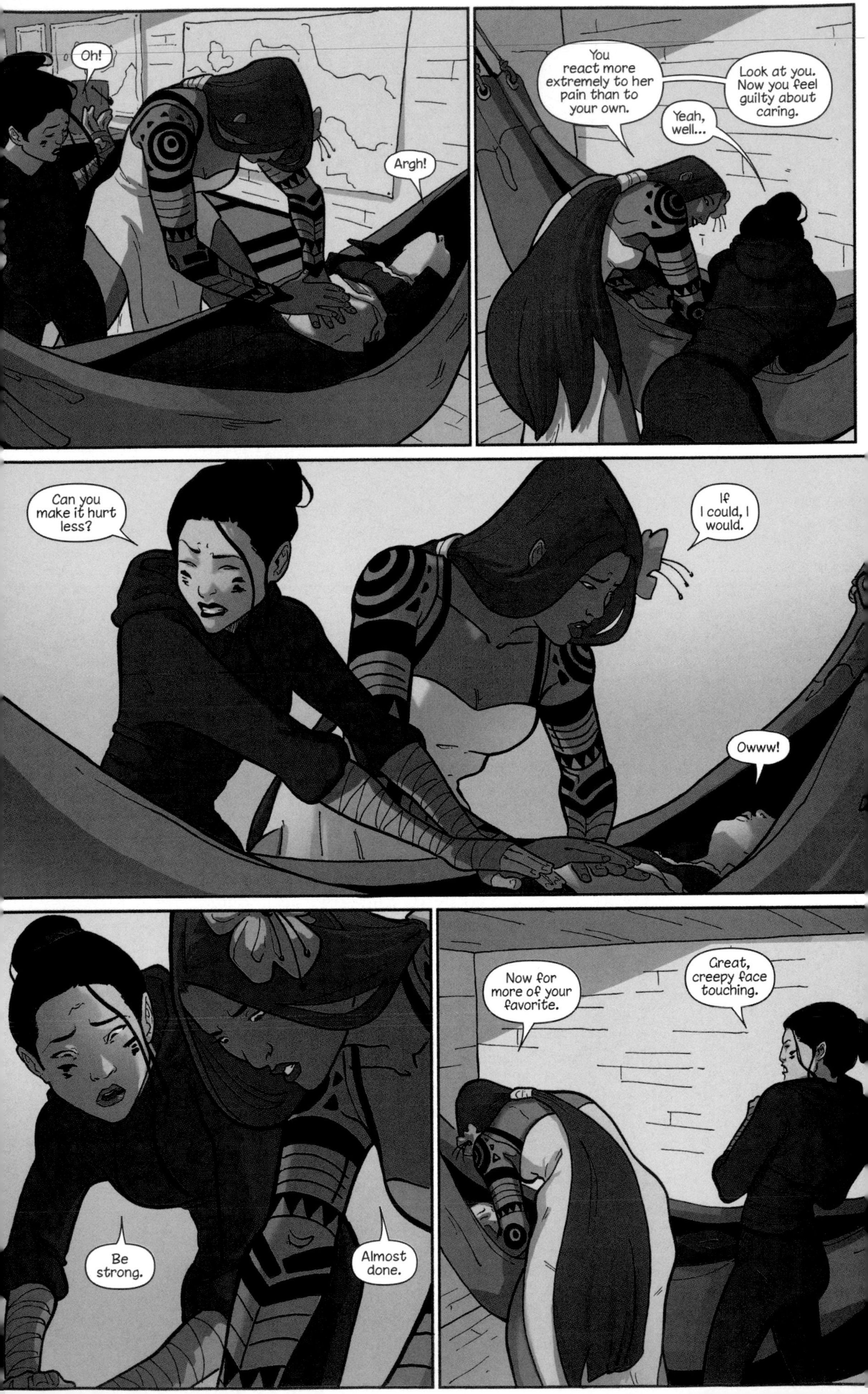
Oh!
Argh!
You react more extremely to her pain than to your own.
Yeah, well...
Look at you. Now you feel guilty about caring.
Can you make it hurt less?
If I could, I would.
Owww!
Be strong.
Almost done.
Now for more of your favorite.
Great, creepy face touching.

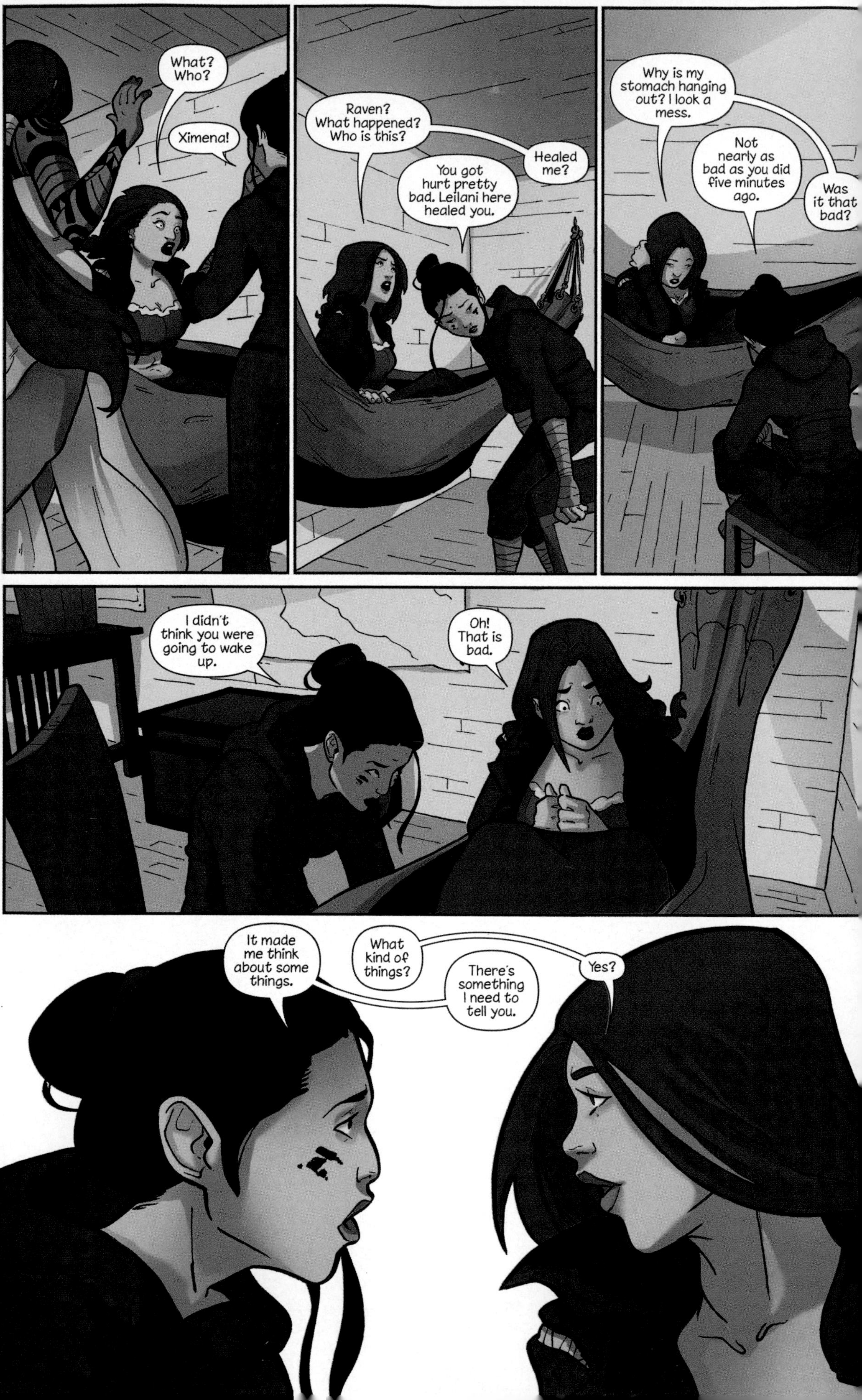
What? Who?
Ximena!
Raven? What happened? Who is this?
You got hurt pretty bad. Leilani here healed you.
Healed me?
Why is my stomach hanging out? I look a mess.
Not nearly as bad as you did five minutes ago.
Was it that bad?
I didn't think you were going to wake up.
Oh! That is bad.
It made me think about some things.
What kind of things?
There's something I need to tell you.
Yes?

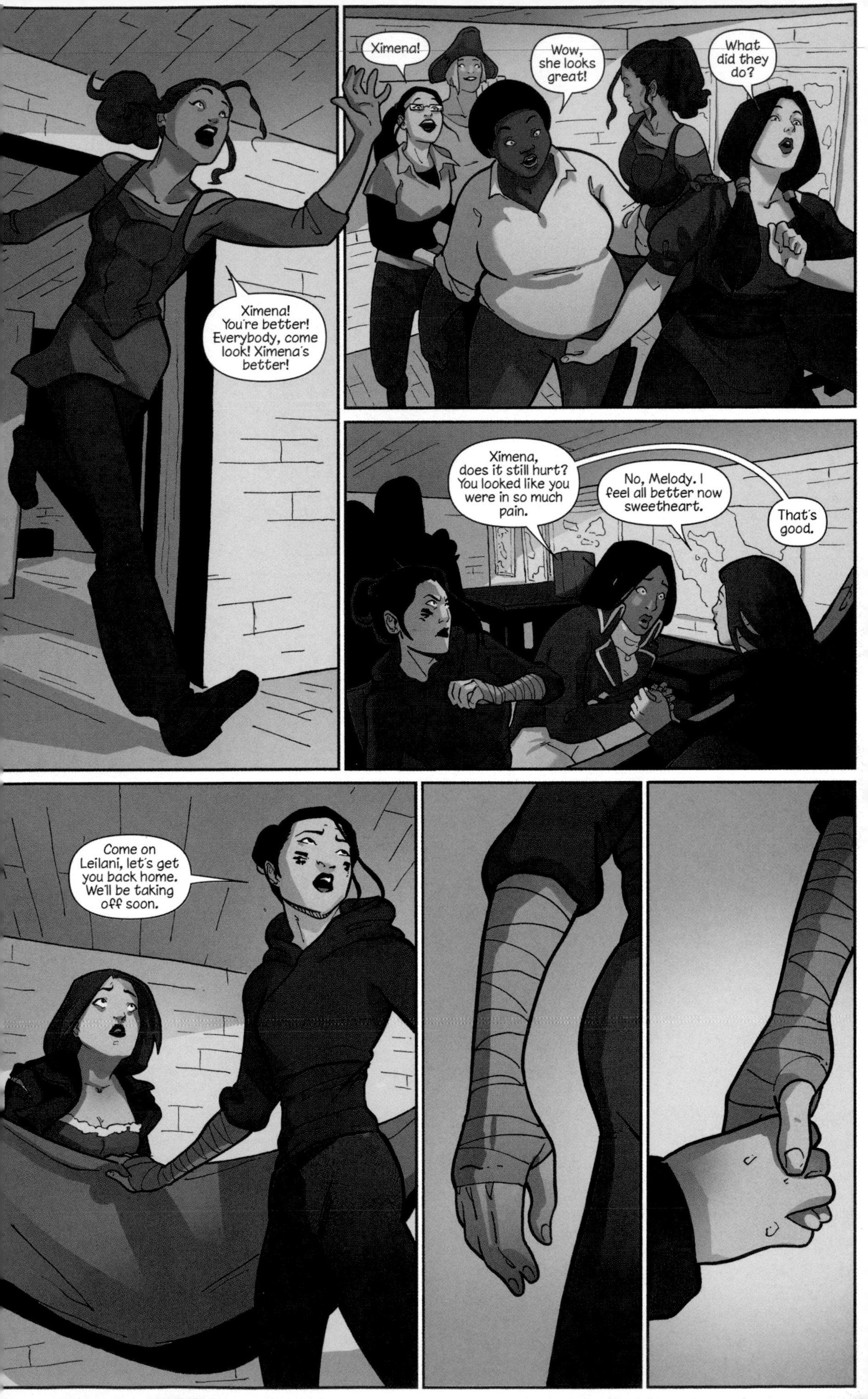
Ximena! You're better! Everybody, come look! Ximena's better!
Ximena!
Wow, she looks great!
What did they do?
Ximena, does it still hurt? You looked like you were in so much pain.
No, Melody. I feel all better now sweetheart.
That's good.
Come on Leilani, let's get you back home. We'll be taking off soon.

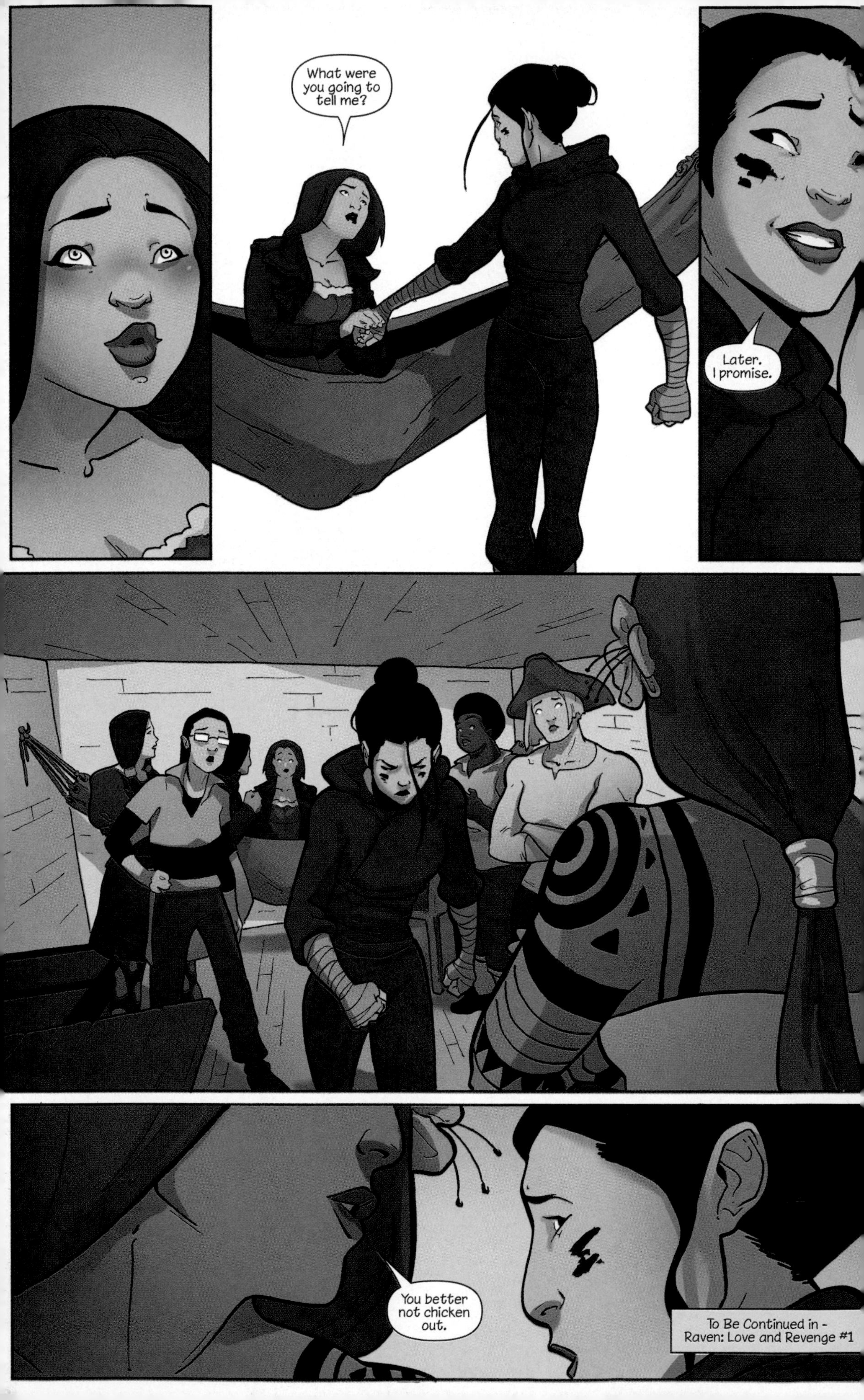
What were you going to tell me?
Later. I promise.
You better not chicken out.
To Be Continued in - Raven: Love and Revenge #1

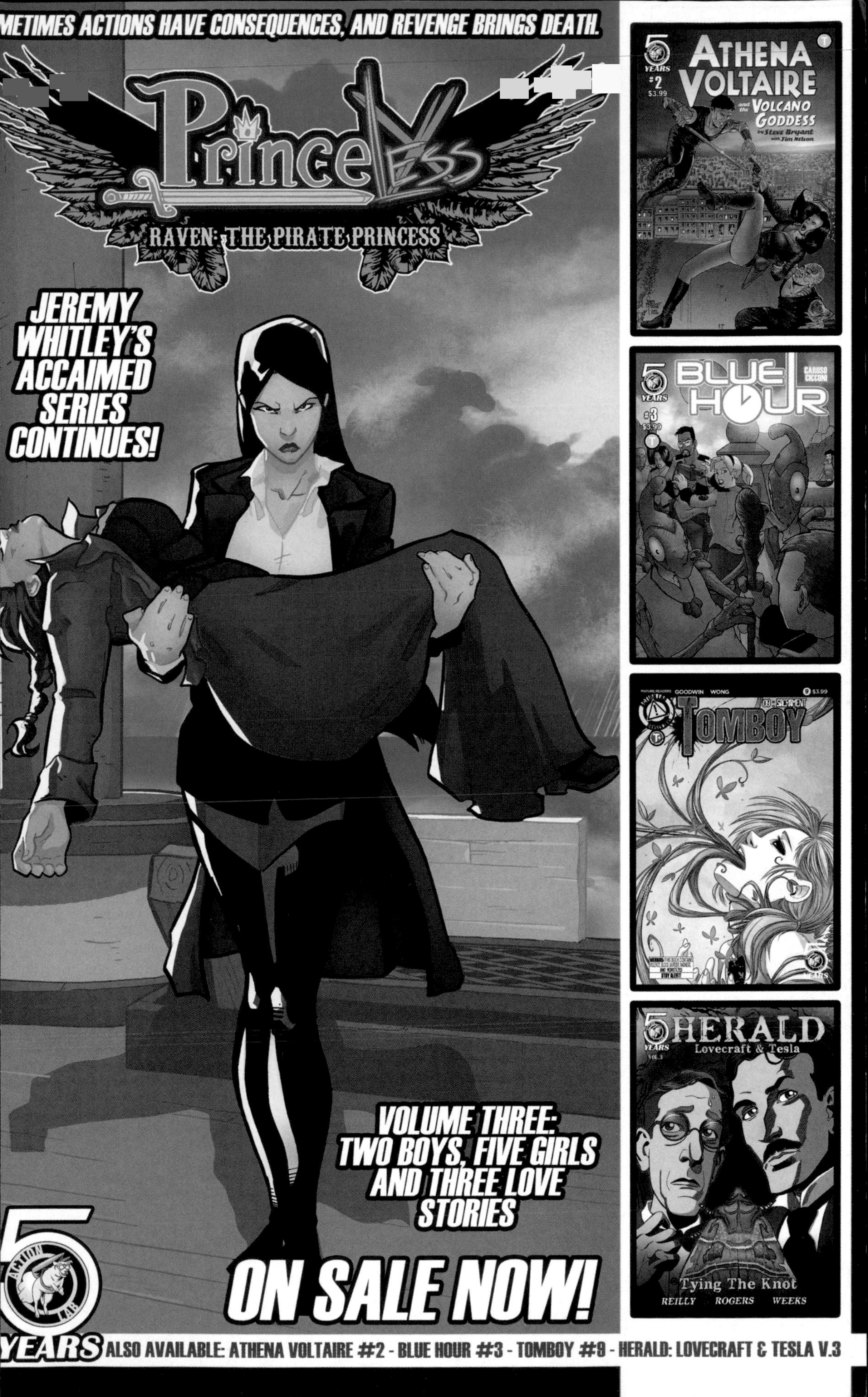
METIMES ACTIONS HAVE CONSEQUENCES, AND REVENGE BRINGS DEATH.
Princeless
RAVEN: THE PIRATE PRINCESS
JEREMY WHITLEY'S ACCAIMED SERIES CONTINUES!
VOLUME THREE: TWO BOYS, FIVE GIRLS AND THREE LOVE STORIES
ON SALE NOW!
5 YEARS
ACTION LAB
ATHENA VOLTAIRE
#2 $3.99
and the VOLCANO GODDESS
by Steve Bryant with Jim Nelson
BLUE HOUR
CARUSO CICCONI
#3 $3.99
MATURE READERS GOODWIN WONG
$3.99
09 - SACRAMENT
TOMBOY
HERALD
Lovecraft & Tesla
VOL.3
Tying The Knot
REILLY ROGERS WEEKS
ALSO AVAILABLE: ATHENA VOLTAIRE #2 - BLUE HOUR #3 - TOMBOY #9 - HERALD: LOVECRAFT & TESLA V.3

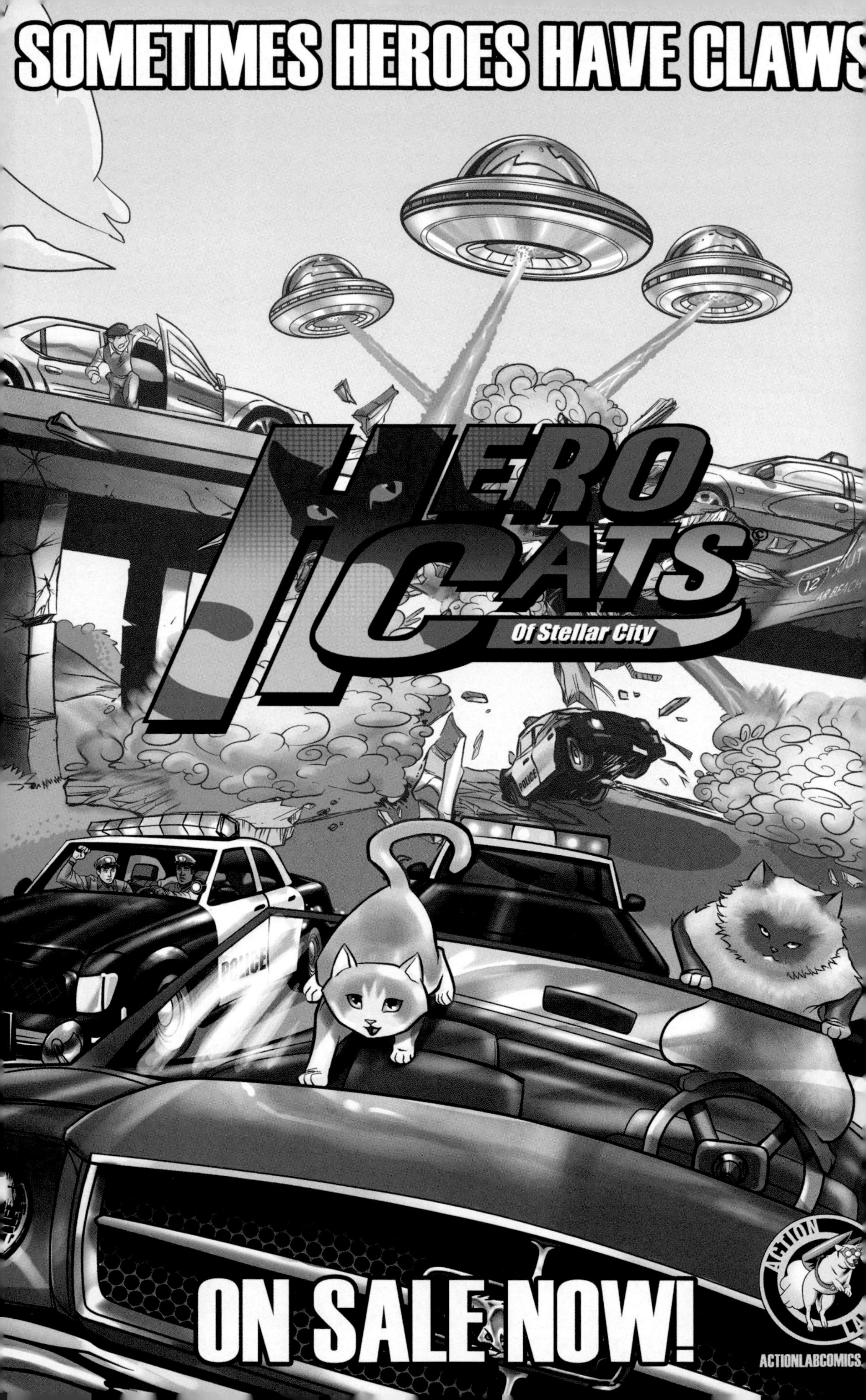
SOMETIMES HEROES HAVE CLAWS
HERO CATS
Of Stellar City
POLICE
POLICE
ON SALE NOW!
ACTION LAB
ACTIONLABCOMICS.

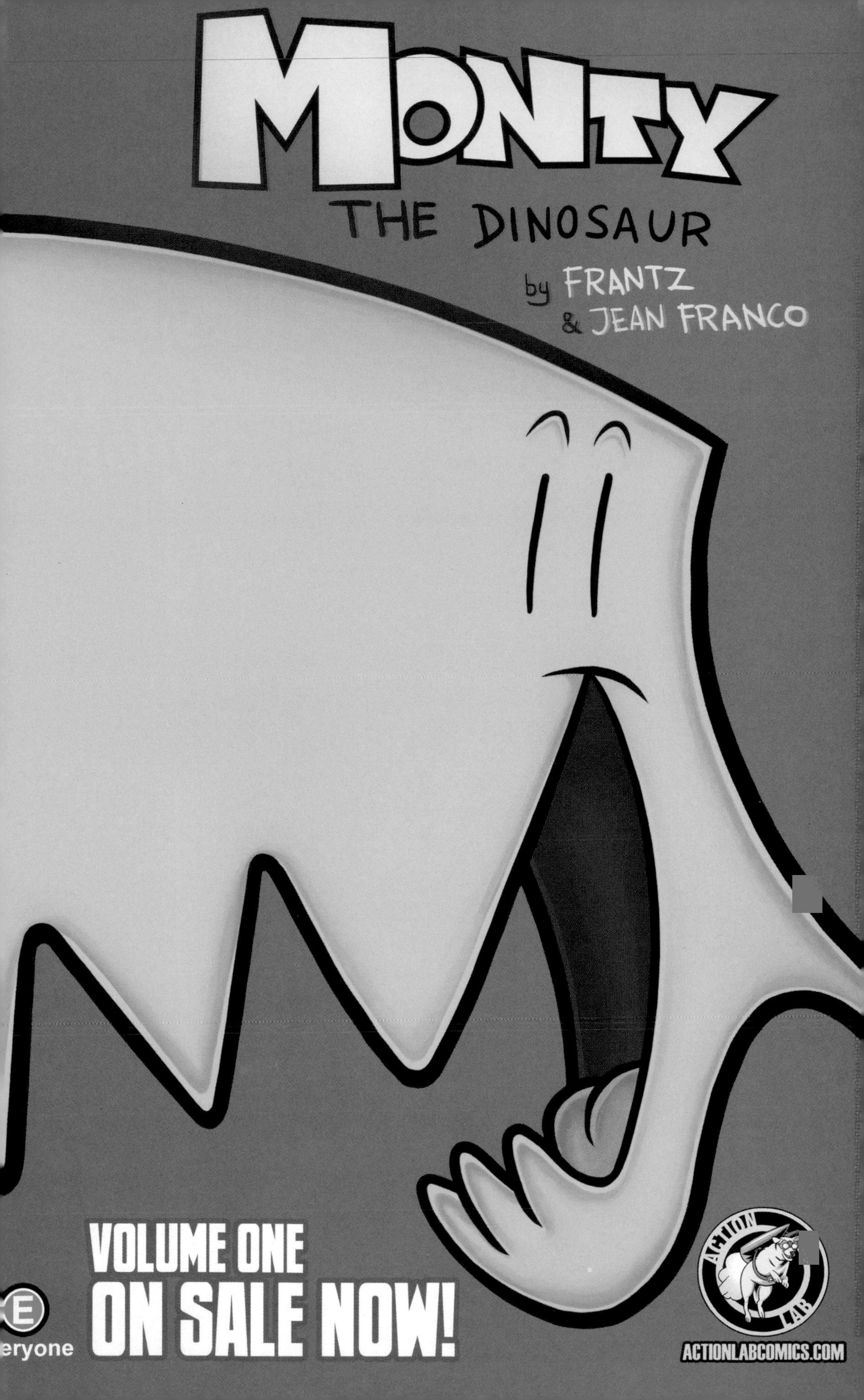
MONTY
THE DINOSAUR
by FRANTZ
& JEAN FRANCO
VOLUME ONE
ON SALE NOW!
E
eryone
ACTION LAB
ACTIONLABCOMICS.COM

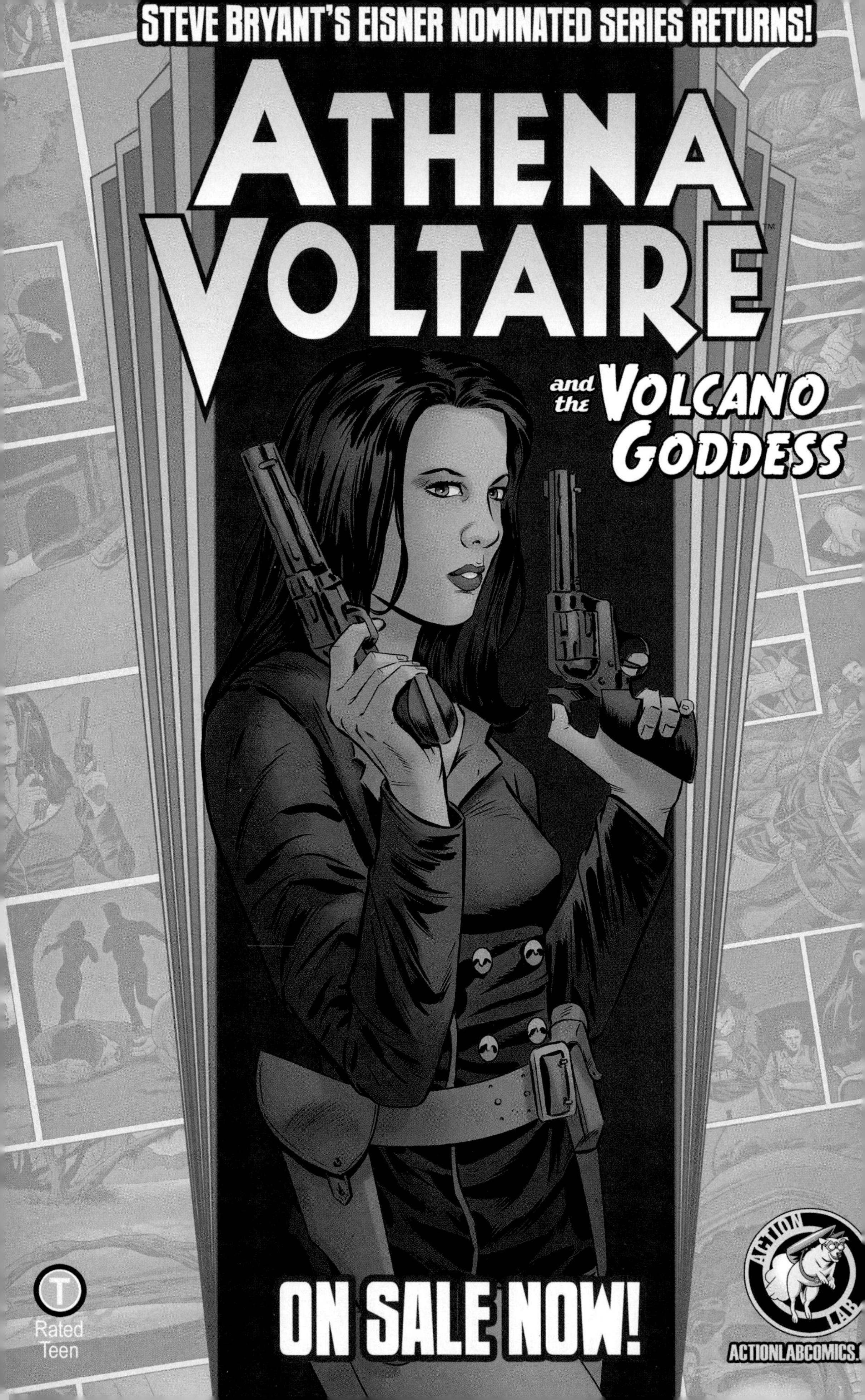

STEVE BRYANT'S EISNER NOMINATED SERIES RETURNS!
ATHENA VOLTAIRE™
and the VOLCANO GODDESS
ON SALE NOW!
T
Rated Teen
ACTION LAB
ACTIONLABCOMICS.

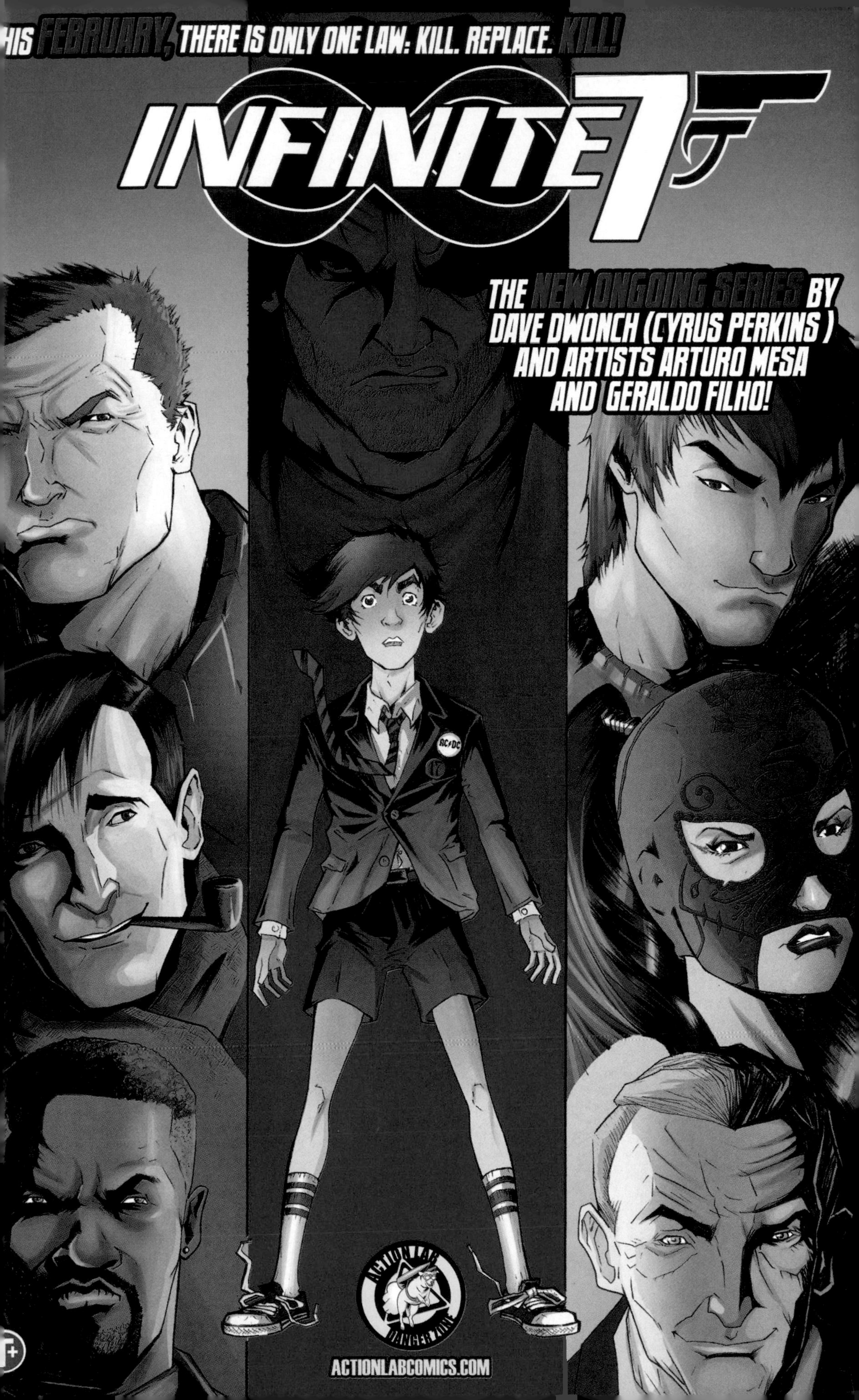

HIS FEBRUARY, THERE IS ONLY ONE LAW: KILL. REPLACE. KILL!
INFINITE 7
THE NEW ONGOING SERIES BY
DAVE DWONCH (CYRUS PERKINS)
AND ARTISTS ARTURO MESA
AND GERALDO FILHO!
AC/DC
ACTION LAB
DANGER ZONE
ACTIONLABCOMICS.COM

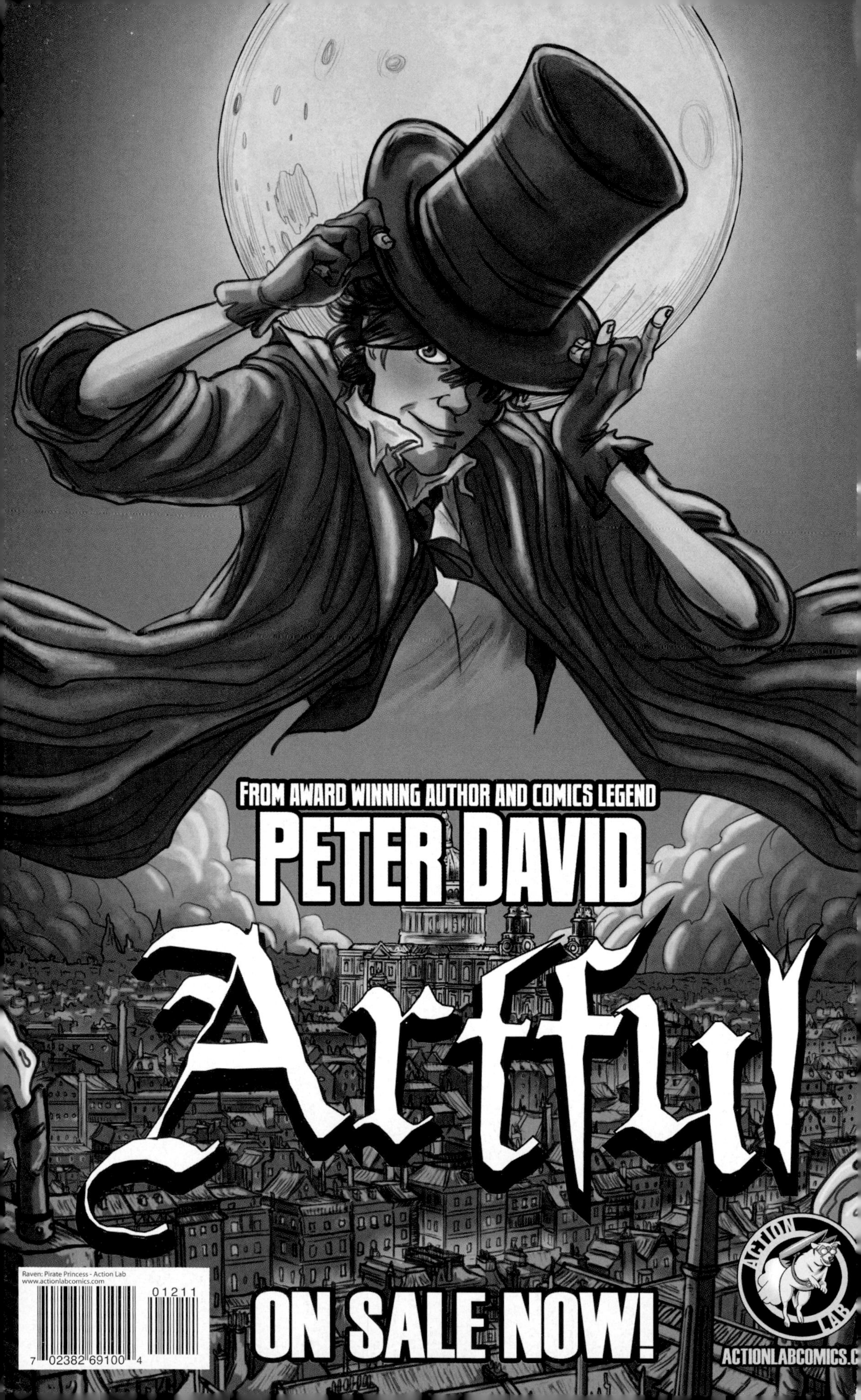
FROM AWARD WINNING AUTHOR AND COMICS LEGEND
PETER DAVID
Artful
ON SALE NOW!
ACTION LAB
ACTIONLABCOMICS.C
Raven: Pirate Princess - Action Lab
www.actionlabcomics.com
01211
7 02382 69100 4